Our Time Is Now

Also by Chloe Douglas

A Love for All Time

Our Time Is Now

CHLOE DOUGLAS

FOREVER
YOURS

New York Boston

Forever Yours
Hachette Book Group
1290 Avenue of the Americas
New York, NY 10104
Hachettebookgroup.com
Twitter.com/foreverromance

First ebook and print on demand edition: December 2014

Forever Yours is an imprint of Grand Central Publishing.
The Forever Yours name and logo are trademarks of Hachette Book Group, Inc.

The Hachette Speakers Bureau provides a wide range of authors for speaking events. To find out more, go to www.hachettespeakersbureau.com or call (866) 376-6591.

ISBN 978-1-4555-8507-6 (ebook edition)
ISBN 978-1-4555-8508-3 (print on demand edition)

Our Time Is Now

Chapter 1

McLean, Virginia
March 2014

Like duelists on the field of battle, they faced one another from opposite sides of their king-sized bed.

" 'Until death do we part.' Or have you forgotten?"

"It's just that we're not…I mean, I thought it would be better for me…for us, that is, if—" Jessica stopped in mid-plea, knowing that beneath her husband's eerily calm exterior, there lurked a very angry man.

"I'm only going to say this one time, Jessica. I have no intention of ever letting you go."

"Richard, please hear me out." She took a deep breath, hoping to steady her faltering nerves. "I don't want any alimony. There will be no scandal. And no divorce lawyers to—"

"Obviously, I need to remind you that, seven years ago, we took a vow before Almighty God, pledging ourselves in holy matrimony," Richard intoned as he stepped toward her.

Staring at her husband, she noticed that the tips of his ears were bright red. Had his ears always been that color? Surely, she hadn't pledged herself in holy matrimony to a man with terra cotta-colored ears?

Jessica choked back a hysterical laugh, knowing that if she remained in the room with Richard much longer, she might go off the deep end. After weeks of nail-biting vacillation she'd finally gotten up the courage to ask him for a divorce, and he'd shot her down with no more effort than it took to swat a fly.

Unable to look her husband in the eye, Jessica dropped her gaze, noticing the small, precise monogram stitched onto the cuff of his Brooks Brothers shirt: RB. Richard Bragg. The "wonder boy" of the ultra-right wing, he was the chief spokesman for the Traditional Family Movement, able to make or break political careers with a single, glib sound bite.

"Perhaps it would help things…um, our marriage, that is, if you would be willing to—"

Jessica didn't see the blow until it was too late; the force of Richard's backhanded slap whipped her head to the right. As she gasped for breath, her cheek felt like it had just been blow-torched, the pain radiating along her jawbone and up to the top of her skull. It was the first time that Richard had ever hit her, Jessica was stunned by his show of violence.

Knowing that her husband despised any type of emotional display, she hastily wiped at the tears that rolled down her cheeks.

Richard stepped over to the nightstand and snatched a tissue out of the box. "You drove me to that," he said without apology as he handed her the Kleenex. "After all that I've done to provide for you, I can't believe this is how you repay me."

"I…I'm sorry, Richard." Despite the ready words of contrition, Jessica knew there was no reason to apologize. She'd always been a dutiful wife.

"Being an understanding husband, I'm willing to overlook your irrational behavior. Dr. Metzer mentioned that the drugs might have some ill side-effects."

The drugs. By that he meant the pharmaceutical cocktail that was supposed to change the indicator on the home-pregnancy test from pink to blue. It had been Richard's idea to send her to an infertility specialist. A woman incapable of bearing children had little to no worth in his carefully scripted world. As the barren months had slipped past, the deprecating glances at her midsection had made Jessica feel like some worthless abomination. Richard didn't want a wife; he wanted a womb. And yet he refused to divorce her to seek out more fertile fields. Because he was one of the more visible leaders of the Traditional Family Movement, Richard would never willingly grant her a divorce. The pundits would skewer him alive on the flames of public opinion if that ever happened.

"Did you take your temperature this morning?"

Hesitantly, she nodded, fearful of what that loaded question portended.

Without so much as a glance in her direction, Richard began to loosen his silk tie, causing Jessica to inwardly cringe at the thought of his pale, brittle hands perfunctorily moving across her body. Years ago, she'd stopped pretending to enjoy it, even as Richard had stopped acting as though it was anything other than a reflexive biological act. Place part A into socket B. The bodily symbol of a loveless marriage. *Until death do we part.*

Resigned to her fate, Jessica automatically started to unbutton her blouse, stopping in mid-motion when her husband's wristwatch emitted a high-pitched chirp.

Brusquely, Richard pushed at the buttons that rimmed his

expensive timepiece. "I've got to catch a flight to New York," he muttered, yanking his tie back into place.

Knowing that she'd been dismissed, Jessica hurriedly left the room. Grateful for the reprieve, she headed to the living room to await Richard's departure.

When, several minutes later, she heard the heels of Richard's Italian loafers rhythmically click against the polished marble floor as he strode down the hall, she steeled her emotions, telling herself that he'd soon be gone. Plastering a demure smile onto her face, she watched as he set his garment bag down before he approached her.

"I haven't previously mentioned it, but I made arrangements for a contractor to come by tomorrow morning to install a wall safe in my study." As he spoke, Richard jingled the coins in his pants pocket. Merely annoying in the early years of their marriage, his habitual coin jingling had begun lately to grate on Jessica's nerves with a wracking intensity. "I need a place to store the deed to the house, wills, that sort of thing."

About to point out that was why they had a safe deposit box at the bank, Jessica held her tongue. She'd learned long ago never to contradict him.

"And don't forget to pick up my dry-cleaning," Richard continued. "I need my tux for a fund-raiser on Friday night."

"No, I won't forget," she replied dutifully.

Placing a hand on her shoulder, Richard leaned over and kissed her on the cheek, the same cheek that he'd earlier brutalized with the back of his hand. "While I'm gone, I want you to reflect on the reasons why we committed ourselves to one another."

"Yes, Richard. I will do that," she acquiesced without argument, willing to say anything to get him out the door.

Moments later, as she watched the gray Lexus back out of the driveway, Jessica clutched her stomach and moaned, assaulted with waves of pent-up anxiety.

Well, there's one surefire way to cure that, isn't there?

Like an addict in search of a fix, she made a beeline for the kitchen. As she reached for the cookie jar, she caught sight of a framed picture with the embroidered words "Home, Sweet Home." Averting her gaze, she sank her teeth into a double-fudge cookie, needing the comfort that only chocolate could provide.

Admittedly, it hadn't always been like this. There had been a time, early in the marriage, when she'd believed that if she tried hard enough to be a good wife, Richard would reward her with affection and respect. She didn't require love—merely the occasional kind word.

Who am I kidding? Everyone needs love.

As that thought crossed her mind, Jessica wondered when she'd become so pathetic. On days like today, it was hard to recall that she'd once been a free-thinking college graduate bent on a career in journalism. Particularly since she now guarded her every word, her every gesture. Richard had long ago sapped the *joie de vivre* right out of her, like some blood-sucking parasite.

Glancing at the crumbs littering the floor and countertop, she angrily shoved the cookie jar away from her. Unable to even enjoy the simple pleasure of a sugary treat, she stepped out of the kitchen to retrieve the vacuum cleaner from the hall closet.

As she walked past the oversized mirror in the foyer, Jessica came to a standstill. Shoving a hank of shoulder-length, auburn hair behind her ear, she stared at her reflection. Her hazel-green eyes were red-rimmed, and her left cheek was splotchy from where she'd been hit: a visible reminder that something had dramatically changed in the dynamic of their relationship. It wasn't simply the fact that her husband had struck her; it was that some dark, malevolent force had finally bubbled to the surface. Before today, Richard's abuse had always been verbal in nature; the man was an expert at battering her to a pulp with a disparaging turn of phrase. Now that the abuse had been ratcheted to the next level, she feared what he would do next, well aware that there was nothing she could do to protect herself from—

No. That's not true. I can walk away from the marriage.

Longingly, Jessica stared at the front door, imagining the freedom that beckoned from the other side. While the will was there, she had no means with which to leave. Unlike the average person who could simply go to an ATM machine or get a cash advance on their credit card, she had no direct access to monetary funds other than the household allowance that Richard doled out at the beginning of each week. That would buy her an airline ticket and a night's hotel room, but little else.

Suddenly inspired, her gaze darted to the closed door of Richard's study. On numerous occasions, she'd seen him exit from there with her weekly cash allowance in hand.

Galvanized into action, Jessica rushed down the hall and flung open the door to her husband's home office. With a confidence she didn't necessarily feel, she walked over to Richard's imposing antique desk and yanked open the center drawer. At a glance, she could see that it contained nothing more valuable than a few pens, some pencils, and several rolls of antacids. The next two drawers were equally disappointing.

Not about to retreat, Jessica tugged on the bottom drawer, surprised to find that it was locked. Certain that was where Richard kept his petty cash, she dashed out of the room, quickly making her way to the attached garage next to the kitchen. A few seconds later, rummaging through the tools stored on a shelf affixed to one side of the garage, she found what she was searching for.

With the tool clutched to her chest, Jessica made her way back to Richard's office. Unraveling the cord, she plugged it into the wall socket behind his desk. The electric pruning saw jerked slightly against her tightly clutched hand.

"*Carpe diem*," she murmured. Time to seize the day.

Pressing the saw blade against the wooden drawer, Jessica felt a giddy burst of excitement as small chips of wood flew up at her. It gave her a sense of empowerment that she was unaccustomed to feeling, unable to stifle a peal of hysterical laughter at the sight of the metal blade working its way through her husband's hundred-year-old mahogany desk.

It didn't take very long to saw through the locked drawer. Setting the tool aside, she thrust a hand into the butchered opening, her fingers making contact with a metal strongbox. Anxious to see what it contained, she placed it on top of the desk. Then, taking a deep breath, she lifted the lid.

The moment she did, Jessica's mouth fell open.

Oh, my God … can all of this money be for real?

Trembling, she slid a hand across the neatly stacked rows of green and white. "Yep, it's real, all right."

Picking up one of the banded packs of crisp hundred-dollar bills, Jessica guesstimated that she was holding $10,000 in her hand. Given that there were many more packs of similar size and denomination still in the box, Richard must have over a million dollars hoarded in his desk drawer.

No wonder he wanted a wall safe installed.

Where in heaven's name did all of this money come from? Richard surely didn't accrue it by putting his loose change in a jelly jar every night. Was he skimming from the coffers of the

Traditional Family Movement? Was he taking bribes from lobbyists? Did she even care? She wanted her freedom, and here it was staring her right in the face.

Because she'd entered into her marriage with $300,000—the inheritance that she received after her parents, Benjamin and Glenda Reardon, were tragically killed in an auto accident—she decided that she would take half that amount. A fair settlement by anyone's standard.

After grabbing fifteen banded packs of hundred dollar bills, Jessica hurried back to the kitchen, retrieving a canvas shopping bag. After dumping her booty into the sack, she snatched the framed piece of embroidery from the wall.

"Home, sweet home," she snickered before smashing the frame against the granite countertop. Twisting her wedding band off of her finger, she carefully placed it on top of the broken glass. Then, removing a banana-shaped magnet from the refrigerator, she retrieved a numbered receipt, which she carefully placed beneath the gleaming gold ring. "Heaven forbid that I should forget Richard's dry-cleaning."

As she marched down the hall a few moments later, canvas bag in hand, Jessica brightened at the thought that, at thirty-one years of age, she was about to become her own woman.

Chapter 2

Greenbrier County, West Virginia
September 2014

Give 'em hell, boys!"

Although it was late in the day, the sulfurous tang of gunpowder hung thickly in the air as volley after volley of intense firing raged between the two battle lines. Trying to rally his troops, a blue-clad officer scrambled over a rocky ravine waving a bayonet. A group of soldiers followed close behind, the thrill of combat gleaming in their eyes.

Rising from an earthen embankment, a line of gray-uniformed skirmishers met them head-on, yelling raucously as they fired their muskets.

Jessica Reardon jerked like a puppet on a string, startled to find herself in the path of a charging cavalry trooper. Before she could leap out of the way, the soldier's mount came to an abrupt halt, showering her sneakers with a layer of dirt. The uniformed rider thrust his arm in her direction, the elaborate gold braid on his gray coat sleeve glistening in the fading sunlight.

"Miss Reardon, the 4th Cavalry under the command of General Sitwell is preparing to charge. Are you ready to shoot?"

Jessica removed the lens cap from the camera that hung around her neck. "Ready to fire at will, Captain Stoddard."

It was the 150th anniversary of the Battle of Lewis Creek, and as a reporter for *The Greenbrier Dispatch*, Jessica was there to cover all the action. The event had drawn throngs of Civil War reenactors, intent on recreating a bit of West Virginia history—although, one hundred and fifty years ago, it'd been hotly contested as to whether this area of the eastern Alleghenies belonged to the Commonwealth of Virginia or to the newly formed state of West Virginia.

"Ma'am, would it be impertinent to ask if you will be in attendance at this evening's regimental ball?"

Jessica gulped, unnerved to discover that beneath Captain Stoddard's nineteenth-century uniform and courtly manners, there lurked a twenty-first century man on the make. "To tell you the truth, Captain Stoddard—"

"Please, call me Bruce."

Jessica nervously fumbled with the menu button on her camera. "Um, as you can see, Bruce, I left my hoop skirt at home." Hopefully, her would-be admirer had the smarts to know that no self-respecting southern belle would dare dance the Virginia Reel garbed in khaki shorts, a T-shirt, and an Orioles baseball cap.

"Without your fair beauty to grace this evening's festivities, I shall be a lonely cavalier, indeed." With a theatrical sweep of the arm, Bruce removed his plumed hat. "Farewell, dear lady! I am afraid that duty calls." That said, horse and rider charged across the battlefield.

Watching Bruce Stoddard disappear over a grass-covered knoll, Jessica exhaled a pent-up breath. She was there on a journalistic assignment and not to fill her dance card for some ridiculous reenactment ball. To prove, if only to herself, that she really was a newspaper reporter-at-large, she raised the digital camera and took a few snaps.

Admittedly, "reporter-at-large" primarily meant doing the human interest stories that no one else at *The Dispatch* wanted to do. Last week, she'd interviewed Okie Phelps, head of the Greenbrier Turkey Shoot Club, who was kind enough to go through his entire repertoire of wild animal calls. The week before that, she'd gotten the big scoop on how Mrs. Lucy Albright, 87, resident of Big Stink Lick, kept raccoons out of the cornfield.

While she'd never win a Pulitzer reporting on how pumpkin vines deter furry trespassers, working as a journalist—even if it was for a small town paper that only went to press three times a week—was reward enough. And if the editor liked her piece on this weekend's reenactment, she had a shot at getting bumped from freelance reporter to full-time news writer. She could certainly use the extra money.

Turning away from the battlefield, Jessica retrieved her car keys from the zippered pocket on her knapsack before making her way down a well-worn footpath toward the rows of parked cars in the lower field. It was late in the day, and she'd already gotten enough interviews to write a story for next week's paper.

As she neared her vehicle, Jessica inwardly cringed at the sight of her sixteen-year-old Ford Bronco sandwiched between a luxury SUV and an aerodynamically designed mini-van. No doubt about it, her three-thousand-dollar clunker stood out like the proverbial sore thumb.

Opening the car door, she readjusted the faded T-shirt that covered the ripped driver's seat before easing herself behind the wheel. As she did, she wrinkled her nose at the Bronco's musty smell, a permanent odor that no amount of air freshener could alleviate.

Fingers crossed, she turned the ignition key. "Okay, Houston, all systems are go," she chirped happily at hearing the engine roar to life. The Bronco was less than perfect in the reliability department.

After shifting into reverse, Jessica slowly backed out of her parking space, ignoring the noxious, gray smoke spewing from the tail pipe. Once clear of the parking area, she made the turn onto Route 219.

Jessica knew that she'd eventually have to fork out the money for an auto mechanic: the Bronco was in desperate need of a tune-up. As well as a new starter. And though money woes were a regular obsession, she didn't mind living hand to mouth. Tucked away in the back of her mind was the memory of the alternative. So while she was currently strapped for cash, at least she was forging her own life. Footloose and fancy free. Or at least she would be once her divorce was finalized.

"Holy crackers! Where did *that* come from?" Flipping on the windshield wipers, Jessica glanced at the dark clouds suddenly storm-trooping across the western sky, a doozy of a storm that had just rolled over the mountains with no advance warning.

When, in the next instant, the engine suddenly stalled, she let the Bronco coast to the side of the road as she berated herself again for not having bought a new car battery when she'd had the extra money. Fortunately, she didn't have too far to walk because the Bronco had petered out only a hundred yards from the turnoff to the house. From there, she only had to traverse half a mile to reach dry clothing, freshly brewed coffee, and a warm meal.

With a resigned sigh, Jessica pulled the keys out of the ignition, depositing them in the pocket of her khaki shorts. After tucking her ponytail into her baseball cap, she stepped out of the vehicle. The moment she did, a logging truck, heading in the opposite direction, splashed a sheet of water across the front of her body.

"Just what I need," she muttered, the misery index instantly compounded.

Long minutes later, catching sight of her house through the grove of sugar maple and oak that timbered the hillside, Jessica's shoulders sagged with relief. Barely able to put one foot in front of the other, she had a whole new appreciation of why her hilltop residence was called Highland House.

Six months ago, she would never have guessed that she'd be living in a two-hundred-year-old house that actually came with its own name. And it was all hers—lock, stock, and barrel—bought at auction on the Greenbrier County courthouse steps for the sum of $125,000. Paid for in cash. Although there was no getting around the fact that the ramshackle, two-story, red brick house was in desperate need of some TLC. Which, loosely translated, meant another $125,000 would be needed for essential repairs. It would take at least three times that amount to bring Highland House back to its former glory.

Feeling an ache in the back of her calves, Jessica slowed her pace. As she did, she glimpsed a lightning strike in the near vicinity, the stentorian crackle followed by a stereophonic *boom*. Then, as though it was hurled by Zeus himself, another bolt plunged from the sky. Stunned, she watched it make contact with an ancient maple tree, a heavy limb crashing to the ground, fissured by nature's most merciless slayer.

Terrified of being struck by lightning, Jessica tucked her head and sprinted in the direction of the house.

She was almost to the front porch when, out of the corner of her eye, she saw a flash of motion in the trees. In the next instant, she heard a spine-tingling, lion-like roar. Curiosity getting the better of her, Jessica came to halt and stared at the stand of maples. Unnerved, she had the distinct impression that some sort of otherworldly creature with glowing red eyes was peering at her through the foliage. Which was a totally preposterous notion. Given the large deer population in the area, it was probably a doe or a buck.

But could a doe or a buck have made that bone-jarring roar?

Since she didn't think it likely, Jessica wondered if it wasn't a bear. Or perhaps a—

Suddenly, without warning, a burst of orange flames jettisoned across the wooded grove. The fiery blaze lasted for several seconds, as if it had been shot from a gigantic flame torch.

"Oh my God!" she screamed, petrified.

Worried that this was fast turning into a storm of biblical proportions, she rushed toward the porch, making a beeline for the front door. Yanking it open, she lunged inside the dimly lit foyer. After bolting the door, she fumbled for the light switch.

"Could things get any worse?" she muttered, disheartened to discover that there was no electrical power. Since it would soon be nightfall, there was no time to wallow in self-pity. She needed to locate a flashlight and some basic emergency provisions before it turned pitch dark.

Several minutes later, flashlight and candles in hand, she decided to set up camp in the library. It had more furniture than any other room in the house and boasted a beautiful set of French doors that would provide ample daylight if she was still without power come morning. It also happened to be her favorite room in the house.

With the toe of her wet sneaker, Jessica pushed open the library door. The flashlight cast a golden beam that illuminated the room's peeling wallpaper and cracked plaster ceiling. Buster, her recently adopted Maine Coon cat, lazily stretched his orange and white body along the back of the sofa.

"Hello, big guy. Hope you don't mind the company."

After setting the flashlight on top of the mantel, Jessica placed several candles in strategic places out of Buster's reach. The constellation of flickering lights created a soft, romantic ambiance. She only needed Mister Darcy to walk through the door to complete the fantasy.

Oh, be still my heart.

Just then, Buster lurched from his cozy perch and Jessica was surprised to see that the fur on the back of his neck was standing on end.

"Hey, what's the matter, fella?" When her question met with a feline growl, she smiled and said, "Surely, a mighty hunter like you isn't afraid of an old thunder—"

Jessica's breath caught in her throat when she suddenly heard the unmistakable sound of the porch floorboards creaking and groaning under a heavy weight. When she next heard a loud, rattling sound, her heart forcefully pounded against her breastbone.

Someone is trying to open the front door!

Terror-stricken, she rushed over to the mantel and grabbed the flashlight, clutching her pitiful weapon to her chest. Long seconds passed as she stood rooted in place, the rattling sound eventually ceasing.

On the verge of giving the "all clear," Jessica instead shrieked as the French doors suddenly swung open. The swoosh of cool, moist air caused the candles to erratically sputter. In the next instant, a tall, soaking wet man stepped into the library.

Seized with a burst of unadulterated fear, Jessica let the flashlight slip through her fingers, and it shot frenetic beams of light onto the baseboards as it rolled across the floor.

Deciding to make a run for it, Jessica spun on her heel.

Only to pull up short when she saw that the intruder had a gun in his hand. And it was pointed directly at her.

Chapter 3

Terrified, Jessica opened her mouth to scream, but the shriek was so firmly lodged in her throat that she barely produced a tinny squeak. The fact that the gunman's face was obscured by a wide-brimmed hat and thick, overgrown beard amplified her fear, inducing a full-body paralysis.

"What are you doing in this house?" the intruder demanded as he lowered his revolver and shoved it into the holster belted around his waist.

He wants to know what I'm doing in my own home?

Quite frankly, she didn't know how to reply. Particularly since the fiend could rape and murder her, in her own home, and it would be days before she would be missed by anyone.

Because the intruder had the advantage of size, standing several inches over six feet, her only hope was to land a perfectly executed kick to his testicles.

About to launch her attack, she was thrown off-kilter when her assailant unexpectedly staggered toward her. Doing a fair impersonation of a Weeble, he wobbled to and fro before crash-landing on the sofa with a heavy thud. He rolled his head as he made one of those uniquely male sounds, midway between a groan and a grunt. After that, he went eerily silent.

In a state of total shock, Jessica hurriedly retrieved her flashlight from the floor and shined it over the intruder's prone body. At seeing the Confederate uniform jacket, she exhaled a gusty sigh of relief.

"Oh, for Pete's sake," she huffed. Not only was he one of those Civil War reenactors that she'd seen earlier in the day, he was also stinking drunk. Why else would he have passed out on the couch like that? Given that the house had been vacant and abandoned for several years, her Confederate intruder probably thought that Highland House would be a good place to wait out the storm.

As she inched closer to the sofa, Jessica closely scrutinized the drunken man. "Kinda difficult to guess your age, let alone your species, with all of that facial hair," she muttered, suspecting he wore a fake beard that he'd pasted on for the reenactment. In the real world, men didn't grow beards like that unless they were Amish or they spent their days pushing a shopping cart and begging for quarters.

Curious, Jessica impulsively reached down and tugged on the reenactor's beard. "Oh, Lordy! It's real."

In the next instant, a bolt of lightning discharged nearby, brightly illuminating the library. The man jerked slightly. Then, to Jessica's horror, his eyes opened.

"My beloved," he whispered hoarsely, before his eyes again closed.

Yep. Drunk as a skunk.

Annoyed that the inebriated man had picked her sofa to pass out on, Jessica strode over to the French doors and closed them, noticing for the first time a leather saddlebag in the corner of the room. Hoping there wasn't a horse hitched to the front porch, she tucked the flashlight under one arm as she crouched beside it. She needed to find some ID to contact the man's family, so she unbuckled the clasp and unceremoniously dumped the saddle-bag's entire contents onto the floor.

She was surprised by the odd assortment of items she found as she rummaged through an old-fashioned toothbrush with prickly bristles, a sterling silver cigar case, several half-burnt wax candles, a wooden comb, an ivory-handled knife and fork, a worn-out pack of playing cards, and a pair of wool socks that looked like they'd seen better days. She next unfolded a newspaper clipping from *The Richmond Times* dated September 20, 1864. A fake, obviously. Earlier in the day, she'd seen plenty of "authentic" nineteenth-century wares for sale at the reenactment.

"Okay, so where's your wallet?" she muttered.

Discovering a pair of leather packets that looked promising, Jessica opened one of them. Rather than the man's ID, it instead contained a wad of phony Confederate paper money and several gold coins. To her dismay, the other leather purse only contained bullets and gun cartridges.

Her frustration fast mounting, she plucked a soiled envelope out of the pile. Shining the flashlight on it, she could see that it was addressed to a Colonel Gideon MacAllister.

"Finally, a name. Sometimes snail mail really is the best way to go," Jessica opined, as she stuffed all of the items back into the saddlebag.

At hearing Gideon's ragged breathing, Jessica rose to her feet and tiptoed over to the sofa. For several seconds, she stared at the man who was sprawled across it. "A little gamey smelling, aren't you?" she said to her drunken guest, able to detect the scents of gunpowder, campfire smoke, and pine needles.

Noticing the way that Gideon's legs were shoved against the side of the coffee table, Jessica put down the flashlight so that she could grasp his booted feet by the ankles, enabling her to swing his legs into a less contorted position. Then, telling herself that she was simply being a Good Samaritan, she grabbed a throw pillow. Removing Gideon's rain-dampened hat, she gently placed the pillow behind his head. When she did so, she experienced a strange tingling sensation in her fingertips. As though she'd been hit with a low-voltage burst of electricity.

Chalking it up to some kind of weird electrical discharge caused by the raging thunderstorm, she immediately withdrew her hand.

Deciding to leave the room, Jessica's gaze fell upon the gun holster and sheathed sword belted around Gideon's waist. Inwardly groaning, she knew both items had to be removed. Even though the revolver was undoubtedly loaded with blanks—per reenactment regulations—she didn't want him accidentally setting it off, or ripping a hole in her couch with his sword.

After she unhooked the metal buckle at his waist, she grasped hold of Gideon's upper shoulder and rolled him toward her, no easy feat given his size. Then she yanked the belt out from under him because she simply wanted to get the unpleasant task over and done with. She then eased Gideon onto his back, relieved that he was three sheets to the wind and therefore blissfully unaware of what was happening to him.

Setting the menacing-looking weapons on top of the coffee table, Jessica took one last gander at her unwelcome houseguest. There was something hauntingly familiar about him, although she felt certain they had never previously met.

Flashlight in hand, Jessica headed for the door. "Pleasant dreams, Gideon MacAllister."

* * *

Certain that he'd just heard a woman's voice, Gideon vainly struggled to open his eyes. *What is she doing here?* The house had been empty since the fire. Perhaps she was fleeing from the Federal troops and had sought refuge there. If so, he must tell her that there was no refuge to be had at Highland House. As he knew all too well, the only refuge was in death.

Now, with the end close at hand, Gideon felt a profound sense of relief. He had been waiting for death, longing for it even. So many deaths on his hands. His beloved's death on his hands.

Feeling a heavy, oppressive weight on his chest, he tried to pull some air into his weakened lungs. His efforts were to no avail; each breath was more shallow than the one before it. Perhaps he was already dead. That would certainly explain the demoniacal, red-eyed beast that he'd glimpsed as he'd approached the house, the winged serpent looking as though it'd been spawned in the fiery abyss. He had expected Charon to ferry him across the River Styx. But Satan's dragon could perform the task just as well, he supposed.

Enveloped in a still silence, Gideon wondered what had become of the auburn-haired woman with the steadfast gaze. *It doesn't matter*, he told himself. Nothing in this world was of any consequence. Soon enough, he would arrive at Hell's gate.

Punishment for a life that could have been better lived.

* * *

Still navigating by flashlight, Jessica wearily headed upstairs, irked that the telephone book had no listing for a Gideon MacAllister. Although she wouldn't have been able to call anyway because the land line was dead, and she'd left her cell phone in the Bronco to keep it from getting wet.

Entering her bedroom, her gaze was immediately drawn to Buster. The furry imp had already settled in for the night, curled on the pillow next to hers.

"Don't look at me like that. I didn't invite him," Jessica said in response to Buster's inquisitive stare.

Normally, she'd be scared to death at having a stranger asleep on the sofa. But because this particular stranger was out like a light, she wasn't as worried as she might have been. In fact, she suspected that come daybreak, her "guest" would cut bait and run—a killer hangover and shamefaced embarrassment dogging him all the way home.

"I should probably have left some Alka-Seltzer on the coffee table," she said with an amused chuckle.

In a hurry to get out of her damp clothing, Jessica strode over to the armoire. Opening it, she set the flashlight on one of the shelves. She then kicked off her tennis shoes, too tired to bend over and untie them. Next, she yanked off the T-shirt, unsnapped her bra, wiggled out of the khaki shorts, and removed her panties, carelessly flinging all four items into the nearby laundry basket. Having brought a towel with her, she quickly dried off before she donned clean panties and a ribbed tank top.

No sooner had she pulled the tank top over her head than the flashlight went dead, throwing the room into complete darkness.

"That's just great," Jessica muttered disagreeably when the flashlight failed to magically turn back on after she gave it the time-honored whack.

Unable to see a thing, she carefully maneuvered over to the four-poster bed, managing to bang her knee in the process. The day's events had taken their toll. She plunked down on the edge of the mattress. The last hour had unraveled like a bad Fellini film, except in this instance truth really was stranger than fiction.

As if sensing her distress, the big Maine Coon positioned himself on her lap, gently kneading Jessica's thighs with his paws before curling into a fluffy ball. The soothing sound of Buster's purr worked its magic, and Jessica happily reciprocated by stroking her cat under his chin.

Just feed 'em, give 'em shelter and affection, and in return they give you unconditional love. Why can't all relationships be like that? Why couldn't my marriage have been like that?

It had been six months since she'd walked out on her husband. Her legal separation from Richard Bragg incited a brouhaha, and his reputation had been sliced and diced by a public eager to yank the right-wing poster boy—who'd always been quick to lambaste the lack of morals in Washington—off his self-righteous high horse. Not that Jessica cared. To her mind, Richard had dug his own grave, although she suspected that he blamed her entirely for his fall from grace.

She also suspected that Richard was none too pleased about the $150,000 that she'd taken from his desk drawer, but he'd made no mention of the money in the deposition that he'd given as part of the divorce proceedings. Well and good since she'd already spent the cash, having used most of the money to buy her house. Granted, Highland House wasn't much of a residence, not yet anyway. But it was hers, and she would never give it up.

"What's your take on all of this, kitty?" She gently rubbed Buster behind his ears. "Is love nothing but a dirty, four-letter word?" Her query was met with one of those disinterested, leisurely yawns that felines seem to have perfected over the ages.

Pulling back the quilted coverlet, Jessica snuggled into the feather-tick mattress. For several seconds, she restlessly tossed and turned until her body finally settled into a comfortable position. She then slowly descended into the enticing realm of deep sleep.

As her unconscious self stood on the periphery of a dream, she caught sight of a glowing light in the shrouding darkness. Intrigued, she walked toward it. No—"walk" wasn't the right word—she floated toward the light, her body unfettered by the gravity of the waking world.

No sooner had she passed through the luminous sphere than Jessica emerged in a wooded ravine. Standing in the middle of a path that was illuminated by dappled sunlight, she knew that she was in a place called Sweet Springs. How she knew this, she couldn't say. The name had simply popped into her head as though it was common knowledge. Or a bit of hidden knowledge that had suddenly been revealed.

Her attention drawn to the sound of rustling leaves, Jessica turned her head, smiling at the sight of a fawn nibbling on a bush. Startled by her approach, the animal quickly scampered through the woodland.

Farther down the path, Jessica saw a lone woman, her long, plaid dress seemingly out of place in the midst of the forested wilderness. Because the woman seemed vaguely familiar, Jessica moved toward her, not stopping until she and the other woman collided, their bodies, their thoughts, their joys and fears melding together.

In that instant, they became one and the same woman. A fusion of body, mind, and soul.

Chapter 4

Sweet Springs, Virginia
Summer 1860

Grabbing hold of her voluminous skirt, Miss Sarah Pemberton carefully navigated her way over the rocky terrain.

Moments earlier, she'd glimpsed a fawn darting through the forest, the reason she'd strayed from the path. A mountain wilderness such as this was a thoroughly exotic realm to a young lady born and raised in the port city of Norfolk, Virginia. Indeed, nearly everything about this Allegheny paradise was enchantingly beautiful, putting her in mind of a Highland scene from a Sir Walter Scott novel.

Gazing across the verdant hillock, she sighed pensively. Although she'd arrived several days ago, she'd had scant free time to explore the scenic wonders that surrounded the mountainside spa. Because of her father's death two years ago, she'd been forced to act as a lady's companion to her stepmother, Mrs. Etta Pemberton. Despite the fact that her father had financially provided for Sarah in his will, her stepmother obstinately refused to turn over her inheritance, claiming that her father had intended for the money to be used as a dowry.

While Sweet Springs was, without question, the most elegant of all the Virginia spas, and even though, by all accounts, the 1860 summer season would likely be the grandest in recent memory, her stepmother had made it abundantly clear that she was there *only* to take the water cure. It was her stepmother's adamant contention that a regimen of hydro-therapy, administered three times daily, would alleviate her chronic rheumatism. Soirees, dancing, and musical evenings would do nothing to aid the curative process.

Rendered awestruck by the majesty of a centuries-old oak tree, Sarah failed to notice the pitted ground beneath her booted feet. Suddenly thrown off balance, she pitched forward, her foot ensnared in a hole. To her utter embarrassment, not only did she land in an ungainly heap of plaid poplin and starched muslin petticoats, but her straw bonnet flew off her head, landing in a blueberry bush several feet away.

As she drew herself into a seated position, Sarah heard the pounding reverberations of an unseen horseman's mount. Hurriedly, she tried to stand up, dismayed to discover that her right foot was thoroughly wedged in the hole, and that she was unable to pull it free.

"Whoa!"

She winced at hearing that deep, masculine command, mortified that a stranger might be privy to her absurd predicament.

A few seconds later, as the horseman dismounted and approached, her breath caught in her throat. Standing before her was surely the most handsome, finely fashioned man she'd ever set eyes upon. Without question, he had a more manly bearing than her fiancé, Mr. Oren Tolliver.

The gentleman bowed at the waist and said, "Allow me to introduce myself: I am Gideon MacAllister. And I am at your service."

"I can assure you, Mr. MacAllister, that your help is entirely unnecessary," she replied, extreme embarrassment lending a churlish note to her voice.

"I beg to differ." As he spoke, the horseman plucked a leafy twig from her coiffure, presenting it to her as proof.

Unable to help herself, Sarah smiled. The handsome stranger had rightly taken her to task for her peevish remark. "As you can see, my foot is stuck in this hole, and I am unable to extricate it," she informed him, lifting her skirt a few modest inches in order to reveal the extent of her predicament.

Immediately going down on bent knee, Gideon said, "I shall be happy to assist."

Without further ado, he took hold of her foot and began to gently jiggle it. Due to their close proximity, her gaze roamed to his broad shoulders, superbly outfitted in a coat of dark blue broadcloth.

"How long do you and your stepmother intend to stay at Sweet Springs?" Gideon politely inquired.

Taken aback by the question, her jaw slackened. "How on earth did you know that I'm here with my stepmother?"

"I know a great deal about you, Miss Pemberton," the rascal had the audacity to reply as he liberated her foot from the hole. "After catching sight of you at the springs, I took the liberty of making a few inquiries."

Sarah could feel her face pink with heated color. Never before had so a handsome man sought her favor.

Taking hold of her hand, Gideon assisted her to her feet.

Goodness, but he's a tall man, she mused as they stood side by side, gauging Gideon to be nearly a foot taller than her betrothed.

"While there's a bit of swelling, I didn't detect any broken bones."

"Your prognosis relieves me," she said in a staid tone of voice, self-consciously aware that she lacked the vivacious charm of a belle.

"You will do more harm than good, Miss Pemberton, if you continue to stand on that injured foot. Will you allow me to carry you to my mount?"

Unable to meet his gaze, she breathlessly nodded.

Swinging her into his arms, Gideon carried her to his horse, which was tethered to a low-hanging tree limb. As he lifted Sarah to the saddle, he instructed her to hook a leg around the pommel. He then retrieved her straw hat from the blueberry bush.

"I thank you, sir." After securing the hat on her head, Sarah straightened her shoulders, attempting to regain her ladylike composure. No small feat given the unusual circumstance in which she now found herself.

Taking the reins in his hands, Gideon walked beside the horse as he led it along the bridle path. In the near distance, she heard the insistent hammering of a determined woodpecker, the sound mimicking the insistent pounding of her heart.

They'd not gone far when Gideon began to softly chuckle.

"And what, may I ask, do you find so amusing?"

He turned his head in her direction, sunlight brightening his eyes to one of the most mesmerizing shades of blue that she'd ever seen. "I'm delighted at my good fortune. It's not every day that a man is able to rescue a damsel in distress."

"So you fancy yourself a knight errant, do you?"

"Alas, I'm only a gentleman farmer come to Sweet Springs on holiday."

"Allow me to rectify that." Sarah leaned toward him. Lightly touching, first one shoulder, then the other, she said playfully, "I dub thee, Sir Gideon, Knight of the Allegheny Mountains."

His smile broadened. "I am honored, fair lady."

Flustered, Sarah redirected her attention to the red brick hotel that was just coming into view. Replete with neoclassical pediments and porticos, it caused many a traveler to approach Sweet Springs in a state of awe, mistaking the magnificent, white-columned piazza for a far-flung, ancient temple. Unlike her stepmother, whose sole purpose in visiting the spa was to take the cures, the vast majority of guests were southern-born aristocrats who retreated to these mountains in droves to escape the debilitating heat of their native climes, as well as partake of the endless rounds of balls and social outings. With good reason, Sweet Springs had earned its reputation as the Almack's of the Allegheny Mountains.

"Were you aware of the fact that Thomas Jefferson designed the hotel's main building?"

"I am impressed, Miss Pemberton. Clearly, you are as intelligent as you are beautiful."

Uncertain how to respond to such warm-hearted praise, Sarah nervously fidgeted with her skirt. Educated at the Westbrook Ladies Academy, she had once hoped to enter the teaching ranks. However, having recently been apprised by her stepmother that she was to be given in marriage to a distant relative of her stepmother's, Mr. Oren Tolliver of Wheeling, Virginia, her dreams of becoming a teacher had been thoroughly dashed.

Not wishing to dwell on her unhappy situation, Sarah turned her gaze to the emerald green lawn that surrounded the hotel, where swarms of elegantly attired guests leisurely strolled the manicured paths.

"Miss Pemberton, are you all right? You suddenly have about you a forlorn expression."

"There is no need for concern. I am quite all right." As she spoke, Sarah furtively perused the vicinity, relieved to see neither her stepmother nor Mr. Tolliver. Earlier in the week, Mr. Tolliver had joined their party, ostensibly so that the two of them could become better acquainted before their upcoming nuptials.

"Since I must shortly beg leave of your company, may I ask for the honor of dancing the first waltz with you at tomorrow's ball? Assuming, of course, that your ankle has sufficiently healed."

Unschooled in the art of coquetry, Sarah blurted the first thing that came to mind, "Sir, I will gladly dance the first waltz with you."

"Truly, you've made me a happy man, Miss Pemberton."

The ardent reply caused her to heatedly blush. Perhaps a more devoted woman would have refused to dance the first waltz with a man who was not her betrothed. She, however, could not lay claim to such devotion.

When they reached the end of the drive, a livery servant took the reins from Gideon. Hands freed, Gideon reached up and effortlessly plucked her from the saddle, cradling her close to his chest. More than a few heads turned in their direction as he proceeded to carry her up the long row of stairs that led to the hotel's grand piazza. She noticed that a few gentlemen even went so far as to wink in approval.

Horror struck, Sarah caught sight of her stepmother and Mr. Tolliver waiting for them at the top of the steps.

As Gideon set her upon her feet, Sarah immediately tried to explain the reason for her odd predicament. "I was out taking the mountain air when I…I had an accident. Fortunately, Mr. MacAllister came to my rescue."

Etta Pemberton shot Gideon a withering glance. "Mr. MacAllister, you say? I do not recollect making this man's acquaintance. How could you permit a stranger to take such liberties? Not to mention the fact that you have made an utter spectacle of yourself."

"I don't really have…that is to say that…" Sarah's explanation faded into silence, words escaping her.

Stepping forward, Gideon said, "While my actions may seem somewhat inappropriate, the seriousness of your stepdaughter's injury warranted bold action. If any blame is to be cast, it should fall upon my shoulders, and not Miss Pemberton's."

"Be that as it may, Miss Pemberton's thoughtless behavior caused us to miss our afternoon tea," Oren scolded, openly glaring at Gideon as he spoke.

Forcing a smile onto her lips, Sarah hastily attempted to make the proper introductions between the two men. "Mr. MacAllister, may I present Mr. Oren Tolliver."

While Gideon bowed respectfully, Oren did not return the courtesy, much to her chagrin.

"I will have you know that I am Miss Pemberton's fiancé," Oren asserted.

"Then you are an enviable man, indeed," Gideon said with a wistful expression.

Just then, a group of distinguished-looking gentlemen strolled past, including the governor of the state, all of whom greeted Gideon in passing. Although it seemed an innocuous exchange, she could see that it infuriated Oren, who did not have the benefit of so esteemed an acquaintanceship.

Knowing that her fiancé was overly sensitive about his humble origins, Sarah attempted to smooth his ruffled feathers. "Mr. Tolliver is a newly elected member to the Virginia legislature," she informed Gideon, trying, without much success, to infuse a note of pride into her voice.

Gideon raised an interested brow. "These are troubling political times, to say the least. Clearly, our state's legislature has a great task before it."

"And where do you stand, Mr. MacAllister, on the troubling issue of secession?"

In the wake of Oren's blunt query, a tense silence ensued.

"It will cause me great pain should Virginia fall victim to the tide of extremism that is sweeping across the South," Gideon replied after a lengthy pause, obviously taking care with his words.

"Humph!" Oren's lips twisted into a nasty sneer. "While that is a fine sentiment, I happen to know that you Virginia bluebloods can't wait to march into battle so as to maintain your cherished institution. You and your kind would willingly throw the whole country into war before you let anyone take your slaves from you."

"Not every landowner in Virginia is a slaveholder," Gideon said quietly. "Slavery is an institution that I find particularly repugnant. Moreover, I will not take up arms to safeguard one man's right to own another. However, if Virginia becomes a battleground, I will fight to defend my home."

"You Southerners should be forewarned that God is on *our* side." Oren emphasized the pronouncement by puffing out his chest like a bantam cock. "And he will smite all rebellious sinners from the face of this hallowed ground."

"Sir, I shall not dignify your remarks with a reply," Gideon countered with an air of cool self-assurance. He then reached for

Sarah's hand and, bowing gallantly, he grazed his lips across her knuckles. "Until tomorrow evening, Miss Pemberton."

As Gideon took his leave, Oren snorted derisively and said, "The gall of the man to think that he'll see you again. These Virginia cavaliers are as arrogant and self-serving as they come."

Sarah made no reply as she watched Gideon descend the long flight of steps.

Good-bye, my handsome knight. Until we meet again.

Chapter 5

"You're still here? I was sorta hoping you'd be gone by now," Jessica muttered as she entered the library, annoyed at finding Gideon MacAllister up and about. Particularly since last night he'd taken center stage in the strangest dream she'd ever had, a full-length costume drama right out of *Gone with the Wind*.

It made Jessica think that she'd spent *way* too much time at yesterday's Civil War reenactment.

As they stood across from one another, Jessica couldn't help but notice that Gideon possessed a pair of brilliant, cerulean blue eyes. As in truly dazzling. Not to mention, he had a beautiful head of wavy, sandy-brown hair. Although there was no getting past the long, bushy beard.

Glowering, Gideon grabbed a newspaper off of the nearby end table. "How in God's name can you possibly explain this?" he demanded to know as he thrust the paper in her direction.

Jessica snatched yesterday's edition of *The Greenbrier Dispatch* out of his hands. "School Board Approves Auditorium Fund," she read aloud, puzzled by his heated reaction. "I admit it's not the catchiest of headlines, but the kids need a new basketball court."

Gideon jabbed his finger at the front page. "Look at the date!"

"September 25, 2014." Still baffled, she shrugged and said, "What's the problem with that?"

"The problem is that when I awoke yesterday morning, it was September the twenty-fifth...eighteen sixty-four."

Oh, God. He's a certifiable wacko.

The instant that fearful thought crystallized in Jessica's mind, the newspaper slipped through her fingers, falling in a heap onto the floor.

"Have you nothing to say, madam?"

"I, um, don't know what to, um—" Jessica broke off in midstammer, unable to form a single coherent thought.

Abruptly turning away from her, Gideon stepped over to the coffee table and retrieved a large, hardbound book. "And I would be most interested to hear what you have to say about this." He held the volume in front of his chest, enabling Jessica to see that it was a *Time-Life* book on the Civil War that she'd checked out of the Lewisburg public library in order to gather background material for the reenactment.

Jessica stared at the volume, at a loss to know how to respond. Either the guy was off his rocker or he was playing the mother of all practical jokes. Given that his revolver and scabbard were in plain sight, she sincerely hoped that it was the latter.

As Jessica nervously peered at Gideon, she noticed that his face was flushed an unnatural color. Moreover, his breathing had become labored, and there was a feverish glimmer in his eyes.

Suddenly struck with the uneasy realization that Gideon MacAllister might be gravely ill, she pried the *Time-Life* book from his hands. Then, taking Gideon by the elbow, she guided him toward an armchair. "Perhaps you should sit down and rest."

Wordlessly he slid into the chair, his head slumping against his chest. Despite his height and broad-shouldered mass, he didn't appear to have the strength to shoo a fly.

When, a few seconds later, he began to shiver, Jessica hurried over to the other side of the room and snatched a throw blanket out of a wicker trunk.

"Is there anyone I can call for you?" she anxiously inquired as she tucked the woolen plaid around his chest and shoulders.

The question met with an unresponsive silence.

"My Bronco conked out yesterday," she continued, hoping to get a reaction from him. "But as soon as I get a jump-start, I'll drive you home, okay?"

To her relief, Gideon's eyelids slowly opened. "I am home," he murmured hoarsely.

In your dreams, fella.

On the verge of setting Gideon straight, Jessica instead clamped her mouth shut, thinking it best not to berate a sick man. As his eyelids again draped over his pupils, she surmised that Gideon MacAllister needed to see a doctor ASAP. The man was so far-gone he had no idea as to his whereabouts. Unfortunately, with the Bronco out of commission, she had no way of getting him to a medical office.

Hit with a sudden idea, Jessica lunged to her feet and dashed to the telephone stand in the hallway. Grabbing the phonebook, she turned on the table lamp and quickly perused the yellow-page listings for "physicians." The only bit of luck to come her way so far this morning was that the electrical power and telephone service had been restored sometime during the night.

Although most of the advertisements were for slickly managed health care clinics, she did finally hit upon a listing for a Dr. Raymond Whitecastle, MD. He was apparently the last of a dying breed—a family physician who still made house calls. Fingers crossed, she punched in the number.

A few minutes later, greatly relieved, Jessica hung up the phone. Dr. Whitecastle's answering service had informed her that he was currently visiting another patient in the area and would be at Highland House within the hour.

She next flipped to the S's in the white pages, locating the listing for "Captain" Bruce Stoddard. Since Gideon had obviously participated in yesterday's Civil War reenactment, she was hoping that Bruce would be able to give her Gideon's address and telephone number.

When the call was bounced to Bruce's voicemail, Jessica left a brief message asking him to call her with any information pertaining to a Confederate reenactor named Gideon MacAllister. That done, she returned to the library.

At a glance, she could see that Gideon's condition had worsened in the few minutes since she'd left the room. Sprawled in the armchair, eyes closed, he labored to pull a ragged breath into his lungs.

Rushing to his side, Jessica put a hand to his forehead. Even without a thermometer, she ascertained that he was running a dangerously high fever.

Suddenly feeling an unexpected static charge against the palm of her hand, she hastily removed it from Gideon's brow.

"The doctor will be here shortly," she said in a chipper tone as she knelt on the floor beside Gideon's chair. Wanting to reassure him that all was well, she awkwardly patted his hand. Not only was it exceedingly warm to the touch, but she experienced another static charge that caused a strange tingling in her fingertips.

Bewildered by the odd sensation, she moved her hand to the

cuff of his uniform jacket. As her fingers lightly traced the frayed trim, she felt as though her digits were enlivened with some sort of hypersensitivity. The sensation enabled her to see in her mind's eye a woman's hand as it slowly and precisely sewed several stitches into the garment. Closing her eyes, Jessica was struck with a sudden mental image; she was actually able to envision how the well-worn garment had appeared before it'd gotten into its present "distressed" condition. *Stiff gray wool. A bold serpentine pattern of gold braid on the cuff. A row of stamped brass buttons shining brightly in the noonday sun.* No sooner had those images flashed through her mind than Jessica saw Gideon, with a warm smile on his clean-shaven face, lean over to kiss—

Jessica's eyes popped wide open, and the image instantly vanished. She felt as though she'd just recalled a long-lost memory.

But how can I have a memory of a man I don't even know? she wondered, flustered by the weird interlude.

Just then, Gideon thrashed his head from side to side, frantically grabbing the arm of the chair. "Two will die in the fast, green water! So sayeth the Beast!"

Given that his eyes were closed, Jessica surmised that Gideon was having a doozy of a nightmare.

* * *

Lost in the throes of a dark delirium, Gideon forced the disturbing image of the green water out of his mind. Thinking about it only made his head ache. Instead he focused on the woman, the one with the steadfast gaze, who knelt beside him.

However, when he turned and looked back, Gideon could see his beloved. Strangely enough, it seemed as though he was peering at the same woman in both directions.

Had his ravaged heart conjured the mirage simply to mock him? No, he was certain that his beloved was with him. He recognized the touch of her hand, just as he remembered the feel of her lips against his.

Memories, like warm blood, soon rushed through his veins, warming him, then just as quickly chilling him to the bone. There had been so many endless nights spent without her...

Yet she was now achingly near.

Sensing that they were as close to one another as the breadth between two heartbeats, he struggled to rouse himself.

"Come back to me, Gideon...Come back to me."

Hearing her plea, Gideon turned his head, desperately trying to find his beloved in the murky depths. As he did, he suddenly knew that he must cross the Rubicon of his last life in order to reach his beloved on the opposite shore.

Although he was determined to take the first step, he was halted by the demons of remembrance. After the unforgivable transgression he'd committed, why would his beloved return for him? His words, uttered in anger, had been unjustly cruel. And his agonized torment was that they had been the last words spoken between them. His lament was in knowing that he'd sought forgiveness too late, his plea for repentance muffled by the vagaries of war and the eternal silence of the grave.

Before him, death beckoned, a siren's song, luring him with its haunting melody.

On the verge of surrendering to it, Gideon felt his beloved reach out to him, pulling him away from the Stygian blackness. Taking him by the hand, she led him across the deep, swift flowing waters of time. As they neared the end of their journey, she turned and smiled at him.

In that instant, Gideon realized that it was the woman with

the steadfast gaze who had brought him home to Highland House.

* * *

"Exactly how long has the patient been in this condition?" Finished taking Gideon's pulse, Dr. Raymond Whitecastle next pried open an eyelid and examined a very bloodshot blue eye.

"Well, he came back yesterday evening from the reenactment looking kind of, um, down and out," Jessica hedged, still guilt-ridden that she'd erroneously assumed Gideon had been suffering from drunkenness when he first arrived at Highland House.

"Do you mean to tell me that in such a weakened condition, this man actually attended yesterday's Civil War reenactment?"

"Oh, he was there, all right." Jessica lamely gestured to Gideon's woebegone Confederate tunic. "That's why he's still wearing his uniform."

Dr. Whitecastle made a *tsk*ing sound as he opened his doctor's bag and pulled out several metal instruments. "Is this man your hus—"

"He's an old family friend," Jessica interjected. While she hated to tell such a bald-faced lie, she knew that gossip could spread like a mountain brushfire in a rural community. Because she was still a relative newcomer to the area, she didn't want anyone to know that she was temporarily sheltering some strange man at Highland House. In fact, her plan was to contact Gideon MacAllister's family and arrange for them to retrieve him with as little fanfare as possible.

"Why are you doing that?" Jessica anxiously inquired when Dr. Whitecastle began to unbutton Gideon's jacket.

"I need to remove some of your friend's clothing so that I can properly examine him," the doctor said matter-of-factly. "Will you give me a hand with his jacket?"

Somewhat reluctantly, Jessica reached over to help the doctor remove the well-worn garment, revealing a dark gray vest beneath.

"You don't often see a fine, old timepiece like this," Dr. Whitecastle said admiringly as he plucked a gold pocket watch from the vest pocket and passed it to Jessica. "I'm no expert, but my guess is that's a very valuable watch."

Stepping over to the fireplace, Jessica carefully placed the pocket watch on the mantel for safekeeping. As she turned back around, her breath caught in her throat—Gideon's vest and white linen shirt were both fully unbuttoned, revealing one of the most incredible upper bodies she'd ever set eyes upon. Absolutely ab-tastic! She'd thought that only Hollywood actors with personal trainers had washboard abs like that.

Boy, was I ever mistaken.

"Your friend appears to keep himself in excellent shape," Dr. Whitecastle remarked off-handedly as he lifted a stethoscope to Gideon's chest.

"I'll say," Jessica murmured, small rivets of tension pulsing along her spine as she continued to stare at what could only be called a beautiful male torso.

"Do you happen to know who sutured this chest wound?"

"Hmm?" Jessica tore her overly avid gaze from Gideon's bare chest, chagrined that she'd actually been ogling a sick man. One who boasted a very bushy beard. *Surely, I'm not that desperate.* "I'm sorry, doctor, but I didn't hear what you just said."

The doctor poked his finger at a raw-looking scar located near Gideon's underarm. "This is new scar tissue. Whoever sewed him up did a very sloppy job of it," he stated in a disapproving tone of voice. "Why, I'm surprised that anybody could get through medical school with such a crude technique."

"Two will die in the fast, green water! So sayeth the Beast!"

Jessica and Dr. Whitecastle jerked in unison at Gideon's loud exclamation.

"Two will die in the fast, green water!" Gideon again bellowed, his body heaving with exertion.

Concerned that he might come bodily out of the chair, Jessica unthinkingly placed a restraining hand on Gideon's bare chest. Immediately feeling a tingling heat radiate from his pectoral muscle through her palm and along the length of her arm, she quickly removed her hand.

Clearing her throat, Jessica peered at the doctor and said, "I should probably mention that Gideon was a little confused earlier this morning as to his whereabouts." *Not to mention, his whenabouts.*

"Given the fact that he's running a temperature of 104.2 degrees, disorientation is not uncommon," Dr. Whitecastle informed her. "Once we get his temperature down, his mental state should return to normal."

Jessica's shoulders sagged with relief. "You don't know how happy I am to hear that." It meant that Gideon made those screwball remarks because he'd been in a fevered state of mind. *1864, indeed.*

"Incidentally, your friend is an extremely lucky man. Even with all of the advances of modern medicine, pneumonia can still be a deadly killer if not treated early."

"Pneumonia!" she exclaimed, shocked by the diagnosis.

"No need to worry. It's not contagious," Dr. Whitecastle said reassuringly as he removed a small glass vial and a wrapped syringe from his leather bag. "From the preliminary exam, it's evident your friend is suffering from the early stages of pneumonia, as well as extreme physical exhaustion. Of course, in the old days, before antibiotics, he wouldn't have stood much of a chance. But with plenty of bed rest and lots of fluids, he should be on the mend soon enough." That said, he unwrapped the syringe, tipped the bottle upside down, and pierced the protective seal with the syringe's needle.

Sympathetically flinching, Jessica watched as the doctor jabbed the syringe into Gideon's right arm.

"Speaking of bed rest, does this couch convert into a bed?" Dr. Whitecastle inquired as he inserted the used syringe into a plastic tube.

"As a matter of fact, it does pull into—" Jessica halted in mid-sentence, belatedly realizing where the conversation was headed. Allowing a man to sleep on her sofa fully dressed was one thing. Permitting that same stranger to recuperate on her sofa bed was an entirely different matter, one that placed her in an extremely awkward position.

"After he's recovered a bit, you can move him to a proper bed. I want to him get at least a week's worth of bed rest," the doctor instructed in a tone of voice that would brook no argument. "Also, try to get as many fluids into him as you can, because we don't want him to become dehydrated. And, lastly, keep a close eye on his fever. If it doesn't come down by tomorrow, give me a call."

Tongue-tied, Jessica mutely stared at the doctor. Even though she very much wanted to tell him that she had no intention of playing nursemaid to a complete stranger, for some inexplicable reason she couldn't bring herself to do so.

Finished administering the meds, Dr. Whitecastle retrieved a prescription pad from his bag. "What's your friend's name?"

"Gideon. Gideon MacAllister," she woodenly replied, watching him scribble something indecipherable onto the pad.

Ripping off a total of three prescriptions, the doctor handed them to her just as his cell phone began to trill loudly.

"Excuse me," he said before taking the call. A moment later, Jessica overheard him say, "I'll be there in ten minutes."

With a discernible frown etched onto his face, Dr. Whitecastle stuffed the mobile phone into his jacket pocket. Muttering something about mailing Jessica the bill, he hurriedly closed his medical bag.

"Is everything all right?" she asked, noticing that the doctor's demeanor had greatly altered since taking the call.

"I wish that I could say yes, but unfortunately I've just been informed that there's been a tragic rafting accident on the Greenbrier River. Apparently two rafters drowned and several others have been severely injured."

Two will die on the fast, green water.

Recalling Gideon's cryptic utterance, Jessica felt the proverbial chill course along her spine.

Chapter 6

I took the liberty of filling your prescriptions," Jessica said in a breezy tone as she entered the library.

To her dismay, the announcement was met with a pronounced silence.

At a glance, Jessica could see that Gideon was still sacked out on the sofa bed. Whatever had been in the injection that Dr. Whitecastle had administered had completely knocked him out. Despite the fact that it was late in the day, the "patient" gave no indication that he would be awakening any time soon. And though Gideon needed his rest in order to recuperate, she desperately needed to learn some vitally important information: his address and phone number, for starters.

In all honesty, she was halfway tempted to call the county sheriff's department and demand that they take Mr. Gideon MacAllister off her hands. Why should she be responsible for taking care of him? He was a stranger who'd landed on her doorstep and collapsed on her couch, and now she was supposed to feed, clothe, and care for him? Well, forget it. Nothing doing. Gideon MacAllister would have to find some other sucker to play nursemaid.

As she placed the prescription bottles on the end table, Buster, reclining in the armchair, gave her a heavy-lidded glance.

"I just put some fresh kibble in your bowl."

Hearing that, the big Maine Coon instantly morphed from drowsy kitty into speeding feline bullet, hightailing it to the kitchen.

With a weary sigh, Jessica stepped over to the sofa bed. Within micro-seconds, all thoughts of throwing Gideon to the wolves instantly vanished. Along each side of his face, she saw dried tear tracks that meandered down his cheeks before disappearing into his bushy beard. It was a sight that instantaneously kick-started all of her protective instincts.

Worried that he may have worsened, Jessica sat on the edge of the sofa bed. Leaning over him, she placed the back of her hand against Gideon's forehead, ignoring the tingling sparks that immediately radiated from his brow.

To her relief, his skin was cool to the touch.

"While I know that personal hygiene is a somewhat delicate matter, I went ahead and bought you a new toothbrush, some deodorant, and a bag of disposable razors. Although from the looks of it, you're gonna need a pair of garden shears to get rid of that bushy beard," Jessica muttered under her breath. Gideon seemed unaware of the fact that he was being spoken to.

Because he was oblivious, Jessica succumbed to temptation, letting her gaze errantly roam across the muscled planes of Gideon's bare chest. Despite the fact that he was in a weakened condition, Gideon MacAllister possessed the well-honed body of an athlete.

As she continued to watch his chest rise and fall with each measured breath, she gently laid a hand on his bare skin. The instant she did, she felt another heated tingle in her fingertips, a sensation that was akin to plunging a cold hand into a tub of hot water.

Unable to stop herself, Jessica let her fingers glide across one of Gideon's pectoral muscles. Figuring no red-blooded woman would blame her, she next ran her fingers through his chest hair, pleasantly surprised at its soft texture. Then, leaning forward, she impetuously laid her cheek against his naked chest.

The moment she did, Jessica was hit with a barrage of images. *A woman in a hoop skirt. A four-poster bed. A candlelit chamber.* The images flashed across her mind's eye in such fast succession that it was as though she'd glimpsed them through a kaleidoscope.

With a gasp, she pulled away from Gideon's chest. Obviously, her all too vivid imagination was working overtime. "I, um… was just checking your heartbeat," she fibbed, on the off-chance that Gideon was aware of what she'd just done. "And, FYI, it's beating just fine."

My heart, I'm not so sure about, she silently appended, stunned that she could even be remotely attracted to the big, bearded man.

"I think you ought to know that I, um…" Her voice faded into silence as Jessica worriedly gnawed on her lower lip. Inundated with guilt, she finally drummed up enough courage to say, "I'm really sorry, but I had to pawn one of those gold coins that you had in your saddlebag."

Since leaving Bud's Pawn Shop, she'd come up with every excuse imaginable for filching the coin. But the simple truth of the matter was that she hadn't had enough cash to pay for Gideon's three prescriptions with payday still a week away. Whether that justified petty thievery would be for him to decide.

"And let me tell you, I was absolutely floored to find out that one coin alone was worth two thousand dollars," she informed her sleeping patient, figuring the dry-run was good practice for when she'd have to make the actual confession. "The man at the pawn shop said it was an authentic, 155-year-old golden eagle coin. But you probably already knew that, huh? And don't worry, I've got receipts for everything."

Alarmingly, Gideon's eyelids suddenly began to flutter. Moaning softly, he moved his head from side to side, as if he was trying to rouse himself from a deep slumber. A split-second later, Jessica found herself gazing into a pair of mesmerizing blue eyes.

In those super-charged moments, a spark of recognition flashed between them. Jessica became absolutely certain that she knew Gideon MacAllister from *somewhere*.

Without so much as moving a muscle, Gideon stared at her with what could only be described as a look of profound longing.

Continuing to hold her in that steadfast gaze, Gideon secured a hand around each of her upper arms as he pulled her toward him. There was nothing rough or forceful in his manner; he was merely determined. Inexplicably excited, Jessica drew in a serrated breath. Having lost the ability to think clearly, she instinctively anchored her hands against Gideon's shoulders. As though she'd just stuck a wet finger in a light socket, all ten fingers began to tingle.

In slow, unhurried fashion, Gideon appraised her flushed face before his gaze slid down her neck, finally coming to a rest on her visibly heaving chest. Glancing downward, Jessica saw that her nipples were indecently outlined against her cotton T-shirt.

Breathlessly attuned to the impassioned silence that vibrated between them, Jessica knew that she had to pull away from him. Now. Before it was too late.

Although that was what she'd intended to do, her body simply refused to comply with her brain's "retreat" order. If anything, her heart contrarily demanded that she stay put, certain that if she remained there long enough, Gideon would—

Yes. Just as her rebellious heart had hoped, Gideon raised his head to kiss her.

The instant that his lips touched hers, Jessica insanely thought that she may very well have been waiting for this moment her entire life. Even crazier than that, she was hit with a jolt of all-encompassing familiarity, too enthralled to ponder how such a thing could even be possible.

What began as a sweetly tender kiss snowballed into something else entirely. Gideon deepened the kiss, one intimate degree at time. As he suckled on her lower lip, a muffled whimper of pleasure lodged in Jessica's throat. Welcoming his ardent exploration, she opened her mouth, reveling in the twining of lips and tongues.

And, boy, did it feel good. The kind of good that made her heart pound and her hips twitch. Eager for more, she brazenly smashed her breasts against Gideon's torso. When he shuddered against her, Jessica deduced that he was as deeply affected by the kiss as she was.

Needing to pull air into her lungs, Jessica had no choice but to break the connection between their two mouths. With his eyes closed, Gideon moved a hand to the back of her neck and let his lips blaze a trail along the column of her neck.

"I've missed you so much," he murmured, his lips now traversing the line of her jaw.

Jessica instantly froze, disbelieving what she'd just heard.

How can you miss someone that you don't even know? Unless you think you're kissing someone else.

Jerking away from Gideon, she saw that his eyes were still

firmly closed. She had the sudden, sickening realization that he was sound asleep. Completely lost in the land of Nod from the looks of it. And obviously in the throes of one heck of a hot dream.

With an undignified shriek, Jessica lunged off the sofa bed. Grabbing the nearby armchair for support, she inhaled several deeps gulps of air, her legs wobbling unsteadily beneath her.

Just then, Gideon moaned in his sleep, his hips erotically thrusting upward.

"I can't believe that I just saw that," she gasped, horrified to think that Gideon was doing a lot more than merely kissing his dream woman.

Appalled, she yanked the woolen blanket up to his chin, hoping that if she covered his writhing body, she could pretend that she wasn't in the company of a sexually aroused male.

Turning her back on him, Jessica touched her swollen lips, her body quivering with humiliation. That it could've happened in the first place was beyond comprehension. Gideon, at least, had the excuse of being asleep. Which was a lot more than what she had.

But what about that heart-stirring interlude when he'd gazed up at her, peering into her eyes as if he could see into her very soul? In those electrifying seconds, Gideon had appeared very much awake.

Suddenly hearing the peal of the hallway telephone, Jessica rushed out of the room to answer it, relieved when it turned out to be Bruce Stoddard.

"We sure missed you last night at the reenactment ball."

"I'm sure that a good time was had by all." As she spoke, Jessica impatiently drummed her fingers against the telephone stand, not in the mood for idle chitchat.

"Although it took a bit of digging, I was able to uncover some facts about your mystery man Gideon MacAllister."

Elated to hear that, Jessica snatched a pencil and pad of paper out of a drawer. "Go ahead, Bruce. I'm ready."

"Well, I checked with our regimental historian and found out that Colonel Gideon MacAllister commanded the 8th Virginia Cavalry."

"Cavalry, gotcha." Jessica quickly scribbled "8th Va Cav" onto the notepad. "Okay, what's his phone number?"

Her question was met with a boisterous chuckle.

"First, you'll have to find a long-distance telephone company that can connect you to the great beyond," Bruce said, still chortling.

"Huh? What are you talking about?"

"Colonel MacAllister died in 1864, shortly after the Battle of Lewis Creek."

At those words, the pencil slipped from Jessica's fingers, rolling along the table top before landing on the wood-planked floor.

Desperately trying to collect herself, Jessica took a stabilizing breath before she said, "Are you absolutely certain about that, Bruce? Maybe one of your reenactors has the same name."

On the other end of the line, she heard Bruce rifle through several sheets of paper.

"Nope, sorry," he said a few seconds later. "There's no Gideon MacAllister on the list. Like I said, Colonel MacAllister died in September of 1864 from pneumonia."

"Pneumonia!" Jessica was unable to hide her stunned disbelief. "You didn't say anything about pneumonia."

"What's wrong? Was this guy a relative of yours or something?"

"No, um, not exactly," she mumbled, wondering how Bruce Stoddard would react if she told him that, right before he called, she'd been groping a man who'd supposedly died a hundred and fifty years ago.

"According to our historian, MacAllister and his men were covering the rear flanks during the Confederate retreat. Apparently, his horse was shot out from under him and, to escape capture by the Federals, he hid on the mountainside," Bruce told her. "The records are kinda hazy as to where exactly he died. His home was in the vicinity, and it's believed that he somehow managed to make his way there. No one really knows for sure since there's no recorded grave site."

Jessica struggled to catch her breath, absolutely floored by what she'd just heard.

"Jessica, are you still there?"

"Yeah…yeah, I'm still here." She glanced down, absently noticing that she'd twisted the telephone cord around her wrist. Slowly, she unraveled it. "Um, I need to go now." That said, Jessica hung up the phone, forgetting to say good-bye.

Reluctantly, she turned and walked toward the library, telling herself that there was a logical explanation for all of this. *People cannot, repeat, cannot travel through time.*

As if it was a magical incantation, Jessica uttered the phrase several times, astounded that she'd even briefly considered such a ridiculous thing possible. It only testified to the strain she'd been under these last twenty-four hours.

Intending to get to the bottom of what was fast becoming a deep, dark mystery, Jessica decided that the time had come to confront "Gideon MacAllister," uncover his true identity, and then put him in the Bronco and drive him home. Obviously, her uninvited guest had taken his Confederate role-playing too far, which was why Bruce had been unable to identify him. Because Civil War reenactments drew throngs of people, many of whom traveled from miles away, she suspected that it was impossible to keep track of all the participants.

Moments later, as she purposefully strode into the library, Jessica came to a shuddering halt. The entire room was blanketed in an inky darkness, the sun having set while she'd taken the call.

Standing in what she gauged to be the middle of the room, Jessica used an outstretched arm to navigate her way toward the end table so that she could turn on a lamp.

"Damn!" she cursed aloud as she stubbed her big toe against an unseen piece of furniture. Fumbling for the lamp, she accidentally knocked over a water glass. "Oh, for Pete's sake."

Finally locating the light switch, she turned it on. The moment she did, she was grabbed from behind.

Chapter 7

I intend you no harm," Gideon assured the skittish female as he placed a hand on the small of her back in order to prevent the two of them from tumbling backward onto the bed. Given her loud shriek of surprise, he surmised that she'd not seen him sitting on the edge of the mattress.

Caught off balance, the woman nonetheless toppled onto his lap.

The instant that their two bodies came into contact, physical desire—raw, potent, and wholly unexpected—pulsed between his hips.

It'd been nearly a year since his wife's passing. Still in mourning, he'd not so much as glanced at another woman. After his beloved's tragic death, he'd lost all interest in fleshly desires. And though his mind now commanded otherwise, his body, too long deprived, responded to the squirming female.

At a loss for words, he tried not to stare at the woman's immodest apparel. The auburn-haired beauty was garbed in trousers made from a well-worn, denim fabric and a shirt, such as it was, that resembled an abbreviated undergarment. If her aim was to look like a man, she fell short of the mark, for her garments only accentuated the fact that she was most definitely a woman.

Ashamed of his wayward thoughts, Gideon hastily lifted the strangely clad female off of his lap.

"I wasn't expecting you to be up and about," the lady said stiffly, protectively crossing her arms in front of her waist as her gaze nervously darted from his face to his torso.

Gideon glanced downward, surprised to see that he was bare-chested. Mumbling an apology, he reached for his shirt, which was hanging from a nearby chair. Avoiding her gaze, he hurriedly plied his fingers to the buttons. As he did, his mind conjured an elusive memory of the auburn-haired beauty tenderly caressing him just before she—

No. It had been his wife who'd caressed him in his dream. His wife who had kissed him so sweetly, so passionately. And it had been his wife whom he'd touched, held…*Loved.*

Rising to his feet, Gideon teetered unsteadily, hit with a jolt of pain in his right temple. He pressed a hand to his head; the pain was nearly unbearable. Since arriving at Highland House, he'd not had a moment's respite from the agonizing headache. As though his skull was encircled by an ever-tightening cinch.

"I know that you're not feeling up to par right now, but I need your telephone number so I can contact your family," the woman announced in a brusque tone of voice.

Only able to decipher a few of the words spoken to him, Gideon replied, "I have no family. Everyone I have ever known has long since become food for worms. Moreover, I am at a loss to understand why I have been spared."

An uneasy expression crept into the lady's eyes as she shifted her weight from one foot to the other. "The doctor said that you might be somewhat, um, disoriented on account of your high fever."

"I am orientated enough to know that I am at Highland House," he affirmed, suddenly feeling like the fabled storybook character Rip Van Winkle. "What I cannot account for is how so much time could pass in the blink of an eye."

Clearly displeased with his answer, the lady's gaze narrowed. "Rather than playing this silly game, why don't you tell me where you live? My Bronco is up and running, and I'd be only too happy to drive you home. In fact, we can leave right now. No doubt, your family, your neighbors, and even your dog, are all worried about you."

"Highland House *is* my home, madam."

"No. Highland House belongs to me," the woman slowly enunciated, as though she was speaking to a half-wit. "And I've got a bill of sale and a property title to prove it."

Rightly brought to task, his ownership of Highland House very much a thing of the past, Gideon acquiesced with a deferential nod. "My apologies for being so presumptuous."

"No doubt, things are a little fuzzy around the edges because of your illness," his hostess said with a hesitant smile. "Although you have to admit that it's awfully odd for a man to walk into a stranger's house, uninvited, and just collapse on the couch."

"I am as perplexed as you to know how I came to be here." Gideon peered around the room, his gaze eventually landing on the strangely fashioned table lamp that brightly illuminated the entire room. Truly bewildered, he said, "A man traversing the boundaries of time is an absurd proposition, is it not? And though preposterous, that is exactly what seems to have transpired."

"Did you make the trip on a magic carpet or did the extraterrestrials teleport you to the twenty-first century?"

Detecting a note of derision in her voice, Gideon said, "There are many mysteries of the universe for which I have no explanation."

"That's it? That's your answer? You're just going to write this off as an unidentified, cosmic blooper, and expect me to believe you?"

"Rest assured, madam, I am no charlatan."

"Will you please stop calling me 'madam.' It makes me feel like a—" The lady abruptly shook her head as she waved away the unspoken thought. "Never mind what it makes me feel like. My name is Jessica. Jessica Reardon."

He bent at the waist and said, "And I am Colonel Gideon MacAllister."

A discernible spark of annoyance immediately flashed in his hostess's hazel-green eyes. "I know for a fact that your name is not Gideon MacAllister. Just a few minutes ago, I was on the telephone with someone who informed me that this Gideon MacAllister character died one hundred and fifty years ago. Now I'm no doctor, but you look very much alive to me."

"Be that as it may, 'this Gideon MacAllister character' and I are one and the same," he doggedly maintained.

Clearly exasperated, the lady rolled her eyes heavenward. "All right, fine. If you want me to call you 'Gideon,' then that's what I'll call you. Now will you please tell me where you live so I can take you home?"

Gideon had only to glance at what used to be his library to know that, despite the neglect and damage of a century and a half, he was standing in the only home he'd ever known: Highland House.

Suddenly restless, he walked over to the French doors on the other side of the room. "'Things are not, and yet appear to be,'" he murmured dejectedly, thinking there was more than a germ of truth contained in Epictetus' immortal observation.

As he stared at the overgrown woodland that bordered the lawn, Gideon was certain that somewhere in the dark grove the beast still lurked. The same red-eyed, winged serpent that he'd glimpsed upon his approach to Highland House.

Otherworldly creatures. Unexplained rifts in time.

Have I gone completely mad?

He'd known more than a few soldiers who'd lost, not only their will to live, but their wits as well. War could do that to a man. Drive him to the brink of self-destruction. Yet earlier in the day, he'd seen with his own eyes the newspaper printed with the date 2014. Even more damning, he'd perused the history book entitled *Time-Life's Illustrated Guide to the Civil War* that detailed how the Confederacy had been defeated, General Lee having surrendered the army of northern Virginia at a place called Appomattox. The evidence was incontrovertible. He did travel through time.

But how? And, more importantly, why?

"Gideon, are you all right?" his hostess worriedly inquired, her image suddenly reflected in the window panes. "Maybe you should sit down," she suggested, placing a solicitous hand on his forearm.

Almost immediately, Gideon felt a tingly heat course up and down the length of his arm. Turning his head, he peered into Jessica Reardon's eyes, noticing how the green irises were tinged with flecks of yellow and brown. The mirrors of the soul, her eyes seemed hauntingly familiar to him. Transfixed, he wondered why this woman, upon whom he'd never set eyes before yesterday, had repeatedly appeared in his fevered reveries.

Could it be that, in his dream, he kissed *her* rather than his beloved wife?

Angered that he would do such a thing, Gideon inwardly berated himself. Even if the kiss had only occurred in a dream, in that unconscious realm where no man had control, it felt like a betrayal to his beloved. No matter that she'd been dead nearly twelve months. No matter that he'd traversed one hundred and fifty years into the future. Their love had no beginning and no end.

My heart shall forever belong to her.

Somewhat guiltily, Gideon glanced at the feminine hand that rested lightly upon his forearm. It did not escape his notice that the lady wore no wedding band.

As the tingling sensation became more pronounced, Gideon abruptly pulled away, perplexed by his strange reaction to the woman. Then, his mind made up as to what had to be done, he purposefully strode over to his saddlebag, in plain sight where he'd dropped it on the floor the previous evening. Going down on bent knee, he unbuckled it. When he found what he was searching for, he rose to his feet and approached Miss Reardon.

Taking hold of the lady's right hand, he braced himself against the electrifying reverberation that passed between them as he deposited four gold coins into her palm. "I trust that this will sufficiently pay for my lodging."

* * *

Flabbergasted, Jessica stared at the four coins nestled in her open palm.

"I don't understand," she murmured, admittedly dazzled by the gleaming bits of gold.

"It would be remiss not to offer fair recompense for your hospitality."

Jessica shook her head to clear the proverbial cobwebs. "Are you asking me to rent you a room?"

"That is precisely what I am doing." Gideon jutted his chin at the four coins. "Is that a sufficient amount to cover my room and board?"

After doing a quick mental calculation, she gulped and said, "More than sufficient. You've just given me somewhere in the neighborhood of a year's worth of rent. Which is beside the point because— What I mean to say is—"

At a sudden loss to remember the point that she wanted to make, Jessica involuntarily closed her fist around the four gold coins. Because of her dire monetary situation, she'd considered getting a roommate, albeit a female one, to help with the household expenses. Lord knew she could use the extra money.

Whether Gideon MacAllister knew it or not, he'd just dangled a very alluring carrot in front of her. Certainly, his tempting offer would solve many of her short-term financial woes. Four coins at two thousand dollars apiece—more if she sold them to a certified coin dealer instead of a pawn broker—amounted to at least eight thousand dollars. Which meant that she could now afford to pay for some of the more urgent home repairs that she'd had to put on the back burner. And while there was no getting around Gideon's weird delusion about traveling through time, for eight thousand dollars, she was willing to chalk it up to a case of temporary insanity induced by a high fever.

Shifting the coins to her other palm, Jessica thrust out her right hand. "All right, Gideon MacAllister. You've got yourself a deal."

Visibly taken aback by the gesture, Gideon stared at her extended hand for several seconds before he finally sealed the agreement with a time-honored handshake. The moment their two palms touched, Jessica realized her mistake. A heated discharge ignited between them, one that instantly made her wonder if letting Gideon remain at Highland House was such a good idea after all.

What if he tries to kiss me again? What if he tried to do more than kiss her? She hadn't exactly spurned his advances the first time around. Even more worrisome, what if he turned out to be some sort of deranged sex maniac?

"Miss Reardon, you're staring at me as if I was Mephistopheles."

Oh, great. A well-read sex maniac.

"I'm sorry for staring. It's just that I, um…" Her voice trailed into silence as Jessica realized that she'd jumped to a completely unfounded conclusion. Since waking up, Gideon had been a perfect gentleman. More than likely, he had no conscious memory of the frenzied lip-lock that had earlier taken place between them.

Affecting a cheery demeanor, she pocketed the four coins in her well-worn Levis. "Gee, I feel like the richest girl in Greenbrier County."

"It has always been my contention, Miss Reardon, that true wealth cannot be measured in terms of money," Gideon intoned, the huskiness in his voice lending the sentiment a certain gravitas.

Maybe it was because of Gideon's long beard and sad, forlorn gaze, but for some inexplicable reason Jessica was suddenly put in mind of a woodcut engraving she'd once seen of a medieval crusader. A knight of old who'd sacrificed everything for his cause, his cross, his crown.

"Don't you think you should call me by my first name?" she invited with a friendly smile. "We are, after all, going to be roomies."

"As you wish," he consented with a courtly nod of the head.

Glancing at the open door, he then said, "If it wouldn't inconvenience you, I'd like to be shown to my room now."

"Of course. I'll take you right up. You look like you could use some rest."

Deciding to put him in the upstairs bedroom at the far end of the hall—the complete opposite end of the hall from her bedroom—Jessica grabbed the plastic pill bottles on the side table. "I had to pawn a gold coin to pay for your medicine," she told him. "But don't worry. I have your change. And all of the receipts, too."

"I am in your debt," Gideon said as he started to gather his belongings. After tossing his saddlebag over his shoulder, he picked up his boots, gun holster, and scabbard. The effort evidently cost him as he immediately drew in a ragged breath.

As they made their way to the foyer, Jessica warily glanced at the revolver protruding from his leather holster. Although it was menacing-looking, because Gideon was a Civil War reenactor she knew that it would be loaded with blanks per reenactment regulations.

However, per Bruce Stoddard, there'd been no one at the reenactment by the name of Gideon MacAllister. Furthermore, Bruce had been unaware of any reenactor playing the role of the nineteenth-century Confederate colonel. Unwilling to dwell on that particular conundrum, Jessica shoved the inconvenient factoid into mental cold storage.

When they reached the foot of the staircase, she came to a standstill. "I can give you the full tour when you're feeling better. For the time being, all you really need to know is that the kitchen is behind the staircase, and the living room is on the opposite end of the house from the library."

A rueful expression crept into Gideon's eyes as he glanced at the hallway's dreary walls and drab woodwork.

"I'm in the process of renovating, but it's slow going," Jessica explained, well aware that Highland House wasn't exactly a model home.

Slowly, Gideon ran a hand over the carved newel post, the gesture putting her in mind of a lover's caress. "It used to be the color of Devonshire cream," he remarked.

Refusing to comment—figuring it would only lend credence to the outlandish notion that he'd magically beamed down from the nineteenth century—Jessica started up the stairs with Gideon following in her wake. Entering the guest bedroom a few moments later, she flipped on the overhead light. Out of the corner of her eye, she noticed that Gideon's awestruck gaze immediately focused on the wall plate before shifting to the ceiling fixture.

Ignoring his rapt expression, she gestured to the naked bulb and said, "I'll get a shade on that ASAP." She was conscious of the fact that not only was the fixture an inhospitable eyesore, but that for eight thousand dollars Gideon deserved more than an old brass bed, a badly scarred writing desk, and a metal clothes cabinet.

"Please do not trouble yourself," Gideon said as he deposited his boots on the floor and set his weapons on top of the desk. "The accommodations suit me just fine."

"Since the doctor wants you to stay in bed, I'll bring you a dinner tray," Jessica said as she turned to leave.

Taking her by surprise, Gideon gently took hold of her by the wrist, preventing her departure.

"You do so remind me of someone," he murmured. "But I am at a complete loss to know who that somebody might be."

So, he felt it too, she thought with no small measure of surprise as she gazed into Gideon's cerulean blue eyes. Eyes that put her in mind of a clear sky on a bright summer's day. Which was kind of ironic given that Gideon MacAllister seemed so utterly forlorn. Like he was present in body, but his mind, as well as his heart, were faraway.

"I know what you mean. I keep thinking that we've previously met, but—" Jessica stopped in mid-sentence, belatedly realizing that she was being lured into a conversation that she did not wish to have. "But seeing as how you supposedly rode the magic bus through the mystical time portal that would be next to impossible."

Gideon held her gaze, a beseeching look in his eyes. "Is it so very difficult to believe my tale?"

"Try flat-out impossible."

* * *

Jessica closed her book, the words having begun to blur on the page.

"Lily Bart and everyone else in *The House of Mirth* will have to wait until tomorrow to board the yacht," she murmured as she set the volume on the nightstand and turned off the bedside lamp.

No sooner was the room plunged into darkness than Buster leaped onto the mattress, taking his customary place on the pillow next to hers.

Smiling, she rolled over and gave her purring feline an affectionate rub under his chin. "Night, sweetie."

Utterly exhausted, it didn't take long for Jessica to drift into a deep sleep, leaving the waking world far behind.

Once she entered the dream realm, a door began to materialize within the murky shadows of the dreamscape. Opening it, she peered into an unfamiliar room where she saw a woman garbed in a long, white nightgown. Jessica immediately recognized the woman, who was her dream world avatar, a character named "Sarah."

As she stood on the threshold between the two worlds, Jessica waited for an invitation. Slightly turning her head, Sarah made eye contact with her.

Connection made, Jessica stepped into the room and merged with her dream persona. The moment she did, she could feel Sarah's every emotion, able to know her every thought.

And there was no doubt in her mind that Sarah was mad as hell.

Chapter 8

Sweet Springs, Virginia
Summer 1860

Oh, but she was furious.

Her stepmother had capriciously forbidden her from attending the Sweet Springs grand ball. Not only did her stepmother and fiancé Oren Tolliver disapprove of her newly formed acquaintance with Gideon MacAllister, but, in a cruel act of spite, her stepmother had locked her in their suite, making it impossible for her to inform Gideon that she would not be in attendance at the ball.

To add insult to injury, she could now hear strains of music emanating from the hotel's main ballroom. Crestfallen, her shoulders sagged as she exhaled a dejected sigh, the lively tune depressing her all the more.

Certain that the Fates had plotted against her, Sarah shut the window and pulled the draperies closed. Since she was already dressed for bed, she decided to take what comfort she could in sleep.

No sooner had she settled herself on the feather tick mattress than she heard a strange *rat-a-tat-tat*. Had it not been a clear August night, she would have sworn that hailstones were hitting the window pane.

Curious, she pulled the heavy drapery aside to peer outside. Aghast at what she saw, she immediately yanked the drapery to one side and opened the window.

"Whatever are you doing here?" she demanded to know as she leaned over the window sash.

Standing several feet below her, resplendent in black evening attire, was Gideon MacAllister, the devil's own grin stamped onto his handsome face.

"The Knight of the Allegheny Mountains has once again come to your rescue."

"Mr. MacAllister, have you lost your mind?"

"Only my heart, fair maiden."

His lighthearted reply caused Sarah's breath to catch in her throat. What would make him say such a thing? Surely he jested.

"Your presence confounds me, sir. Should you not be at the ball?"

"May I respectfully remind you, Miss Pemberton, that you did promise me the first waltz of the evening?"

"And I was very much looking forward to the pleasure of your company; however—" Her fingers nervously toyed with the drapery material, uncertain how much of the humiliating tale she should divulge. "I'm afraid it's utterly impossible for me to keep my promise," she said a few seconds later, opting for the full truth. "If I were to be seen in the ballroom, my stepmother would never forgive me."

"There's no need to fear on that account."

Baffled by Gideon's reply, she made haste to point out the

obvious. "If I'm not in attendance at the ball, how can we possibly dance with one another?"

"Who said anything about attending the ball?" Gideon opened his arms as he gestured to the expanse of lawn outside her bedroom window. "This looks as good a dance floor as any."

At hearing that, her eyes opened wide. She was utterly flabbergasted. "You cannot seriously be asking me to dance with you on the lawn."

"I've never been more serious in all my life. Can't you hear the music, Miss Pemberton?" Gideon cupped one hand to his ear, while the other hand swung in time to the music. "The musicians at Sweet Springs are so accomplished that you may very well think you've been spirited off to the ballrooms of Vienna."

Torn between reason and desire, Sarah was forced to surrender to the former. Even if she dared to defy her stepmother, she was still a virtual prisoner.

"My stepmother has secured the door from the outside," she informed him, shame-faced at the disclosure.

"Where is your sense of adventure, Miss Pemberton? No one is about, and the window at which you stand is no more than four feet above the ground. It would be easy enough for me to lift you over the sill."

Worried that she might be possessed by some form of lunar madness, Sarah said, "I feel compelled to remind you that I only agreed to the one waltz."

Gideon's tall body bent into a sweeping bow. "And you have my word, as a gentleman, that I shall keep to my end of the bargain."

About to acquiesce to his proposal, Sarah belatedly realized that, not only was her hair unbound, but she was garbed in her nightdress and chintz wrapper. Moreover, because she would have to dress unattended, she would need at least twenty minutes to change into more suitable attire.

"Is something the matter, Miss Pemberton?"

Hopes dashed, she gestured to her wrapper. "As you can plainly see, I am not dressed for the occasion."

Gideon's eyes twinkled with obvious amusement. "Perhaps I should return to my room and don my nightshirt and bed slippers."

"Really, Mr. MacAllister!"

At hearing her indignant retort, Gideon assumed a more serious air as he said, "I admit to knowing little about ladies' fashions; however you appear modestly clad to my eyes."

Indeed, he made a valid point. Her watered silk ball gown—which revealed a fair amount of bosom—did make her high-necked dressing robe seem chastely modest.

Her mind made up, she decided to embark on the impetuous adventure attired in her night clothes.

Opening the window as high as it would go, Sarah gingerly maneuvered herself onto the edge of the sill. After assuring her that she had nothing to fear, Gideon placed his hands around her waist and lifted her out of the window. Her wrapper and night-dress billowed behind her as he swung her through the air.

"You smell of vanilla and summer flowers," he whispered, his hands still clasped around her waist.

For a brief moment, their two bodies touched before Gideon took a deferential step backward. With a demure smile, she gave him custody of her right hand as she placed her left one upon his shoulder. A few seconds later, they began to waltz across the soft pelt of grass, their movements illuminated by colorful Chinese lanterns strung in the nearby tree limbs. Even though Sarah knew that she was bound to the earth, it seemed as if she were dancing on a cloud, all of her senses attuned to the magic of the moment.

"I must confess, Miss Pemberton, that I was taken aback to hear of your impending marriage to Mr. Tolliver," Gideon remarked, his earlier smile eclipsed by a more sober expression.

"No more than I," she informed him, the magical moment instantly shattered.

"Do you mean to say that the engagement was arranged without your consent?"

Not wishing to dwell on the fact that she would soon be wed to a man she did not love, she confirmed with a doleful nod. "Alas, the situation is hopeless."

"Perhaps your predicament is not as dire as you maintain."

"You would not say that if you were the one engaged to Mr. Tolliver."

The hand at her waist tightened ever so slightly as Gideon peered deeply into her eyes. "What I would like to say is that you are remarkably different from any other lady of my acquaintance."

Unwilling to read too much into his remark, she said, "I suspect that's because I'm the only one foolish enough to dance in the moonlight garbed in a nightdress."

Gideon slowly shook his head, disavowing her of the notion. "What I meant is that you possess a spirited beauty wholly lacking in other women."

The comment had a dizzying effect upon her, warm blood instantly rushing to her cheeks. Enthralled, she said, "I will cherish this night forever, Mr. MacAllister."

Gideon pulled her closer to him, causing her heart to skip a beat.

"Since I've been pondering the notion of kissing you, perhaps you should call me by my first—"

"Gideon. Dearest Gideon," she amended with a warm smile.

Not missing a single dance step, he inclined his head. Then, ever so gently, Gideon kissed her. And though they continued to waltz across the lawn, their lips danced to a wholly different tune.

Certain that she'd been waiting her entire life for this one glorious moment, Sarah reveled in the sweet pleasure of Gideon's kiss. Indeed, it made her wonder if this was the ecstasy which the poets wrote of, the spellbinding tumult that accompanied true love.

Managing to overcome her shy tendencies, Sarah moved her hand across Gideon's shoulder. Possessed of a hunger she could not comprehend, her body and, yes, even her soul, yearned for a deeper intimacy.

To her complete and utter frustration, Gideon broke off the kiss. Coming to a standstill, he said, "I know that you are forsworn to another. And though we have known one another only a brief time, I must confess that I—"

He was interrupted by a burst of animated laughter that originated in the near vicinity. Hurriedly, Sarah pulled away from him, terrified of being seen. Sensing her distress, Gideon took her by the hand and led her to the open window. Wordlessly, he lifted her to the sill, standing guard while she scurried back into her bed chamber.

As she made a move to close the window, Gideon caught her by the wrist, forestalling their inevitable farewell.

"Will you meet me at the garden pavilion tomorrow morning before breakfast?"

* * *

Murmuring to herself, Jessica snuggled against the down-filled pillow, caught midway between sleep and wakefulness. Her dream had been so real, so vivid, it was as though she'd been watching one of those old Technicolor costume dramas on TCM.

Although why she would be dreaming about a strange man she barely knew was a complete mystery. This was the second night in a row that she'd dreamt about Gideon MacAllister.

I hate to think what that says about me.

Perhaps the bone-deep loneliness of the last several months had finally started to catch up to her. Maybe she'd been wrong to turn down every man who'd asked her out on a date. Maybe if she'd been out there getting a little nookie, she wouldn't be having these weird, inexplicable dreams. Weird because the Gideon of her dreams was nothing like the man who was currently asleep at the other end of the hall.

Which made her wonder what Gideon MacAllister might be dreaming about.

Chapter 9

Gideon tried to awaken from the hideous dream. Unable to do so, he took stock of the nightmarish scenario that was spread out before him.

Twilight had fallen upon the blood-drenched meadow at Lewis Creek, the setting sun having put an end to the savage contest. In the far-off distance, he could hear the roar of thunder, and the slender saplings that lined the creek bed shivered in the aftermath. Before him lay a scene of indescribable brutality. Even as the falling rain tamped out the torches of those who wandered the battlefield in search of fallen comrades, the muffled cries of the wounded—a cacophony of moans, grunts, and tearful pleas—remained unceasing.

Gideon craned his neck and stared at the gloomy sky above. How could a loving, benevolent God wreak such havoc upon His peaceful kingdom?

"What did any of us do to deserve this?" he bellowed at the night sky, berating God, the Yankees, and the Southern Cause. But mostly he railed at himself for having been such a damned fool of a man. For having forsaken everything he knew and loved for this.

As he stood in the rain, a dark shadow spread across the devastated landscape. A few seconds later, he heard a low, baritone roar.

Gideon strained his ears, knowing that what he'd just heard hadn't been the roar of thunder or the more familiar roar of cannon. When he again heard the ominous rumbling emanate from the nearby woodland, his battle-hardened senses went on alert. A twig snapped behind him and he reflexively drew his revolver, spinning on his booted heel and pulling the trigger.

In the next instant, his bloodlust congealed into outright horror. Standing before him, dressed in a flounced, ivory gown, was his beloved wife. Blood poured from an open gunshot wound; the bullet had pierced her heart.

"No!" he hollered, rushing forward to catch her as she fell.

Lowering his wife to the ground, Gideon clasped her tightly against his chest, one hand pressed to her breast to stem the flow of blood.

"Come back to me, Gideon…come back to me," she murmured weakly, turning her head to peer at him.

Stunned, Gideon stared at the woman he held in his arms. For it was not his wife who now gazed at him…it was Jessica Reardon.

Just then, the ground beneath him shook. Again, he heard a low, thundering roar. A primitive, unearthly sound, it raised the hair on the back of his neck. Straining his eyes, he saw a huge winged beast emerge from the murky shadows, its red eyes demonically gleaming. It stood nigh on thirty hands high with a wingspan of equal measure. As it lumbered toward him, Gideon intuitively knew that it would take more than a lead ball to fell the winged colossus.

Perhaps he could slay it with his cavalry saber. That was,

after all, how the knights of old had slain mythical dragons, was it not?

As he started to rise to his feet, the woman in his arms frantically clutched his arm. "Come back to me, Gideon…come back to me," she pleaded, her voice little more than a breathless whisper.

Gideon paused in mid-motion, torn between protecting the woman and doing battle with the beast.

As if sensing his dilemma, the beast opened its mouth and released a fiery breath, the red-hot flames scorching the leaves on the nearby trees. Almost immediately, Gideon clutched his temple, hit with an excruciating burst of pain.

Despite the agonizing spasms, he heard a deep, unfamiliar voice inside his head loudly proclaim, "Evil will descend upon the land of the Greenbrier. The red man cometh. Those in high places will perish in the flames of hell. So sayeth the Beast."

Although he tried to make sense of it, he could not. The words were like so much gibberish to him.

Suddenly, the beast moved its leathery wings, leaving Gideon certain that it intended to attack him. Struggling to his feet, he drew his sword and charged forward.

* * *

Gideon awoke from the nightmare with a violent start.

Thrashing his legs, he tried to disengage himself from the bed sheets. To his frustration, his limbs would not do as he commanded, and his body was seized with a shuddering spasm. Panting, he finally managed to throw the quilt onto the floor. Swinging his legs to the side of the bed, he sat upright, his body trembling in the dream's aftermath.

Damn the creature for tormenting me like this.

He'd been at Highland House seven days now, and on each of the seven days, the winged beast had invaded his sleep, taking possession of him, body and soul. The dream never varied—the beast continually taunted him with those inscrutable words: *Evil will descend upon the land of the Greenbrier. The red man cometh. Those in high places will perish in the flames of hell. So sayeth the Beast*

What did it mean? Did it mean anything? Or was he was suffering from a dark dementia, the sins of his past having finally caught up to him? Perhaps Hell did exist, here on Earth, and he was being punished for his beloved's death. And for the deaths of all the brave men who'd lost their lives under his command.

As Gideon sat hunched on the side of the bed, the windows suddenly rattled in their frames. From outside the house came a thunderous roar, an ungodly sound, as though hell's pantheon was flying overhead.

The beast had returned!

Opening the nightstand drawer, he grabbed his Colt revolver and staggered to his feet. Moaning, he swallowed a mouthful of stomach bile, overcome with nausea, the pain in his head unbearable. To keep himself from tottering over, he slapped his left palm against the wall. Holding the revolver in his right hand, he eased himself around the perimeter of the room, using the wall to hold himself upright.

Within moments, the unearthly rumbling ceased.

Admittedly relieved, Gideon lurched back to the unkempt bed. Slowly, with his every movement exacerbating the pain inside his skull, he eased himself onto the mattress. He sagged against the bed pillows, his energy depleted.

What am I doing here, one hundred and fifty years in the future? Since his arrival at Highland House, he'd been doing nothing but killing time. Or maybe time was killing him, he amended, thinking that the more likely scenario.

Pushing out a deep breath, he glanced at the nightstand. There, in plain view, was the small brown bottle which contained the restorative that had cured his pleurisy. An antibiotic, Jessica had called it. He reached for it, but it was as though he suffered from apoplexy. His hands trembled uncontrollably as he attempted to remove the white cap. He knew he had to push and turn, but he couldn't manage to—

Gideon cursed aloud as a handful of colorful pills flew through the air, spilling all over the bed.

Frustrated, he flung the brown bottle against the wall. The damned pink and blue pills had brought him back from the brink of death, but had anyone thought to ask beforehand if he wanted to remain amongst the living?

Leaning over, he retrieved an envelope from the nightstand drawer. Although he'd long since committed the words to memory, he carefully removed the single sheet of paper from its wrapping. Wear and tear, dirt and blood, had rendered a good portion of the letter indecipherable. It mattered not. The few words that he could still read were punishment enough.

…regret to inform you…tragic death…Mrs. MacAllister shall be deeply missed…with heartfelt condolences.

As he stared at the letter, it felt as though the devil's blacksmith was continuously banging an anvil against his skull. And though he was pain-wracked, he suddenly heard the soft murmur of a woman's voice.

Come back to me, Gideon…come back to me.

A tear rolled down his cheek, splattering onto the letter,

smudging the ink. In the next instant, the sheet of paper slipped through his trembling fingers.

"I know but one way to return to you, my beloved," he whispered, raising the Colt revolver to his right temple.

His finger poised over the trigger, Gideon took a deep, ragged breath, his mind made up. He did not belong here. Moreover, he did not wish to be here. Everyone he'd ever known or loved was dead. His beloved waited for him on the other side. All he had to do was—

"Yoo-hoo, Gideon! I come bearing gifts."

Gideon froze at Jessica's insistent knock. Gasping for breath, he immediately lowered the revolver. *God Almighty! Have I taken leave of my senses?*

Shame-ridden, he shoved the revolver inside the nightstand drawer and slammed it shut.

"I know you're awake, oh, bearded one," Jessica said from the other side of the door. "I can hear you moving around in there."

"A moment, if you will," he hoarsely called out, shoving himself off the bed. "I am not properly attired."

Hurriedly, he snatched his gray woolen trousers from where they hung on the end of the brass bed frame. Gritting his teeth against the pain inside his head, he yanked the trousers over his hips. It took several moments of fumbling with the buttons, but he finally managed to make himself decent. He then slowly ambled over to the door and opened it. On the other side stood a brightly smiling Jessica Reardon, several blue bags looped over her wrist. He stepped back, motioning for her to enter.

"I'm sorry for banging on the door like that, but you've been sleeping for hours and—" Her brow suddenly furrowed as she stared at his face. "You've had a relapse, haven't you?"

Grimacing, he shook his head. "I am well."

"You're lying," she said flatly, tossing the bags onto the bed. "Your cheeks are flushed, your eyes are bloodshot, and you're—" she placed the palm of her hand on his forehead—"running a fever. I'm going to call the doctor."

The instant that Jessica's hand touched his brow, a pulsating tingle spread from the front of Gideon's face to the crown of his head, all the way to the back of his skull, causing the pain to immediately dissipate.

Unaware of the curative effect that she had on him, Jessica began to remove her hand from his brow. Impulsively, Gideon grabbed her by the wrist. Unable to stifle a moan, he placed her palm against his cheek and firmly held it there. At that moment, Jessica Reardon was his only link to the land of the living.

"Gideon, I can see that you're not feeling well."

"I am not…I am not ill." Worried that he may have inadvertently frightened Jessica, he relaxed his grip on her wrist. "A dream…it was only a dream."

She tenderly cupped his cheek for a few seconds before removing her hand from his face. "A dream did this to you?"

"In truth, it was more like a nightmare," he confessed. "I have not been sleeping well."

"I've recently had a few strange dreams, myself."

But not as strange as his dreams, he'd warrant.

"If you like, I can bring a dinner tray to your room," Jessica offered.

He shook his head, afraid of what he might do if left alone. "I have been imprisoned in this room for the last seven days," he told her. "I would like to dine downstairs this evening."

"In that case, dinner will be ready in an hour." Gesturing to the blue bags that she'd flung onto the bed, she said, "I stopped at Walmart and got a refill on your meds. And since I was there,

I went ahead and bought you some clothing. Nothing fancy. Just a few plaid shirts and some denim jeans. And I, um, also bought you some shaving gear in case, you know, you want to, um—" she swirled her right hand in front of her chin—"update your look. It's been quite a few years since ZZ Top last had a hit single."

Unable to decipher the meaning of her last remark, Gideon nodded his head and said, "I am most grateful. If you will give me a tally of the expenses incurred, I shall gladly reimburse you."

"I left the receipt in the bag."

No sooner did Jessica take her leave than Gideon slumped against the back of the door, the last bit of strength ebbing from him.

In the wake of Jessica's departure, he felt anxious and unsure of himself. The fact that he felt so filled him with self-loathing, making him wonder what kind of man he'd become. Before the war, before his wife's death, he'd been afraid of nothing, certain beyond all reason that he was the master of his fate. Now he dreaded falling asleep at night. Dreaded having to relive the sins of his past. Dreaded having to face the beast yet again.

Surely I am one of God's damned.

Disgusted with himself, Gideon snatched a blue bag emblazoned with the word "Walmart". Removing a red plaid shirt, he held it against his chest, quickly surmising that it would fit. The garment put him in mind of his old friend General A.P. Hill, who'd always worn a red plaid shirt into battle as a clarion call to his opponents. The blood-red shirt had served notice that Hill intended to fight to the death.

Isn't that what I should do also?

As he pondered the notion, it suddenly dawned on Gideon that two paths lay before him—either he could take his own life or he could fight to the death. To end his life here, tonight, was the craven, albeit easy, choice. The more treacherous path lay in navigating a future not of his own making. But navigate it, he would.

From this moment forward, he would no longer wallow in self-pity. He would no longer cower before his fate. He didn't know how he'd come to be at Highland House, one hundred and fifty years in the future. He might never unravel the mystery behind that strange riddle. Nevertheless, he would not be defeated by this unexpected turn of the screw. He'd survived worse ordeals.

He would survive this one as well.

Chapter 10

J eez, Louise!"

Startled by the ear-splitting buzzer, Jessica rushed toward the oven, fumbling with the knobs as she turned off the shrill timer. Donning a baking mitt on each hand, she swung open the oven door. Met with a blast of fruit-flavored steam, she smiled.

While she wasn't intentionally trying to impress Gideon, this was the first time since he'd arrived that he'd been well enough to join her downstairs for dinner. After seven nights of serving him bland microwaved meals in his room, she thought it might be nice to cook something special.

Okay, it wasn't that special. Just a simple pasta primavera. And because she'd recently bought a bag of apples at a roadside stand and had to do something with them, she'd made a *tarte aux pommes* from scratch. She'd also decided, at the last moment, to pull out a bottle of Tuscan Chianti that she'd been saving, the wine more for her benefit than his. Impressed with her reenactment story, "Another Time, Another Place," the editor-in-chief at *The Dispatch* had promoted her to full-time staff reporter. As expected, she was in a celebratory mood.

And hopefully, the meal would cheer Gideon up a bit.

When she'd earlier delivered her store purchases, he'd seemed utterly bereft. In fact, she'd felt guilty leaving him alone and had been sorely tempted to give him a comforting hug. But she'd stopped herself from doing so because the last time they'd had intimate contact, she'd nearly combusted. Even though the incident in question had happened a week ago, the memory of that ill-fated, explosive kiss still sent a shiver down her spine. Mercifully, Gideon seemed to have no conscious memory of the passionate interlude.

Then again he seemed to have little to no conscious memory of anything. Either that or he was the most intensely private man she'd ever encountered. He'd yet to speak of his family or friends, and she still had no idea where he came from or how he'd arrived at Highland House. Other than his name, she knew absolutely nothing about him.

Which was why, soon after Gideon's mysterious arrival, she'd contacted a crony at the newspaper office to find out if there'd been any local reports of missing persons in the area. The only report, to date, was of a woman who'd mysteriously vanished. She'd even spent several hours on the Internet perusing various "Missing Persons" sights. Unable to find anyone who matched Gideon's physical description, she'd been forced to abandon the search.

Admittedly, she felt responsible for Gideon. Not to mention that it seemed *right* having him at Highland House. In his weakened condition, he needed her, and she liked being needed. More to the point, she liked being needed by him.

Baffled by her growing attachment to her reticent housemate, Jessica couldn't help but wonder if she'd been living alone too long. Perhaps she'd "adopted" Gideon because she enjoyed having somebody to talk to, even if their conversations rarely went beyond "Good morning," "Good night," and "Did you remember to take your medication?" Maybe she'd gone all-out on making dinner because this was the first time since she'd walked out on her husband that she would actually be sitting across from someone at the dining room table. Maybe she even secretly hoped that, in time, something would develop between her and Gideon.

Oh, for the love of Pete.

Had she really just contemplated falling into the sack with Grizzly Adams? It wasn't like her to have lurid imaginings about some man she barely knew. Or any man, for that matter.

Bad enough she was fantasizing about her new roomie during her waking hours. But more unnerving was that fact that her nighttime reveries had become full-length, costume productions that featured people riding horses, driving carriages, and wearing hoop skirts. Most mornings, she was too embarrassed to look Gideon in the eye when she took up his breakfast tray, afraid he might somehow deduce that the previous night they'd laughed, flirted, and danced on wide-screen Dream TV.

"May I say that whatever it is you are preparing, it smells delicious."

Taken off guard, Jessica spun on her heel, surprised to find Gideon standing in the kitchen doorway.

"You shaved!" she unthinkingly blurted, nearly dropping the apple tart on the floor.

Unable to stop staring, she stood motionless, the piping hot baking dish held in front of her. To her stunned amazement, beneath the bushy beard Gideon had been hiding a face of leonine male beauty: strong-jawed, lean cheeked, and bronze-skinned. But what really floored her was that he looked exactly like the clean-shaven man who'd been haunting her nightly dreams.

Gideon rubbed a hand along his jaw. "I trust that it meets with your approval."

My approval? What woman wouldn't approve of this big, oak tree of a man with thick, tawny brown hair and piercing blue eyes? If that wasn't reason enough to gawk, the way he filled out his red flannel shirt and new jeans was—

"Wow," she murmured, too overwhelmed to think in full sentences.

Gideon shot her a quizzical glance. "Is 'wow' good or bad?"

"It's good...Wow is good." Flustered, Jessica abruptly turned toward the kitchen counter, putting the baking dish on a metal trivet.

Wow is good. Did she really just say that? It made her sound like some pathetic, star-struck groupie. *The man shaves off his beard and suddenly I'm reduced to monosyllabic baby talk.*

Rallying her defenses—not that a simpering mush pile had much to work with—Jessica turned back around. "Would you mind putting the wine and the salad bowl on the dining room table?"

Gideon reached for the bottle of Chianti. "I'd be only too happy to oblige." As he fingered the wrapped straw on the bottom half of the bottle, he said, "You honor me with such indulgence. I would have been content with another desiccated meal."

"A desiccated— Oh, you must be referring to those Hungry Man microwave dinners that I've been feeding you." Belatedly it dawned on her that Gideon was making a concerted effort at small talk, a first for him. "As you astutely noticed, a microwave oven has the power to zap the life out of any meal. Lucky for you, the other day I got a promotion at work and...well, I was in the mood for a little celebration." She self-consciously finished, well aware that she was nervously babbling.

"Thus far, you've made no mention as to how you earn a living."

"Oh, haven't I?" Jessica unwillingly recalled how Richard used to denigrate her journalistic aspirations. Bracing herself for a similar reaction, she said, "I'm a, um, news reporter for *The Greenbrier Dispatch*."

"A lady journalist...I am impressed."

To her surprise, Gideon appeared genuinely intrigued, which made her realize that there was something different about him. As if he'd somehow morphed into another man since she'd last set eyes upon him.

"Well, it's not like I'm Lois Lane. You know, Lois Lane, Superman's main squeeze," she elaborated at seeing Gideon bewildered expression. When it became evident that he still had no idea who she was talking about, she waved away the comment, refusing to indulge his time-travel fantasy.

Courteously bowing his head, Gideon carried the Chianti and wooden salad bowl into the other room.

Wanting to get the food on the table while everything was still hot, Jessica quickly heaped pasta noodles into two large bowls, topping each with a generous serving of sautéed vegetables.

Bowls in hand, she made her way to the dining room. Gideon rose to his feet the instant she crossed the threshold. Taking both bowls from her, he set them on the table, then stepped behind her chair and politely waited for her to take her seat.

"Thank you," she murmured, feeling a heated tingle pulse up and down her spine.

As Jessica placed her napkin on her lap, Gideon poured wine into each of their glasses. For all his bizarre claims of leapfrogging through time, he was, without a doubt, the most well-mannered man she'd ever met. And even though she was garbed in her usual around-the-house attire—yoga pants and a tunic top—the deferential treatment made her feel like the belle of the ball.

"The aroma is deliciously pungent," Gideon complimented, taking an appreciative sniff.

"Oh, it's just a simple pasta primavera. Although I should warn you that I tend to go a little heavy on the basil and garlic."

"'Pasta primavera.' A most melodic-sounding name."

"Yes, it is," she agreed with a smile.

As she gazed across the table at Gideon, for one charged instant, nighttime dreams and daytime reality collided, creating an unnerving sense of *déjà vu*.

* * *

Leaning against one of the front porch columns, Gideon slowly moved his knife blade across a small piece of maple, savoring the peacefulness of the moment. Mercifully, the pain in his head had ebbed; it was now little more than a dull throb.

To his surprise, he'd greatly enjoyed dining with Jessica Reardon. It had been eleven months since he'd last shared a meal with a member of the fairer sex, that woman having been his wife.

Eleven months. It seemed like an eternity.

Gazing at the moonlit sky, Gideon tried to reckon the passage of time. As he did, it suddenly occurred to him that time might be similar to a railroad track on which trains traveled from one station to the next. The year 1864 was one of many stations along the route, the year 2014 yet another. If that was true, then it might be possible to travel in the opposite direction. Although, having no knowledge as to how he'd arrived at this future terminus in time, he had small prospect of returning to the past. And even if such a thing were possible, he would be returning to a brutal war that could not be won and should never have been waged.

In the heady days after Fort Sumter's fall, there'd been no question that he would take up arms to protect his home and loved ones from Northern invasion. A native-born Virginian, his sense of honor had compelled him to join the Confederate army. But his allegiance had blinded him, and his so-called honor had ultimately destroyed everyone and everything he'd ever held dear.

Taking a deep breath, Gideon filled his lungs with the sweet night air as he gazed at the western horizon. While this century was unfamiliar to him, the mountains that saw-toothed across the evening sky were unaltered by time.

Everything else, however, had changed dramatically.

He'd always assumed that when he returned home from the war, he would pick up where he'd left off—managing his property. But with Highland House now owned by another, there was no hope of reviving his fortunes by working the land. Be that as it may, the twenty-first century was an uncharted wilderness, waiting to be explored. And though he felt like a blind wayfarer in this land of gadgetry and mechanical devices, he was determined to traverse the path set before him.

For the time being, that path included the enigmatic Miss Jessica Reardon, a lady who was without a doubt the most unusual woman he'd ever encountered. At times, her manner was brash and her speech rather brazen. Nonetheless, there was a femininity about her, a gentleness that was wholly at odds with her masculine attire. Moreover, he suspected that her outward façade was a suit of armor that she donned to hide the loneliness that he occasionally glimpsed in her eyes. Suffering from the same ailment, he wondered why so beautiful a woman would live in a state of near-solitude.

As he contemplated the conundrum, Gideon carefully slid his knife along the length of wood, shaving thin slices of maple with each pass of the blade. To take their minds off the homes they'd left behind, the men in General Lee's ragtag army had invariably turned to gambling, drinking, praying, or whoring. Having lost his faith in God and not interested in pursuing vice, Gideon had turned to whittling to help calm his mind and to stave off the endemic boredom of camp life.

"Mind if I join you?"

Upon hearing Jessica's voice, Gideon quickly rose to his feet. "I would greatly enjoy your company," he said, ushering her to the porch stoop.

Tilting her head upward, Jessica peered at the sky. "It's a perfect night for star gazing, isn't it? And look, there's a shooting star," she exclaimed as she excitedly pointed toward a flash of celestial light. "Quick! Make a wish."

"I've always believed that it's 'not in the stars to hold our destinies, but in ourselves,'" Gideon said, tongue in cheek.

"That's from Shakespeare, isn't it?"

"Act One of *Julius Caesar*. Do you read the bard?" he inquired conversationally as he reseated himself.

"Not lately," Jessica replied. "Not since college, anyway."

"A lady reporter with a college education. I am doubly impressed."

"Don't be. I mean, it's not that big a deal," Jessica demurred with a shrug.

Detecting a measure of unease in her voice, Gideon thought a change of subject was in order. "When the white settlers first arrived in the valley of the Greenbrier, they referred to the Alleghenies as the Endless Mountains," he told her as he gestured to the rugged expanse outlined against the night sky.

The new topic clearly met with the lady's approval because

Jessica smiled at him as she said, "I once read that the word 'Allegheny' is an Indian word that means eternity. Nice to know that some things in this world last forever."

As Jessica continued to gaze at the peaked horizon, the enraptured expression on her face inexplicably put Gideon in mind of his wife. Although the two women bore no physical resemblance, he couldn't help but notice—

Suddenly realizing that he'd been comparing them, Gideon pushed the errant thought from his mind, considering it a betrayal of his vows. His wife's death notwithstanding, his feelings for her were as strong this day as they had been the day they'd wed. Neither time nor death could diminish the love he bore for her; that love, like the mountains on the horizon, was eternal.

Crossing her arms over her chest, Jessica leaned her back against a rounded column. "Since we're playing the name game, why is it called Highland House?"

The question surprised him. Although the lady had refused to countenance the fact that he'd traveled through time, evidently her curiosity had finally gotten the better of her.

Gideon leaned against the opposite column, mimicking Jessica's pose. "Since the house sits high atop a knoll, my grandfather, a practical man if ever there was, decided it should be called Highland House."

Jessica's delicate features instantly scrunched into a disappointed pout. "And here all along I thought the name had to do with Scottish lords roaming the mist-covered Highlands."

"There is no reason why you shouldn't continue to think thusly," he told her. "Given that Archibald MacAllister was exceedingly proud of his Scottish forbears, I suspect those mist-covered Highlands held a more powerful sway over my grandfather than he cared to admit."

"Do you mind telling me what you did before the, um, Civil War broke out?" Jessica next inquired.

Given the lady's intent gaze, Gideon deduced that he was being tested as to the veracity of his time-traveling claim. And while he could offer no proof that he had traveled through time, Jessica could offer no proof that he had not.

"I oversaw affairs at Highland House," he informed her.

Hearing that, a pucker materialized between Jessica's brows. "What was there to oversee? The property is less than a hundred acres."

"Though you may find it difficult to believe, Highland House used to be one of the more sizeable properties in the county. In its day, the farm surveyed at roughly five thousand acres," he stated, the words tinged with a hint of manly pride. For one profane moment, Gideon wished that he could pull back the curtain of time so that Jessica could see how grand Highland House had been before the last fifteen decades had taken their toll.

"So I take it that you were some sort of gentleman farmer."

"While you could have called me that at one time, as you can plainly see, my current holdings are greatly diminished," Gideon quipped, holding up his whittling knife for her inspection.

"Jeez, I can't win for losing," Jessica muttered, clearly exasperated. "No matter the question, you've got a pat answer. Personally, I believe you sniffed too much gunpowder at the Civil War reenactment. And just so we're clear, I don't think that—" The lady stopped abruptly in mid-harangue, her gaze swiveling toward the ringing chimes that hung at the far end of the porch.

Gideon also stared at those gently swinging pieces of metal.

"There's no wind blowing," Jessica remarked, putting into words what Gideon had already observed.

In the next instant, the lights inside the house began to flicker.

Catching the whiff of a sulfurous odor, Gideon leapt to his feet, immediately recognizing the putrid smell. He'd first caught wind of the scent a week ago when he'd staggered through the woodlands that bordered Highland House.

When, a few moments later, he heard a loud rustling noise, Gideon unceremoniously grabbed Jessica by the upper arm and hauled her to her feet.

"What in the world is going on?" Jessica demanded.

Suspecting that she would think him a lunatic if he answered truthfully, he gave no reply as he shoved Jessica behind him, shielding her as best he could with his much larger body. Holding his whittling knife like a dagger, he then braced himself to do battle.

No more than a few seconds passed before Gideon glimpsed a bright discharge of reddish-gold flames through the trees. At that precise moment, he was struck with an agonizing burst of pain, radiating from his left temple.

"Did you see the fiery blaze in the maple grove?" he hissed, barely able to speak through the pain.

"I can't see *anything*," Jessica carped. "I'm standing behind you."

As though it had a life of its own, the torturous staccato inside his skull intensified, causing Gideon to totter unsteadily.

Attempting to support him from behind, Jessica wrapped her arms around his waist. "Gideon, what's the matter?"

Hit with another painful salvo, he grabbed the porch railing with his free hand to prevent himself from toppling over like a felled tree.

"Please, Gideon! Tell me what's wrong," Jessica pleaded.

Gritting his teeth, he said, "The beast has returned."

Chapter 11

Groaning loudly, Gideon wrapped both his arms around the porch column as he slumped against it.

Terrified, Jessica immediately placed two fingers over the pulse point on his right wrist, alarmed to discover that his pulse was beating somewhere in the neighborhood of two hundred beats per minute.

Oh, God.

"Gideon, I need to know if you're suffering any chest pains or—" frantically, she tried to recall the classic symptoms of a heart attack—"or radiating pain down your left arm?"

"Evil will descend upon the land of the Greenbrier," Gideon hissed, his face contorted in an agonized grimace. "The red man cometh. Those in high places will perish in the flames of hell. So sayeth the Beast."

"Cut the mumbo-jumbo! *Are* you having a heart attack?"

"Evil will descend upon—"

"Tell me where it hurts," Jessica yelled over him.

When Gideon suddenly clutched his head with both of his hands, Jessica had her answer.

Trying to keep her voice as calm as possible, she cupped a hand around Gideon's elbow. "I want you to sit down while I go inside and call the paramedics. Okay?"

Evidently, it wasn't, because Gideon suddenly pivoted toward her, grabbing her by the shoulders. "Evil will descend upon the land of the Greenbrier," he rasped, shaking Jessica by the shoulders as he spoke. "The red man cometh. Those in high places—"

Jessica put a hand over Gideon's mouth to quiet him. "I know: the flames of hell. Now how about doing me a favor and sitting down? Please," she implored.

Mercifully, he complied, sinking onto the front stoop in an ungainly heap. Holding his head in his hands, Gideon then brought his knees up to his chin as he began to rock back and forth. Torn between calling the paramedics and staying with him, Jessica decided to remain where she was, afraid that Gideon might get up and wander into the woods if she turned her back on him.

Please, God, tell me what to do, Jessica silently begged as she plopped down beside Gideon. As though divinely inspired, she suddenly recalled what her mother used to do for her whenever she'd suffered from a headache.

Pulling Gideon's hands away from his head, she placed her own hands on either side of his skull. She then began to gently massage his scalp. Within seconds, Jessica could feel the tension leave Gideon's body; his broad shoulders visibly slumped. Pleased by the efficacy of the cranial massage, she scooted behind him, hunkering against his bowed back so that she could more easily reach his brow and temples.

"Are you feeling better?" she asked once Gideon's breathing had returned to normal.

"Yes, thank you. I am much improved."

At hearing that polite response, Jessica bit back a hysterical burst of laughter. Did the man have any idea what a fright he'd given her? She really and truly thought that he'd been in the throes of a full-fledged heart attack. Which begged the question: if not a heart attack, then what kind of attack had he just suffered?

"I'm going to call Dr. Whitecastle first thing in the morning," she said as she moved to a less compromising position, belatedly realizing that she'd been straddling his hips with her thighs. "Maybe you need another prescription or—"

"I beseech you, Jessica. Please do not call the doctor." Turning around to face her, Gideon took hold of her right hand and placed it over his heart—a heart that now beat strong and steady. "It was but a momentary spell."

Thrown into a quandary, Jessica knew that she couldn't force Gideon to see Dr. Whitecastle. And while she happened to think that he was in dire need of a full medical work-up, Gideon was a grown man. If he didn't want to seek medical treatment, that was his right.

"Okay, I won't call Dr. Whitecastle," she relented. "Provided you don't have another of these so-called spells," she added as a caveat.

"I am in your debt," Gideon said in a lowered voice, just before he raised her hand to his lips.

The instant that his mouth lightly pressed against her knuckles, his warm breath grazing her skin, Jessica felt a powerful, pulsating energy course through her hand, traveling the length of her arm. Although she'd grown somewhat accustomed to the weird, tingly sensation that she experienced whenever they touched one another, this was far more potent, causing her to gasp softly in its aftermath.

"If you don't mind, I, um, think I'll call it a night," she croaked, pulling her hand free as she stood upright.

Also rising to his feet, Gideon said, "Sleep well, Jessica."

"Thanks. And if you need anything during the night, you know where to find me," Jessica said over her shoulder as she stepped through the doorway. The screen door banged shut behind her. Too late, she realized how her last remark might be misconstrued.

Way to go, Reardon. Why don't you hand out an engraved invitation while you're at it?

A few moments later, she hurried through her nighttime routine—brushing her teeth, washing her face, moisturizing from the neck up, and gargling a mouthful of Listerine in record time. Finished with her nightly regimen, she padded down the hall to her bedroom.

As she tugged off her pullover and yoga pants, absently tossing both articles of clothing onto a chair, Jessica wondered how everything had gotten so confused so quickly. Without a doubt, what had transpired on the front porch was definitely out of the norm. Not only had Gideon been disoriented, but the physical pain he'd suffered had been heart-wrenching for her to witness.

And what had been the meaning of all that crazy yammering? Did it mean anything? When he'd first arrived at Highland House, Gideon had repeatedly uttered the cryptic phrase "Two will die on the fast, green water." Because he'd been running a high fever and had been deliriously ranting in his sleep, she'd paid it no mind. Until two people had died in a drowning accident on the Greenbrier River. At the time, she'd briefly considered the possibility that he had some sort of psychic or clairvoyant ability.

All of which convinced her that Gideon needed to be examined by a doctor, perhaps even a neurologist. Granted, she was no expert, but to have a debilitating headache come on so quickly suggested there was something seriously wrong with him. Moreover, he was still suffering from the delusion that he'd traveled one hundred and fifty years into the future.

"He probably needs to see a shrink, as well," she said aloud.

Although, to be perfectly fair, if she removed the time traveling and this recent "spell" from the equation, Gideon MacAllister seemed to be a sane, normal man. True, he was a bit old-fashioned in his speech and mannerisms, but that was hardly a reason to send someone to the funny farm.

"Whatever's wrong with him, I'm sure it's nothing that a prescription drug can't cure," she told herself as she pulled back the covers and got into bed.

Shivering from the autumn chill that permeated the room, Jessica cocooned herself in the quilt and flannel sheets. Eyes closed, she concentrated on the patterns of light that played against her eyelids, the colorful images hypnotically swirling at a dizzying rate.

Completely exhausted, she soon fell into a deep slumber and journeyed to the dream plain, gravitating toward a light that was visible at the end of a dark cavern. Catching sight of Sarah, she effortlessly fused with her, the two of them becoming as one.

Emerging from the cavern, she soon found herself standing in a mist-filled landscape...

* * *

As she wended her way along the path which led to the garden pavilion, Sarah could barely see through the dense mountain fog that eerily hovered over Sweet Springs. A blessing in disguise, she supposed—the heavy mist enabled her to tread undetected. On tenterhooks, she lifted her crinoline several inches, her much-anticipated assignation with Gideon causing her to hasten her step.

After last night's unexpected, and rather daring, waltz, Gideon had asked her to meet him at the hotel pavilion. Needless to say, she'd spent a sleepless night speculating on the reason for the early morning rendezvous. Moreover, she knew that by agreeing to meet Gideon, she courted potential disaster. She was, after all, betrothed to another man. Be that as it may, she intended to spend whatever time she could with Gideon. Once she exchanged wedding vows with Oren Tolliver, her life would never again be her own. These few moments with the man who'd stolen her heart would have to last her a lifetime.

Arriving at the designated meeting place, Sarah glanced about, disappointed not to see Gideon.

"Looking for someone?"

Immediately recognizing that thin, reedy voice, she spun on her heel, horrified to find Oren Tolliver standing directly behind her.

"Mr. Tolliver, whatever are you doing here?" she demanded.

One side of his mouth twisted in a nasty sneer. "I thought that you and MacAllister might need a chaperone. Who better for such a task than your intended spouse?"

Flummoxed, Sarah frantically tried to collect her thoughts. "I...I have utterly no idea what...what you're talking about," she sputtered.

"Correct me if I'm wrong, but aren't you here to meet your lover?"

"He is not my lover!"

"Alas, only a dance partner," Oren sniggered.

"How do you know about that?" Too late, Sarah realized that she'd just unintentionally incriminated herself.

"I have my ways."

"As do I," she matter-of-factly informed him, her mind made up as to what action to take. While the situation was regrettably awkward, it did provide an opportunity to do something that, heretofore, she'd only fantasized about. "Circumstances being what they are, Mister Tolliver, I wish to break off our engagement."

A look of surprise momentarily flashed in Oren's eyes. "I advise against that. Being a woman, you are easily prone to foolish sentiments and unwise decisions."

"Believe what you will, but I am steadfast in my resolve."

"Do you think for one moment that I will allow MacAllister to pocket the dowry money which rightfully belongs to me? I have plans for that money, and I won't be cuckolded by some—"

"I will not marry you, Mr. Tolliver," Sarah said in a firm tone of voice. Believing the matter settled, she nodded her head and said, "Good day to you, sir."

Anxious to depart his company, Sarah turned toward the mist-shrouded path. She'd taken no more than a few steps when Oren grabbed her by the elbow, forcefully jerking her around to face him.

"Have you forgotten that your stepmother and I share a familial kinship? If you defy her wishes in this matter, she'll see to it that you don't receive a cent of your father's money."

"She has no right," Sarah retorted, refusing to be browbeaten. "My father bequeathed that money so I would be provided for."

"And he entrusted its dispensation to your stepmother who—"

"Who has designs for me to marry a man whom I don't love, much less respect," she exclaimed, uncaring if she caused offense.

At hearing that, Oren's normally pale face mottled with rage. "MacAllister has you completely under his spell, doesn't he?"

"I assure you, Mr. Tolliver, that I am under no man's spell," she affirmed. "I am my own woman, and as such, I do and think as I please."

"Which apparently includes running around like a two-bit whore."

Shocked by the loathsome insult, Sarah could barely curb the impulse to slap Oren's face. "I will not permit you to speak to me in so despicable a manner."

"A harlot deserves no better."

"How dare you!" Outraged, Sarah acted on her earlier impulse, slapping Oren Tolliver on the cheek. At seeing the red imprint of her hand on his face, she felt thoroughly vindicated.

Her triumph, however, was short-lived. Oren struck her so quickly that she had no time to muster a defense. Physically stunned by the blow, Sarah closed her eyes, struggling against a surge of queasy pain, afraid that she might very well faint.

When, only seconds later, she heard an agonized grunt, her eyelids instantly flew open. Mystified by the scene unraveling before her, she watched as Oren, his nose sitting askew on his face, wobbled to and fro. Wheezing, he took several backward steps as blood streamed down his shirt front.

What in heaven's name had just happened?

She soon had her answer. Gideon MacAllister emerged from the fog like a crusading knight of old. Given that both of his hands were curled into fists, Sarah quickly surmised that he'd hit Oren in the face.

Grabbing Oren by his coat lapels, Gideon hauled him upright. "I'm more than willing to kill you right here with my bare hands, but honor demands that I give you a fair chance to defend yourself."

Dear God! He means to challenge Mister Tolliver to a duel.

With her heart in her throat, Sarah immediately placed a restraining hand on Gideon's upper arm, able to feel the tense bulge of muscle beneath his frock coat. "Please, Gideon, let it be. Should anything dire happen to you, it will be my fault." Throwing caution to the wind, she impulsively added, "I cannot bear the thought of losing you."

Their eyes met for a brief moment before Gideon returned his attention to her estranged fiancé. "Apologize to the lady, Tolliver."

Oren swiped a hand at the copious blood pouring from his nose, smearing it across his face. "My apologies," he muttered. Then, glaring at Gideon, he hissed through clenched teeth, "Satisfied?"

"A real man would never satisfy honor in so meager a fashion. However, given the type of man that you are, I suppose the apology, such as it was, will have to suffice. But I give you fair warning, Tolliver." His gaze resolute, Gideon paused a moment before he continued, "If you so much as pass Miss Pemberton on the same street, I'll kill you. No matter how long it takes me to hunt you down."

Gideon's threat sent a chill down Sarah's spine. She had never seen a man so dangerously earnest, leaving no doubt in her mind that he would absolutely deliver on his promise.

Evidently, Oren thought so as well, for he wasted no time in scurrying away down the garden path.

Concern writ large on his face, Gideon stepped toward her. "Are you hurt? Shall I summon the doctor?"

Sarah shook her head, the residual pain from Oren's blow having diminished to a tolerable ache.

As if to verify her condition for himself, Gideon skimmed his fingers across her cheekbone. "A man like Tolliver will never be content until he has completely destroyed you," he said, putting into words what Sarah had all along secretly feared.

"What am I to do?" she asked, her voice quavering with uncertainty.

"I'm leaving Sweet Springs, and you, my beautiful green-eyed love, are coming with me. That is, if you're willing to accompany me," Gideon amended as he took hold of her hand and placed it over his heart.

"I am more than willing," she assured him. "But…I come to you empty-handed. My stepmother controls my inheritance and—"

"Shh." Gideon pressed the tip of one finger against her lips to silence her. "No price can be placed on true love. But if money concerns you, I have a sufficient yearly income to provide for all our needs and wants."

Overcome with emotion, Sarah trembled with a longing so profound, so soul-stirring, the world and its trappings suddenly lost all meaning for her. "Gideon MacAllister, you are, without a doubt, the most noble-hearted man that I have ever met."

In the next instant, she found herself in Gideon's arms, their two bodies cloaked in the gray mist which still hovered over the pavilion. As he bent his head to kiss her, Sarah experienced euphoria unlike anything she'd ever known, a love so keenly felt that she knew she would take the memory of it to her grave.

Chapter 12

Suddenly aroused from a deep sleep, Jessica woke with a start.

Rubbing her eyes, she stared at the bedside clock in total disbelief. It was a little after nine o'clock in the morning. For a woman who made a habit of being up and about no later than seven, that amounted to a dereliction of duty. Silently berating herself for having overslept, she threw back the quilt and eased herself off the mattress, careful not to disturb Buster, who was snoozing at the foot of the bed.

Having forgotten to set the alarm, she'd been unable to wake up—her dreams had unfolded like a good book that she couldn't put down.

In a rush to make up for lost time, Jessica yanked her T-shirt over her head, tossing it into the laundry basket situated on the floor of her clothes closet. She then stepped over to the second-hand, Colonial-style dresser and opened the top drawer, removing a clean bra. Since yard work was on the morning "to do" list, she'd hold off taking a shower until later in the day.

As she twisted and snapped her bra into place, Jessica couldn't help but wonder why the man of her dreams was so completely different from the real life Gideon MacAllister. Unlike the blue-eyed gallant who haunted her nighttime reveries—a chivalrous cavalier of yesteryear who was always quick with a smile—a discernible air of melancholy hovered about her new tenant.

Perhaps she was having these dreams because deep down inside she wanted to believe that Gideon MacAllister really had traveled through time, a notion that scared the hell out of her.

Over the course of the last six months, she'd worked hard to become self-reliant and emotionally stable, and she had a very real fear of losing her newfound independence. During the seven years that she'd been married to Richard Bragg, her soon-to-be ex-husband had thoroughly stripped away her autonomy by doling out a weekly household allowance, keeping close tabs on her comings and goings, and fashioning her into his ideal Stepford wife. Although she couldn't put the entire blame on Richard. She had, after all, acquiesced to him, having entered into the relationship at a time in her life—shortly after the unexpected deaths of both her parents—when she'd been particularly defenseless.

While she was no longer a vulnerable woman, Jessica was, admittedly, a lonely woman. Sometimes the loneliness was so stark, so palpable, she could almost feel her heart shuddering from the oppressive weight of it. With good cause, she worried that her extreme loneliness might compel her to make another colossal error in judgment.

As she snatched a pair of cargo pants out of the armoire, Jessica glanced at the two framed photographs prominently displayed on the dresser. One was of her parents, Benjamin and Glenda Reardon, on their wedding day; the other was of the three of them taken just before her parents had died in a fatal car crash.

Does the grief ever end? Jessica wondered as she opened the dresser's middle drawer, grabbing a tank top and a denim shirt.

About to don the tank top, Jessica instead stood motionless, surprised to suddenly hear a loud *thunk* emanating from the front yard. Curious, she stepped over to the bedroom window to see what—

Oh my god!

In that instant, a burst of unadulterated lust hit her head-on. From where she stood, Jessica had a bird's-eye view of Gideon, chopping away at the large maple limb that had fallen a week ago during the storm from Hell. Enthralled, she watched him raise the ax above his head, every muscle in his back straining against his new Hanes T-shirt. As he swung downward, his biceps bunched into corded knots. Raising and lowering the ax, his body kept up a perfect rhythm. Thinking Gideon a beautiful Adonis of a man, she couldn't peel her eyes from him.

Not until several seconds of the peep show had passed did it suddenly dawn on her that Gideon had only recently left his sick bed.

The sexual haze instantly vanished, and Jessica rapped on the window pane to get Gideon's attention. As he stopped chopping and glanced up at her, she belatedly realized that she was clad in only a pair of cargo pants and a lacy white brassiere. Snatching the two ends of the muslin curtains that hung at the window, Jessica pulled them across her torso.

"Stop chopping that wood!" she shouted, her head framed by the V of the two curtain panels. "Otherwise you're gonna have a relapse."

Gideon cupped a hand to his ear, indicating that he couldn't hear her.

"Never mind," she said with a shake of her head. "I'll be right down."

As Jessica turned away from the window, her Smartphone

began to ring. Snatching her cell phone out of the charger, Jessica saw that the incoming call was from her editor at *The Dispatch*, Hoyt Jamison.

"Hey, Hoyt. How's it going?"

"Can't complain," her editor replied. "I'm calling 'cause I've got your new assignment. And, boy, it's a real humdinger."

Stepping over to the nightstand, Jessica opened the drawer and retrieved a pen and small pad of paper. "Okay, I'm ready. Give me the low-down."

"I want you to do a piece on the recent Draygan sightings."

Jessica immediately lifted the tip of the pen from the sheet of paper. "Forgive my ignorance, but who or what is Draygan?"

On the other end of the line, Hoyt chuckled, clearly amused. "That's right. You're not from around here. Draygan is kind of like Greenbrier County's Loch Ness Monster or Saskatchewan's Bigfoot."

Jessica snorted, barely able to contain herself. "So which is it: sea serpent or big hairy critter?" Even though April Fool's Day was months away, she wondered if Hoyt and the *Dispatch* gang weren't punking her.

"According to eyewitness accounts, Draygan is more like a fire-breathing dragon."

Oh, yeah. Big-time prank.

Deciding to give Hoyt a chance to come clean, Jessica said, "Didn't dragons go out of fashion with unicorns and griffins?"

The question was met with a long, drawn-out pause.

"Not around here," Hoyt finally answered in a surprisingly sober tone of voice. "We've had at least two dozen calls in the past week."

Hearing that, Jessica wondered what sort of mass delusion had taken hold of the local populace.

"And while I know that you don't think this is newsworthy, there hasn't been a Draygan sighting since 1939," Hoyt continued. "Word on the street is that Draygan's probably been holed up in a local cave, in hibernation for the last seventy-five years."

Jessica rolled her eyes at hearing "word on the street," knowing that probably meant gossip from a couple of old geezers hanging out at Fedder's Barbershop.

Although she diligently scribbled the details, Jessica nonetheless protested the assignment. "I was kinda hoping you wouldn't give me any more human interest pieces. My new job title, in case you've forgotten, is investigative reporter."

"To get the ball rolling, I've compiled a list of people who claim to have seen Draygan," Hoyt said, completely ignoring her last two remarks. "I want you to interview 'em and find out what it is that people think they're seeing."

Resigned to her fate, Jessica's shoulders slumped dejectedly. "I'll get right on the horny-tailed, flying dragon story."

"Who said Draygan could fly? I don't recall saying that."

Stymied, Jessica said, "Well, I just assumed that being a dragon, it could—" At hearing a deep-throated chuckle on the other end of the phone, she stopped in mid-sentence. "That's right. Laugh it up, Hoyt. Your name won't be on the byline, will it?"

"Have the story on my desk by Monday morning. And try to keep your DC cynicism to a minimum. *You* know there isn't a dragon out there, and *I* know there isn't one, but more than a few folks in Greenbrier County are of a different opinion. Folks who happen to subscribe to *The Greenbrier Dispatch*. Do you copy?"

"Loud and clear, boss. Don't offend the paying customers."

"That's right. I'll shoot you an e-mail with that list of names," Hoyt said before he disconnected.

Thinking there were times when being low woman on the

Dispatch totem pole could bite the big one, Jessica slipped her Smartphone into the front pocket of her cargo pants. Because her daily schedule had just become more hectic, she hurriedly finished dressing and rushed downstairs to the kitchen.

Several minutes later, after gobbling a breakfast bar and putting down kibble and clean water for Buster, she stepped through the back door.

As she stood on the stoop, Jessica let the autumn sunshine wash over her, bathing her face in its warmth. With an appreciative sigh, her gaze swept across the panoramic vista. Not only was Highland House situated atop a knoll that overlooked acres of rolling hills, bordered by the high mountain ridge in the distance, but the fall foliage was at its peak. Oaks and maples created a veritable mob scene of color: livid reds, bombastic oranges, and lusty yellows.

"I don't know that I've ever seen anything quite so lovely," she murmured, taking a last gander before she made her way toward the brick carriage house that was situated at the end of the pebbled drive.

Poking her head through the open double doors, Jessica was surprised to find Gideon bent over a long plank of lumber, using a handsaw to cut through the thick board. Since he evidently hadn't seen her enter, she tapped him on the shoulder. The hairs on the back of her neck immediately stood on end when she touched him.

Putting down the saw, Gideon turned around and greeted her with a polite nod of the head. "I thought that I'd repair the floor boards on the front porch as they are in a sad state of disrepair."

Even though she was tickled pink to have Gideon undertake a job that was beyond her skill set, she nevertheless said, "Should you be exerting yourself like this? That was a doozy of a headache you suffered last night."

"I have fully recovered from my unfortunate spell," Gideon said. Turning slightly, he set the handsaw on a nearby workbench. "And I am pleased to be of service to you. In light of all that you have done for me, it is the least that I can do to repay your kindness."

"In that case, I've got a circular saw which will make the job go a whole lot quicker," she told him.

Gideon raised a quizzical brow. "A circular saw?"

"As in *vroom, vroom*. You know, power tools." She could see that the words didn't register one iota of recognition with him. "Okay, I'll play along with you, Gideon. But only because I need the porch fixed." Stepping around him, Jessica grabbed the circular saw, plugging it into the wall socket above the workbench. "Watch closely as I am about to demonstrate how to correctly operate a power-driven saw." As she spoke, Jessica donned a pair of transparent safety goggles. "You simply push this black button and... *Voilà!*"

In a matter of seconds, the thick board was neatly cut, and the smell of sawdust lay thick in the air. Gideon reached over to take the circular saw from her. The awestruck look on his face said it all—the man was totally bowled over by what he'd just witnessed. Pushing the on button, his eyes widened as he watched the blade spin in dizzying fast revolutions.

"Careful! That's not a toy," she cautioned. "You don't want to end up being a nine-fingered carpenter."

"As for the rest of these power tools—" Gideon gestured to the collection of Black & Decker tools neatly stored on the shelf above the workbench—"would you be so kind as to show me how to operate them?"

"Gladly. How about I give you a full tutorial after lunch?"

"I look forward to the lesson." As he spoke, Gideon bent

slightly at the waist. Given that he was attired in denim jeans and a T-shirt, with bits of sawdust clinging to his hair, the courtly gesture was oddly anachronistic.

As were a great many things about Gideon MacAllister.

"If you, um, ever need someone to talk to, I want you to know that I'm available," she said, on the off chance that he might want to discuss last night's strange incident.

Gideon cocked his head to one side, clearly baffled. "We are conversing now, are we not?"

"I meant that if you have anything that…that might be troubling you, I'm a pretty good listener. And you know what they say about confession being good for the soul."

"That is most kind. However I do not wish to encumber you with such matters," Gideon said stiffly. Circular saw in hand, he turned toward the workbench.

As she stared at his broad back, Jessica mentally kicked herself, worried that she'd come on too strong. For all that they were the brawnier sex, men could be ultra-sensitive when it came to their "feelings."

Hearing a car engine, Jessica excused herself and hurriedly made her way toward the front of the house. To her surprise, a fire-engine red Dodge pickup truck, with a horse trailer hitched to the back of it, had just pulled up. Even more to her surprise, Darlene Malone, owner and operator of A Cut Above—a hair, nail and, of all things, tarot card-reading salon—stepped out of the vehicle.

Because of an excessive amount of blond hair, not to mention other excesses more anatomical in nature, Darlene was frequently likened to a young Dolly Parton. The buxom beautician took this comparison as the greatest of compliments. Since Jessica occasionally had her hair trimmed at the salon, she had a passing acquaintance with Darlene. However, this was the first time that Darlene had ever been to Highland House.

"I brought a pot of chicken soup," Darlene announced. "For that sick man of yours."

Dumbfounded, Jessica's jaw slackened. "Gee, thanks," she mumbled as Darlene gave her custody of the soup pot. "But he's not my man. He's simply *a* man. In fact, he's my new tenant. And just how did you learn about Gideon?"

"I found out from my girlfriend Lou Ann who works part-time at the Walmart pharmacy counter. She mentioned in passing that you were there yesterday to get his medicine."

"What a relief to know that the grapevine is operating so smoothly," Jessica deadpanned, annoyed that she and Gideon had been the object of local gossip.

Just then, the man in question came into view, carrying several freshly sawed floorboards on his right shoulder.

Eyes opening wide, Darlene ogled Gideon as he headed toward the front porch. "Honey, if I had a man who looked like that living in my house *and* he was paying me rent, I'd swear I had died and gone straight to heaven."

Desperate to change the subject, Jessica decided to take advantage of the fact that Darlene Malone was the local high priestess of the occult. "What, if anything, do you know about Draygan? I've been assigned to do a story for *The Dispatch*, and I need some background information before I conduct my interviews."

If Darlene was surprised by the sudden change in topic, she gave no indication. "I know that Mother Maebelle used to talk a lot about Draygan."

"'Mother Maebelle? Who is she?'"

"Maebelle Malone was my granny. And like me, she was a conjure woman. In fact, most of the women in my family, going back as far as anyone can remember, have been conjure women," Darlene elaborated, clearly proud of her bona fides.

Jessica shifted the heavy pot of soup onto her hip. "A 'conjure woman'? I'm not familiar with that term."

"That's a woman who has the gift of second sight." As she spoke, Darlene opened her purse and removed a compact and tube of lipstick. "Folks used to come from miles around to have Mother Maebelle toss out the bones and read their fortunes."

"Did Mother Maebelle ever see this so-called dragon?" Jessica next inquired, thinking the information interesting, but not anything that she could use for the article.

"Only from a distance," Darlene informed her. "That was back in '39, during the last Reckoning. Mother Maebelle claimed to have seen Draygan flying over Bobbitt's Knob one night during the full moon."

"What exactly do you mean by a 'reckoning'?" Jessica asked, the word sounding to her as if it were loaded with dire implications.

Opening the mirrored compact and holding it near her face, Darlene meticulously applied a fresh coat of red lipstick. "Whenever Draygan shows up, folks around here call it the Reckoning, on account of the fact that death and destruction follow in the beast's wake."

Amused, Jessica couldn't help but chuckle. Like most fairytale creatures, the mythical Draygan probably got blamed for everything from colicky babies to sick cattle.

"The last time that Draygan appeared, back in 1939, the Greenbrier River flooded, killing a total of fifty people. And the time before that, back in 1864, not only did the Yankees come through and burn all the crops, but there was a smallpox epidemic," Darlene said as she pulled a tissue out of her purse and blotted her lips. "And during the 1789 Reckoning, the Shawnee

Indians attacked the frontier settlement at Tilden's Run, slaughtering every man, woman, and child in sight. As you can well imagine, folks are bracing themselves for what's going to happen this time around."

Although Jessica didn't believe for one instant that the calamitous events just cited had anything to do with a flying dragon, it suddenly occurred to her that she might be able to put a historical spin on the local folktale.

"Thanks Darlene, you've given me a lot to work with. I should be able to access *The Dispatch* archives and pull the stories pertaining to the 1939 flood."

"I can do you one better than that. If you want to talk to someone who came face to face with Draygan back in '39, head on out to Gooseneck Holler and speak to John Henry Burdette. He was just a boy at the time, but he lived to tell the tale."

"I'll be sure to add Mr. Burdette to my interview list." Jessica gave Darlene a grateful smile, the woman proving to be a font of information.

"Be forewarned: John Henry keeps a loaded shotgun at the ready. So you might want to take him a peace offering," Darlene advised in an uncharacteristically serious tone of voice. "As I recall, he likes banana moon pies and cinnamon-flavored Skoal. And he'd probably welcome a case of RC Cola." Then, chortling softly, Darlene said, "If nothing else, you could use it to shield yourself from the buckshot."

"Very funny," Jessica muttered, thinking that she was most definitely going to have to talk to Hoyt about collecting some hazard pay. She didn't make enough money to get shot at by some backwoods hillbilly.

"Hey there, good looking!" Darlene suddenly called out as she enthusiastically waved at Gideon, who was in the process of prying a rotted floorboard from the front porch. "How about coming over here and joining us ladies?" Lowering her voice, Darlene said out of the corner of her mouth, "It's not often we get an eligible bachelor around these parts. What exactly does Gideon do for a living?"

"Actually, he just got out of the military," Jessica hedged. "So he's, um, in between jobs right now."

As Gideon approached, Jessica noticed the interested look in his eyes as he caught sight of the horse inside Darlene's trailer.

"Darlene Malone, I'd like you to meet my new tenant, Gideon MacAllister," Jessica said, making the obligatory introduction. "Darlene was kind enough to bring you a pot of chicken soup."

"That's most kind of you, Miss Malone," Gideon said with a cordial nod of the head. "And I am pleased to make your acquaintance."

Darlene smiled, dimples appearing at the corners of her mouth. "Likewise, Mr. MacAllister. Hey, I just got hit with a great idea: why don't the four of us meet up at McGuff's later tonight?"

Admittedly baffled, Jessica said, "The *four* of us? But there's only three of us standing here."

"In that case, I guess we'll have to ask my brother J.W. to join the party," Darlene said with a sly wink.

Inwardly groaning, Jessica hoped to head the other woman off at the pass. "If you must know, I don't date very often and—"

"Honey, I understand," Darlene said with a commiserating nod. "It can be tough hitting the dating scene. I don't like to admit it, but I hit a six-month dry spell between husbands number two and three. And it darned near drove me crazy. As far as I'm concerned, living alone is for the birds."

"Who technically live in flocks," Jessica pointed out.

"I know that," Darlene countered with a good-natured laugh.

Then, casting Gideon a sidelong glance, she said, "What do you say, big guy? Are you up for having a little fun this evening?"

"I would welcome the opportunity," Gideon replied, quick to accept the invitation.

"Then it's a date!" Slinging her purse over her shoulder, Darlene gestured to the horse trailer. "While I hate to cut my visit short, I need to take Blaze over to Mitch Wilkerson's place. He's agreed to board him until I can scrounge together enough money to put in a new pasture fence. Although given what Mitch is charging, you'd think he had 14-carat-gold grass growing in those fields of his."

Turning his head, Gideon stared admiringly at Darlene's trailer. "Your horse puts me in mind of the stallion that I took with me when I first went away to the University of Virginia. Nicodemus also had a white blaze on his forehead."

"You know, my property is fenced. You could board Blaze at Highland House for free," Jessica impetuously offered: one, because she suspected Gideon would enjoy caring for the horse; and two, she hoped to prevent him from blurting anything about the buggy that had been hitched to his stallion.

"Honey, you are too kind." Reaching over, Darlene affectionately squeezed her arm. Then, turning toward Gideon, she winked and said, "Hey, cowboy, how about helping me unload my horse?"

"I would be only too happy to assist you, Miss Malone."

None too pleased about the upcoming "date night," Jessica watched Darlene and Gideon troop off together. "A rowdy roadhouse, beer on tap, and a man who claims to be from the nineteenth century," she muttered under her breath. "What could possibly go wrong?"

Chapter 13

N̲ow that's what I call a taste of Milwaukee's finest!"
J.W. Malone exclaimed, wiping a ribbon of white foam from
his mouth with the back of his hand.

"Milwaukee? Do you mean to say that the proprietor of
McGuff's can actually secure beer from such a great distance
without it spoiling?"

Hearing the incredulous tone in Gideon's voice, Jessica gulped
down another swig of ice-cold beer. Just as she'd feared, it was
proving to be a very weird night.

J.W. nudged her with his elbow. "Gideon is a real joker,
isn't he?"

"You could say that," Jessica responded with a strained
smile. On the other side of the table, Gideon, seated next to Darlene, was clearly oblivious to the fact that he'd said something
off-key.

As she tapped her fingers in time to the Blake Shelton song
that blared from the sound system, Jessica peered around the
smoke-filled tavern. Having worn a vintage maxi-dress that she'd
recently purchased at the local consignment shop, she definitely

looked out of place amidst the predominantly denim-clad clientele. Darlene, on the other hand, took top fashion prize for the evening in her skin-tight, denim mini-skirt and fringed leather vest. And though her brother J.W. didn't have the same flair for fashion, he'd doused himself with enough Old Spice to ensure that he would stand out in any crowd.

Secretly, Jessica wished that she was sitting on the other side of the booth next to Gideon. Hands down, he was the best-looking man in the joint. Like every other male at McGuff's, he wore blue jeans, but rather than the bold patterned shirts favored by most of the male patrons, he wore a white linen shirt and a dark gray vest—cleaned up remnants from his "Confederate" uniform. Dangling between his vest pocket and a button hole was a gold watch fob.

Beer pitcher in hand, J.W. reached across the table to top off Gideon's half-empty mug. "My sister tells me that you just got out of the military. What branch were you in?"

Nodding his thanks for the refill, Gideon said, "I served in the 8th Virginia Cavalry."

The remark made Jessica instantly jerk to attention. Scrunching her brows together, she silently pleaded with Gideon to put a damper on it.

"The cavalry!" J.W. let out a snort of amused laughter, raising his right hand in mock salute. "Hey, that's a good one, buddy."

"Actually, Gideon was involved in Special Forces," Jessica impulsively fibbed. "Which means he's not allowed to talk about what he did in the military."

J.W. gave her a knowing wink. "Because if he told me, he'd have to kill me."

"Um, something like that."

"Oh, I just think all of that commando stuff is too thrilling," Darlene cooed as she batted her eyelashes at Gideon.

Telling herself that she could care less if "Boobs" Malone put the moves on him, Jessica reached for the bowl of popcorn set in the middle of the table. As she listlessly chewed on the stale-tasting snack food, she watched as Darlene leaned toward Gideon, provocatively smashing a leather-clad breast against his arm.

"So what are you planning to do now that your stint is up?"

"I haven't really given it much thought," Gideon said in reply to J.W.'s query. "My military service ended somewhat abruptly and—"

"Gideon has been busy with the carpentry work at Highland House." Jessica tried to steer the conversation away from dangerous shoals.

"If you're handy with a hammer, I'd be willing to take you on full-time," J.W. offered out of the proverbial blue. "I've been looking to hire an extra man."

"What kind of business are you in?" There was no mistaking Gideon's keen interest.

"Historic reconstruction." As he spoke, J.W. refilled everyone's mug from the new pitcher that the waitress had just placed on the table. "I'll be honest with you; the pay isn't much. But it'll keep you in suds."

"When can I start?"

"How does Monday morning grab ya?"

"That suits me just fine."

Gideon's lightning-fast acceptance of J.W.'s job offer caused Jessica's mouth to fall open. It hadn't occurred to her that he'd seek gainful employment so soon after his illness.

"Only thing is, the job is up in Shepherdstown and—" J.W.

noisily slurped the foam from the top of his beer mug—"Damn, that's good brew. Anyway, as I was saying, the other contractor pulled out at the last minute, and they need someone on the double-quick. The foundation on an old church is disintegrating due to extensive flood damage. Which is good for us 'cause it'll mean a big bonus if we can get the job done in the next four weeks."

"I know Shepherdstown well," Gideon said. "We marched through there on our way to Antietam."

A silence fell over the booth. Unaware that he'd just said something he shouldn't have, Gideon calmly drank his beer.

"Gideon is a, um...Civil War reenactor." Jessica sputtered. Then, hoping to change the subject once more, she plastered a chipper smile onto her lips as she turned to her "date" and said, "How far away is Shepherdstown?"

J.W. reached for a handful of popcorn. "It's a good three-and-a-half hour drive," he answered in between chomps.

"So what you're saying is that you want Gideon to go to Shepherdstown with you, and you want him to stay there for at least four weeks?"

"Yep, that's what I'm saying," J.W. verified with a nod. "Mind passing me a napkin?"

Glumly, Jessica reached over and snatched a wad of napkins out of the metal container on her end of the table. While she desperately wanted to forbid Gideon from going to Shepherdstown, her hands were tied. She'd known Gideon MacAllister little more than a week, and because theirs was a platonic relationship, she had no right to voice an objection or make a big stink. Only in her dreams did she and Gideon share a more intimate bond with one another.

Just then J.W. slid toward her, pressing his jean-clad leg against her outer thigh. "What are you doing tomorrow night?" he whispered in her ear. "I thought maybe we could hook up. Just the two of us."

"Thank you, but I have to work tomorrow evening." Jessica straightened her spine, hoping her overly ardent suitor would take the hint and slide back to his side of the booth. "I don't know if Darlene mentioned it to you, but I'm writing a story for *The Dispatch* about the recent Draygan sightings."

Hearing that, J.W.'s face lit up like a 100-watt light bulb. "Then this is your lucky night. It just so happens that I'm a local authority when it comes to the topic of Draygan."

Anxious to test J.W.'s bold claim, Jessica hurriedly retrieved a pen and reporter's notepad from her handbag. "Okay, for starters, how about telling me why the fabled creature is called Draygan?"

J.W.'s toothy grin instantly faded. "Truth be told, I don't know how the dragon got its name," he mumbled, missing the first pitch.

In the process of raising his beer mug to his lips, Gideon suddenly lowered it to the table. "Do you mean to say that a dragon truly exists?" Clearly, he was spooked at hearing about the local legend.

Darlene placed a perfectly manicured hand on Gideon's forearm. "Not only does the dragon exist, but it can bedevil people in the flesh, as well as in their dreams."

"Getting back to my original question," Jessica said, trying to regain control of the conversation, "why is the mythical beast called Draygan?"

"He's called Draygan on account of how them fellas from Scotland spoke," Darlene informed her. "The Scots were the first ones to cross over the mountains and settle in Greenbrier County."

When Jessica raised a questioning brow, the other woman elaborated by saying in an exaggerated burr, "Look, laddie! It's a flying *dray·gan*."

"I can top that," J.W. announced, not about to be outdone by his sister. "Did you know that the entire North American continent was settled by Indians except for one area—West Virginia? I'm guessing that the fire-breathing Draygan had something to do with it. Let's face it, we've got good soil, good weather, and good water. Like the song says, 'almost heaven.' So what scared the Indians off?"

Jessica looked up from her hastily scribbled notes. "I thought there were Indians here. Earlier today, Darlene told me that there was an Indian massacre at Tilden's Run back in 1789."

"There was," J.W. verified with a vigorous nod of the head, pieces of his lank blond hair falling onto his brow. "That was when the Shawnee swooped down from Ohio. But believe you me, they tucked tail and headed back to Ohio right quick."

"It's true," Gideon piped in. "My grandfather often spoke of those dark days on the Virginia frontier. The 'bloody ground', he called it."

Noticing the way that Darlene's head suddenly whipped in Gideon's direction, Jessica could see that damage control was urgently needed. "His grandfather was a, um, amateur historian."

"Well, he was right on the mark about the 'bloody ground.' Murder and mayhem always follow in Draygan's wake," J.W. intoned with macabre relish. "Yes, sirree. That beast has been the cause of much misery in these parts."

"Misery only befalls those people who don't take heed," Darlene verbally counter-punched. "Mother Maebelle always said that Draygan is merely the harbinger of death, not the instrument of death."

"Well, there's plenty of folks here about who would dispute that claim," J.W. argued.

"In other words, no one knows for certain whether Draygan is sacred or profane," Gideon said in a circumspect tone of voice.

The grim resignation on Gideon's face immediately garnered Jessica's attention. While the Malones obviously enjoyed sharing their vast knowledge of local folklore and history, Gideon was clearly unnerved by the conversation. If it wasn't for the fact that the Draygan deadline loomed, Jessica would have long since changed the topic.

"Every time that Draygan comes a callin', there's more than a few hunters who try to bag 'em a dragon," J.W. said with ghoulish delight. "But in all these years, nobody's been successful. Why? Because Draygan is impervious to a regular lead bullet. The only thing that will kill a dragon is a pure silver bullet."

"What a fascinating bit of folklore," Jessica murmured, wondering where J.W. came by his information. After hastily scribbling the words "silver bullets" onto her notepad, she asked J.W. the question uppermost in her mind. "Have you seen Draygan?"

Folding his arms across his chest, J.W. leaned against the booth. "Not yet. But because I was born right after midnight, I've got as good a chance as anyone of seeing him."

"Only those people born during the witching hour between midnight and 1:00 a.m. can see Draygan," Darlene clarified. "Ghost seers, Mother Maebelle used to call 'em. Although there are plenty of ghost seers whose sight is dimmed by skepticism."

"Hey, not only am I a ghost seer, but watch this!" With theatrical aplomb, J.W. reached for a set of stainless steel flatware that the waitress had placed on the table when she seated them.

Clutching the spoon between the fingers of his right hand, he closed his eyes and then proceeded to perform the impossible: He actually bent the spoon in half!

Flabbergasted, Jessica stared at the contorted piece of stainless steel in utter disbelief.

"What do think of them apples?" J.W. asked, sliding the spoon to the middle of the table.

"That is a very impressive parlor trick," Gideon remarked as he picked up the spoon and carefully examined it.

"You're telling me," J.W. said, still smirking. "The other day I was at the construction site, sitting around shooting the breeze with a couple of my buddies, when I started to roll a 16 penny nail around in my hand. Well, the next thing I know, I'd bent the darned thing in half. The boys on my crew could hardly believe it. I must have bent a hundred nails that day, one right after another."

"But how?" Jessica asked, having yet to get over her shock. "I mean, if I hadn't seen you bend that spoon with my own eyes, I would never have believed it."

J.W. shrugged. "Can't say for sure how I do it."

"I can," Darlene said, quick to jump into the fray. "Whenever Draygan shows up, there's always a lot of unexplained psychic activity that happens throughout the county. Some folks have visions. Others, like J.W., suddenly have a psychokinetic ability. And then there are those who are bestowed with the gift of second sight, some of them able to see into the past, while others can see into the future."

At hearing that, Jessica's stomach muscles suddenly tightened. Was that the reason for her recent dreams? Was she one of those people who could see into the past?

No sooner did she consider the notion than she flat-out rejected it, refusing to believe in the dragon's existence. And though it was an incredibly entertaining tale, being a sane, rational individual, she also knew that it was a load of malarkey.

"Okay, let's suppose that somebody born during the so-called "witching hour" wants to see the mythical dragon. What do they have to do?" she asked, if for no other reason than to play devil's advocate.

Darlene peered at her, a knowing look in her dark eyes. "Are you saying that you were born during the witching hour?"

Jessica wordlessly nodded.

"As was I," Gideon quietly remarked.

Jessica turned her head in his direction. For several prolonged moments, she and Gideon stared at each other across the table. Although they sat a good three feet apart, she felt a heated tingle pulse up and down the length of her spine.

"If you want to see Draygan, I reckon the best way is to go to his lair," J.W. said, answering Jessica's question.

"Which is located...?"

As he topped everyone's mug with more beer, J.W. said, "You'll find Draygan's lair on the other side of Archibald's Wood, at the fork in Devil's Run Creek, up near the old saltpeter cave."

Jessica quickly jotted down J.W.'s directions. If she could locate the saltpeter cave, take a few photographs, it might put to rest the Draygan myth. "And where exactly is Archibald's Wood?"

J.W.'s gaze dropped to the tabletop. The gregarious man suddenly appeared acutely uncomfortable.

"It's located on the western edge of your property," Darlene stated matter-of-factly.

Stunned by the revelation, Jessica glanced up from her notepad. "Are you kidding me?"

Ignoring the question, Darlene shot her brother a purposeful glance. "Why don't you and Gideon shoot a game of pool? Hmm?"

Evidently thinking it a good suggestion, both men wordlessly got up from the table, Gideon politely inclining his head before following J.W. to the other side of the bar.

Opening her purse, Darlene removed a compact and tube of lipstick. "I thought it might be nice if we had a little girl talk." Explanation given, Darlene then carefully applied a shade of lipstick very similar in color to that of her fire-engine red Dodge truck. "Nothing like a fresh coat of war paint to make you feel like a new woman," she said after she'd blotted her lips.

Jessica made no comment, unable to recall the last time she'd worn the stuff.

Finished with her lipstick, Darlene flagged down their waitress. "Trudy, would you mind getting us two ladies a pot of hot tea."

Open-mouthed, the waitress stared at Darlene as if she'd just requested a drink from the sacred waters of the Nile. "I can't make any promises, but I'll try to find some tea in the back room," Trudy muttered before she headed for a swinging door marked with the words EMPLOYEES ONLY.

Darlene waited until their waitress was out of earshot before she said, "It's fairly obvious that J.W. doesn't have a snowball's chance in hell with you."

"Well, it's just that I, um—"

"No need to explain," Darlene said as reached across the table and gave Jessica's hand a reassuring pat. "I can see that you're saving it for someone special."

Uncomfortable talking about her personal life, Jessica glanced at her Draygan notes. "Don't you think that seventy-five years is an awful long time for any creature to stay in hibernation?" she asked, anxious to change the subject. "Surely, in all those years, some hiker or spelunker would have inadvertently stumbled across a sleeping dragon."

Just then, Trudy returned to the booth. Silence ensued while the waitress set two mugs on the table, a limp string dangling from the side of each one. As she and Darlene doctored their tea with cream and sugar, the silence between them lengthened.

"That's just an old wives' tale about Draygan sleeping it off in some local cave for seventy-five years," Darlene said at last, picking up the conversation where they'd left off. "It was always Mother Maebelle's belief that Draygan can pass through the veil of time, from his world into our world. But the problem is that Draygan can't speak our language. Which is why there's so much psychic activity happening to folks who don't even know the meaning of the word 'psychic'. That's Draygan's way of trying to communicate with us, to warn us that there's danger on the horizon," Darlene explained in a noticeably subdued tone of voice. "The problem is that most folks ignore the warnings as nothing more than tomfoolery. They don't realize that the strange symbols they see in their coffee grinds, or what transpires in their nightly dreams, are dire warnings."

Jessica shook her head, refusing to believe that her recent spate of strange dreams had been generated by a winged dragon. Her dreams were just that—dreams. Involuntary images produced by chemicals in her brain. They weren't esoteric messages from some horny-toed chimera. "No offense, Darlene, but I personally think that Draygan is a make-believe monster, and I intend to prove that in my article."

"No offense taken. But you best take care, honey. Draygan ain't Puff the Magic Dragon." Darlene took a sip of her tea. Frowning, she reached for two more packets of sugar. As she ripped them open, she sighed appreciatively. "Now *that* is a sight to die for."

Jessica turned her head from side to side. "What is?"

"Why, Gideon's tush, of course. That man was just made to wear a snug pair of jeans, wasn't he?"

Following Darlene's gaze, Jessica caught sight of Gideon bent over a pool table, angling himself to take a shot. "It's rude to stare," she murmured, trying not to ogle Gideon's long legs and picture-perfect rear end.

Pursing her bright, red lips, Darlene blew on her hot tea. "Have you noticed how different Gideon is from everybody else?"

"Trust me. He's not all that different," Jessica countered, attempting to backpedal out of the conversation.

"Oh, sure, he probably throws his dirty socks on the floor like any other man," Darlene said with an airy wave of the hand. "But what I meant is that he knows how to make a woman feel like a lady."

"So he's a gentleman. I, for one, don't see anything odd in that."

"Just look at him, will you?" Darlene inclined her peroxide-blond head in the direction of the pool table. "You'd think he'd never seen a football game before, huh?"

Looking across the crowded bar, Jessica could see that Gideon had taken his pool shot and that his attention was now focused on the TV set suspended from the ceiling above the bar.

"You know how men are about sports," she mumbled, wishing Darlene wasn't so darned observant.

"It's more than that. He's interested in everything around him. Kinda like a kid in a toy shop. And yet he's gotta be the manliest fella I ever laid eyes upon. A potent combination, don't ya think?"

"Well, I, um—"

"You know, this puts me in mind of a story that Mother Mae-belle used to tell," Darlene blithely continued. "During the last Reckoning, back in 1939, there was this mysterious stranger who walked down the mountain dressed in strange, old-fashioned clothing. Nobody could figure out where he came from, and the only thing the stranger could tell them was that he'd lost his way in time."

Chapter 14

As Jessica put the Bronco in reverse and backed out of the parking space at McGuff's, she automatically raised her left hand, waving good-bye to Darlene and J.W. To her mind, the only good thing to have come from the evening was the extensive Draygan material that she'd gleaned from the Malone siblings.

And though Gideon might consider his new job with J.W. a good thing, Jessica wasn't necessarily sold on the idea. He'd only recently recovered from pneumonia. Not to mention, he was still under the delusion that he was a Confederate soldier. A delusion that could very well land him in the loony bin.

What will happen when I'm not around to cover for his Civil War bloopers? J.W. wasn't stupid. He'd soon figure out that something wasn't right.

Flipping the turn signal, Jessica turned right and headed east on Route 60. As she peered through the windshield, she could see numerous stars twinkling against the night sky.

"I couldn't help but notice that you seemed awfully intrigued with Draygan," she ventured, throwing out an opening gambit.

"I do not wish to speak of the matter," Gideon replied.

Jessica tightened her grip on the steering wheel. "You spoke of it plenty in front of Darlene. Or maybe those D cups were just the incentive you needed to loosen your tongue," she added under her breath.

"Miss Malone lent a sympathetic ear."

"So would I, if you gave me half a chance."

"You, madam, are the quintessential skeptic."

Jessica whipped her head in Gideon's direction, angered by his starched tone of voice. Folding his arms over his chest, Gideon returned her stare, giving as good as he got.

Afraid that she might run them off the road—a very real possibility on a narrow, two-lane, winding stretch of highway—Jessica was the first to look away. "You do know, don't you, that Darlene is determined to get you alone, preferably in a room with a big, fluffy bed."

"You need not worry on that account," Gideon assured her. "Given that Miss Malone is thrice widowed, I shall watch my step."

"Oh, Darlene isn't a merry widow; she's a gay divorcée," Jessica clarified. As she spoke, she flipped on the defrost fan, since the windshield was starting to fog up.

"A divorced woman? I am appalled."

About to swipe her hand across the fogged up glass, Jessica stopped in mid-motion. Gideon's last remark sent a chill down her spine. Although she'd yet to disclose her marital status, she, too, was about to join the ever-expanding ranks of the divorced. According to her lawyer, her divorce would be finalized in just a few weeks' time.

"To listen to you, someone would think that a divorced woman and a fallen woman are one and the same."

Still on his high horse, Gideon said, "Yes, in so far as a

divorced woman has fallen from a state of matrimonial grace. Need I remind you of the Andrew Jackson scandal?"

"Gee, maybe you better." Particularly since Jessica had no idea what he was talking about.

"Andrew Jackson nearly lost the presidential election because he married a divorced woman. Such scandals are to be avoided at all costs," Gideon stated emphatically.

Quickly rallying to the dead president's defense, Jessica said, "If Andrew Jackson loved his wife, it shouldn't matter that she was divorced."

"That is beside the point."

"Well, here's a newsflash for you: more than half of all marriages end in divorce," she informed him. She was not only offended, but deeply wounded by Gideon's high-and-mighty attitude. "Which makes Darlene Malone fairly typical. So I suggest you either get off the soap box or you keep your puritanical opinions to yourself."

Gideon's jaw visibly slackened, his look of stunned disbelief nearly comical. "Half of all marriages, you say. Good God. What has the world come to?"

Jessica snorted, that having to be the mother of all rhetorical questions. While it was none of his business, she'd tried hard to make a go of her marriage. For seven long years, she'd been loyal, faithful, and completed committed to Richard and his unceasing demands. But having given up her friends, her career, her interests, and even her dreams, she'd finally realized the situation was hopeless. When Richard had hit her in the face, it was a wake-up call, a dire warning that things would only get progressively worse if she stayed in the marriage.

"I'll have you know that sometimes, maybe even all the time, there are extenuating circumstances which make it necessary for a person to file for divorce," Jessica stated. "No one should have to stay in an abusive or loveless marriage."

Gideon shot her a quizzical glance. "Why would a husband ever demean his wife? Does a man not take a sacred vow before Almighty God to honor, protect, and love the woman he weds?"

The naiveté of his remarks *almost* made Jessica forgive Gideon for his rigid thinking.

"I guess some people don't place much value on their marital vows," she countered with a weary sigh. "Besides, actions speak louder than words. What good is it to say you love someone if all your actions speak to the contrary?"

"Is that why Miss Malone sought divorce?" Gideon quietly asked, scorn having given way to a more compassionate tone.

"Probably." It certainly was the reason why Jessica had filed.

For the next several minutes, they road in silence, the soft *whrrr* of the defrost fan the only sound in the vehicle.

"Were you aware that there's an old saltpeter cave located near Highland House?" Jessica abruptly inquired, if for no other reason than to break the unnerving silence.

"The cave was part of my grandfather's original land deed," Gideon responded, a guarded look on his face. "During the war, soldiers in General Lee's army mined saltpeter from it in order to make gunpowder."

Although she didn't want to enable Gideon's time-travel fantasy, Jessica couldn't resist asking the follow-up question. "Have you ever gone inside the cave?"

Gideon shook his head and said, "No. But when I was a young boy, I frequently ventured near the cave. In my youth, I was an avid collector of fossils and Indian arrowheads, which I uncovered in abundance in the area surrounding Hell's Hole."

"Hell's Hole?" she repeated, the place name unfamiliar to her.

"That is the name of the saltpeter—"

Just then, from out of nowhere, a burst of golden-orange flames shot across the two-lane highway.

Jessica immediately slammed her foot on the brake, causing the back end of the Bronco to fishtail wildly and sending the SUV into the direct path of a massive tree trunk. Leaning across the seat, Gideon grabbed the steering wheel and gave it a hard yank to the right. In fact, he leaned over so far that Jessica was pinned against her door.

"What in God's name are you doing?" she screamed.

"Driving your conveyance, I dare say."

"Then watch out for that—"

Tree!

Only by the grace of God and Gideon's superior upper body strength did they avoid hitting the sturdy maple. Instead, the SUV plowed through a farmer's fence, which bombarded the vehicle with bits of barbed wire and rotted wood.

"Apply the brakes!" Gideon yelled, still holding on to the steering wheel.

Jessica did as ordered, too terrified to do otherwise. As they gradually lost forward momentum, Gideon steered the vehicle toward the middle of the field, far from any dangerous obstacles. When they finally stopped, he released the steering wheel.

"Thank you, God. Thank you, thank you, thank you," Jessica gratefully babbled as she slumped against Gideon's shoulder. "I can't believe that really happened. I mean, we could have been killed. And where did that blast of fire come from?"

Gideon, his blue eyes fiercely shining, stared at her. "Did you not see the beast?" he hissed between clenched teeth as he pulled away from her.

Jessica wordlessly shook her head.

A split-second later, she watched in stunned disbelief as Gideon opened his car door and lurched out of the Bronco. Then, reeling like a skid-row drunk, he staggered through the overgrown field.

* * *

Hit with a sharp burst of pain in both of his temples, Gideon fell to his knees. Unable to get to his feet, he groped through the tall field grass on all fours, determined to move as far away from Jessica's conveyance as possible. He did not want her to witness this humiliating, pain-wracked spectacle. No man wanted a woman to see him when he was reduced to *this*—a groveling, mewling shell of a human being.

Because the pain had never been so excruciating, Gideon feared it was a prelude to death.

Shuddering violently, he toppled over, drawing his legs up to his chest as he curled in upon himself.

Damn Draygan for bedeviling me this way.

As if he could read his mind, the beast, again, exacted his vengeance. Gideon clutched his head with both hands as he was seized with an agonizing burst of pain.

Shaking violently, he swallowed a mouthful of stomach bile, on the verge of losing the contents of his stomach. With a loud groan he tried to raise himself to his knees, but could not, only able to lift his head several inches off the ground.

"Gideon! Are you all right?" Jessica anxiously inquired as she crouched beside him. "This field grass is so tall that I couldn't find you. I thought that—"

"Leave me be," he rasped, flinging his arm to shove her away from him. "I do not want you to see me like this."

"I'm not going anywhere."

"Damn you, woman. I am ordering you to—" The words froze on his lips as Gideon suddenly sensed an unearthly presence passing overhead. Turning his head, he caught a glimpse of a huge creature silhouetted against the night sky, a gargantuan with a wingspan of some ten feet.

Draygan.

Gideon grabbed Jessica by the shoulders. "Do you not see the beast?" he croaked, following the colossus with his gaze as it flew toward the western edge of the field.

"There's nothing to see," she insisted, refusing to so much as turn her head. "Now I need to know what's wrong with you, and I need to know this instant."

"My head," he muttered, not having the strength to argue with her. "I have a pain in my—" He stopped, suddenly able to hear Draygan speak to him. "Evil will descend upon the land of the Greenbrier. The red man cometh. Those in high places will perish in the flames of hell. So sayeth the Beast," he duly recited.

"Shh," Jessica murmured, gently lifting his head and cradling it in her lap. "Don't say anything."

Slowly, tenderly, she placed her hands on either side of his head and commenced to gently massage his skull. Groaning, Gideon covered her hands with his.

To his astonishment, the pain soon began to dissipate; the heated warmth of Jessica's hands had a curative effect.

"The spell has passed," he told her once the pain had finally abated. Staring in wonderment at his angel of mercy, Gideon rolled toward Jessica and rested his cheek on her upper thigh as she continued to rub his skull.

Inhaling deeply, he breathed in her scent. *Vanilla.* And another scent, this one more tangy, more earthy.

"Are you feeling better?" Jessica inquired as her hands stilled.

"Yes. Thank you," he murmured, knowing those meager words were wholly inadequate to convey the depth of his gratitude.

Acutely aware of their intimate pose, he shoved himself into a seated position. For one brief moment, Jessica's lips were achingly close, her breath fanning his mouth before he scooted to a more seemly position.

"Gideon, I'm really worried about you. It isn't normal to have these kinds of attacks. This is the second night in a row. I want you to see a doctor." As she spoke, Jessica's concern was plain to see; the woman no doubt thought that he'd lost his mind.

Perhaps I have lost my grip on sanity.

"A doctor cannot cure me," he stated matter-of-factly, certain it was no disease that ailed him. It was something far more insidious, an otherworldly creature known as Draygan.

And as long as Draygan roamed these hills, he'd have only temporary respite. The beast seemed able to take control of not only his thoughts, but his body as well. While resigned to his new circumstance—living in the twenty-first century—he would never be the master of his fate while Draygan lurked. If he was to live, the beast must die.

And the only way to slay Draygan was to fire a silver bullet through his twisted heart.

Unwilling to speak of the matter, Gideon scrambled to his feet. He then extended a hand in Jessica's direction and said, "Come. We must return to Highland House."

* * *

Richard Bragg closed the wall safe in his home office. He then carefully rehung the large, framed photograph that concealed the recessed vault where he kept his secret assets.

Long moments passed as he stared at the wedding picture. Jessica had worn a strapless wedding gown which, at the time, had infuriated him. And though seven and a half years had come and gone, he could still vividly recall how he'd felt when he'd seen the dress for the first time, as his bride-to-be slowly walked down the church aisle. In that horrified instant, he'd not given a damn that the dress had been a Vera Wang design; he'd thought it made her look sleazy instead of chaste and virginal, ruining for him what should have been a perfect day.

With a disgusted snort, Richard turned his back on the portrait, refocusing his thoughts on the contents of the wall safe rather than on the picture that camouflaged its location. For six months now, he'd been waiting for Jessica to lower the boom, to publicly disclose the fact that he'd not only skimmed money from the coffers of The Traditional Family Movement, but that he'd had a *very* cozy relationship with several well-funded lobbyists.

So far, Jessica hadn't uttered a peep, a fact that gave him renewed hope.

Obviously, she still loved him. What else could her silence mean? Not only did his estranged wife still love him, but in keeping mum, she was also protecting him from federal investigation and possible prosecution.

And while Richard was absolutely convinced that his wife still held him in tender regard, he was admittedly stymied as to why Jessica had not yet repented and come back to him. Ever since her abrupt and totally unexpected departure, he'd been waiting for her to return. Because he'd always taken care of their finances and made all the major household decisions, he was certain that she lacked the wherewithal to make it on her own.

Does she even know how to write a check?

"I suspect that the only thing she's capable of writing is a mountain of drivel," he muttered uncharitably as he glanced at a back edition of *The Greenbrier Dispatch*. Sitting down at his desk, he picked up the newspaper and stared at Jessica's front page article and its accompanying photograph of a group of Civil War reenactors. "No doubt she thinks this makes her a bonafide journalist."

As he tossed the newspaper into the waste bin, his gaze landed on his desktop calendar. Time was fast running out, the six-month waiting period for a no-fault divorce nearly at an end. The thought caused his gut to painfully constrict because the window for Jessica to come to her senses and resume her wifely duties was about to close.

What is she waiting for?

"Have I not suffered enough?" he murmured dejectedly.

Once it had been publicly disclosed that Jessica had filed for divorce, he'd been crucified by the mainstream media. Because he'd always extolled the virtues of a traditional marriage, one in which the husband was very much the head of the household, and because he'd so often lauded his own marriage as a gleaming example of the perfect marital relationship, he'd been lambasted as a hypocrite. His political enemies had delighted in his downfall. In a particularly devastating blow, he'd even lost his prominent position with The Traditional Family Movement.

Having been figuratively tarred and feathered, he'd had to reinvent himself, managing to carve out a highly visible and very vocal presence in cyberspace with his daily political blog, "The Truth Teller." Not only did his blog site provide commentary on all aspects of the political landscape, he now hosted a weekly video chat. As the executive editor-in-chief of the site, he had a staff that included several writers, political diarists, and a handful of zealous volunteers. Because of the blog's high traffic, he'd recently been invited as a guest on a cable news roundtable, relieved to have muscled his way back into that particular arena. Be that as it may, he'd yet to reclaim his former prestige in Washington political circles.

"For which I have my lovely wife to blame," he muttered angrily as he shoved himself to his feet and strode out to the foyer.

Unnerved by the stark silence that permeated the house, he came to a standstill several feet from the oversized, mahogany front door.

Why did she have to leave? he wondered for the umpteenth time as he peered through the sidelight's beveled Tiffany glass. Any other woman would have been thrilled to call this tasteful, upscale residence home.

As Richard continued to gaze at the front door, his mind conjured a vision of his estranged wife, suitcase in hand, stepping across the threshold.

Damn you, Jessica!

Clearly, the fertility drugs that she'd been taking had caused some sort of emotional upheaval, one that he was willing to forgive. Although he'd carry the indelible memory of the pain she'd caused him to the grave.

Turning away from the door, Richard stormed down the hallway to the master bedroom, trying to focus on the silver lining. In the first two months following Jessica's meltdown, he'd had her movements continuously monitored by a private investigator. Provided with daily updates, he'd taken heart in the fact that she'd not left him for another man. That would have been an unforgivable transgression.

Heavy-hearted, he flipped on the overhead light in the bedroom before stepping over to Jessica's walk-in closet. At a glance, he could see that everything remained exactly as it had been on the day she left. Noticing the jewelry box set on top of the built-in dresser, he opened it and fingered the gold wedding band that he'd placed there for safekeeping, looking forward to the day when he could slip it onto Jessica's tapered finger once they renewed their vows.

Swallowing the lump in his throat, Richard slid the gold band onto his pinky finger before he stepped over to the line of neatly hung garments. Quickly flipping through the rack of expensive clothing, he stopped at his favorite dress, a green silk gown that Jessica had worn to one of the black-tie affairs that he used to be invited to.

Overcome with emotion, he removed the dress from the padded hanger and held it against his chest. Taking a deep breath, he filled his nostrils with the faint scent of Joy perfume that still clung to the fabric.

"Damn you, Jessica," he muttered, tears streaming down his face.

Chapter 15

Do you think it's wise after tonight's episode to go gallivanting to Shepherdstown?"

Taking exception to Jessica's choice of words, Gideon stepped across the foyer and turned on an electrical lamp. He suspected that the lady had purposefully waited until they'd returned to Highland House to toss down her gauntlet.

"I won't be gallivanting," he informed her. "I shall be working. Rather strenuously, I suspect."

"My point exactly." Removing her wrap, Jessica flung it over the newel post.

Wondering at the reason for her concern, he said, "Does it bother you that I'll be away from Highland House for four weeks?"

"It doesn't bother me so much as . . . well, if you must know, I've gotten used to having you around the house. And I'm worried that you haven't given yourself enough time to fully recover from your bout of pneumonia." Gnawing on her lower lip, Jessica slid her fingers over the banister, her movements innocently seductive. "And there is the, um, you know, the time travel thing."

Ah, yes. The time travel thing. That, he'd wager, was the true reason for her opposition.

"Have no fear. I shall endeavor not to embarrass you in any way by mentioning the forbidden subject."

"Like you didn't mention it tonight at McGuff's?"

"Correct me if I am wrong—" and knowing the lady, she would do just that—"but I don't recall mentioning my adventures in time travel to anyone."

"While it's true that you didn't refer to it directly, I had a busy time glossing over your gaffes." As she spoke, Jessica folded her hands primly in front of her waist, looking every inch the stern school mistress. "This is why I want you to see a doctor. These so-called spells, your insistence that you traveled through time— none of it is normal."

Suspecting that she'd been working herself up to this confrontation, Gideon gently brushed the backs of his fingers across Jessica's flushed cheekbone, noticing how her face colored with heightened emotion. "I am a normal man, Jessica."

With all the wants and desires of any normal man, he suddenly realized, surprised to discover that he was highly aroused. And though he couldn't quite put his finger on it, he recognized that this was no ordinary lust. What he was experiencing was more subtle, and far and away more intriguing, than mere bodily desire. Inciting an inner struggle between what he should do and what he wanted to do: head and heart, the age-old battle.

"Whether you know it or not, I'm trying to help you, Gideon. Why do you have to be so darned resistant? To everything," Jessica said with added emphasis, her hazel-green eyes shimmering with unshed ears.

Gideon slid his hand to the back of Jessica's neck as he slowly drew her toward him. "It is not my intention to cause you so much distress."

What occurred next happened so effortlessly, so naturally,

that Gideon could almost believe he'd wrapped Jessica Reardon in his arms a thousand times before. Like carved puzzle pieces, their two bodies fit perfectly together, her head nestled under his chin, his torso aligned against her soft, womanly curves. Male and female. A perfect symmetry of opposites.

Jessica tilted her head upward, her lips achingly close to his.

"I am in awe of you," he confessed, trying to wade his way through the onslaught of emotions that suddenly bombarded him. "In truth, I have not experienced this kind of... yearning in a very long time, and I'm finding it difficult to resist—"

"So stop resisting."

The unexpected challenge instantly sparked the flame, prompting Gideon to lay siege to Jessica's lips with a fierce urgency.

As she clutched the front of his vest Jessica opened her mouth, inviting him to deepen the contact. Capturing her tongue, he thoroughly suckled her, seeking to reinvent the kiss anew. With a soft moan she arched her back, enabling Gideon to feel her nipples as they bore into his chest. Instantly, blood rushed to his groin, hardening him. At that moment, they were as one. No light between them, only a raging fire.

Desiring more intimate contact, Gideon slid a hand down the column of Jessica's spine. He caressed the rounded curve of her buttock before hefting her against his erection.

Sweet bliss.

Unable to control his primal urges Gideon rocked against her, wanting to possess Jessica Reardon, body and soul. Wanting to take her right there in the middle of the front foyer. When she flexed her hips against him, matching his fervor, Gideon groaned with pleasure.

It's been so long. Not since Sarah have I wanted a woman with such ardent—

The wayward thought was a like a sobering slap to the face.

"What in God's name am I doing?" he muttered in stunned disbelief as he yanked his mouth away from Jessica's. Guilt-ridden, his arms dropped to his sides as he stepped away from her.

"I thought you were kissing me," Jessica said, her brows drawing together in bewilderment.

Horrified by what he'd just done, Gideon shamefully glanced heavenward. "Forgive me, dearest Sarah."

Jessica's eyes opened wide; her expression displayed utter shock. "How is it that you know Sarah?"

Forcing himself to meet Jessica's gaze, he said, "Sarah is my wife."

* * *

Emotionally sucker-punched, Jessica gaped at the man standing across from her.

All along, she'd been dreaming about Gideon and his wife Sarah!

Night after night, dream after dream, experiencing some paranormal *ménage à trois*, she'd been eavesdropping on the MacAllisters. Moreover, she'd somehow been able to tap into Sarah's innermost thoughts and heartfelt emotions, experiencing them as if they were her own thoughts and feelings.

But how? And why?

Completely thrown for a loop, Jessica suspected that she'd overheard Gideon mutter his wife's name that first night he'd arrived at Highland House, when he'd been in a feverish delirium. Her subconscious mind must have latched onto that—along with the fact that Gideon had been garbed in a Confederate reenactor's uniform—and had simply run with it, creating a vivid nineteenth-century dreamscape. And because Gideon kept insisting that he was a Confederate soldier, her subconscious mind continued to set the dreams in that time period.

"Sarah died eleven months ago," Gideon said, unprompted.

"I'm sorry for your loss," Jessica murmured, still reeling from the shock of hearing those four damning words—*Sarah is my wife*. Struggling to get a grip on her runaway emotions, she unthinkingly blurted the question uppermost in her mind: "When you kissed me just now, who were you thinking about: me or Sarah?"

Gideon's blues eyes opened wide, telling her he was clearly startled by the question.

"Tell me," she demanded, besieged with jealousy. "I need to know who you were thinking about."

"It was your lips that I kissed," Gideon assured her, his gaze boring into her with a searing intensity. "And it was your body that I held in my arms."

Tears pricked her eyes. "This is more than I can handle right now." Too exhausted to be able to think straight, Jessica turned toward the staircase. "I'm going to bed."

Latching a hand around her upper arm, Gideon prevented her departure. "I didn't tell you about Sarah because, after she was buried, I never again spoke of her death."

Jessica was admittedly surprised by the disclosure. "Not to anyone?"

Gideon dolefully shook his head.

Swallowing the lump in her throat, Jessica couldn't imagine keeping all of that anguish to one's self. If it hadn't been for the months of grief counseling after her parents died, she would have never emotionally survived that tragic ordeal.

"I should have told you," Gideon continued, still maintaining a hold on her arm. "Instead, I behaved like a cad, and I humbly beg your forgiveness. I shall pack my things and leave Highland House first thing in the morning."

"Under no circumstance are you leaving," Jessica declared, placing a staying hand on his chest.

"I do not wish to cause further offense."

"You didn't offend me. But you did hurt my feelings," she reluctantly admitted. "Although that's no reason for you to permanently move out. How about we talk about this tomorrow? I'll be gone most of the day conducting interviews, but when I get home, we can hash this out. All right?"

"As you wish." Gideon released his hold on her arm and solemnly nodded his head. "I bid you goodnight, Jessica."

Jessica tried to summon a smile, but was unable to make her lips curl in the right direction. "I'll see you in the morning," she said, before turning on her heel and ascending the staircase.

Reaching the top of the steps, Jessica made a beeline for the bathroom. In short order, she covered the basics, and a few minutes later, she was safely ensconced behind her closed bedroom door. Her shoulders slumped as it belatedly dawned on her how close she'd just come to losing Gideon. The moment—*no*, the millisecond—that Gideon had expressed a desire to leave Highland House, her heart sank, plummeting to somewhere in the vicinity of her ankles. It was one thing for him to leave temporarily to go to Shepherdstown, but the thought of him leaving forever was more than she could bear.

Making her realize just how important he'd become to her.

Which undoubtedly explained the heartache she'd experienced upon learning that not only did Sarah really exist, but she'd been married to Gideon. Furthermore, she knew that Sarah had been the love of his life, and she dared Gideon to tell her differently. She'd seen it in his sad, mournful face countless times over the last week, but fool that she was she hadn't realized what she'd been seeing.

Knowing that Gideon had loved, and loved greatly, was what hurt the most. That and the fact that he'd made no mention of it.

But do I really have a right to condemn Gideon when I also harbor a secret?

Somewhat guiltily, Jessica thought about her own lie of omission. Of course, her secret was completely different in nature. Her marriage to Richard Bragg had been anything but loving. But given Gideon's puritanical views on the sanctity of marriage, she was now afraid of what his reaction might be if she did spill the beans.

"Since Gideon mysteriously arrived at Highland House, I've been riding an emotional rollercoaster," she muttered, worried that she'd grown so emotionally attached to a man who, more than likely, had hit his head at the Civil War reenactment, suffered a brain injury, and was now convinced he was a time-traveling Confederate soldier.

Removing her dress, Jessica stepped over to the closet and tossed it into the dirty clothes hamper. With a softly uttered "ah," she unsnapped her bra and tossed it into the hamper on top of the dress before slipping into an oversized T-shirt. Padding over to the other side of the room, she turned off the overhead light and climbed into bed.

No sooner did her head hit the pillow than Jessica rode a somnolent wave that crested in a burst of brilliant illumination. Emerging into the light, she found herself standing in the middle of her own living room. Except that it wasn't decorated at all like her living room. Red damask drapes hung at the windows, and the room was filled with very formal, upholstered Victorian furniture. At the far end of the room, she saw Gideon standing next to an ornately carved table.

Still somewhat lucid, Jessica immediately tried to back out of the dream, to turn around and exit the room. She didn't want to be there, privy to Gideon and Sarah's life. But it was as if someone else was driving the dream bus, refusing to let her depart or to even wake up.

As she tentatively approached the table, Jessica heard a woman softly whimper. Recognizing the voice, she reluctantly merged with her dream avatar and let her consciousness fuse itself to Sarah's body... until they were completely bound to one another—one mind, one soul.

Almost immediately, she gasped in pleasurable delight, belatedly realizing that while Gideon was bent over the table, she was on top of it, splayed beneath him...

* * *

Because there was no time to undress, Gideon pried her legs apart, positioning Sarah near the edge of the table. Given the smile that hovered on his lips, she knew that he thoroughly enjoyed the intimate sight visible through the slit in her pantalettes. Lowering himself to his knees, he slid his hands under her buttocks and lifted her to his mouth. She whimpered, shamelessly undulating against him.

His tongue and heated breath soon incited a riot of tiny sparks that pulsed across her lower body and up her spine.

"I want to feel you... inside of me," she whispered, desperate to mate with him.

Gideon rose to his feet and hurriedly unbuttoned his trousers, shoving them to his haunches. Extending her hand, Sarah took hold of his stiffened manhood. As he wedged himself between her thighs, she guided him to her moistened crevice.

In the next instant, she gasped aloud as her body yielded to him. In that charged moment, they were truly husband and wife, profoundly bound together, one to the other.

Like a wanton, Sarah writhed beneath him, her taffeta-clad body sliding across the table as Gideon repeatedly plunged into her. Whimpering insensibly, she reveled in the sensual onslaught, in the burst of passion that gave rise to what could only be called a mindless frenzy.

Peering into Gideon's eyes, she saw that his ardent gaze was enlivened with a wild desperation. Shaken to the core, Sarah sank her fingers into his upper arms, holding onto him as tightly as possible. Their lovemaking had been an impetuous act, both of them having been seized with a sudden need for one last coupling.

Sarah's breath quickened, each thrust taking her ever nearer to love's pinnacle. Then, unable to stop the inevitable, she began to spasm. Arching her neck, she moaned aloud. Oblivious to everything else, she clung to those radiant moments of exquisite bliss.

"You are…my only love," Gideon uttered, just before he began to shudder in the throes of climax.

"And you are my heart's delight," Sarah said softly, her love for him pouring forth in a torrent of murmured endearments and fluttering kisses.

Long moments passed before Gideon finally withdrew from her. Hitching his gray trousers over his hips, he refastened them. That done, he silently offered her a helping hand. Just as silently, she accepted it. Heavy-hearted, Sarah then watched as Gideon donned a resplendent, dove-gray uniform tunic.

"How do I look?" her husband asked as he buckled his gun holster and sword scabbard around his waist.

She stepped toward him and smoothed a hand over the woolen fabric that covered his chest. "Like a soldier," she murmured, her heart so full of sorrow that it washed over her in unrelenting waves.

The day had finally come—the Greenbrier County troops had been ordered by the state governor to report for active duty. In a few minutes' time, Gideon would be heading off to war.

In the two weeks since Virginia had seceded from the Union, there had been an air of barely contained excitement throughout the state. To fill the muster rolls, editorialists at *The Greenbrier Dispatch* had waxed poetic over the gallantry of the county men. A gallantry yet untested in battle.

And she prayed it never would be.

"Why the sad face? Everyone knows the war won't last more than a few months," Gideon said, pulling her into his arms.

"If I'm sad, it's because I can't bear the thought of losing you. I'll never forgive you, Gideon, if you get yourself shot." *Or killed*, she thought, but didn't dare utter those words aloud.

"I shall endeavor to remember that at the start of each battle," he teased, nuzzling his lips against her brow.

A loud knock caused them to pull apart. Excusing himself, Gideon walked into the central hall and opened the front door. A young, fresh-faced private exchanged a salute with him.

"Major MacAllister, the men are assembled on the Lewisburg Pike and are ready to march out, sir."

"Thank you, Private Guthridge. I shall join the troops shortly."

Once more, both men saluted before Gideon closed the door.

Puffed-up gray peacocks, that's what they are, every last one of them, Sarah bitterly ruminated, convinced that they were fools for rushing off to war.

Hoping to forestall Gideon's departure, she said, "Did you remember to pack those winter socks that I knitted?"

"As well as the new woolen vest and flannel scarf." Gideon's blue eyes twinkled mischievously. "I even packed that heavy overcoat you insisted upon, although I don't foresee much snow this summer."

While he meant to cheer her up with his carefree remark, she found no humor in the situation. The man she loved was leaving, quite possibly forever. How could he stand there and make merry of it?

Taking hold of both her hands, Gideon pulled her toward him. Her heart erratically pounded against her breastbone. They had only a few moments left.

As Sarah choked back the tears, she tried to maintain a brave face. "I love you so much, Gideon."

"As I love you, Sarah." Gideon tenderly kissed her forehead, her cheeks, and finally her mouth, his lips conveying the very love he spoke of. "As I shall always love you. Never forget that I am ever yours."

Those were his last words to her.

Dazed, Sarah stood motionless as Gideon took his leave.

Hearing the jangle of harness and stirrups, she rushed to the window and drew aside the heavy drapes. With tears streaming down her face, she watched Gideon mount his horse. Desperately wishing that she could touch him one last time, she placed a hand on the window pane.

Just then, a breeze blew a handful of pink cherry blossoms across the drive. Like those fragile blossoms, she trembled as she watched her husband trot down the pebbled lane to where the assembled troops waited at the bottom of the hill.

At that moment, the future loomed before her, dark and foreboding.

Chapter 16

"Yet another ghost seer who claims to have seen Draygan," Jessica mumbled to herself as she got into the Bronco.

Having just finished her second-to-last interview, she flipped open her notebook and quickly reviewed the notes that she'd taken thus far:

Susan Erskine, Bank Teller, DOB 11/4/70. First saw Draygan on September 28th while walking her dog. The area where she saw the dragon was completely scorched, as if by fire. Subsequently, the witness has developed extraordinary telepathic abilities, able to correctly "guess" the balance of her customers' checking accounts. Witness gave time of birth as 12:52 a.m.

Chelsea Biggs, Student at Bluefield State College, DOB 3/13/95. While leaving the college library on the night of September 26th, she caught sight of Draygan. She has seen Draygan every night since. Per Ms. Biggs, she now has the ability to communicate with spirit apparitions that dwell in her parents' 130-year-old home. Ms. Biggs gave her time of birth as 12:17 a.m.

Tyrone Johnson, Computer Programmer, DOB 4/7/78. On the evening of October 1st, Mr. Johnson saw a large winged creature in the vacant lot next to the First Baptist Church. Since the sighting, he has started to compulsively scribble arcane phrases into a notebook, including the phrase, "Two will die in the fast, green water. So sayeth the Beast." Mr. Johnson was born at 12:39 a.m.

Joseph Whitley, Attorney-at-Law, DOB 7/31/61. To date, Mr. Whitley has not seen Draygan. However, his wife of twenty years, Christine Whitley, told her husband that on the night of September 27th, while driving home from a meeting of the Greenbrier County Historical Society, she saw a large winged beast in the middle of the road. She swerved her vehicle to avoid hitting it. According to Mr. Whitley, his wife arrived home that night visibly upset. The next evening, when Mr. Whitley returned home from his law office, his wife had vanished, "seemingly into thin air," having taken no belongings with her, not even her wallet. The local police have turned up no clues in the case. While they suspect foul play, the police have ruled out Mr. Whitley as a suspect. Mr. Whitley was born at 3:11 p.m.; his wife at 12:22 a.m.

Jessica contemplatively tapped her finger on the Whitley entry. She'd heard about Christine Whitley's disappearance almost as soon as it'd happened. Because the Whitleys were a prominent local family, the story was still front page news. Until she'd interviewed Joe earlier today she'd had no idea that his wife claimed to have seen Draygan the day before she went missing.

Flipping her notebook closed, Jessica stuffed it into her canvas tote bag. Clairvoyance, telepathy, channeling—there was no clear pattern to any of the supposed Draygan sightings other than the fact that it all fell into that murky realm of the paranormal.

Skeptic that she was, Jessica wanted to believe that it was a case of mass delusional hysteria. Like that which had occurred in Salem, Massachusetts, during the famous seventeenth-century witch trials. The problem was that no one she interviewed had been delusional. Or hysterical. Except for claiming they'd seen a fire-breathing, flying dragon, everyone she'd spoken with seemed perfectly sane. Perfectly believable. Assuming you were the kind of person who believed in the phantasmagoric.

As she started the ignition, Jessica glanced at the dashboard clock, double-checking that she had enough time to drive out to Gooseneck Holler and conduct her last interview of the day with John Henry Burdette. According to Darlene Malone, Mr. Burdette claimed to have seen Draygan seventy-five years ago, the last time that the dragon came calling in Greenbrier County.

Despite being exhausted, Jessica was in no hurry to go home. The fact that she'd fallen hard for Gideon MacAllister, a man who claimed not only to have seen Draygan but to have mysteriously crossed the boundaries of time, had her in an emotional tailspin.

After spending a restless night trying to untangle her feelings, it had finally occurred to her that maybe she'd permitted Gideon to stay at Highland House out of need. Uncut, undiluted, desperate need. She'd simply had this urge to be wanted by a man and, lo and behold, she'd latched on to the first one who came down the pike. It didn't matter that he claimed to be a Confederate soldier. Or that he claimed to have once lived at Highland House. Or that he'd even claimed to have seen a fire-breathing dragon. It only mattered that he had two arms, two legs, and the appropriate attachment in between.

Afraid that she might have missed the turn-off, Jessica pulled over to the side of the road and pulled out her map, comparing it with the handwritten directions she'd gotten from Darlene Malone.

Damn. Gooseneck Holler wasn't on the Rand McNally.

Not one to call it quits, Jessica released the emergency brake and kept on driving down the narrow dirt road. The late-day sun shone through the tangled limbs of poplars and maples, casting eerie shadows onto the desolate stretch of woodland. A mile back, she'd passed a hardscrabble farm, the last outpost of civilization.

Spying a wooden bridge up ahead, she breathed a sigh of relief. Darlene had mentioned a bridge in her directions.

The road narrowed considerably once she'd reached the other side of the bridge, becoming little more than a rutted cow path. Throwing the Bronco into 4-wheel drive, Jessica kept on driving, wondering who in their right mind would choose to live in such an isolated place. On one side of the dirt road clumps of scraggly pines blanketed a steep incline; on the other side the road precipitously dropped away to a creek bed below.

When she finally came to the mouth of Gooseneck Holler, Jessica released her death grip on the steering wheel and cut the ignition. Staggering out of the vehicle, she walked around to the back of the Bronco and retrieved her peace offerings from the cargo hold.

Gifts in hand, she headed into the woods. Dressed in a floral skirt, matching sweater set, and a pair of low-heeled leather pumps, she felt as incongruous as she looked.

About twenty yards down the dirt path, nestled amidst a grove of pawpaw trees with branches heavy with ripe fruit, there was a small log cabin. Unlike the modern cabins favored by hunters and outdoor enthusiasts, this was the kind of cabin once favored by Daniel Boone and colonial frontiersmen. While she was no expert, John Henry Burdette's cabin appeared to be at least 200 years old.

As she made her approach, the earthy smell of the woods gave way to the tangy smell of wood smoke. The chirp of crickets was drowned out by the ferocious, crazed barking of four dogs, each canine chained to one of the four corners of the cabin. Darlene had mentioned in passing that John Henry was "a little cantankerous"; she'd failed to relay that the octogenarian was an antisocial nutcase.

Trying her level best to ignore the dogs, Jessica stepped up to the porch and deposited her load onto a rickety camp table. Above the front door, there was a horseshoe with a fresh clump of green houseleek attached to it. An amateur herbalist, Jessica knew the ancient Romans believed that houseleek was a safeguard against lightning, thunder, and fire.

Guess ancient West Virginians believe the same thing.

Holding her breath, she rapped on the front door. Long seconds passed with Jessica unable to hear so much as a creaking floorboard inside the cabin. Out of the corner of her eye, though, she saw the green and white gingham curtain that hung at the front window flutter ever so slightly. Reaching inside her canvas tote, she removed one of her business cards, then stepped over to the window and pressed it to the glass at eye level.

"Hello, Mr. Burdette," she said in a voice loud enough to be heard on the other side of the glass. "My name is Jessica Reardon and I'm a reporter for *The Greenbrier Dispatch*. If you could spare me a few minutes of your time, I'd like to talk to you about the recent Draygan sightings. I brought a case of RC Cola, six cans of Skoal, and enough moon pies to send your blood-sugar level soaring."

"Leave me be," came the muffled reply. "I ain't got nothing to say."

Undeterred, she said, "Mother Maebelle's granddaughter, Darlene Malone, sent me out here to speak to you. I drove a long way, sir, and I'd really like to talk to you…even if it's off the record," Jessica added at the last, hoping that would sweeten the deal.

A few moments later, the front door creaked open. A tall, grizzled, white-haired man, who looked as rugged as the hills he called home, stood in the doorway, a shotgun resting in the crook of his arm. "Lucky for you, you're right purty or I'd send you packing with a load of buckshot in your backside," he muttered, motioning her inside the cabin with a terse nod of his bearded chin.

Jessica grabbed her gifts and followed John Henry inside. The cabin proved to be cozier than she'd expected, and the glow of oil lamps cast a warm, golden light onto the one-room interior. On one side of the cabin there was a dry sink and several kitchen cabinets, and on the other side was a four-poster bed. In the middle there was a table with a set of mismatched chairs. The centerpiece of the cabin was the massive stone fireplace, large enough to roast a side of venison in it. This she knew because that's exactly what was hanging on the spit.

"I had a bit of trouble finding your place," she remarked conversationally as she set the case of cola and other items on the table. "Gooseneck Holler isn't on the map."

"It don't have to be," her host snarled, his rheumy blue eyes narrowing as he sized her up. "Everybody knows where Gooseneck Holler is."

Well, everybody wasn't driving my Ford Bronco, Jessica nearly retorted, managing to bite her tongue at the last second. Instead, she smiled sweetly as she pointed to the ceiling, where there were at least a dozen bundles of dried yarrow hanging from the rafters. Their stems were wrapped in twine. "What do you use the yarrow for?"

"Ward off evil spirits," John Henry replied laconically as he propped the shotgun next to the front door.

Not so much as glancing at her, he stomped over to the kitchen area and removed an earthenware jug from the cupboard. Grabbing two enamel mugs, he stomped back to the table.

"Well, don't stand there gawking. Have a seat," he said irritably as he set the cups on the table. Not bothering to ask if she wanted any, he proceeded to pour a healthy measure of a very potent-smelling beverage into each of the cups. "Make yourself useful and open that box of moon pies."

"Right away," Jessica murmured, more than a little intimidated by her host's gruff demeanor.

Reaching inside the open box, John Henry snatched two moon pies, handing her one of them.

Not about to inform her host that she absolutely loathed banana-flavored anything, Jessica bit into the iced confection. Trying not to gag, she chewed and swallowed as quickly as possible. Without thinking, she grabbed her enamel cup and took a big gulp. The liquid hit her gut with a fiery impact, and Jessica worried that it may have burned a hole in her esophagus on the way down as well. Hacking, she slapped a hand over her mouth to keep both the liquor and the marshmallow yuck from making a return trip.

John Henry didn't so much as bat an eye as he grabbed an empty coffee can and spit a wad of brown tobacco juice into it before calmly taking a bite of his moon pie. "How does your snack taste?" the old fart had the gall to ask.

"It's yummy," Jessica told him, forcing herself to take another bite. "What a tasty treat, moon pies and moonshine."

To her surprise, the wisecrack elicited a rusty-sounding chuckle from her host.

"You're all right, girl," John Henry said with a smile, and Jessica was able to count on one hand how many teeth he had.

Pleasantries out of the way, Jessica decided it was time to get down to business. "I understand that back in 1939 you saw the mythical beast Draygan," she remarked, deciding at the last minute not to pull out her notepad. She had, after all, given her assurance that his comments would be off the record.

John Henry took a long swig from his mug, wiping his mouth with the back of his hand. "Draygan ain't no myth. And I saw him a heap of times."

"How many is a 'heap'?"

"Five or six times, I reckon."

"And you were how old at the time?"

Her host reached inside the chipboard box and removed two more moon pies. When he offered her one, Jessica shook her head. Since she'd yet to finish the first one, she figured that got her off the hook.

"I was 12 years old at the time," John Henry said, a faraway look in his blue eyes. "Which is why, when I started to get the fits, everyone thought I'd plum lost my mind."

Confused, Jessica shook her head. "What do you mean by 'the fits'? I'm not familiar with this term."

"It started out as just an ache in my head." John Henry wrapped both of his gnarled hands around his enamel mug, contemplatively staring at it as he spoke. "As time passed, it got so bad, I thought my head would burst open like a smashed pumpkin. Then I took to shaking and trembling, like I was possessed by the devil himself. But when I started mumbling crazy stuff, that's when folks begun to whisper as to how I was bewitched; particularly since I was born at the stroke of midnight, right at the start of the witching hour. Ma had that conjure woman, Mother Maebelle, come up here to take off the hex, but it didn't do no good on account as how it weren't a case of conjuration."

Jessica reached for her mug and took a neat swallow, actually welcoming the burning warmth this time. John Henry's "fits" were so similar to what Gideon called his "spells" that she was left dumbfounded.

"Well, if it wasn't a case of conjuration—" whatever that was—"what was wrong with you?" she asked, after she'd had a moment to collect herself.

"Mother Maebelle said that Draygan was using me as a vessel."

Uncomprehending, Jessica said, "I'm sorry, but you lost me."

"Since Draygan can't speak directly to us, he has to find a vessel he can speak through," John Henry clarified as he opened another moon pie. "And that damned dragon chose me. But it was a poor choice on account of me being just a kid and folks payin' no mind to what I was spoutin'. Except to say I was crazy. And because no one paid me any mind, all them people drowned when the flood waters came through. Fifty of 'em died in one single day."

"Do you remember what it was that Draygan used to say to you?" she quietly asked, wondering if this traumatic episode from John Henry's childhood hadn't permanently scarred him. That would certainly explain why he chose to live isolated from the rest of the world.

"I expect I'll take them words to my grave. 'Two score and ten will die in the fast, green water. So sayeth the Beast,'" he recited, before taking another swig from his mug.

Like a puppet on a string, Jessica's head instantly jerked. The wording was almost identical to what Gideon had babbled just before two rafters were drowned on the Greenbrier River—*Two will die in the fast, green water. So sayeth the Beast.* A cryptic phrase that had then proven tragically prophetic.

"Did Draygan say anything else to you?" Jessica inquired, still reeling from shock.

Her host shook his shaggy head. "Nope. And after the Reckoning, I stopped having my fits."

The Reckoning. Jessica recalled that was how many locals referred to the Draygan epochs.

"For how long a period did you experience these fits?" she next asked, tempted to pull out her notepad and record all of this while it was still fresh in her memory.

"Nigh on six weeks."

"Have you seen Draygan recently?"

Again, John Henry shook his head. "And I'm doin' everything in my power to make sure that I don't see hide nor hair of him. I got my Dragon Dogs at the four corners of the cabin keeping vigil. Ain't no way Draygan is going to pester me this time around."

"I hope that he doesn't," Jessica said in all sincerity. John Henry Burdette sounded as if he'd been pestered enough for one lifetime. Slipping her canvas tote over her shoulder, she rose to her feet. With a grateful smile, she extended her hand toward her host and said, "Thank you, Mr. Burdette. This has been an illuminating conversation. And I promise that nothing you said will be printed in *The Dispatch*."

For several seconds, John Henry stared at her proffered right hand. Then, getting to his feet, he took her hand in his. "You best take care, Miz Reardon. That dragon can cause you a world of misery if he puts his mind to it."

"Yes, I know," she murmured, reminded of the pain that Gideon endured each and every time he suffered one of his spells. She didn't believe in dragons, but she did believe that some unseen force, something possibly malevolent, was at work. The coincidences were too striking to be written off as chance occurrences.

As she turned to leave, John Henry cleared his throat. "Hold your horses...I got something for you." Stomping over to the other side of the cabin, he removed a floral garland from a wall peg. "This will protect you from any evil spirits that might be lurking," he said as he placed the garland around her neck.

Jessica gently fingered the dried blossoms of sweet woodruff, rue, and yarrow. "Why, thank you...this is the nicest gift that anyone has ever given me."

A few moments later, ignoring the ferocious barking of John Henry's four Dragon Dogs, Jessica made her way back to the Bronco. Just as she was about to open the driver's side door, she stopped in her tracks, her breath catching in her throat.

In the layer of dust that covered the hood of her SUV, somebody had written the words "Ever yours."

* * *

Gideon raised his head, letting the warmth of the autumn sun caress his face as a gentle breeze wrapped him in its embrace. Not nearly so complacent, the horse beneath him nickered.

"You're quite right, Blaze. Walk on," he said to his equine companion, nudging him behind the girth.

The black gelding obediently set off at a leisurely pace toward the hillock just yonder. While it was only half a mile from Highland House, the small hilltop fell outside the boundary of Jessica's property. No matter. He had a reason for committing the trespass.

As they crossed the verdant pasture, everywhere that Gideon gazed, the hills were festooned in a patchwork of vibrant color: the flaming reds of sourwoods and maples, the golden yellows of hickories and poplars. Beauty of such magnitude took a man's breath away. The roots that bound him to this place ran deep, going back to his great-grandfather Fergus MacAllister, one of the first white men to cross into what was then a forbidding wilderness. It had been a place fraught with danger, but also holding the promise of untold bounty for those bold enough to tame it.

Having reached his destination, Gideon dismounted and wrapped the horse's reins around the wrought-iron fence that enclosed the small hilltop cemetery. From his saddle horn, he untied the bundle of yellow goldenrod and blue asters that he'd picked earlier. As he opened the gate, he winced at the loud, grinding creak that broke the peaceful silence.

While the fence was encrusted with the rust of several decades, Gideon was pleased to see that some kind soul had recently tended to the area. The brush and debris had been cleared, and save for a trailing vine of myrtle, the head- and footstones were all plainly visible. Here, guarded by a pair of ancient maples, were the mortal remains of three generations of MacAllisters.

And here it was that his beloved Sarah had been laid to rest.

Finding her grave, Gideon went down on bent knee. As he stared at the tombstone he lightly fingered the incised epitaph.

" 'So I turned to the Garden of Love that so many sweet flowers bore,' " he read aloud. To ensure that his wife had a proper burial and that the quotation from Blake was inscribed upon her tombstone, he'd forwarded every Confederate dollar and Union greenback that he'd had to his name.

"This is not how I envisioned our lives unfolding," he whispered as he placed the bundle of wildflowers at the base of the weatherworn headstone. "I have so many regrets. There are so many things I could have done differently...should have done differently. It weighs heavy on my mind that I cannot atone for the grievous sin I committed against you, dear Sarah. I took a vow to always protect you. I broke that vow, and I shall spend the rest of my days living in the shadow of that broken promise."

As he spoke, a cloud passed overhead, casting a dark shadow over the cemetery.

"I dare not ask your forgiveness, Sarah...I have not earned it. Indeed, I may never earn it." As his eyes blurred with tears, Gideon stared at the headstone, at those damning words—*Beloved Wife of Gideon*. Shamefully, he bent his head, unable to gaze at the inscription. "You must believe me...If I could do over, if I could somehow pull back the curtain of time, I would do differently. If given a second chance, I would stay by your side, and no force under the heavens would be able to separate us."

But as he knew all too well, he would never have that second chance. Time flits past on wings made of quicksilver, there but for an instant.

Inundated with self-recrimination, Gideon wiped the tears from his eyes. As he did, the sun broke through the clouds in a dappled burst.

Still on bended kneed, he raised his face heavenward. "Even though we are separated by death, once again I feel your presence, dear Sarah. When you died eleven months ago, it was as though that piece of you that had hovered ever near took flight. And try as I might to call it back to me, I could not. But now, once again, I—" He lowered his head and stared at the ground beneath him, unsure of what it was he wanted to say.

How could he explain to his beloved that once again he felt her presence—her beautiful, compassionate essence—but in the guise of another? He could not. He did not have the words at his command to articulate so mysterious a conundrum. Moreover, he had yet to sort through his feelings for Jessica Reardon. He only knew that the time had come to begin again.

Slowly, Gideon rose to his feet." My darling Sarah, I shall never forget the love we shared...never."

It is done, he acknowledged as he turned to leave, having made his peace as best he could. He'd deliberated long into the night, his heart torn between the woman who was lost to him forever and the woman who'd mended his broken body, even as she'd helped to heal his broken heart.

As the hour was late and he still had a great many preparations to make, he quickly mounted and headed back to Highland House.

Setting a brisk pace, Gideon reflected on the many changes he'd recently undergone. When he'd first arrived at Highland House, he'd been dispirited, his grief an unbearable crucible. He'd seen so much senseless carnage, been witness to so much human misery, that he'd wanted nothing more than to close his eyes one last time and put it all behind him. But then a courageous and steadfast woman had entered his life, ushering him back to the world of the living.

In so many ways, Jessica Reardon put him in mind of Sarah. Although, curiously enough, it was the differences between the two women that he found most appealing. At first, he'd been consumed with guilt whenever he made the comparison, but that guilt had now given way to a hope for the future.

In order to secure that future promise, he knew he must break free of his shackles and escape the beast that held him in its thrall.

Coming to a halt at the old corn crib that served as a stable, Gideon dismounted. Since he would later have need of the gelding, he put down a supper of hay, but left the horse saddled. That done, he strode toward the carriage house, opened the double doors, and stepped inside.

Once his eyes had adjusted to the dim lighting, he strode over to the workbench. There he retrieved the bullet mold that he'd earlier discovered hidden in the bottom of a box with other "junk," as Jessica had referred to the miscellaneous collection of ancient odds and ends. While she'd deemed it worthless, the bullet mold was highly valuable to him. His great-grandfather had used this very mold to fashion his own bullets when he'd fought with Washington's troops during the Revolutionary War.

Just as Gideon intended to fashion the silver bullet that he would use to kill Draygan.

To that end, he slipped a hand inside his coat pocket, removing the sterling silver cigar case that his father had given to him upon his graduation from the University of Virginia. As he removed the lid, he stared ruefully at the family crest that was engraved upon it. He was the last of his line. A lone twig on a venerable old tree. When he died, so, too, the name MacAllister in Greenbrier County.

So be it.

His future course set, Gideon cast a quick glance at the western horizon. The sun was low in the sky, and he had much work to do before he set out on his quest.

Chapter 17

Exhausted, Jessica pulled the Bronco up to the front of Highland House and cut the engine. Grabbing her purse and canvas tote, she opened the door and got out. There was a distinct chill in the air, the sun having already started its descent behind the western ridge.

Hearing the front door open, she turned and watched as Gideon stepped onto the porch and waved to her. Attired in his cleaned-up, gray uniform trousers, which were tucked into a pair of polished, knee-high boots, and a flowing, white linen shirt, he looked like he'd just walked out of her nightly dreams.

"You were gone so long that I'd begun to worry about you," Gideon said as he held the front door open for her.

"My interviews took a bit longer than expected," Jessica told him, managing to drum up a smile.

Depositing her things on the hall table, Jessica headed to the living room with Gideon tagging along. With a weary sigh, she plopped into one of the wingback chairs situated in front of the fireplace.

"And were you able to solve the Draygan mystery during the

course of your interviews?" Gideon inquired, seating himself in the chair opposite hers.

Jessica plucked at a loose thread that protruded from the armrest. Then, having had her fill of Draygan for one day, she said, "There is no dragon. However, I am convinced that some very strange psychic phenomenon is happening throughout the county. For whatever reason, it's only happening to people born between the hour of midnight and one a.m."

Gideon raised a questioning brow. "Should you not be affected by this strange phenomenon? As I recall, last night at McGuff's, you acknowledged that you were also born during the witching hour."

Uncertain if her nightly dreams could rightly be classified as psychic phenomenon, Jessica shrugged, faking a nonchalance she didn't feel. "I guess some people are less susceptible than others."

"Then you live a more charmed life than the rest of us doomed ghost seers."

As she stared at Gideon Jessica's gaze was suddenly drawn to the gray woolen fabric of his trousers and the welt of yellow that was sewn on the outer seam of each pant leg. "You have a closet full of new clothes. Why are you dressed like that?"

Gideon peered down at his uniform. "I don't see anything wrong with my attire. Men in this day and age also wear shirts and trousers."

"True. But unless it's Halloween, or they're extras on a Hollywood movie, or going to an historical reenactment, they don't wear Confederate cavalry uniforms," she snapped, making no attempt to curb her irritation.

"As much as the thought is objectionable to you, I did travel one hundred and fifty years into the future," Gideon stubbornly maintained. "I cannot alter reality simply to suit your skepticism."

Still reeling from the Draygan interviews, Jessica didn't have the patience or wherewithal to deal with Gideon and his purported adventures in time travel. "Well, guess what? Your whole story smacks of altered realities, conspiracy theories, and alien abductions."

"Might I point out that your argument is utterly nonsensical?"

"Oh, that's rich," she snickered. "What could be more nonsensical than you claiming that one moment it's 1864, then all of a sudden, *poof,* it's the twenty-first century? And don't bother answering that. It was a rhetorical question," she muttered disagreeably as she got up from the chair.

Also rising to his feet, Gideon said, "Why is it so difficult to believe that I hail from another century?"

"Maybe because I stopped believing in fairytales a long time ago," she informed him, terrified that she might lose her claim to sanity if she acquiesced.

"This is no fairytale, Jessica. As well you know." Bowing his head, Gideon added, "Please forgive me if I have distressed you in any way."

Apology issued, Gideon strode across the room and retrieved the gray tunic hanging from the back of a ladder-back chair. Without uttering a word, he slipped it on. That done, he reached for the leather gun holster and sword belt which also hung from the chair.

"Wh-what are you d-doing?" Jessica stammered, hit with a potent sense of *déjà vu.* Last night in her dream, she'd watched Gideon perform this same ritual.

"I must leave now," Gideon answered as he pulled on a pair of leather gauntlets.

Leave? Surely, he wasn't intending to return to the nineteenth century via the same time portal that had brought him here?

Which, of course, would be an impossible feat, given the fact that there was no time portal.

But what if I'm wrong? What if a time portal really does exist?

Panic-stricken, Jessica rushed across the room. "You can't leave," she cried, grabbing hold of his arm.

Gideon gently disengaged himself from her grasp. "But I must," he insisted, a determined look in his eyes. "I shall not have a moment's peace until I confront the beast known as Draygan."

Flabbergasted, Jessica said, "That might not be such a good idea. Hunting a fire-breathing dragon could prove very danger-ous." Not to mention, it was an utterly quixotic venture, right up there with tipping windmills.

"And here I thought that you didn't believe in the beast's exis-tence," Gideon countered.

"While I don't believe there's a fire-breathing dragon on the loose, I am convinced that there is some force—some inexplica-ble phenomenon—happening here in Greenbrier County," Jes-sica conceded, hoping to talk some sense into him. "But whatever it is, this mysterious force is beyond our comprehension."

"I do not mean to comprehend the beast," Gideon declared. "I mean to slay it."

His resolute tone of voice caused Jessica's panic to instantly transmute into acute fear. "But what if Draygan slays you instead?" she argued.

"That is always a possibility when one meets a deadly foe on the field of battle," Gideon said matter-of-factly. "A battle is, by its very nature, a contest to the death."

"This isn't a game of *Dungeons & Dragons*," she told him, dis-believing what she was hearing. If, on the outside chance, there really was a fire-breathing dragon, Gideon could very well walk out the front door, never to return. Wasn't that what had happened to Christine Whitley? According to Joe Whitley, after catching sight of Draygan, his wife had vanished without a trace. "Please, Gideon. Don't do this."

"Ask anything of me but that."

"Then take me with you!" she said impetuously, refusing to surrender. "It just stands to reason that two people can slay a dragon better than one."

Her plea caused Gideon's stoic expression to soften ever so slightly. "You, Jessica Reardon, are the most stout-hearted woman that I have ever known. But this is my fight, not yours." Snatching his gray slouch hat from the table, Gideon set it on his head at an angle.

Because there was nothing she could do to stop him, Jessica stood silent as Gideon strode out of the room. Hearing the soft jangle of his scabbard as it bumped against his thigh, she experienced another burst of *déjà vu*.

Overcome with a dark premonition, she darted over to the window and watched as Gideon left the house. In that charged instant, Jessica couldn't distinguish where her nightly dreams ended and reality began.

* * *

Telling herself for the umpteenth time that Gideon would safely return to Highland House, Jessica glanced at the stack of dragon lore and other related material that she'd printed off the Internet. Despite the lateness of the hour—a few minutes before midnight—she'd decided to put a dent in her research since she was too wired to go to bed.

Nearly five hours had passed since Gideon had departed, his foolhardy quest putting her in mind of one of King Arthur's knights setting out to find the mythical Holy Grail. As any-one familiar with those legends knew, more than a few gallant knights had never made it back to Camelot. A fact that she pre-ferred not to dwell upon.

Picking up the first page of the printed stack, Jessica quickly perused an article written by an accredited folklorist who explained that, in the Asian world, dragons represented wis-dom and hidden knowledge; while in the West, winged serpents were considered evil and destructive. Which meant that Dray-gan could possibly embody both positive and negative aspects. Assuming, of course, that the mythical beast actually existed. Jessica was still highly skeptical.

After highlighting a few passages that she intended to cite in her article, Jessica put the printout aside and reached for the next sheet of paper, a list of documented dragon sightings over the last fifty years. To her surprise, there had been sightings of the mythi-cal beast all over the globe—Bangkok, Helsinki, Rio de Janeiro, Cape Town. Moreover, all of the sightings coincided with peri-ods of intense psychic phenomena, deadly disasters, and in one case—reported in Wiltshire, England in 1965—of time travel.

As she re-read the last entry, her jaw went slack.

"Oh my god," she murmured. "What if it's true? What if Gideon MacAllister somehow fell through a crack in time?"

And could that possibly be what had happened to Christine Whitley? Maybe Christine didn't "vanish into thin air" so much as she vanished into another century. Every year thousands of people went missing. What if some of them were actually time travelers? Just ordinary people going about their daily lives when they were unexpectedly jettisoned to a different time period.

But how could such a thing happen? Jessica's rational mind demanded. Time travel was a mind-boggling premise.

Suddenly envisioning a mad scientist standing at a chalkboard writing out a mathematical formula a mile-and-a-half long, she pivoted toward her laptop, pulled up an Internet search engine, and typed "Is time travel scientifically possible?" Clicking on a recent entry, she carefully read an extract written by a particle physicist—*no dummy there*—who claimed that, according to Einstein's general theory of relativity, traveling into the future was scientifically possible!

If that was true, it meant that one hundred and fifty years ago Gideon MacAllister really did fight in the Civil War.

"It also means that Gideon once owned Highland House," she murmured, shell-shocked.

In dire need of fresh air, Jessica got out of her chair and walked over to the French doors, pulling them wide open. Bombarded with more questions than answers, she gazed at the night sky. Spying Orion, the celestial hunter, she thought of Gideon. At that moment, he was out hunting for Draygan, the same beast who might very well have brought him forward in time.

That she was actually starting to believe such a preposterous notion prompted a burst of hysterical laughter. Jessica's notion of reality had just taken a turn for the weird.

* * *

Standing beside a massive pine tree, Richard Bragg stared at Highland House, his estranged wife's ramshackle abode.

"That she bought with my money," he muttered. Anger was getting the better of him, and the list of Jessica's sins seemed a long one indeed.

Be that as it may, he was still willing to show mercy and to forgive her willful behavior, provided that she not only return to him but also agreed to renew their marital vows. More than generous terms, given the hell that she'd put him through.

Having decided that the best course of action was to confront his wife directly, Richard had driven to Greenbrier County, West Virginia. Earlier in the evening, he'd checked into a local motel in Lewisburg, planning to pay Jessica a visit after he attended Sunday church service tomorrow.

However, anxious to catch a glimpse of her, he'd driven to Highland House, which was set on top of a steep knoll. He parked his Lexus at the bottom of the hill.

He peered down at the sudden rustle of shrubbery, catching sight of a large marmalade cat that immediately hunched its back and hissed at him. Richard knew from the private investigator's dossier that Jessica had adopted a cat from the local animal shelter.

The creature will have to be put down, he thought dispassionately, tempted to kick the cat in the face. Like women, cats were devious creatures.

Stepping around the ill-tempered feline, he cautiously made his way to the front yard, grateful for the full moon that clearly illuminated the grounds.

Despite the fact that they'd had no contact in the last six months, there was no doubt in his mind that he could persuade Jessica to return to him. She was, after all, malleable as clay. Moreover, she belonged to him, and Richard was intent on reminding his estranged wife of the sacred vows that they'd exchanged on their wedding day.

Noticing the golden light that spilled from one of the downstairs rooms, he headed in that direction, keeping his footfalls as light as possible as he traipsed toward a set of French doors. Able to see Jessica, in profile, seated at a wooden desk, he came to a standstill some ten feet from the house.

The mere sight of her caused the breath to catch in his throat.

As he stared at the loose, auburn tresses that framed either side of her face and grazed the upper curve of her breasts, Richard became highly aroused.

Unable to stop himself, he lowered a hand and rubbed his crotch. Stimulating himself to erection, he called to mind their wedding night. While Jessica had kept her eyes shut and her mouth tightly clenched, he knew that she'd found him virile. At the time, he'd foolishly imagined himself in love with her. This had been a short-lived belief, as Jessica soon proved herself unworthy of his affections. Too late, he'd discovered that his wife was a freak of nature, possessed of a barren womb and breasts that would never suckle a child.

The unpleasant memory caused Richard to immediately lose his erection.

Cursing under his breath, he glared through the glass panes, watching as Jessica speedily clicked away on a laptop computer. No doubt she was busy writing more drivel for the local newspaper. Because she had a degree in journalism, she'd always had aspirations to work as a newspaper reporter—an ambition that he intended to squash as soon as she returned to him. As his wife, her job—her only job—was to tend to his needs.

"To love, honor, and obey me," Richard murmured.

Until death do we part.

Chapter 18

It's a killing moon, Gideon noted as he rode across the dew-dampened meadow. The luminous, orange orb was bisected with inky bands of striated clouds, making it appear as though the full moon bled from a fatal, celestial wound. A bracing wind blew against his back, causing the leaves on the nearby trees to quiver on their branches.

On such a night, death seemed to lurk in every shadow.

Suddenly catching sight of twinkling lights about half a mile distant, Gideon urged his mount to quicken its pace. The mysterious lights were the first sign he'd had all night that something was afoot.

He'd been riding for hours now and had yet to see the winged beast. Earlier, he'd gone to the abandoned saltpeter cave near Devil's Run Creek, but had determined that Draygan was nowhere in the vicinity.

Approaching the spot where he'd seen the twinkling lights, the only discernible illumination was that cast by the moon. Scanning the meadow, Gideon saw that the lights now beckoned from the other side of the meadow. As he gamely ventured forth, he couldn't help but wonder if Draygan was toying with him.

When, a few moments later, he arrived at the new location, once again the twinkling lights seemed to emanate from a different direction. Vexed, Gideon was on the verge of kicking Blaze into a gallop—determined to outrun the lights—when he saw a crouched figure standing near a towering oak tree. The lone figure immediately put him in mind of Hecate, the ancient patroness of witchcraft. Legend had it that she appeared nightly at a crossroads to aid anguished mortals haunted by the spirits of the dead.

To Gideon's surprise, rather than the fabled Hecate, the solitary figure turned out to be an old, white-haired woman. She was garbed in a faded dress and wore a shawl tied around her frail shoulders.

"Have you lost your way?" he inquired, reining Blaze to a halt beside the mighty oak tree.

"'The night was dark, no father was there, the child was wet with dew. The mire was deep, and the child did weep, and away the vapor flew,'" the old woman intoned in a sing-songy voice.

"Ah! You are familiar with the poetry of William Blake," he remarked as he dismounted.

Softly cackling, the crone peered up at him and said, "Such words are in your head, ain't they?"

Admittedly perplexed by her cryptic reply, Gideon unbuttoned his jacket. "It is a chill night for you to be about without a proper coat," he remarked, solicitously offering her the tunic.

With a shake of her head, the old woman refused the garment. "What need have I of such raiment? 'Tain't the least bit cold."

Although thinking otherwise, Gideon shrugged back into

his jacket. "Have you perchance seen the great winged beast that inhabits these environs?"

"Ain't seen Draygan tonight," she responded. "Although I know where he be a-hiding."

His interest instantly piqued, Gideon asked the obvious question. "And where might that be?"

"In your heart, boy…in your heart." Cocking her head to one side, the old woman silently appraised him. "Most everyone hereabouts is familiar to me, but I've never seen your face before."

"Forgive my lax manners. I am Gideon MacAllister." As he introduced himself, Gideon bent slightly at the waist. "And might I inquire with whom I have the pleasure of speaking?"

"Folks call me Mother Maebelle."

Ah, yes. Miss Malone's grandmother.

Craning her neck, Mother Maebelle stared at the night sky. "The moon just moved into Gemini, sure enough."

Gideon gave the sky a cursory glance. "Is that significant?" he asked, beginning to suspect that Mother Maebelle might well suffer from an unsound mind. It would certainly explain her wandering the hillside so late at night.

"It be of great significance to those who come a-searchin'. Are you a seeker, Gideon MacAllister?"

"In so far as I seek the beast known as Draygan."

"Others have come before you, and they rued the day they set out on that ill-fated quest. Only those pure of heart can know the mind of Draygan," Mother Maebelle informed him.

Bewildered, Gideon shook his head. "What does my heart have to do with this matter? I only need a strong arm and a steady gaze to slay the beast." And the silver bullet that he'd earlier cast.

"Mark my words, you'll need more than that. You best think long and hard before you venture into them hinterlands," Mother Maebelle warned, pointing to the mountain in the distance. "You could lose your way if you're not careful. Maybe even lose your soul. Draygan is only a reflection of you. What you do unto Draygan, you do unto yourself."

Again, her meaning eluded him. The old woman was speaking in riddles. "I do not intend to kill Draygan for the mere thrill of the hunt," Gideon said in his own defense. "For ten days now, Draygan has been bedeviling me, insinuating himself into my waking thoughts and sleeping dreams. To free myself from this dark malady, I must slay the beast."

Extending her right arm in his direction, Mother Maebelle placed a gnarled hand over his heart. "There is a dark force that haunts you, but it's one of your own making. To cure yourself, you must make amends for the sins that you committed against your beloved."

"It would be impossible for me to make amends … My wife is dead."

"Nothing is impossible," the crone countered with a toothless smile as she removed her hand from his chest. "The time is now, the place is here. You must complete the circle. Kill Draygan and you will die. Learn from the past and you will live."

Yet another senseless riddle, Gideon silently fumed, fast losing his patience. "My course is set," he stated, more brusquely than he intended. "I cannot change my destiny."

"And I say your destiny ain't yet been revealed to you. But I'd be willing to give you a look-see," Mother Maebelle offered as she gestured toward the sinkhole on the other side of the oak tree.

With a wary nod, Gideon followed her to the small pond.

While he placed little faith in the superstitious practice of scrying—gazing into a pool of water to "see" one's future—he also didn't think any harm would come of it. When she directed him to get down on his hands and knees in front of the water hole, he obediently complied.

"This will help you see the truth," Mother Maebelle said, retrieving a small burlap pouch from her skirt pocket. Untying it, she reached inside and grabbed a handful of dried dandelion petals, which she sprinkled over his head and shoulders. "Now hold your gaze steady and soon enough a vision will come to you."

Taking a deep breath, Gideon did as ordered. Uncertain as to what he would see, if anything, he stared, unblinking, into the still water.

Just as he expected, nothing happened. All he could see in the inky surface of the pool was his own reflection, juxtaposed beside that of the full moon.

"Keep looking, boy," Mother Maebelle hissed. "The vision is inside of you just waiting to be conjured forth."

As if those words had some magical effect, Gideon's reflected image suddenly blurred, giving way to another image in the stygian depths, that of his beloved Sarah. Although faint and diaphanous, the image was heartbreakingly familiar. Mesmerized, Gideon's heart slammed against his ribcage.

With a sorrowful expression on her heart-shaped face, Sarah slowly raised a framed picture of an upright triangle encircled by an Ouroboros, a dragon biting its own tail.

Come back to me, Gideon . . . come back to me.

Able to hear Sarah's insistent plea inside his head, Gideon shuddered. In the next instant, the waters rippled and the reflection dissolved into an ever-widening blur.

Desperate to hold onto Sarah's image, Gideon squinted his eyes in order to sharpen the vision. Yet even as the first image faded, a new one materialized, and Gideon was taken aback to see Jessica Reardon's image reflected in the water's surface. As with Sarah, she held in front of her a framed picture of an upright triangle contained within an Ouroboros.

With an expression as bleak as Sarah's had been, Jessica softly whispered, "Come back to me, Gideon…come back to me."

Startled to hear the very same words spoken by both women, Gideon jerked his head. At that point, the image instantly vanished.

Scrambling to his feet, he turned to Mother Maebelle. "What does it mean?" he asked, his voice hoarse with shock.

The old woman shrugged and said, "Only you know what it means. The vision is yours to do with as you see fit."

"Admittedly, I am at a loss to understand what I just saw." Not only was he puzzled that both Sarah and Jessica had appeared in his vision, he could not even begin to decipher the meaning of the framed picture that each woman had shown to him.

Taking him by the arm, Mother Maebelle led Gideon away from the pool of water. "Nothing in this ol' world is carved in stone. The Lord, he taketh, and the Lord, he giveth. You remember that, boy. You learn from your past mistakes, or the Lord, he'll taketh all over again."

Gideon came to a halt, her dire warning sounding like a death knell to his ears. "Would the Almighty be so cruel as to take yet another love from me?"

Chortling, Mother Maebelle shook her head. "There be but the one love. And she's been with you forever and a day. Your two lives are woven together like the gossamer threads of a spider web. But you best take care, Gideon MacAllister, because that web is a fragile thing, sure enough."

Could the old woman only speak in riddles? he wondered, utterly confounded.

At hearing a screech owl hoot, Mother Maebelle suddenly went as still as a megalith. Long seconds passed as the old woman appeared to listen to a silent communiqué that only she could hear. "You must return from whence you came, to the house on the hill," she said suddenly. "There is no time to lose."

"Can you not tell me more than that?" he asked, alarmed by her urgent tone.

"Go to the house. 'Tis there that the danger lurks."

Gideon swung himself into the saddle. "Shall I notify your granddaughter and tell her of your whereabouts?"

Mother Maebelle shook her head. "She knows where to find me if she has need of me. Now you best hurry, boy. When the moon next enters into Gemini, redemption can be found. But only if you be of true and courageous heart."

Gideon doffed his hat. "I thank you for the wise counsel."

* * *

Jessica worriedly glanced at the mantel clock. Gideon had been gone for hours, and she was beginning to worry about him.

When, a few seconds later, she heard a loud rustling sound, she turned her head and peered out the window that was adjacent to her desk. On the other side of the glass pane, the full moon hovered above the tree line, shedding an eerie, silver illumination onto the landscape.

Shivering from the autumn chill, she got up from her desk and walked over to the fireplace. Highland House had never been updated with a furnace, and while many of the rooms had been retrofitted with electric baseboard heaters, the library wasn't one of them.

Not particularly in the mood to build a fire, Jessica nonetheless plucked several sheets from a stack of old newspapers that she kept at the ready. Going down on her knees, she grabbed a handful of twigs and broken tree branches from the large basket beside the hearth. She placed the kindling around three sturdy logs, shoving the balled-up newspapers in between the gaps. She then struck a large kitchen match, wrinkling her nose at the sulfurous smell.

In no time at all, she'd built a roaring fire. As she was about to close the fireplace screen, Jessica heard a loud *whoosh* as the French doors suddenly blew open, leaving both panels wildly swinging to and fro.

"Criminy!"

Lunging to her feet, Jessica rushed over and closed the doors. No sooner had she secured them than she noticed that the draft from the open doors had blown several burning embers onto the hearth. To her horror, the pile of newspapers combusted into a burst of orange flames.

With a horrified shriek, she dashed over to the fireplace and immediately began to stomp out the flames. It wasn't until she'd gotten the worst of it under control that Jessica suddenly realized the bottom half of her long skirt had caught fire. Panic-stricken, she frantically swished the sides of the skirt from side to side, trying to keep the fabric away from her body.

Unable to extinguish the flames, Jessica's terror escalated as images flashed across her mind's eye in a rapid, almost dizzying succession. *Burning embers showering her head. A bundle of hay violently igniting. Falling roof timbers creating a deadly inferno.*

Seized with a fear unlike anything she'd ever experienced, she was so petrified that she could no longer move. Could no longer breathe. She could only wait for what she was certain would prove to be a fiery death.

* * *

Although tempted to rush to his estranged wife's aid, Richard Bragg stood rooted in place.

Taken aback by the unexpected turn of events, he watched Jessica's sudden capitulation as orange flames aggressively danced around her skirt hem. While her quick surrender was deplorable, he found himself inexplicably engrossed by the scene. Aroused even, his heart wildly thumping as the blood surged to his groin.

It was a trial by fire for the grievous sin that she'd committed against him.

That realization filled him with a sudden burst of euphoria. What he was witnessing—immolation by fire—was the ultimate purification, the flames burning away the dross that had accumulated in the wake of Jessica's terrible transgression. A fitting punishment given that she'd abandoned their domestic hearth, with the sentence perfectly matched to the crime.

This is what happens when a wife repudiates her sacred marital vow, he told himself, tamping down on his initial impulse to go to her rescue.

But if he let her burn at the proverbial stake, how would she ever be able to beg his forgiveness?

Seized with indecision, Richard gnashed his teeth together. "As her husband, I must save her," he muttered as he stepped away from the pine tree so that he could go to Jessica's rescue.

He'd gone no more than several feet when he suddenly

glimpsed a pair of gleaming red eyes in the depths of the nearby grove. Able to smell a distinctly gamey odor, he feared some feral animal was afoot.

When, a split-second later, he unexpectedly heard the steady pounding of hooves, the heroic impulse to save his wife was instantly doused as Richard dashed back to the sheltering pine tree.

In the next instant, he watched as a horseman galloped past.

Chapter 19

Panic-stricken, Jessica opened her mouth to scream, but her terror was so extreme that her vocal cords froze up on her, rendering her mute.

"Jessica!" Gideon shouted as he charged toward her.

In the next instant, she felt cool water splash against her legs. Still in a daze, it took several moments for her to realize that Gideon had snatched the vase of fresh-cut flowers from the coffee table and tossed the water onto her burning skirt. Going down on bent knee, he hurriedly unbuttoned her it. Then, without bothering to ask permission, he slid the smoldering garment off her hips and tossed it into the fireplace. He wrapped her lower body with a plaid throw blanket grabbed from the couch.

Suddenly dizzy, Jessica felt as light as the smoke that permeated the room. Wobbling unsteadily, she focused on Gideon's broad shoulders as she pitched forward.

Catching hold of her, Gideon wrapped his arms around the backs of her legs and hoisted her over his right shoulder. He carried her down the hallway to the living room, easing her into a wingback chair a few moments later.

"I tried to put out the flames. But I couldn't," Jessica told him, wheezing slightly, still struggling to catch her breath. "And then I became so petrified that—" Embarrassed by her bout of pyrophobia, Jessica stopped speaking mid-sentence. She'd always been a bit nervous around fire, but she'd never before experienced a panic so severe that it left her completely debilitated.

"You're safe, Jessica. No harm can come to you," Gideon assured her as he pulled the blanket up to her knees and inspected her lower legs. Both had turned a vivid shade of pink. "Your calves appear to be slightly burned. Do you have any laudanum in the house? It will help to ease the pain."

"I'm afraid they outlawed that decades ago," she said, smiling weakly.

"Then perhaps a tincture of willow tree bark?"

Shaking her head, Jessica said, "There's none of that in the medicine chest either. But I do have some aspirin in the kitchen cupboard where I keep my vitamins."

"I'll be right back," Gideon said before he hurriedly left the room.

"It's in the yellow bottle," she called after him, just in case he didn't know what aspirin was.

Moments later, hearing the clang of metal pans, Jessica wondered what Gideon was up to. She soon had her answer when he returned bearing a large stock pot. In addition to the two towels that were slung over his shoulder, he had a bottle of spring water and the Bayer aspirin tucked under his arm.

"The cold water will hopefully prevent any swelling," Gideon told her as he set the stainless steel pot on the side table.

Jessica glanced into the pot; there were a dozen or so ice cubes bobbing in the water.

Muttering "push and turn" under his breath, Gideon opened the bottle of aspirin. "How many of these should you take?"

"Two ought to do it, I think."

Shaking out two caplets, he handed them to her, along with the spring water. Then, reading from the front of the aspirin bottle, he said, "This is reputed to be a wonder drug."

"Let's hope there's truth in advertising," Jessica said before she popped the aspirin into her mouth and washed them down with a gulp of water.

Setting the bottle of Bayer aside, Gideon stuck his index finger into the pot. "I think this has chilled enough," he said as he squatted beside her chair.

With a true economy of motion, he dunked both towels into the water. After wringing them out, he lifted the tartan blanket to her knees. He then gently wrapped a wet towel around each of her calves. Even though he didn't touch her skin directly, Jessica immediately felt an electric tingle, one that had nothing to do with her burned skin.

"Thank you. That feels much better," she told him. Fixing her gaze on Gideon's bent head, she resisted the urge to run a hand through his hair.

"I apologize for having tossed your frock into the fireplace," Gideon said as he peered up at her.

"There's no need to apologize. It was just an old frock—er, I mean skirt," she amended.

"That doesn't detract from the fact that you looked quite lovely in it." Still looking deeply into her eyes, Gideon gave her the sort of heated glance that made Jessica's heart thump and her stomach flip-flop.

"You appear to have a bit of experience with this sort of injury," she remarked, hoping she didn't sound as nervous as she felt.

"There was more than one man under my command who rolled too close to a nighttime campfire." No sooner was the remark made than one side of Gideon's mouth turned down at the corner. "Although I suspect you'd prefer that I not speak of such things, given that my wartime service is a forbidden topic."

Recognizing Gideon's last remark as the perfect segue, Jessica said, "Actually, I'm glad that you mentioned the war because I've had a change of heart. About the time travel thing," she added a split second later.

"Pray continue. You have my full attention," Gideon said as he seated himself in the wingback chair opposite hers.

"While I need to do more research, I now have reason to believe that time travel might very well be possible."

"Alas, only a mere possibility."

Ignoring Gideon's sardonic rejoinder, Jessica said, "Possible because it has to do with the theory of general relativity and the fact that you somehow got tossed across the space-time continuum."

Hearing that, Gideon raised a quizzical brow.

"Space-time has to do with different dimensions on subatomic and super-galactic levels," she elaborated. "And while I'm still grappling with the *how* of it, the important thing is that time travel is scientifically possible."

"Since I have no recollection whatsoever of the event, I'm unable to verify what precisely occurred," Gideon acknowledged. "Additionally, I am at a loss to understand what the cursed beast Draygan has to do with any of this."

"I'm not sure either," Jessica confessed with a shrug. "However, according to Darlene Malone, Draygan not only exists on a different plane of existence from us, but he has the ability to cross through the veil of time. Which I'm guessing is a quaint expression for the space-time continuum." Because she'd already plunged into uncharted waters, Jessica decided to go ahead and dive into the deep end. "So if Draygan can cross through time, what's to stop him from bringing a human passenger along for the ride?"

Gideon took a moment to digest that before he said, "But why then is the beast bedeviling me?"

It was a good question, one for which Jessica didn't have a ready answer. Earlier in the day, John Henry Burdette had informed her that, as a young boy, he'd been under the influence of Draygan for "nigh on six weeks" before his so-called fits finally abated. Granted, she wasn't keen on Gideon going to Shepherd-stown; however, putting physical distance between him and his nemesis might diminish, if not completely alleviate, his painful symptoms.

"I honestly don't know why Draygan is bedeviling you. Or why he ushered you across the veil of time." Then, hoping to put a happy spin on things, she smiled and said, "But whatever the reason, it's brought the two of us together. So while I could never replace your wife Sarah, I hope that, um…" Finding it difficult to articulate her feelings, Jessica paused a moment to collect her thoughts.

"It is true that you could never replace Sarah."

The rebuff stung. Jessica instantly shifted from high gear to low. Sandbagged, she struggled to get a grip on her emotions. "Gee, did you have to be so agreeably blunt?"

"Forgive me. I've done this badly," Gideon apologized as he reached for her hand.

A noticeable silence ensued as he stared at their entwined fingers.

"Whenever I am with you, I'm reminded of that time before

the war when Highland House was filled with love and laughter," Gideon said at last, raising his gaze to peer directly into her eyes.

"After witnessing so much horror during the war years, it's only natural that you'd want to remember more pleasant times," Jessica said tentatively, uncertain where the conversation was leading.

"It is more than that," Gideon clarified, a pensive frown having worked its way onto his face. "Since traveling forward in time, I've sensed Sarah's presence at Highland House."

The admission took Jessica by complete surprise. "Are you saying that the house is haunted by Sarah's ghost?"

He shook his head, disavowing her of the notion. "What I'm trying to say is that I sense Sarah's presence when I'm with you. Indeed, there are times when I'm unable to differentiate where one woman ends and the other begins."

"Oh my god, tell me I'm not hearing this!" Forcefully yanking her hand free of Gideon's grasp, Jessica covered her ears and closed her eyes, refusing to look at him.

In the next instant, she felt, rather than saw, Gideon move toward her, going down on bent knee beside her chair.

"Please look at me, Jessica," he urged as he pried her hands away from her ears.

Jessica reluctantly opened her eyes. "Well, at least you got my name right."

"Do you think that I don't know who you are?"

"I'm beginning to wonder," she told him as she removed the towels from her lower legs and set them on top of the stock pot.

"Above all else, I know you to be your own unique woman," Gideon said, holding her gaze as he spoke. "And it is that unique woman who has touched my heart so deeply these past ten days."

Certain that he was about to lower the boom—and wanting to get it over with as soon as possible—Jessica said, "But…?"

"But I've had reason to wonder if you and Sarah are not kindred in some way."

"You just want me to be a replacement for Sarah," she said sullenly. His explanation certainly did little to assuage her hurt feelings.

"Nothing could be further from the truth." Gideon emphasized the point by raising her right hand to his lips and placing a soft kiss on her knuckles. "Furthermore, it is the differences, rather than the similarities with Sarah, that I find so compelling."

At a loss for words, her thoughts and emotions in a jumble, Jessica stared at him. *Could there possibly be some sort of kindred connection between me and Sarah MacAllister?* Truth be told, she'd felt the connection in her dreams, the bond so close, she'd been under the delusion that it was her, Jessica, wearing the hoop skirt, riding the horse, and making love to him.

Gideon traced the curve of her cheek with his finger. Even though his touch was sweetly demonstrative, it caused a tingly sensation to course along her spine, a tingly sensation that quickly turned into a full-blown, passionate pulse between her hips.

"Yesterday evening when you kissed me, I wanted you to—" Hit with a sudden burst of timidity, Jessica had to take a deep, fortifying breath. Then, mustering her courage, she said, "I wanted you to make love to me."

The flash of uncensored emotion that Jessica saw reflected in Gideon's blue eyes completely disarmed her. No man had ever looked at her with such passion. Such longing. With perfect clarity, she knew that she and Gideon were meant to be together.

Maybe that's why Draygan brought Gideon across the veil of time.

"When we kissed, I, too, longed for a deeper communion," Gideon told her, his voice tinged with a husky drawl.

Jessica's lips curved in a flirtatious smile. "I believe this is the part where you're supposed to whisk me off to the boudoir."

"I would be only too happy to oblige." Taking hold of her hand, Gideon urged Jessica to her feet…just before he swept her into his arms.

* * *

"My room," Jessica whispered as Gideon carried her up the flight of steps, hoping the more familiar surroundings would alleviate her sudden attack of first-night jitters.

At least I'm wearing a matching bra and panties.

Nudging the bedroom door open with his boot tip, Gideon stepped across the threshold.

Because of the moonlight that streamed through the windows, Jessica could see that her bedroom had a lived-in look, with various articles of clothing strewn over the backs of chairs and door knobs. Not wanting to spoil the mood, she decided not to switch on any lights.

Easing her out of his arms, Gideon set Jessica on her feet. The moment her toes touched the wood floor, he cradled her head between his hands, his mouth capturing hers in a soulful kiss that completely reassured her that they were doing the right thing.

In no time at all, sweet tenderness gave way to a passionate fervor, with Gideon stoking the fire as his tongue boldly slid in and out of her mouth. Up to the challenge, Jessica met each thrust with an equally sensuous parry, and their lips glided in perfect concert with one another.

With a groan of pleasure, Gideon wrapped an arm around her

lower back, pulling her closer to him. In turn, Jessica clutched the front of his tunic. When the incredible kiss finally came to an end, both of them were left panting softly in its wake.

"May I?" Gideon asked, taking hold of the hem of her jewel-neck sweater. When she nodded her consent, he pulled the garment over her head, tossing it onto the nearby chair.

Cupping his hands around her lace-covered breasts, Gideon traced feathery circles around her nipples with his thumbs before he reached behind Jessica and unhooked her bra.

The muscles in Jessica's legs tightened as she felt a sudden, unanticipated spasm between her hips. "I'll give you this: for a man born in the nineteenth century, you're a quick study in the women's lingerie department," she said breathlessly, finding it more and more difficult to pull air into her lungs.

"It's much easier than unlacing a corset," Gideon said as he slowly dragged the bra across her distended nipples before consigning it to the chair.

As he slid his hands down her bare back, the leisurely caress incited a trail of puckering gooseflesh. Smiling, Gideon snagged two fingers under the plaid blanket that was still wrapped around her waist, removing it from Jessica with one quick twist of the wrist before flinging it aside. His smile broadened as he gently held Jessica's arms out to the side, enabling him to fully appraise her nearly naked body.

"This isn't fair. You're wearing way too many clothes," she complained, seized with an urgent desire to see, to taste, to feel his bare skin. Pulling her hands free from his grasp, she shoved Gideon's uniform jacket off his shoulders, carelessly tossing it onto the growing pile of discarded clothing.

"I am overdressed," Gideon agreed as he undid the top four buttons of his shirt. "A situation that I will gladly rectify." Tugging at the garment, he freed the tails from the waistband of his trousers. That done, he reached behind his neck and yanked the shirt over his head in one sure motion.

It was all Jessica could do not to lick her lips. The sight of his broad, well-muscled chest made her go weak in the knees. With her heart pounding like a jackhammer, she plopped down on the edge of the bed, unable to take her eyes off Gideon as he seated himself on the arm of the chair. Bending at the waist, he removed first one boot, then the other, tossing both aside with a dull *plunk*. Her attention was completely focused on him as he stood up and unbuttoned his trousers, shoving them, along with his boxers, off his hips.

Hurrying to play catch up, Jessica wiggled out of her panties. In the beam of pale moonlight that slashed across the room, she could see that Gideon was fully aroused, his penis proudly springing upright from a thatch of tawny curls. As she unabashedly stared at him, her breath caught in her throat.

Now that's what I call a well-hung man. "And if it feels half as good as it looks, this is gonna be an unforgettable night." Too late, Jessica realized that she'd actually given voice to the brazen thought.

Approaching the bed, Gideon came to a standstill directly in front of her. "I shall do everything in my power to accommodate your desires."

"Likewise," she murmured.

Eager to explore Gideon's firmly muscled torso, Jessica extended a hand in his direction. To her astonishment, everything about his naked body, from the crinkly feel of the hair on his chest to the smooth texture of his sculpted pectoral muscles, was so uncannily familiar that it was as if she were rediscovering something that she'd once known all too well, but had long since forgotten. And though the electrical sparks that had been so keenly felt when he first arrived at Highland House more than a week ago had greatly diminished in intensity, Jessica could still feel a tingly sensation in the palm of her hand as she continued to caress his body.

Moving her hand lower, Jessica squeezed a sinewy thigh muscle before fanning her hand to the side of Gideon's hip. Quite intentionally, she bypassed the swollen flesh between his legs, secretly pleased when she observed his erect organ anxiously twitch against his lower belly.

"I suspect you'll be the death of me before this night is finished," Gideon rasped as he placed his hands on her shoulders and gently nudged Jessica against the mattress. "But then, *le petit mort* is the desired outcome, is it not?"

"I wouldn't know," Jessica confessed, sighing contentedly as Gideon settled himself beside her. "Although I'm anxious to find out," she told him, hoping that, for the first time in her life, she'd actually experience the big O.

"Do you mean to say that you've never been with a man?" Gideon propped himself on his forearm as he trailed a finger down the middle of her chest.

"No. It's just that—" The last thing Jessica wanted to think about, let alone discuss, was her and Richard's pathetic sex life. This wasn't the time or place to dwell on such unpleasant memories. "Without going into any detail, let's just say that I've never been able to finish the race."

"Then tonight shall be a first," Gideon assured her, nuzzling the crook of her neck with his lips. Sliding a hand under her back, he lifted her several inches off the mattress, his warm breath caressing a pert nipple before he ever so gently began to suckle her.

"So…so wonderful," Jessica whimpered as she arched her back, enabling her to thrust her breast more fully into his mouth.

Just when she thought she might actually fall into an old-fashioned swoon—it felt that good—Gideon's lips roamed to the other breast. Switching gears, he plucked the nipple between his teeth, the pleasure so intense that it bordered on pain.

Needing, *wanting*, more, Jessica spread her legs, silently imploring Gideon to touch her in that most intimate of places. Seemingly attuned to her every desire, he stroked her damp folds with his fingertips, causing Jessica to gasp aloud from the sheer pleasure of it.

"You're like a camellia in full bloom," Gideon said in a lowered voice.

Sexual inhibitions thrown to the wayside, Jessica writhed against his palm. "Call me a wanton hussy, but I don't think it can get any better than this."

As if to prove her wrong, Gideon brushed the pad of his finger over her clitoris.

Blindsided, Jessica frantically grabbed hold of Gideon's wrist, if for no other reason than to ensure that he didn't stop, that he continued to administer the most exquisite pleasure she'd ever experienced.

Suddenly feeling the insistent nudge of Gideon's penis against her thigh, Jessica intuitively knew that his body was as tightly wound as hers. Snuggling a hand between them, she began to fondle his erection. Gideon groaned his approval, the sound rumbling deep within his chest.

Delighted with his reaction, Jessica rubbed her thumb over the tip of his penis, smearing it with a silken drop of pre-ejaculate.

"Now, Gideon." She rhythmically ground her hips against his muscled thigh. "I need to feel you inside of me."

In the next instant, Gideon rolled on top of her, insinuating himself between her splayed thighs. A welcome invasion.

"I don't want to hurt you," he said, a ragged edge to his voice.

"I told you... I'm not a virgin." Assurance given, Jessica guided him toward her.

A heartbeat later, Gideon entered her with a mighty thrust.

Jessica stifled a yelp. Despite her avowals to the contrary, she suddenly felt like a reborn virgin. Gideon was too thick. Too hard. As he continued to stretch her, she didn't know how much more she could take, worried that—

Just then, her body gave way, allowing him full penetration, and the pain was replaced with a potent, rapturous kind of pleasure.

"Faster," she panted, no longer in the mood for slow and leisurely.

Supporting his upper body on outstretched arms, Gideon immediately complied, furiously pumping his hips. In a sensual haze, Jessica locked her legs around the backs of his thighs as she clutched his shoulders.

"I can't get enough of you," she told him, moaning aloud when he pressed more forcefully, imbedding himself that much deeper. Together their bodies moved in frantic harmony, erotically in sync.

I never thought it could be so good, she thought dazedly, fast losing herself in a passionate tumult, the likes of which she'd only read about in romance novels. Bucking and writhing in wild abandon, Jessica clawed her fingers into Gideon's buttocks, straining for an even closer contact. She was so close. All she needed was—

Hit with an intense, climactic burst, Jessica held on as long as possible to that ecstatic detonation, sobbing with joy when she was hit again. And then, again.

A moment later, Gideon groaned as his big body powerfully shuddered against her.

Still trying to catch her breath, Jessica smoothed her hands across his back, surprised to feel Gideon tremble in her arms as he nestled his head in the crook of her shoulder. Lovingly, she stroked the back of his head, threading her fingers through the damp mass of thick, sandy-colored hair.

When Gideon finally pulled out of her and rolled onto his back, Jessica experienced a momentary flash of disappointment. She could easily have stayed with him, joined at the hips, forever.

* * *

Feeling as though his heart had been lanced with a red-hot poker, Richard Bragg staggered down the hillside toward the lone car silhouetted in the pale moonlight.

After he'd caught sight of the same man who'd earlier arrived on horseback carrying his wife up a staircase, presumably to a second-story bedroom, Richard had waited for what seemed an interminable length of time for the bastard to emerge from the house and tend to the horse that was still tethered to a fence railing. When that didn't happen, he came to a hideous realization: the stranger was fucking his wife and wouldn't be leaving the house anytime soon.

"How could Jessica betray me like this?" he hissed. "She took a vow before Almighty God to always be my faithful spouse."

Obviously, the sacred vow had no meaning for his harlot of a wife. Jessica was willing to spread her legs for any man. It was the reason why he'd always kept close tabs on her—he knew women were promiscuous by nature. No better than cats in heat, they were ruled, not by their hearts, but by an animalistic urge to mate.

God, how I hate her, he inwardly seethed, staggered by the depth of his wife's infidelity.

No sooner had he reached the parked Lexus than Richard felt his Smartphone softly vibrate. Shoving a hand into the pocket of his jacket, he snatched hold of the device and read the text message—"Last minute cancellation on Sunday talk show. Are you available?"

Normally, he'd be thrilled at the chance to appear on a political roundtable, even as a last-minute guest. But there was nothing normal about this night. Hands down, it'd turned into the most horrific, sickening episode of his entire life. Even more terrible than the night he'd come home to an empty house and discovered that his wife had deserted him.

Though he was in no mood to make the drive back to D.C., Richard nonetheless got behind the wheel of the luxury sedan and jammed the key in the ignition.

Before driving away, he craned his neck and took one last look at the old brick house at the top of the hill. Unbeknownst to Jessica, he wasn't about to let another man take what was rightfully his.

"You're mine, Jessica. To do with as I please."

And nothing would please him more than to mete out the only punishment suitable for an unfaithful woman: a blazing fire.

Chapter 20

As she stood trapped in the raging inferno, burning embers fell upon Sarah's head like fiery raindrops and the crackling flames voraciously consumed everything in sight. When another ceiling beam suddenly crashed to the barn floor, it instantly ignited several stacked bundles of hay.

Terrified, she saw that the hem of her skirt was aflame. Oblivious to the pain, she frantically swatted at the burning fabric with her hand.

Realizing that she'd lost the battle, that the fire was raging out of control, she screamed . . . a lost soul cast into a fiery hell.

"Come back to me, Gideon! Come back to me!"

Forcing herself to return to the waking world, Jessica's eyes popped wide open as she roused herself from the clutches of a hideous nightmare. The dream about Sarah was undoubtedly the result of her own skirt having earlier caught fire, her subconscious mind having fused its current nineteenth-century obsession with a traumatic event from the here and now.

Taking care not to awaken Gideon, she reached for the quilt

that had been kicked off the bed. After pulling it over the two of them, she snuggled against Gideon's warm body.

As she shifted her weight, Jessica felt an achy tenderness between her legs. Reflecting on the reason for the slight discomfort, her lips curved in a smile. Finally, she understood how all the different pieces—male/female, soft/hard, love/sex—fit together.

Not only had she discovered the true meaning of the word "passion," but she'd learned that intimacy didn't have anything to do with fear or degradation. Grounded in trust, true intimacy between a man and a woman was one of the most uplifting forces in nature. Even now, several hours after the fact, merely thinking about her and Gideon's lovemaking was empowering, making her feel upbeat and sexy.

Before Gideon had mysteriously appeared at Highland House, there'd been a lonely void in her life, one which no amount of self-discovery could fill. That loneliness was now gone, making Jessica wonder if their two aching hearts had somehow reached across the boundary of time to find one another. A lovely sentiment, but it also made her fearfully worry that Draygan might capriciously snatch Gideon from her and return him to the nineteenth century.

As Jessica stared at the heavy, early-morning fog that was buttressed against the window pane, it suddenly occurred to her that the horror of the Civil War was a recent memory for Gideon. It was to him, after all, only ten days ago that he'd fought in the Battle of Lewis Creek.

At the thought of all the brutality that Gideon had been forced to suffer during the war, tears pooled in Jessica's eyes. Unwillingly, she envisioned some of the horrific battlefield tableaus that had been captured on daguerreotype by nineteenth century photographers. Gruesome images of unspeakable carnage, they caused a well of latent emotions to spring forth from some hidden reservoir deep within her.

Beside her, Gideon stirred to wakefulness. "Jessica, whatever is the matter?"

"I'm so sorry that I didn't believe you sooner...about the time traveling," she said, her voice thick with emotion. "I didn't realize until now just how much you've suffered." Embarrassed by her wayward emotions, Jessica burrowed her head in the pillow.

Gideon pulled her toward him, wrapping her in his arms. "There's no need for tears."

"Yes, there is," she said on a noisy sob. "There must be people—family and friends—that you left behind. Back in the past, that is."

"They have all since gone to the grave," Gideon said quietly as he blotted her tears with the bed sheet. "I have no one."

"That's not true," she told him. "You have me."

Long seconds passed as Gideon silently stared at her. Jessica worried that she may have pushed the intimacy envelope too far, too fast.

"I would think that after tonight we have each other," Gideon said at last, a tender smile on his lips. "And because of that, I am disinclined to continue our present relationship without the sanctity of nuptial bonds."

Jessica's jaw slackened. "Are you...are you asking me to...to *marry* you?" she sputtered, not quite believing what she'd just heard.

Confirming with a nod, Gideon said, "While our acquaintanceship is admittedly of short duration, given what earlier transpired between us, I believe that marrying you is the honorable thing to do."

Jessica immediately pulled away from Gideon, his proposal

rubbing her the wrong way. "From which, I deduce, our lovemaking was less than honorable." Rolling toward the nightstand, she switched on the lamp, illuminating the room with a soft, golden light.

Gideon raised a quizzical brow. "Your sarcasm is most unexpected. Only an unprincipled rogue would continue to share your bed without the benefit of matrimony." Shifting into a seated position, he leaned his back against the four-poster's wooden headboard. After tucking the quilt around his lap, he then said, "In my day and age, unabated lovemaking was not without consequence. I take it things have not changed that much in the intervening years."

"Now who's being sarcastic?"

"If I get you with child—"

"I can't have children," Jessica interjected, cutting him off at the pass.

Her announcement was met with a palpable silence.

"Do you mean to say that you're barren?" Gideon finally asked in a measured tone of voice.

Jessica dejectedly nodded her head. "Yeah, barren. That's exactly what I meant to say," she muttered, loathing that particular word with a passion. Not only did the word "barren" rankle, it reminded her of the humiliation she'd suffered at Richard's hands because she'd been unable to conceive. At the time, it'd made her feel like an utter failure as a woman.

"Although there is a silver lining," she said a few seconds later, putting on her best game face. "It means that we can have all of the risk-free sex that we want."

"Nothing in this world is wholly without risk," Gideon countered. "If we continue to have intimate relations, we should do so within the banns of marriage."

"Seeing as how I can't have children, I'm surprised you'd still want to marry me," she said, inwardly despising the weak-kneed insecurity that underscored her reply.

Cocking his head to one side, Gideon peered at her as though she'd just uttered something nonsensical. "I cannot change God's will. Just as I cannot change my feelings for you."

"Your feelings?" Admittedly stymied, Jessica said, "I thought this impromptu proposal had to do with your antiquated sense of honor. By bringing your feelings into the mix, you've just changed the whole equation."

Gideon put his arm around her shoulders and pulled her close to him. "I had not thought to ask for your hand in so ungallant a fashion," he said as he pressed his lips to her forehead.

Jessica pulled back slightly, enabling her to look him in the eye. "Do you mean to say that you've actually given this some thought?"

"I have thought of little else since I went to visit— Since yesterday."

Hearing that, Jessica inwardly groaned; the situation was becoming more complicated with each passing second. "Don't take this the wrong way, but I don't think we should get married," she informed him point-blank. Then, realizing how heart-wrenchingly final that sounded, she hastily added, "At least not right now."

"I see."

"No, you don't," she retorted. "For your information, you're the best thing to ever come my way. But I'm not ready to give up my independence just yet." Jessica paused a moment to collect her thoughts, wishing that she'd had some time to rehearse her answer. "I've worked too hard to get to this place in my life. And, yes, I know to most people it doesn't look like much of a life, but it's one of my own choosing. Before, when I was—" Jessica clamped her lips together, have nearly uttered the ill-fated words, "*Before, when I was married to Richard.*"

Because of the sensitive nature of the situation, this wasn't the appropriate time to mention her previous marriage. Particularly since her divorce hadn't yet been finalized. Also, given Gideon's prudish, Victorian objection to divorce, she wanted to wait until they were further along in their relationship, when things were more emotionally congealed, before she made a full disclosure.

Somewhat hesitantly, she met Gideon's gaze, well aware that she'd done more than simply wound his manly pride. She'd hurt his feelings in the bargain.

"While I'm deeply honored that you want to make an honest woman of me," she continued, tacking in a different direction, "the fact of the matter is that we've only known each other a scant ten days."

"I feel as though I've known you much longer than that," Gideon said.

"I know what you mean," she readily agreed. "But no matter how you cut it, ten days is too short a period to be talking about something as life-altering as marriage. Besides, these days most men and women live together before they walk down the aisle. Think of it as a trial run," she said, striving for an upbeat tone.

"Am I to understand then that you're not entirely opposed to marriage?"

"I'm not opposed in the least." As she spoke, Jessica lovingly brushed a lock of tawny hair off of Gideon's brow. "I just need more time."

"Four weeks from now, when I return from Shepherdstown, may we revisit the matter?"

Touched by his earnestness, Jessica smiled and said, "Of course we can."

Relieved that they'd gotten past what could have been an insurmountable hurdle, Jessica leaned over and turned off the lamp.

Snuggling close to Gideon, her thoughts turned decidedly wanton as she admired his naked torso. With his broad shoulders, contoured pecs with small brown paps, and, her favorite bit, the washboard abs, he was the most gorgeous man she'd ever set her gaze upon. And though the impressive physique was a testament to the fact that Gideon was physically strong, Jessica knew that he could also be, oh, so tender. A potent combination.

As she took note of the battle scar near his underarm, she leaned toward him, placing a soft kiss on the welt of raised flesh.

* * *

Gideon's entire body jolted, startled to suddenly feel Jessica's warm mouth moving across his chest. Astonishment, however, quickly gave way to a burgeoning desire as her tongue painted a moist pattern onto his battle scar.

Utterly bewitched, he threaded his fingers through Jessica's auburn tresses, his gaze drawn to her pale breasts that impudently jutted out between the silken strands. Bathed in the light of early dawn, they resembled a pair of ripe pears. Hungrily he reached for one, surprised when Jessica swatted his hand.

"I won't be able to concentrate if you do that," she said. "And to ensure that you don't do it again, I want you to lie flat on the mattress."

Gideon smiled broadly. Unless he missed the mark, his lady

love intended to play bawdy with him. Eager to comply, he winked slyly and said, "Your wish is my command."

Anxious to see where the enticing game would lead, he watched as Jessica knelt beside him. As she did so, her breasts dangled near his face, a puckered nipple seductively abutting his mouth. But no sooner did his lips close around the tender morsel than she pulled away from him. Undeterred, he craned his neck, hoping to recapture the delectable prize. Jessica made a *tsk*ing sound, reproving him with a shake of the head. Then, smiling playfully, she shoved the bedding to his lower abdomen.

At seeing the prominent bulge that was clearly outlined beneath the colorful quilt, her eyes opened wide, a look of astonishment on her face. "My, goodness. Whatever could it mean?"

Gideon pulled the quilt away from his groin, desperately needing to fill Jessica's hands with the heavy swell of his erection. "A little exposure might clarify the matter," he said as he molded her fingers around his shaft, only to suffer a frustrated pang when the spirited vixen pulled away from him.

"We do it my way or not at all," she said petulantly, punctuating the threat with a stubborn thrust of the chin.

Muttering under his breath, Gideon closed his eyes as he took several deep, stabilizing breaths. *Why is she torturing me like this?* Why incite a raging inferno, if she had no intention of dousing the flame? It was obvious to him that Jessica needed to be tutored in the ways of a man's body. Because, clearly, she didn't understand that a man could only endure so much physical stimulation before he lost control. Which he was very near to doing, lust and love converging on Gideon in equal measure.

And he did love Jessica Reardon, greatly admiring her beauty, her compassion, and her indomitable will. And, yes, he even loved the fierce independence that set her apart from any other woman he'd ever known. Although it went without saying that her rejection of his marriage proposal had been maddening. What they were doing, here, right now, should be sanctioned by—

"God Almighty," Gideon groaned as his hips jerked off the mattress. Through half-closed eyes, he stared in utter disbelief as Jessica's tongue flirtatiously laved at his fully engorged organ. Never had a woman pleasured him in so intimate a fashion.

Barely able to pull air into his lungs, Gideon couldn't have imagined a more erotic vision than Jessica bent over him, her silky mane blanketing his hips, her breasts cushioning his thighs as she took him deep into her mouth.

But even as he watched the highly arousing sight, he knew that his pleasure would be more keenly felt if she would partake in the ecstasy with him, as shared bliss was always more gratifying.

As if attuned to his every desire, Jessica suddenly ceased her love play. Gracefully swinging a leg over his prone body, she sat astride his hips. Encircling her waist with his hands, Gideon hoisted her upward, the tip of his manhood poised at the entrance of her moist slit.

Splaying her hands on his chest, Jessica lowered herself upon him. "Time to put you through your paces."

"Have mercy on me," he rasped as he watched his swollen rod disappear into her wet and welcoming body. Already dangerously close to climax, he grasped hold of Jessica's buttocks, enabling him to guide her along his entire length.

During the long moments that followed, the friction between their two bodies was a pleasure beyond compare. Mesmerized, Gideon watched as Jessica suddenly threw back her head. Breasts proudly thrust forward, back provocatively arched, she began to shudder. The sight of her caught in the throes of orgasm caused the seed to gush from his body in a powerful burst.

In pleasure's aftermath, neither spoke. In those dizzying moments, words were entirely unnecessary. They'd each freely given to the other, their bodies having eloquently and passionately spoken for them. And though they'd only known each other a total of ten days, their coupling had exhibited none of the awkward fumbling of a new union. It was as if they'd danced this particular waltz many times before.

When Jessica suddenly slumped against him, Gideon belatedly realized that she'd fallen into an exhausted slumber.

" 'To sleep, perchance to dream,'" he whispered as he wrapped his lady love in his arms and clasped her to his chest.

Chapter 21

Good God," Gideon bellowed, clearly appalled. "What is that woman doing?"

Seated next to him on the library sofa, Jessica glanced at the writhing bodies on the music video. "She's twerking. It's a type of, um, dance movement."

"Dancing, you say? With the exception of a few bits of clothing, it puts me in mind of—"

"How about we watch a cable news channel?" Hoping that would prove more tame fare, she flipped through a dozen or so cable stations, finally landing on a political roundtable.

Because she'd recently used some of the proceeds from the sale of Gideon's gold coins to purchase a 46-inch TV, the two of them had been able to spend the last several hours vegging out, his-and-her couch potatoes.

Since Gideon was leaving tomorrow morning for Shepherdstown, Jessica had spent a good part of the day tutoring him on pop culture. The Kardashians, hashtags, zombies, SpongeBob, and breast implants gave him some trouble, but, all things considered, he'd aced the crash course.

Reaching for the remote control, she muted the sound on the TV. As she did, Gideon turned his head and peered at her, a questioning look on his face.

His attention garnered, Jessica smiled hesitantly, about to broach a subject that had been weighing heavily on her mind. "Do you ever think about…about returning to the past?"

Smiling warmly, Gideon caressed her cheek with the backs of his fingers. "Even if I could find a way to return, I would choose to remain here. You, Jessica, are my future."

Deeply touched by his response, Jessica impulsively took hold of his right hand and placed it on her left breast. Right above her heart. "Can you feel what you do to me?"

In like manner, Gideon reached for her free hand, placing her palm squarely on his chest. "It is no more than what you do to me."

Thus posed, each could feel the drumbeat of the other's heart.

Enthralled, Jessica noticed how the lamplight burnished Gideon's hair and highlighted the specks of gold in his blue eyes. This was how she'd always envisioned the archangels, as fiercely beautiful as Gideon MacAllister.

Snuggling against his shoulder, Jessica aimed the remote at the TV screen, switching the sound back on. "It looks like a political discussion," she said, recognizing the speaker as a prominent member of the ACLU.

As the television camera panned to the other guests on the panel, which included "Conservative Blogger Richard Bragg," the remote slipped through Jessica's fingers.

"Oh, God," she groaned, feeling like she'd just been ambushed in a dark alley. "It's Richard."

His attention focused on the TV, Gideon spared her a quick sideways glance. "I take it that you know this man?"

"Er, I know of him," Jessica hedged, affecting a disinterested shrug.

Attired in one of his Brooks Brothers suits, his strawberry-blond hair immaculately groomed, Richard appeared exactly as he had on the day she'd walked out on him. Unless she was greatly mistaken, he was even wearing the same tie.

When, a few seconds later, the program broke away for a commercial, Jessica breathed a sigh of relief. "How about we change the channel?" she suggested. "They're showing *Gone with the Wind* on TCM. I bet you'd get a big kick out of that."

"If you don't mind, I would like to continue watching the debate," Gideon said politely. "I have always had a keen interest in politics."

Too guilt-ridden to look at the TV screen, Jessica reached for a magazine, feigning a sudden interest in kitchen and bath design as she debated her next move. Despite being unplanned, the opportunity had just presented itself to tell Gideon about her marriage to Richard Bragg.

But if I do, he might suddenly decide that he isn't so keen to stay with me in the twenty-first century after all.

For the first time in her life, she was genuinely happy. She enjoyed her work. She took pleasure in her dilapidated home. And she loved Gideon MacAllister. But for all his admirable qualities and sexy as sin physical attributes, he was still very much a man of yesteryear. To such a man, the dissolution of a marriage brought dishonor to all involved.

In truth, that wasn't too far off the mark; she had felt defiled by her marriage. What's more, deeply ashamed that she'd ever wed Richard in the first place, she'd kept mum about the divorce, having mentioned it to no one. If she came clean, she'd then have to own up to the fact that, for seven years, she'd completely sublimated who she was as a person, having sacrificed her friends, her interests, and even her dreams.

Shivering slightly, she set the magazine aside and wrapped her arms around her torso.

"You're chilled." Getting up from the sofa, Gideon walked over to the hearth. "I'll build a fire."

"Please don't," she said, her voice catching on a ragged breath.

Hunkered in front of the fireplace, Gideon dropped a log onto the grate, apparently not hearing her request.

Jessica clicked off the TV. "Gideon, I'm begging you, please don't build a fire," she pleaded, this time in a louder tone of voice.

Still squatting, Gideon pivoted on his heel, a baffled expression on his face. "Is something the matter?" he asked as he rose to his feet. "You appear vexed."

No doubt she did. The previous night she'd had at least three nightmares, all involving her, or rather Sarah MacAllister, being trapped in a burning barn.

Unable to mentally erase those terrifying images from her mind's eye, Jessica said, "I need to know how Sarah died."

Gideon's broad shoulders immediately stiffened. "As I am wholly responsible for Sarah's death, it would pain me to speak of the matter," he said brusquely.

Taken aback, Jessica shook her head. "How can you possibly be responsible?"

"My wife was killed in a fire," Gideon told her, grim-faced. "But the truth of the matter is that she died on account of my unforgivable arrogance. And because of my soldier's honor," he added with a brittle, humorless smile. "There. Are you satisfied?"

Not by a long shot. Particularly since she'd seen the raging inferno in last night's dreams, still able to hear Sarah frantically scream Gideon's name. "If you were away fighting in the war, why would you blame yourself for Sarah's death?"

The muscles in Gideon's jaw visibly tightened. "If you must know, I was here at Highland House, home on furlough, the day that Sarah died."

Hearing that, blood instantly rushed to Jessica's head, furiously pounding in her temples. "If you were at Highland House, why in God's name didn't you save Sarah?" she demanded to know. When Gideon gave no immediate answer, Jessica lurched off of the sofa. Rushing over to where he still stood at the fireplace, she grabbed hold of his shirt with her balled fists. "Answer me, damn it!"

Gideon stood motionless, his eyes glazed with unshed tears. "I couldn't save Sarah on account of the fact that I wasn't home when the fire started. I was supposed to be here, but...I had left the house earlier in a rage. And because of my cursed pride, I lost my beloved wife."

No sooner had Gideon finished speaking than he reached up and clutched his head between his hands.

"Gideon, are you all right?" Worried when he didn't reply, Jessica wrapped a hand around each of his wrists. Feeling his arms forcefully quiver, her concern instantly spiked. "Please tell me what's the matter."

"Evil will descend upon the land of the Greenbrier," Gideon hissed between clenched teeth. "The red man cometh. Those in high places will perish in the flames of hell. So sayeth the Beast."

He's channeling Draygan, she realized with no small measure of fear, wanting nothing more than to hurl the damned creature into whatever black cave it had slithered out of.

"Let me help you," she offered, bracketing his head with her hands.

Gideon pulled free of her grasp. "Leave me be." With a muttered oath, he stormed out of the library. A few seconds later, Jessica heard the front door slam shut.

"I just wanted to help you," she murmured, heartsick that Gideon had spurned her.

In hindsight, she had no one but herself to blame. She had, after all, needled him into talking about Sarah's death. She also suspected that Gideon's tormented memories were the reason he had no desire to return to the nineteenth century, not that things were peachy keen in the here and now. They were going to get even worse if she didn't come clean soon about her divorce from Richard.

Dispirited, Jessica wandered over to her desk and plopped down in the chair. Quickly booting up the laptop, she opened her e-mail account and typed a missive to her attorney, inquiring as to when the divorce would be finalized. That done, she glumly stared at her desktop. Needing to do a final edit on her Draygan article, she plucked a red pen out of the flower pot that doubled as a pencil holder.

Long minutes passed as she absently stared at the printed pages, unable to summon the will to read through the article. Hoping to jump-start her creative juices, she began to doodle on a sheet of clean paper.

When did my life get so confusing?

The dreams about Sarah and Gideon's courtship, the nightmare about the fire, all seemed so vaguely familiar. As if Sarah MacAllister's life was right there on the tip of her memory. A wild flight of fancy that—

"Oh, God."

The pen dropped from Jessica's fingers, rolling several inches across the wooden desktop.

Stunned at what she'd unconsciously scribbled, Jessica stared at the sheet of paper. Not only had she written the name "Sarah MacAllister" in elegant penmanship, resplendent with the curlicues and squiggly flourishes that were typical of the nineteenth century, but the signature bore absolutely no resemblance to her own handwriting.

Jessica slumped over her desk, resting her head on her folded arms. Why was this happening to her? Why was she obsessing over a woman who'd died a century and a half ago?

"I've gotta buck up and put Sarah MacAllister behind me," she muttered as she pushed herself upright. Purposefully folding the sheet of paper in half, she deposited it in the recycling box that she kept next to her desk.

Damn you, Draygan.

* * *

"Have you come to bid me farewell?"

To Gideon's dismay, his question was met with an indecipherable grumble.

Shuffling past him, Jessica reached for the coffee pot. Not wishing to incite her ire, he opened a kitchen cupboard and retrieved a coffee mug. Wordlessly, he handed it to her. They'd yet to reconcile, and it weighed heavy on his mind. Particularly since his departure was imminent.

"Actually, I thought you'd already left for Shepherdstown," Jessica said after imbibing several swallows of freshly brewed coffee. "I heard the front door open and close."

"I walked down the hill to retrieve the morning post." He

motioned to the pile of mail on the kitchen table. "Although J.W. should be here shortly to pick me up."

A ponderous silence ensued. Jessica was clearly not interested in making small talk.

Yesterday, several hours after their verbal clash, he'd made an attempt to bridge the divide. But when Jessica once again asked about his wife's tragic accident, wanting to know the reason why he'd left Highland House in a rage on the day that Sarah died, he'd instantly regretted having made the overture. His refusal to speak of the matter had unfortunately triggered yet another dispute. Which had then resulted in their retiring to separate bed chambers.

"Did you sleep well?" he asked, worried about Jessica's noticeably wan appearance.

"I suffered from a recurring nightmare. But I'm fine now." As she raised the coffee mug to her lips, her hand visibly trembled, belying the disclaimer.

"I hope that you can find it in your heart to forgive me for being such a bull-headed lout," Gideon said, the apology long overdue. "While I don't understand your fascination with the past, that is no excuse for my—"

"I forgive you."

Those three words, softly spoken, came as a great relief. Having missed his lady love, Gideon made haste to pull Jessica into his embrace. When she reciprocated, wrapping her arms around his waist, he smiled gratefully.

"You have a way of bringing out the best, and the worst, in me," he confessed, cognizant of the fact that only one other woman had ever had that effect on him.

"That goes double for me." Jessica chuckled, the sound muffled against his shirtfront. "Maybe even triple."

Gideon's smile widened. As always, he wondered how this intrepid woman could remind him of Sarah—not that Sarah couldn't be bold; she could be, particularly when pushed.

God knows I pushed her that last day. If it was in his power, Gideon would retract every hurtful, acrimonious word that he'd spoken to his wife during that last tragic interlude. But more importantly, he'd give anything, even his life, if he could somehow relive that one day and snatch Sarah from the arms of death. But he couldn't, and so absolution would forever remain an unattainable dream.

"Let us speak no more of this," he murmured in Jessica's ear. "It only mars our happiness to dredge up the past. Instead, let us focus on the future. Our future."

No sooner were the words spoken than Jessica wiggled free from his embrace. Wide-eyed, she stared at him. As though he'd just made an outlandish request.

"You want me to shove Sarah's death into cold storage. But I can't," she informed him. "Not until I know everything that happened on the day that Sarah died."

Bewildered by her morbid curiosity, Gideon stood his ground. "I will not speak of that atrocity." Then, suspecting that nothing less than a full-blown ultimatum would deter her, he said, "And you will never again broach the subject. Am I making myself clear?"

"But I—"

"Never again."

Even to his own ears the finality of those two words struck a harsh note. To temper the command, Gideon reached for Jessica's hand. The moment he did, a horn blared just outside the kitchen window.

"J.W.'s here," Jessica said, her fingers slipping from his grasp as she stepped away from him. "Time to hit the road."

Sadly aware that a true reconciliation had just eluded them, Gideon reached for his jacket. "I will call you this evening on my new Smartphone device," he said as he placed a hand on Jessica's shoulder. Inclining his head, he kissed her on the cheek. "Try to get some rest."

She graced him with a forlorn smile. "I'll give it my best shot."

Chapter 22

*I*nundated with fear, Sarah shrieked loudly as she watched the nearby hay bales combust, orange flames shooting in every direction. Peering above her, she saw that the loft was now completely consumed. Soon the entire barn would become a raging furnace. The sight of that fast-moving inferno caused her heart to slam against her breastbone, her entire body shaking as though palsied. She was looking death in the face, and it incited a frenzied panic. And though there was no one to hear her pitiful cry for help, she cried nonetheless.

Just then, she heard a loud, crackling hiss. It was the only warning she had before the entire hayloft suddenly collapsed, fiery beams crashing to the ground. Within moments, a furious rumble shook the barn as several roof timbers plunged from the ceiling in a roaring blaze of fire, igniting everything they came into contact with. As her lungs filled with smoke, she began to gasp for air, her chest violently heaving with each wracking cough.

Terror-stricken, Sarah knew she had to move away from the scorching flames that steadily encroached upon her. Gritting her teeth, she tried to scoot toward the barn door. But the moment she *moved, she was hit with a burst of excruciating pain that radiated the length of her lower leg. In agony, the pain more than she could bear, she opened her mouth and screamed.*

"Gideon!"

Like some wild, feral animal, Jessica desperately tried to claw her way back to wakefulness. Although it took several seconds, she finally crash-landed in the conscious realm, relieved to feel wet drops of cool water splashed against her face. That is, until she glanced up at the ceiling.

At seeing the brownish stain above beaded with water, Jessica pounded her fist against the mattress in sheer frustration, realizing that the water was leaking from the ceiling onto the bed.

Having awakened from one nightmare only to enter another, she stared at a piece of damaged plaster that precariously dangled above her head. "Like I have the money for a new roof," she muttered. While she'd managed to tuck away some of the proceeds from the sale of Gideon's gold coins, it wasn't nearly enough money to have an entire roof replaced.

As she considered her options, another drop of water fell from the ceiling, singling her out. With a muttered oath, she rolled over to the dry side of the bed, trying her utmost to ignore the steady *plop plop* of water.

Having suffered through another night filled with tormented dreams, Jessica slung an arm over her eyes, utterly exhausted. Over the nearly four weeks since Gideon had left for Shepherdstown, she'd been hounded nightly by the same recurring nightmare. And though she knew it was Sarah MacAllister who was trapped in the burning barn, it was Jessica who felt those scorching flames, who choked on the smoke-filled air, who heard the crashing roar of falling beams and timbers as the fire raged all around her.

It was Jessica who always awoke terrified, a silent scream lodged in her throat, her body quaking with fear.

Because of the recurring nightmare, she'd been averaging only 4-5 hours of real sleep per night. Desperate to get a good night's rest, she'd tried any number of natural sleep aids—chamomile tea, melatonin, and the time-honored glass of warm milk—all of which conked her out. Invariably, however, her sleep was interrupted by the hideous dream.

Unable to ignore the dripping ceiling, Jessica threw back the sheet and got out of bed, grimacing when she caught sight of her soggy pillow. Suffering a sudden surge of nausea, she opened her nightstand drawer and reached for the bottle of Tums. Lately her stomach hadn't been agreeing with her—the weeks of sleep deprivation were taking a toll on her body. After popping two peppermint-flavored tablets, she quickly pulled on an old sweater and a pair of yoga pants.

As she reached for her hairbrush, Jessica glanced at the bureau mirror, instantly wishing she hadn't. The dark circles that rimmed her eyes and the gaunt cast to her features gave her a haggard appearance. Not only did she feel sleep-ravaged, she looked it as well.

Just as she was about to fetch a plastic bucket to collect the dripping water, her cell phone rang. Removing the phone from its charger, Jessica glanced at the display.

"Another blocked call," she grumbled, refusing to answer it.

Ever since her first Draygan piece had run in *The Greenbrier Dispatch*, she'd been the recipient of a slew of hang-up calls. Even though the article made no claim as to whether or not the mysterious creature actually existed, numerous readers had sent their personal testimonials to the newspaper office via snail mail and e-mail. That first story had also attracted its fair share of criticism, and several outraged readers had vented their disbelief by writing some very harsh words. Unfortunately, a few of those readers had crossed the line with nasty, anonymous phone calls.

Her editor, Hoyt Jamison, was delighted with the response—"irate readers sell newspapers"—and he had assigned Jessica a weekly column he'd dubbed *The Draygan Chronicles*. While she still wasn't completely convinced the beast was real, she did believe that something otherworldly, something that had to do with that murky realm of the sixth sense, was occurring throughout the county. Those people who were familiar with the old legend, and who did believe in Draygan's existence, were bracing themselves for a catastrophic "Reckoning"—something along the lines of a flood, an earthquake, or a tornado—that could bring death and destruction to the good folks of the Greenbrier Valley.

In no mood to deal with a home maintenance emergency, Jessica swung open the door that led to the attic. When she'd first bought Highland House, she'd made only one ill-fated attempt to explore the upper regions of the house. That exploration had lasted all of thirty seconds, since after hearing what sounded like an army of rodents scampering in the eaves, she'd hightailed it to safer environs on the double-quick. Hopefully, the attic vermin had gone south for the winter.

With bucket in hand, Jessica ascended the rickety flight of steps. She hacked loudly as her lungs filling with a toxic combination of dust and mold. Reaching the top of the stairs, she flipped on the flashlight that she'd brought with her, then directed its beam across the accumulated junk that had been stored in the attic—out of sight, out of mind—a veritable menagerie of lamps, chests of drawers, ancient fans, metal bed frames, and old hat boxes.

Trying her best to ignore the scratchy pitter-patter of unseen animals scurrying for safe cover, Jessica headed for the area of the attic that was directly above her bedroom. There she discovered a puddle of water on the rough-planked flooring.

Dismayed by the sight, she aimed the flashlight toward the heavy support beams directly overhead, able to see that the dark-stained wood was beaded with droplets. Since it appeared to be the only place where rainwater was coming into the attic, it meant that she could possibly have just that one section of the roof repaired. That would be a slapdash Band-Aid until she had enough money to replace the entire roof. For now, the bucket, placed to catch the raindrops, would have to do

As she turned to leave, Jessica's eye fell upon a large, old-fashioned trunk that was wedged into one nearby eave. Curious, she shined the flashlight across it, able to discern the initials "G.M." engraved on a tarnished metal plate affixed to the top of the trunk.

Gideon MacAllister!

Stuffing the flashlight under her arm, Jessica grabbed hold of the trunk by one of its ancient leather straps and hauled it down the staircase to the second floor. From there, she dragged it to the first floor. Then she immediately took it to the library.

Keen to explore the contents of the trunk, she plopped into her office chair, throwing aside her reservations about opening something that didn't belong to her. The trunk had, after all, come with the house, she told herself. Ergo, she owned it along with all the other junk that was stored in the attic.

With building excitement, Jessica undid the antique latches and threw open the lid. Wrinkling her nose at the not-so-pleasant scent of mildew, she could see at a glance that the trunk contained half a dozen ornately designed cases, an assortment of leather-bound books, numerous envelopes, and sundry documents, all of which appeared to be from the mid-nineteenth century.

The butterflies in her stomach were beating fast and furious as she grabbed several of the cases. Unlatching the first one, which measured approximately five by six inches, she was delighted to discover that it contained a gray-toned image of Highland House, inscribed "1859."

"It's lovely," she murmured, marveling at what a beautiful, stately home Highland House had once been.

After setting the first case aside, she opened the next one, stunned to realize that she was peering at a daguerreotype of Gideon in full-dress uniform. Because he'd been clean-shaven in all of her dreams, she was surprised to see him with a swooping mustache. Furthermore, the beautifully tailored tunic was a far cry from the ragtag uniform that he'd worn when he arrived at her house one dark, rainy night.

"I think I like you better without the mustache," she said after a moment's consideration.

As Jessica glanced at the third case, which was far more elaborate in design than the first two, her hands began to tremble. Taking a deep breath, she unlatched the small metal eye-hook that held the two hinged halves together and slowly opened the case. On the left side was a crimson velvet insert; on the right side, housed beneath a brass frame with an ornately patterned design, was a portrait of Gideon and Sarah. As was customary for the period, he was seated in a chair with Sarah standing beside him, one hand resting upon his shoulder. Also, as was typical of nineteenth-century portraiture, both of them stared directly at the camera, unsmiling.

Gasping softly, Jessica couldn't pull her gaze from the image of the woman who'd been haunting her dreams. Sarah MacAllister's heart-shaped face had been captured for posterity on the framed copper plate. Dressed in a light-colored gown, with all the frills and flounces of the period's fashion, Sarah's solemn, sad-eyed visage seemed at odds with her almost frivolous attire.

Carefully returning the framed pictures to the trunk, Jessica next reached for a pile of old documents. As she set them on her desk, one piece of paper fluttered to the floor. She immediately bent over to retrieve it, handling the aged document with great care.

"I don't believe it…it's Gideon and Sarah's marriage certificate."

As she stared at the signatures affixed to the yellowed document, Jessica suddenly gasped, shocked to the core.

I've seen that signature before. Unwillingly, her eyes darted to the recycling bin beside her desk.

Pushing her chair back, Jessica reached for the bin and turned it upside down, emptying its contents onto the floor. One by one, she methodically examined each item, searching for the particular piece of paper she'd tossed into the bin nearly four weeks ago.

Midway through the collection of article drafts, grocery lists, junk mail, and other bits and pieces of her life that she was willing to recycle, she found what she was searching for: the sheet on which she'd scrawled "Sarah MacAllister."

Taking hold of the marriage certificate in her left hand and the piece of scrap paper in her right, Jessica compared the two signatures.

"No…it can't be."

To her utter disbelief, Sarah MacAllister's signature from 1860 exactly matched the signature she'd subconsciously written several weeks ago. Feeling the sting of tears, Jessica rubbed the back of her hand against her eyelids.

Am I losing my freakin' mind? How could I have duplicated Sarah MacAllister's signature?

The only rationale that seemed halfway plausible was that she'd seen Sarah's signature in one of her dreams. She'd once read in a scientific journal that everything perceived by the ocular nerve was encoded and stored in the brain. Every sunset, every license plate number on every automobile, every face in the crowd. If that was true, then it stood to reason that—

What in God's name am I thinking? There wasn't anything reasonable about any of this, or anything else that had happened in the last five or six weeks, for that matter. Gideon traveling through time, then a fire-breathing dragon appearing on the scene, and now this…this *whatever.*

Worried that she might be possessed by some type of ghostly spirit—how else to explain the duplicated signature?—Jessica snatched her cell phone and hurriedly scrolled through her contacts. When she found the name of the person she hoped could solve the mystery, she pressed the call button.

*   *   *

Glancing at the New Age artwork and astrology charts that adorned the back room of A Cut Above, Jessica immediately began to have second thoughts about consulting with the local "conjure woman."

"Honey, when was the last time you got some decent shuteye?" Hands set firmly on her hips, Darlene gave Jessica a critical once-over. "Don't take this the wrong way, but you look like hell."

Aware of how bad she looked, Jessica shrugged and said, "As I told you on the phone, I haven't gotten a decent night's sleep in weeks."

"And you actually think that's happening because you're possessed by a ghostly spirit?" Darlene shot her a dubious glance, clearly not on board.

Prepared to make her case, Jessica opened her canvas tote and retrieved a file folder. "If you don't believe me, maybe this will convince you." Opening the folder, she extracted two pieces of paper. "That's my handwriting," she said as she gave Darlene the first slip of paper. Then, handing her the 1860 marriage certificate, she said, "And that's the signature of a woman who died during the Civil War. Who, by the way, also happened to live at Highland House."

Darlene held both pieces of paper at arm's length as she carefully scrutinized them. "I'm no handwriting expert, but these signatures look identical to me." As she glanced away from the two pieces of paper, her brow furrowed. "And do you mind telling me what Gideon's name is doing on this old marriage certificate?"

"Well, um…" Jessica self-consciously cleared her throat several times before she said, "He used to be married to the woman that I've been dreaming about."

"I knew it!" Darlene's frown instantly morphed into a dimpled smile. "That man had time wanderer written all over him. Now don't that beat all?"

"You don't seem too surprised," Jessica remarked, taken aback by Darlene's ready acceptance of what could only be called a mind-blowing fact.

"Mother Maebelle often spoke about the time wanderer who showed up in '39 during the last Reckoning," Darlene said in a nonchalant tone of voice. "As I recall, he was a surveyor for George Washington, back before the Revolutionary War. According to Mother Maebelle, time wandering happens more often than people realize."

Trying to stay on topic, Jessica said, "I'm not here to discuss Gideon's time wandering. My problem has to do with his dead wife, Sarah. Ever since he showed up at Highland House, I've been seeing her—" Jessica tapped the signature on the marriage certificate for added emphasis—"in my nightly dreams. Which wasn't so bad in the beginning. But for nearly the last four weeks, I've been having this recurring nightmare in which Sarah is trapped in a fire."

Darlene placed the two pieces of paper back in the folder. Then, folding her arms over her chest, she gnawed on her lower lip for several seconds before she said, "As far as dreams go, there's a lot of mystical symbolism attached to fire. Since ancient times—"

"No, you don't understand. Sarah MacAllister died in 1863. In a fire," Jessica clarified. "But I didn't discover that fact until after I started having the nightmares."

Striking a thoughtful pose, Darlene tapped a manicured finger against her chin. "Hmm. That certainly adds spice to the stew. Have you talked to Gideon about this?"

"I've tried, but he refuses to discuss Sarah's death with me."

"Typical male response." Darlene punctuated the dig with a headshake and a theatrical roll of the eyes. Then, with her expression sobering considerably, she said, "From everything that you've told me, it sounds like you've hit up against an unresolved problem from a previous incarnation. It's what's known as a past life scar."

Shocked, Jessica's jaw dropped. "A past life! You're not actually suggesting that Sarah and I... that the two of us are—"

"One and the same," Darlene confirmed with a vigorous nod. "This is a case of reincarnation, pure and simple."

Hearing that, Jessica's natural skepticism immediately kicked into high gear. "Come on. Everyone knows that reincarnation doesn't happen to real people. It only happens to vegetarian gurus in India."

"For your information, reincarnation happens to garbage men, gurus, you, me. Everyone," Darlene said succinctly. "To put it in layman's terms, you once lived a life as a woman named Sarah MacAllister. She died, and now you're reincarnated as Jessica Reardon."

Stubbornly shaking her head, Jessica said, "Nope, I'm not buying it. I happen to know from my dreams that Sarah and I are nothing alike."

"I never said anything about the two of you being carbon copies of one another," Darlene retorted. "Reincarnation doesn't work like that. You need to remember that what we're talking about is two different bodies, two different minds, two different hearts. But only *one* soul. In your present incarnation, you've had a whole different set of life experiences which have made you the unique woman that you are today. However, if you scratch beneath the surface, I'd wager that you and Sarah are more alike than you realize."

As Jessica pondered the ways in which she and Sarah were similar, she suddenly realized that Sarah had gone against convention when she broke off her engagement to Oren Tolliver, enabling her to marry Gideon. This was comparable to how she'd walked out on Richard so that she could have her own life. An act of defiance that eventually led to her relationship with Gideon.

"Let's suppose for argument's sake that reincarnation does

take place," Jessica said hesitantly, not entirely convinced. "What then is a past life scar?"

As Darlene motioned for her to have a seat on the nearby sofa, she said, "Simply put, a past life scar is an unresolved traumatic event that gets carried over into another lifetime. There's a lot of karmic energy attached to a tragic or violent death that can emotionally scar a person in their next incarnation. In fact, most phobias are nothing more than carryovers from a past life."

The explanation gave Jessica food for thought. Like a lot of people, she had her share of inexplicable fears. Nonetheless, it was still a mind-boggling concept. "So what you're saying is that I'm not losing my mind. I'm just a little karmically battered."

"In a nutshell. Which is nothing that you and Gideon can't work out between the two of you," Darlene added with a knowing glance.

Thinking that the other woman was too perceptive for her good, Jessica said, "You've known all along about me and Gideon having a thing for each other, haven't you?"

One perfectly plucked eyebrow noticeably raised. "Just who did you think you were fooling with that cockamamie story about being platonic housemates? Even J.W., as dense as he is, noticed that you and Gideon seemed kind of tight."

"Without spending a fortune in therapy bills, how do I go about healing my past life scar?" Jessica inquired, trying to steer the conversation back on track.

"You do that by first healing the past," Darlene answered matter-of-factly. "And that can easily be done through a past life regression."

Jessica's eyes opened wide. "Come again?"

"Since Gideon refuses to discuss Sarah's death, you need to go back in time to 1863 and find out what caused the fire. Once you've done that, your recurring nightmare should cease and desist," Darlene stated in a professional, almost clinical, tone of voice.

"And how exactly am I supposed to go back to the year 1863?"

"By letting me put you into a deep trance."

"You're kidding," Jessica croaked, unnerved by the idea.

"Honey, there's no need to worry," Darlene said reassuringly as she patted Jessica's hand. "Us conjure women do this sort of thing all the time."

Still a Doubting Thomas, the best Jessica could manage was a weak smile.

"Buried deep within each of us are all the memories from all our past lives," Darlene continued. "That's the reason why we're attracted to certain things or certain people. For instance, I suspect that not only were you inexplicably drawn to Highland House, but you and Gideon were hot for each other at the get-go."

Jessica felt her cheeks flush. "Even before he shaved off his burly beard, I was strongly attracted to him," she confessed.

"That's because, on a subconscious level, you and Gideon immediately recognized each other as soul mates."

"Gideon and I are soul mates." Jessica gave herself several seconds to test drive the idea before she smiled and said, "I like the sound of that."

"All right, then. How about making yourself comfortable on the couch while I take care of a few things." Stepping over to the doorway that separated the back room from the salon, Darlene poked her head through the opening. "Lacey, I need you to take my eleven o'clock appointment. It's Mrs. Arbuckle's weekly wash and set. And make sure you use that special silver highlights shampoo." Orders issued, she closed the door.

Jessica fluffed a couple of pillows behind her head before

stretching out on the sofa. As she tried to relax, she was suddenly struck with a worrisome thought. "What if, while I'm deep in the trance, I get stuck in some alternate dimension?"

"It's not going to happen," Darlene assured her as she lit a long stick of incense, causing a plume of sickly sweet smoke to waft through the air. "Now I want you to close your eyes, breathe deeply, and concentrate on relaxing your body."

As she listened to Darlene's carefully worded commands, Jessica soon succumbed to a weightless sensation, and felt her inner self untethered from the here and now. Continuing to follow Darlene's voice, she descended to a shifting plane of time where images zoomed past like photographs in an album. When she caught sight of the precise picture that she was searching for—Sarah MacAllister sitting at a roll-top desk in the library—Jessica entered into the scene.

She wasn't altogether certain, but she thought Sarah glanced up as she approached. Then, as had happened so often in Jessica's dreams, the two of them merged, becoming one.

Chapter 23

Having removed a ledger from the drawer, Sarah opened a bottle of ink and reached for a pen, not particularly in the mood to post the monthly farm accounts. It was one of the more tedious responsibilities that she'd been forced to undertake in the wake of Gideon's war time service. And while he was currently at home on a medical furlough, it seemed pointless to ask him to post the ledgers.

Why bother when he would soon be leaving again?

Although glad-hearted that Gideon was nearly recovered from a bullet wound to the chest, she was fearfully aware that, had the bullet struck a few inches closer to his heart, the wound would have been fatal. Needless to say, she'd had many a sleepless night worrying about the dangers he would face once he returned to active duty.

Too listless to put pen to paper, Sarah stared at the book.

In addition to her concern for Gideon's safety, there was another crisis to contend with—Highland House was going to rack and ruin, and their creditors were threatening to sell the place out from under them. Moreover, she'd been without hired domestic help for months now, tending to all the household chores herself. How Gideon expected her to pay the accounts, put food on the table, and keep the farm running while he was off crusading for a lost cause was a mystery to her. Indeed, there were many mornings when it was a struggle for her to simply get out of bed, each day looming more hopeless than the one before it.

Even with Gideon home on furlough, there was no respite from her melancholia.

About to dip her pen into the ink bottle, Sarah paused in mid-motion as Gideon entered the library, resplendently attired in a new uniform. For some inexplicable reason, the sight of him in that gray tunic angered her, bringing to the fore emotions long held in check. It reminded Sarah that Gideon no longer belonged to her; he now belonged to the Confederate army.

"Well, what do you think?" her husband asked, rubbing his hand back and forth along his jaw, drawing Sarah's gaze to his clean-shaven face. "Personally, I thought the mustache gave me a certain gallant air."

"I don't know what to think anymore," she retorted. "The man I married didn't wear a uniform or walk about the house with a gun strapped to his hip."

"I know why you're upset." Gideon stepped behind her chair and placed his hands on her shoulders. As he gently kneaded the muscles in her upper back, he said, "These last two and a half years have been hard on you. You're dispirited, as am I, by the long separation imposed upon us. But you must learn to be more self-reliant."

"Why must I learn to be more self-reliant?" she snapped in a noticeably peevish tone, twisting in her chair so that she could look him in the face. "You are my husband. You took a vow to protect and cherish me. I am but a woman. I know nothing about running a large farm or managing thousands of acres."

"Need I remind you, Sarah, that there is a war being fought not far from here?" As he spoke Gideon emphatically gestured to one of the opened windows. "The world is not as it once was. You must adapt to these uncertain times. If I do not survive the war—"

"No! I beg you, Gideon. Do not utter those words."

Grim-faced, her husband exhaled a deep breath. "I understand the hardships that you face. And I know that you must feel—"

"How could you possibly know my feelings?" she interjected, unable to temper her runaway emotions. "Your only concern these days is for the Confederate army."

"That is an unfair accusation, as well you know."

"Is it? If you had to choose between the Confederate army and your wife, which would you choose, Gideon?"

Clearly astounded by her brazen question, he said, "Good God, woman. How can you even think, let alone ask, such a thing?"

"Because I am interested in hearing the answer." Refusing to back down, Sarah leveled her husband with an unrelenting stare. "Which would you choose, Gideon…me or the army?"

"You might as well hold a double-edged sword to my throat as to ask a question like that." Gideon ran a hand through his hair, his expression one of beleaguered frustration. "Truth be told, I don't know what it is that you want from me."

"I want you to remain at Highland House. Today, and all the days to follow," she informed him, refusing to mince words. "You can receive a medical discharge by informing your commanding officer that—"

"You know full well that I cannot," Gideon affirmed.

"And why is that? Plenty of men have received medical discharges. You've served long enough. Let some other poor deluded fool take your place."

The muscles in Gideon's jaw visibly clenched. Absent for more than two years, he was clearly unaccustomed to his wife playing the shrew.

"Is that what you think I am, Sarah—a deluded fool?"

"Can you honestly claim otherwise?" she scoffed, not knowing what hidden demons drove her to malign him so. "Indeed, the Confederacy is full of men just like you, parading around in fancy uniforms and charging into battle like a pack of overgrown schoolboys."

"Despite your lowly opinion of the Confederate army, I have a responsibility to the men under my command who—"

"Spare me the soliloquy," she interjected, raising a hand to forestall his explanation. "Obviously, being promoted to the rank of colonel has gone to your head. You also have a responsibility to your wife. Or have you conveniently forgotten about that?"

A deep furrow materialized between Gideon's brows. "How can you throw these accusations at me when our country is at war? Have you no patriotism?"

"Patriotism?" she parroted with a full measure of sarcasm. "What good is the Confederacy to me if you are killed in battle?"

Letting the question go unanswered, Gideon began to restlessly pace back and forth in front of the desk. Sarah observed his every expression, able to discern in his silent deliberation a fierce inner conflict between honor and duty. And love.

Coming to a halt, Gideon executed a crisp, soldierly about-face. From his steadfast expression, Sarah could see that he'd come to a decision.

"I know this is not how we'd planned to live our lives," he said.

"Unfortunately, we cannot subvert the course of history to suit our individual needs. This cruel war will soon end. And when it does, everything will be as it once was."

At hearing that, Sarah mockingly laughed aloud. "Do you have any idea what I do after each battle? I search the casualty lists, all the while praying to God that I won't see your name. Once I've ascertained that you aren't listed among the dead, I am filled with a joyful euphoria." As she spoke, Sarah held up her fist, clutching an imaginary casualty list. "Can you not see what this unholy war has done to me that I can hold a list with the names of hundreds, sometimes thousands, of slain men, and be rendered deliriously ecstatic? No, Gideon, we shall never again be as we once were. Those days ended when you ran off to join the army."

"Even as we speak, invading troops are marching through the whole of Virginia, burning and vandalizing every step of the way," Gideon said, a hard cast to his features. "I refuse to stand by and allow that to happen. The very reason I put on this uniform was to safeguard our home."

Her lips twisted, a bitter smile in the making. "So you claim."

"Are you actually questioning my motives?"

Pointedly ignoring him, Sarah dipped her pen into the open bottle of ink. Putting pen to paper, she very neatly wrote out the day's date on a clean page of the ledger. As she stared at the date that she'd just written—November the 7th, 1863—she mentally calculated it had been two years, seven months, and eight days since her husband first left for the army.

Without warning, Gideon slapped his palm on the open book. "Damn it, Sarah. I'm talking to you."

"You can talk all you want; however, I have no intention of listening to you."

Again, she dipped the pen, startled to have the ink bottle snatched out from under her. With a muttered oath, Gideon hurled the bottle against the library wall.

"Maybe you'll listen to me now."

"You've killed so many men, violence has become second nature to you," she said stiffly as she rose from her chair. "I want nothing further to do with you. If you will excuse me, I need to—"

"Sit down!" Grabbing her by the upper arm, Gideon shoved Sarah back into the chair. "You're not going anywhere."

A tense silence stretched between them, each armored behind an impregnable wall of anger.

"You are not the man I married," Sarah said at last, the truth painful to acknowledge.

"Don't you think I know that?" Gideon rasped, his voice thick with emotion. "If I could somehow change all of this, spirit us away to another time and place, I would do so. You must believe that."

"Unlike you, Gideon, I no longer have the capacity for such fanciful dreams. All I ask is that you resign your commission and—"

"Stay here at Highland House tied to your apron strings." As he spoke, Gideon straightened to his full, imposing height. "Even then, I suspect you wouldn't be satisfied until you had completely divested me of my manly honor."

"If your manly honor is so important to you, then by all means return to your Confederate comrades. Go on, leave! Get yourself killed and be done with it," Sarah lashed out, her fury fueled by too many months of lonely separation.

Wordlessly, Gideon slipped a hand into the inner pocket of his uniform tunic and removed a leather purse. With careful deliberation, he extracted from it a large wad of paper money. "It's obvious, madam, that I'm no longer welcome in my own home," he said, disdainfully tossing the money onto the desk. "I trust this will sufficiently cover my funeral expenses." That said, he stormed out of the room.

Trying to collect her shattered emotions, Sarah focused her attention on the rivulet of ink that stained the far wall, strangely fascinated by the tentacle-like ribbons of dark color. How long she sat there, she had no idea. It wasn't until she heard the front door slam shut, followed soon thereafter by the reverberating pounding of horse hooves that she realized Gideon was taking his leave of Highland House.

Her heart in her throat, Sarah rushed over to the French doors and flung them wide open. Without a thought to propriety, she raised her skirts to her knees and raced across the lawn, hoping to stop him. "Come back to me, Gideon…come back to me!" she yelled.

Her wild dash was in vain. By the time she got to the front of the house, he was nowhere in sight.

Dear Lord. Why had she said all of those hateful things to him? If she could, she'd take it all back. Every spiteful word.

Heavy-hearted, Sarah returned to the house. Once inside, she went about her household chores, much like a puppet on a string, afraid to do otherwise. Certain that if she stopped long enough to think, she would surely lose her mind.

And so she didn't think.

Instead, she posted the farm accounts, wrote a letter of condolence to a neighbor who'd recently lost her son, and tried, without much success, to clean the ink spot off the wall. After that, she stripped the beds, boiled water, and nearly rubbed her knuckles raw scrubbing bed sheets.

One hour bled into the next until, finally, near collapse, she stepped onto the front porch to catch a breath of fresh air. Overhead, four black ravens ominously circled. A bad omen. An even worse omen was the thunderous roar she heard in the distance. Shielding her eyes from the late afternoon sun, she sighted a group of riders, ten to twelve men in all, galloping at breakneck speed toward the house.

Frantically, she tried to determine whether they wore blue or gray.

Biting back a horrified shriek, she saw that they wore Federal blue—the Huns about to descend upon Highland House.

Amid shouts and hoarsely barked commands, the detail of riders stopped en masse several yards from where Sarah stood at the edge of the porch. Trying to affect a calm manner, she stepped toward them, her legs shaking beneath her skirt. Mercifully, she'd had the foresight to bury the silver and other valuables beneath the azalea bushes.

Several of the Union soldiers dismounted, two of them doffing their hats as they approached.

"Good afternoon, gentlemen." Sarah clenched her hands at her sides, determined not to show them any fear. "There's water for your horses around back, and…and I have a pot of beans stewing in the kitchen if you are hungry," she said, thinking it best to make the offer before they commenced to steal her provisions out from under her.

The officer in charge stepped forward, his kepi politely held in his hands. "Would you by any chance be Mrs. MacAllister?"

"Oh, it's Mrs. MacAllister, all right," one of the men in the party remarked snidely.

Sarah turned her head, taken aback to hear a long forgotten, yet eerily familiar, voice. Surely, it couldn't be—

Her hand flew to her mouth, unable to stifle a gasp at seeing Oren Tolliver standing several feet away from her. "Mr. Tolliver! This is a surprise, to say the least."

"A pleasant one, I hope."

Sarah dropped her gaze, unwilling to confirm a lie.

"We're looking for your husband," the commanding officer said. "It's our understanding that he's here at Highland House."

Taken aback, Sarah stared at the officer, uncomprehending. "What business have you with my husband?"

Oren, evidently amused by her response, snickered. Sarah paid him no heed, thinking it best to direct her remarks to the officer in charge: a major who, thus far, had conducted himself with a measure of civility.

"Begging your pardon, Mrs. MacAllister, but I don't like this any more than you do," the major commiserated in a courteous tone of voice. "Capturing an enemy soldier on the field of battle is one thing. Sneaking up on him while he's sitting down at his own supper table is a different matter, altogether. Be that as it may, I've been ordered to—"

"Apprehend your traitorous husband and see that he's remanded to a military prison," Oren interjected, taking an almost gleeful delight in doing so.

Sarah silently contemplated the man to whom she'd once been engaged, baffled as to why he had accompanied the detail of Federal soldiers given that he was the only man present who was garbed in civilian attire.

"I hate to disappoint you, Mr. Tolliver, but my husband is not at Highland House."

"I happen to know differently," Oren countered. "A loyal Unionist informed us that Colonel MacAllister is home on furlough."

"And did your informant also mention that Gideon returned to his regiment earlier today?"

Although the upper half of Oren's face was obscured by the brim of his hat, Sarah could see that his lips had flattened into a thin, hard line. When he purposefully took a step in her direction, she fearfully backed away from him, recalling how he'd struck her that long ago day at Sweet Springs.

"If I discover that you're lying to me, I'll—" Oren left the threat unfinished.

"By all means, Mr. Tolliver, search the house if you don't believe me," Sarah invited with an expansive gesture to the front door.

Oren turned to one of the soldiers still on horseback. "Sergeant, take two men and search every room of the house."

"Yes sir, Governor."

Hearing that, Sarah's jaw slackened as she wondered what misbegotten folk would ever elect Oren Tolliver to govern them. "Mr. Tolliver, I am confused as to why that soldier addressed you as 'Governor.'"

Oren hooked a thumb into each of his vest pockets. "I've recently been elected provisional governor," he informed her, his narrow chest visibly expanding as he made the announcement.

"Provisional governor of what, may I ask?"

"Obviously you haven't been apprised of the news yet. Greenbrier County is to be included in the boundaries of what will be the new loyal state of West Virginia," Oren said in a self-important tone of voice. "Which makes your treacherous husband guilty of committing high crimes against the people of West Virginia. Crimes for which he must now answer to me."

"Ha! That will be the day," Sarah exclaimed defiantly. Her husband was guilty of no crime save love of homeland.

Scowling, Oren stepped to within inches of where she stood.

"Never forget, Mrs. MacAllister, that vengeance is mine," he whispered in her ear.

"Sayeth the Lord," she chastised, appalled to hear him utter such blasphemy.

Oren negligently shrugged. "It matters not who said it, given that the sentiment is one which I wholeheartedly endorse."

Just then, the sergeant who'd been searching the house stepped through the front door. "The lady was telling the truth. Ain't nobody here, but her."

Visibly angered, Oren turned to the commanding officer. "Major, I want you to take these men back to Lewisburg. I'll be along shortly."

"Governor, I think it would be prudent to leave a small escort detachment," the major advised.

"That's entirely unnecessary. Mrs. MacAllister and I have some unfinished business which shouldn't take long to conclude."

Sarah turned her head in Oren's direction. To say that she was confounded would be an understatement. As far as she was concerned, she and Oren Tolliver had long ago severed all ties to one another.

Dutifully, the soldiers mounted their horses, the major issuing the order to ride out.

"Mr. Tolliver, I see no reason for you to—" Sarah stopped in mid-sentence as Oren removed his wide-brimmed hat. "Good heavens! What happened to your face?" Where there had once been a nose, there was only a bulbous hump of scarred flesh.

"Not a pretty sight, is it? Thanks to your husband, I now possess a most distinctive profile."

Unwillingly, Sarah recalled that long ago morning at Sweet Springs. A shudder passed over her at the memory of that violent day.

"Is that what this is all about? Is that why you came looking for Gideon?"

"It's one of the reasons," Oren admitted. "Now, as to our unfinished business, I noticed a barn in the distance and wondered if you would be kind enough to show it to me?"

Thinking it best to humor him, Sarah led Oren to the back of the house, and from there, out to the barn. Overhead, the four ravens that she'd earlier observed gracefully circled, not so much as flapping their wings as they effortlessly rode the wind. In the olden days, her superstitious forbears would have taken that as an ominous harbinger of death. Now she was simply struck by the majestic beauty of their soaring.

When she and Oren passed the line of clean sheets flapping in the breeze, her former fiancé gestured to the unfurled bed linens. "It would appear that Colonel Gideon MacAllister, the paragon of virtue who was so opposed to slave labor, has made a slave of his own wife. Thus proving, Mrs. MacAllister, that you chose the wrong man to marry."

"Surely, you're not suggesting that I should have married you?"

"If you had, you wouldn't be reduced to wearing homespun and scrubbing dirty linen like some lowly house servant."

"I married the man who stole my heart," she informed him, taking a small measure of delight in doing so. "You, on the other hand, wanted only to steal the money that my father had bequeathed to me."

Oren stopped in his tracks, forcefully pulling Sarah around to face him. "You were a fool then, and you are being no less of a fool now." To her acute unease, he ran his hand along the length of her arm, his fingers grazing the side of her breast. "It's a pity that I don't have more time to avail myself of that which should rightfully have been mine."

"How dare you speak to me in so loathsome a manner!" Disgusted with his lurid insinuations, Sarah turned abruptly and started back to the house.

She didn't get far. Oren clamped an imprisoning hand around her elbow.

"We shall see how steadfast your convictions are without your husband here to protect you," he snarled.

Outraged, Sarah tried, unsuccessfully, to pull free of him. "I demand that you release me, Mr. Tolliver."

Refusing to comply, Oren roughly jerked on her arm, nearly pulling it from the socket. Then, with a muttered oath, he dragged Sarah to the barn, shoving her through the open doors and pushing her onto a bale of hay.

"I don't understand why you've dragged me all the way out here," Sarah complained as she rubbed her arm, infuriated with his roughshod treatment of her.

"Because your house is made of brick," Oren matter-of-factly replied. "Setting fire to a wood barn requires far less effort."

Horrified, Sarah lunged to her feet. "You can't get away this!"

"Oh, but I can…and I will." Oren Tolliver's lips curved in a mirthless smile, making his face appear all the more grotesque. "And there's nothing that you can do to stop me." Still smiling, he grabbed a length of rope hanging on a nearby hook.

When Sarah attempted to run past him, he grabbed her by the shoulder and threw her to the floor. Entangled in her own skirts, she was powerless to stop him from tying her hands together.

"For the love of God! Don't do this," she pleaded. "I appeal to your sense of honor and—"

"Save your breath."

Unable to detect any mercy in his harsh voice, Sarah knew that Oren Tolliver intended to kill her, and in the most cruel, inhuman way imaginable. Gesturing toward the ladder which led to the hayloft, he indicated that he wanted her to climb it.

"That shall be somewhat difficult," she told him, holding her bound hands before her as she scrambled to her feet.

From the narrowing of his eyes, Sarah could see that her remark riled him. Cursing aloud, he placed a hand square across her lower back and shoved her toward the ladder. As she began the precarious ascent, Oren remained close behind her, his hand and upper body preventing her from falling backward. When she reached the top, she fell forward onto a bundle of hay.

Out of the corner of her eye, she watched as Oren retrieved a silver vesta case from his inside coat pocket. Removing a match, he struck it against a nearby beam. He then tossed the flaming match onto a bale of hay.

Sarah gasped, her heart beating an erratic, fear-induced tattoo. "Don't do this," she pleaded as she struggled to her feet. "If you set fire to the barn, I will likely perish in the flames."

"That is the point, Mrs. MacAllister." Chortling, Oren struck another match. With a negligent air, he tossed it aside. "You must pay for the humiliation that you made me suffer when you broke off our engagement."

As Sarah watched him strike two more matches in quick succession, she was hit with an almost paralyzing sense of dread. "Forgive me, Oren. It was…it was wrong of me to…to treat you so callously," she stammered. Suddenly lightheaded, she began to sway on her feet. "Is there nothing I can do to make amends?"

"There is something you can do." Clearly amused, Oren smiled as he lit yet another match. "You can die. *That* will settle our debt."

At hearing his heartless reply, Sarah's eyes welled with tears, blurring her vision. "There's some money in the library desk drawer," she told him, unable to hide the desperation in her voice. "Will that not settle the matter?"

"I shudder to think what a low price you would place on my honor. As if it could be bought with a few coins," Oren added as he descended from the hayloft.

Sarah hurriedly made her way to the edge of the loft, alarmed to discover that Oren had removed the ladder. As she stood there, pondering her dire situation, her nostrils began to twitch, assailed by the acrid scent of smoke. Peering behind her, she saw that several of the hay bales had burst into flames. Gripped with fear, she knew that it was more fire than a single person could hope to extinguish, particularly without any water.

Stifling a panic-stricken cry, Sarah caught sight of Oren standing near the open barn door.

"I thought you should know that my true purpose in coming here today was to kill your husband. Arranging for his arrest was merely a pretext," Oren informed her. "But rest assured, I shall have a reckoning all the same." With a casual flick of the wrist, he tossed a final lit match onto the hay bales neatly stacked beside the door, gleefully cackling as the dry hay burst into flames. "Good day, Mrs. MacAllister."

"I beg you! Don't do this!" she called after him.

Without a backward glance, Oren Tolliver left the barn. A moment later, the double doors banged closed, throwing the interior of the barn into a semi-darkness relieved only by the light of the growing flames.

"No!" Sarah screamed, tears coursing down her face.

She didn't want to die; that was the one certainty in this evil madness. But in order to escape, she had to get down from the loft. Which would be an impossible feat without the ladder. Unless…

Not giving herself time to deliberate on the matter, Sarah stepped off the edge of the hayloft, her long skirts ballooning around her as she soared through the air, her bound wrists preventing her from breaking the fall as she landed on her right side.

Almost immediately, an excruciating pain traversed the length of her lower leg. Gritting her teeth, Sarah tried to pull herself upright, but was unable to do so—her leg was bent at an unnatural angle, the bone broken.

Just then, a furious rumble shook the barn, and the hayloft plummeted to the ground in a roaring blaze of fire, barely missing Sarah. With it came several roof timbers, igniting everything they came into contact with. Gritting her teeth against the pain, she desperately tried to move away from the searing flames. In the next instant, another ceiling beam crashed to the barn floor, torching several stacked bundles of hay. All around her, burning embers fell like rain. Terror-stricken, Sarah saw that the hem of her long skirt had caught fire. Oblivious to the pain, she frantically swatted at the burning fabric.

"Gideon!"

Over and over, she screamed her husband's name…even though she knew he would never reply. She'd run him off with her scornful words.

But if I hadn't driven Gideon from Highland House, he would now be dead. Oren Tolliver had openly admitted that his sole purpose in coming to Highland House had been to kill Gideon. Despite her terror, Sarah's heart sparked with a moment's joy.

Unable to pull air into her lungs, she began to choke on the heavy smoke, the life force slowly ebbing from her. As it did, she thought of Gideon and the love she bore him. A love that she would carry with her to the hereafter. And beyond.

"I am ever yours, my darling Gideon." Those were Sarah's last words, her last thought, before her spirit drifted upwards, leaving the fire far behind…

* * *

"…and you'll awake on the count of three. One. Two. Three. Open your eyes."

Grateful the ordeal was over, Jessica heeded the command. As she sat upright on the sofa, she pushed out a deep, uneven breath.

"It's all right, honey. You're back in the here and now." As Darlene gently patted her on the hand, a look of utter shock flashed across her face. "Lord Almighty! You're burning up."

"That's an understatement," Jessica muttered as she recalled the last few moments of Sarah's life. However, more distressing than that horrific memory were the acrimonious words she'd hurled at Gideon just before he'd left Highland House. *Go on, leave! Get yourself killed and be done with it.*

"Because I cruelly taunted him, Gideon never knew how much I loved him," she moaned, salty tears meandering unchecked down her face.

Snatching several tissues from a nearby box, Darlene handed them to her as she said, "He knows, honey. That's why he traveled all this way to find you. Talk about a long distance romance." Clearly amused, she began to chuckle softly.

"You don't understand. Gideon traveled through time to find Sarah, only he ended up with *me.*"

"You being exactly the person he's supposed to be with."

"But I'm not Sarah," Jessica stubbornly maintained, wondering why the other woman failed to see what was so plainly obvious.

"Because that life cycle has been completed." With an almost maternal look on her face, Darlene took hold of both of Jessica's hands as she said, "I want you to listen to me very carefully. There's no force in the universe stronger than love. Not only is love a potent glue in the here and now, it can bind two people together throughout time. And this time around, you happen to be Jessica Reardon."

"Yeah, but—"

"You're not listening to me," Darlene said sternly, stopping Jessica in mid-argument. "Gideon MacAllister loves you for who you are. So stop thinking of yourself as a consolation prize at the county fair."

"But you weren't there, Darlene. You didn't see what happened." As she envisioned Sarah's last day, Jessica closed her eyes and shuddered. "Isn't there some way I can go back and make amends?"

"I'm going to give you the straight scoop. There's nothing you can do to change what happened in a past life." Smiling sympathetically, Darlene then said, "All you can do is make certain that you don't commit the same mistakes this time around."

"But what if I screw up all over again?" she fretted, wondering if that was what was meant by the karmic wheel. "Every now and then, when I least expect it, I can feel Sarah's anger and resentment toward Gideon welling up inside of me, and before I can even stop myself, I'm reacting to her feelings."

"But by the same token, you can also feel her love for Gideon welling up inside of you. Am I right?"

"I felt that from the very start," Jessica shyly confessed, having fallen in love with Gideon when he was still a virtual stranger to her.

"Until you can temper the good with the bad and forgive past transgressions, lasting happiness will elude the two of you. Just as it did one hundred and fifty years ago," Darlene said in a serious tone of voice. "However, this time around, you're going into the relationship with eyes wide open. Remember, you're not Sarah. You're Jessica. And that means you're—"

"Self-reliant," Jessica chimed in, recalling Sarah and Gideon's last heated argument.

Darlene shot her a quizzical glance. "What in tarnation does that mean?"

"It means that I really have changed. And for the better," she affirmed, realizing that after one hundred and fifty years, she'd finally become a strong, independent woman.

"Well, in that case, I suggest you go home and figure out what you're going to say to that man of yours when he gets back from Shepherdstown," Darlene advised as she got up from the sofa. "When I last spoke to J.W., he mentioned they would be returning to Greenbrier County early Friday evening. So that gives you nearly three days to catch up on your beauty sleep."

Also rising to her feet, Jessica took Darlene's measure, the other woman making quite the fashion statement with her peroxide-blond hair, cowboy boots, and flaming red fingernails. "You're one heck of a wise conjure woman, Darlene Malone."

Blushing all the way to her dark roots, Darlene said, "It's too bad you never got to meet Mother Maebelle. Now there was a wise woman."

"Unless I'm greatly mistaken, you're following right in her footsteps."

A mischievous, double-dimpled smile suddenly broke out on Darlene's face. "Speaking of following in someone's footsteps, what are you planning on naming that baby that's on the way?"

Flabbergasted, Jessica's mouth fell open. "I can't…can't have children," she stammered.

"Says who?"

"Says Dr. Harvey Metzer at the McLean Infertility Clinic, for one."

Darlene's smiled widened. "In case you haven't noticed, there's a lot of magic in these old mountains. Especially when Draygan is roaming hither and yon."

In a state of shock, Jessica placed a hand on her lower belly. True, she'd suffered from nausea recently, but she'd just assumed that had to do with a lack of sleep. That she might possibly be pregnant had never crossed her mind.

"How can you be so certain? If anything, I've lost weight these last few weeks."

Affecting a look of mock indignation, Darlene said, "I'm a psychic, aren't I?"

Chapter 24

A hh…it doesn't get much better than this," Jessica said with an appreciative sigh as she sank into the fluffy mound of vanilla-scented bubbles.

After moving her neck rest to a more comfortable position, she reached for the sea sponge and, lifting her leg onto the rim of the claw-footed bathtub, she lathered her foot. While others might laud the superiority of the shower, she'd always been a hardcore fan of the leisurely bath.

Because Gideon was due to return home in a few hours' time, she'd had a busy day cleaning house, planning a romantic dinner for two, and grocery shopping. She'd even finished next week's installment of *The Draygan Chronicles*, having earlier e-mailed the completed article to her editor. Nervous about her and Gideon's upcoming reunion, she wanted to clear her weekend slate.

Hopefully, the bubble bath would calm her frazzled nerves.

Although her nerves weren't nearly as frazzled as they had been. Since her past life regression, she hadn't had a single dream or nightmare about Sarah. In fact, for the last three mornings, she'd awakened, bright-eyed and bushy-tailed, relieved that she was back to having the usual run-of-the-mill, nonsensical Freudian dreams. But even though she was grateful that her sleep patterns had returned to normal, there was no sidestepping the fact that she now had a whole new set of issues to contend with.

Somewhat anxiously, her gaze darted to the plastic shopping bag hanging off the bathroom door knob. Inside the bag was a home pregnancy kit, a purchase she'd never thought she'd ever have to make. Despite the fact that Darlene had assured her that there was a "baby on board," she needed incontrovertible proof. However, before she shared the good news with Gideon, she had to first tell him about her past-life regression and her soul connection to Sarah MacAllister.

Admittedly, she'd yet to figure out how to spin the news that Gideon's dearly departed wife had a new lease on life. Space stations and cruise missiles had thrown him a real curve ball. She had no idea how he'd react to karmic wheels and multiple past lives. The man was, after all, a card-carrying Methodist.

Reincarnation wasn't the only newsflash she had for Gideon. Because her divorce from Richard Bragg would be finalized in just few days time, she absolutely had to come clean about her marital status. A confession long overdue, it was one that she was already dreading. Gideon haled from an era in which divorce was unthinkable. The few brave souls who did seek divorce during the nineteenth century had been shunned by polite society, condemned to spend the rest of their lives as *persona non grata*.

Somehow she had to convince Gideon that divorce no longer had a scandalous taint attached to it. That rather than stay in an unhappy or abusive marriage, spouses now had the freedom to sever their marital ties, and that no one thought less of them for doing so. She just had to make him understand that—

Oh God, what was that?

Panic-stricken, Jessica sat upright in the tub, the sponge clutched to her chest. Holding her breath, she listened attentively, certain that she'd heard a footfall in the downstairs foyer. Since Buster was outside, that eliminated her Maine Coon cat from the suspect pool.

What if my nasty, anonymous caller has decided to take his harassment to the next level? In the last three days, there'd been numerous calls. In fact her phone bully had recently begun to angrily hiss the word "Bitch!" before hanging up.

What was to stop him from entering the house and accosting her? As near as she could tell, the answer to that was nothing.

When she suddenly heard a loud creak on the staircase, Jessica frantically searched the bathroom for a weapon with which to defend herself. While she didn't see anything weapon-worthy, there was some hair spray in the armoire. If she aimed it directly at the goon's face, it should stop him long enough for her to make an escape. And though it was a good plan, she would've liked it a whole lot better if she were wearing some clothing.

Trying to make as little noise as possible, Jessica slid out of the tub. Frothy, white bubbles clung to her body, a garb of sorts. Too scared now to be embarrassed, she opened the armoire.

Crappola! Where's my can of hair spray?

Jessica bit back a groan of despair, her plan shot to hell.

Hearing footsteps approach the closed bathroom door, she knew that she had only a few seconds to come up with Plan B. Desperate, she grabbed her curling iron and held it over her head. Prepared to launch her attack, she held her breath and waited.

Like a scene from a bad horror flick, the bathroom door slowly creaked open. Her heart pounding madly, Jessica waited until the intruder stepped across the threshold before she threw her makeshift weapon as hard as she could.

"Take that, you—Gideon! What are you doing here?"

Possessed of quick reflexes, Gideon raised his arm to rebuff the blow, and the curling iron harmlessly bounced off his forearm. "Unless you've forgotten, I live here," he said in response to her shrieked query. "Moreover, I thought you'd be happy to see me."

"Yes, I'm...er, delighted," Jessica stammered, still trying to catch her breath. "But why didn't you call and let me know that you'd be arriving earlier than expected?"

"I did call. Several times, in fact," Gideon said pointedly as he picked up the curling iron and set it on a nearby shelf. "For whatever reason, I kept getting your automated greeting, instructing me to leave a message. Which I did, I might add."

"Oh...I, um, turned off the ringer so that—" she wouldn't have to deal with her harassing cell phone bully. While it wasn't the homecoming that she'd envisioned, Jessica impulsively threw herself into Gideon's arms. "Welcome home! I'm thrilled to see you."

"Words to warm my heart," Gideon murmured in her ear as he held her in a fiercely tight embrace, the kind of body-smashing hug that left her weak-kneed and warm-hearted. Even though they'd exchanged calls nearly every day, there was something to be said for bodily contact.

When Gideon finally pulled away from her, his gaze appreciatively swept the length of Jessica's wet body. "I see that I've caught you unawares."

"That's putting it mildly."

With a courtly sweep of the arm, he gestured toward the bathtub. "Far be it for me to interrupt a lady's bath." Then, with a suggestive twinkle in his eyes, he said, "Perhaps you need some assistance?"

Jessica returned the smile, her pulse immediately kicking up a few notches.

"Now that you mention it, I probably could use a hand," she murmured as she smoothed her palm over Gideon's flannel-covered chest, the blue plaid turning his eyes an electric shade of cerulean. "Although, as a matter of principle, I refuse to be the only naked person in the room."

"I wouldn't dream of coming between a lady and her principles."

While Gideon undressed, Jessica climbed back into the tub, the warm water erasing the goose bumps that had sprouted all over her body. As she caught sight of Gideon wrapping a towel around his bare hips, she opened her mouth to protest, only to think better of it at the last minute. For the time being, she decided to let her Victorian lover keep his modesty. She'd have that towel off of him soon enough.

Grabbing a stool from the corner, Gideon placed it next to the porcelain tub. As he seated himself, Jessica caught an enticing glimpse of a firmly muscled thigh. Automatically, she extended a hand in his direction. After four weeks of intense longing, she couldn't wait to touch him.

"And here I'd mistaken you for a lady," Gideon teased as he placed her straying hand back into the water.

"Can I help it if I'm feeling a bit frisky? It has been four long weeks. If you know what I mean," she added with flirtatious wink.

"I know exactly what you mean. Which is why I intend to savor our reunion."

"Personally, I think you're being a bit of spoilsport." Reclining against the back of the tub, Jessica arched her back, impudently thrusting her breasts into the air. *Savor that, big guy.*

Gideon reached for the bath sponge. "Very pretty," he complimented with a wry grin as he took hold of Jessica's right wrist and commenced to wash her arm.

"So how did you enjoy your four-week stint with J.W. Malone?" she asked, as streams of frothy soap sluiced off her arm and splattered onto the surface of the water.

"If you must know, J.W. has taught me a great deal about modern-day society."

Rolling her eyes, Jessica said, "I'm almost afraid to ask what you've learned."

In no apparent hurry to answer, Gideon moved the sponge over the length of her other arm, lavishing it with an inordinate amount of attention. After a considerable pause, he finally said, "J. W. has a penchant for speaking at great length, and in fine detail, about 'buns of steel', 'hotties', and 'awesome ta-tas'. Not wishing to appear uninformed, I oftentimes remained silent throughout his colorful soliloquies. But now I put the question to you: What is an awesome ta-ta?"

Jessica bit back a smile. "Not is, *are*. And surely a man who's as imaginative as you can figure that one out."

Clearly up to the challenge, Gideon slid his hand under the water to cup Jessica's derriere.

Giggling, she shook her head and said, "Nope. Guess again."

Clearly enjoying the game, Gideon slowly moved his hand across her abdomen, coming to a halt at her bosom. Grinning broadly, he palmed a soapy breast.

"Bingo," Jessica exclaimed, her breath catching in her throat when Gideon gently tweaked her nipple. "And if J.W. ever asks you to go with him to an exotic dance club, you are to flat out refuse the invitation."

"Well, I, um…"

Jessica twisted around in the tub so that she could face Gideon, the sudden movement causing bathwater to splash onto the floor. "That lowlife took you to a topless bar, didn't he?"

Given the reddish stain on Gideon's cheekbones, she could see that he was acutely embarrassed.

"All I can say in my defense is that I have no desire to ever return."

"Good answer," Jessica said, resettling herself in the tub. "Just wait until I get my hands on J.W."

"In light of the fact that he considers you a 'hometown hottie,' that may not be such a good idea," Gideon advised as he slowly dragged the sponge across her chest.

Jessica gasped softly; the wonderful, tingly sensation of having her breasts thoroughly washed was pleasure taken to the nth degree.

"I take it that you are enjoying your bath?" Gideon inquired.

Not in the mood to play coy, she said, "I'd enjoy it more if you were in this tub with me."

Gideon slowly sponged her hardened nipples. "Is that an invitation?"

"Actually, it's an order. And an adamant order, at that," she added.

As Gideon rose to his feet, Jessica grabbed hold of the towel still wrapped around his waist. It only took one good tug for her to yank it from his body. With an impish smirk, she purposefully cast her gaze upon her lover's blatant arousal. "Very pretty."

As he lowered himself into the bathwater, Gideon said, "I have never been thusly complimented."

Scooting to make room for him, she smiled and said, "There's a first for everything."

Despite the fact that the ancient clawfoot tub was commodious by modern standards, Gideon still had trouble situating his 6'4" frame. Jessica quickly remedied the problem by cinching her legs around his waist.

"Now that we're entwined like sardines in a can, what do you propose we do?" Gideon asked, a seductive glimmer in his blue eyes.

"Hmm, good question." Tilting her head to one side, Jessica assumed an air of mock contemplation. "Well, for starters, we can always do this." Placing her hands on Gideon's shoulders, she leaned forward and nibbled on his lower lip. As he shuddered against her, she slid a hand across his pectoral muscles, thrilled to feel the pounding of his heart against her palm.

With a hand braced on the back of her head, Gideon returned the kiss, his tongue nudging between her lips as he explored the inner recesses and outer contours of her mouth. In the next instant, a spasm of pleasure shot through Jessica as she felt Gideon's hardened desire insistently throb against her lower belly. At that moment she felt a yearning so palpable, so exhilarating, it almost had material substance.

"A most propitious beginning," Gideon said once the kiss had ended. "But I think we can do better." Reaching for the sponge that bobbed on the surface of the water, he nestled it at the juncture between her legs. In tortuous slow-motion, he then moved it back and forth, causing Jessica to whimper softly. In no time at all, whimpering gave way to a lusty moan, pleasure transmuting into a full-bodied passion.

"How about we skip the preliminaries and just rush ahead to the finale?" she suggested, having fantasized about this moment for the last four weeks.

"We are of like mind, sweet lady."

Putting his hands on her hips, Gideon eased Jessica upward, enabling her to position above him. That done, he lowered her back down, completely embedding himself in her body. She shuddered, savoring the feel of having him inside of her, the most intimate bond that she could share with him.

In that sweet, glorious moment, Jessica had never felt so cherished. So desired. *We are fated to be together.* And though she'd lived thirty-one years, she now knew that her life truly began on the stormy night when Gideon MacAllister mysteriously arrived at Highland House.

"Ride me, Jessica. Ride me as fast and furious as you can," Gideon whispered, suddenly tightening his hold on her bottom.

Breathlessly nodding, she did just that, holding onto the edge of the tub as she pumped her hips up and down, her own pleasure heightened with each deep, guttural groan that she elicited from him. In those passion-laden moments, neither took heed of the fact that waves of bathwater noisily sloshed over the rim of the tub.

All too quickly, Jessica reached her peak. Throwing her head back, she opened her mouth and moaned, the moment too primal, too visceral for words. Firmly clasping her to his hips, Gideon incoherently grunted, his body shaking as he climaxed. Unable to speak, Jessica collapsed against his chest with a soft splash.

With a gentle hand, Gideon brushed aside the wet hair from Jessica's face before he placed a finger under her chin, urging her to look at him.

"It's good to be home," he said with a tender smile.

* * *

Her stomach in knots, Jessica snatched a wool sweater and hurriedly pulled it on. When she'd seen Gideon step outside a few minutes earlier, she had decided the time was finally right to tell him about her past life regression and her connection to Sarah.

Exiting the house, she made her way toward the pasture fence where Gideon stood watching Blaze frolic in a nearby field. The horse was clearly happy to see him after his prolonged absence.

As she gazed toward the western horizon, Jessica noticed that the late-day sun hung low in the sky. The days were getting shorter. Soon the low-riding orb would make its way down the backside of the mountain, disappearing from view altogether. Weather-wise, they were in the throes of Indian summer, the mild temperature a pleasant respite from the usual November chill.

With each footstep that she took, Jessica could hear the crunch of brittle leaves—the mighty oaks and maples had lost their foliage several weeks ago. It bespoke of a death that wasn't really a death. Spring would, after all, usher in a glorious rebirth of all that had gone before.

As with nature, so it was with the human soul.

Still grappling with the idea of reincarnation, she found it mind-boggling that the whole of Sarah MacAllister's life was stored in that vast mainframe known as her subconscious mind. And though she'd spent an inordinate amount of time pondering the significance of Sarah's death, she couldn't figure out why—if Draygan could bring Gideon across the boundaries of time—the wily dragon hadn't sent Gideon back in time so that he could save Sarah from the fire. Why bring him forward to the twenty-first century? Truth be told, she didn't need to be saved.

But she did need to be loved. Now more than ever.

Smiling, Jessica placed a hand over her still-flat belly. About to embark on a life-altering, miraculous journey, maybe she had no business wondering why Gideon traveled forward rather than backward through time. Maybe she should instead focus on what color she was going to paint the baby's room.

I'm really and truly going to have a baby, she marveled, having gotten a positive result a short while ago when she took the home pregnancy test.

Admittedly nervous, Jessica wiped her clammy hands against her denim jeans as she approached the pasture fence. At hearing her footfall, Gideon turned, welcoming her with a warm smile.

Sidling next to him, she said, "Since you didn't suffer a single headache or spell while you were in Shepherdstown, I was wondering how you're feeling now that you've returned to Highland House."

"I'm pleased to report that I feel as fit as the proverbial fiddle," Gideon informed her.

"Good news, indeed." Hopefully, Draygan would keep his distance.

Turning around, Gideon leaned his back against the top rail of the fence. "Have I told you how much I enjoy living in the twenty-first century?"

Surprised by the abrupt change in topic, Jessica swiped the back of her hand across her brow, wiping at imaginary beads of sweat. "Phew! What a relief. Because if you weren't happy—" Hit with a sudden change of heart, she waved away the errant thought, not wanting to toss a negative vibe into the universe.

As they watched the sunset in companionable silence, Jessica had a strong, intuitive feeling that she'd known Gideon MacAllister throughout the ages, in other times and other places.

Taking a deep breath, Gideon stared at the western horizon, the sky just beginning to turn a vibrant shade of salmon pink. "This is a century full of promise and possibility. But it's also one in which the past is clearly cherished." Pausing briefly, he tore his gaze from the sunset so that he could look at Jessica directly. "During my tenure in Shepherdstown, I came to realize that there's a growing demand for historic restoration."

"Which means that you can put your knowledge of the nineteenth century to good use," she said, surmising where the conversation was headed.

"Moreover, I'm convinced that if I pursue this avenue, it will enable me to secure a financially stable future." Gideon spared a quick glance at the house. "You did say something about a new roof, did you not?"

"I did." Having delayed the inevitable long enough, Jessica took a deep, fortifying breath, about to open a very big can of squiggly worms. "We need to talk about Sarah's death," she announced without fanfare.

Almost immediately, a ghostly specter of grief flashed across Gideon's face before he hid it behind an impenetrable stone mask.

"Don't do that. Don't emotionally retreat on me," Jessica implored, convinced that their future happiness hinged on getting everything out into the open. "That's how this whole tragic business got started in the first place."

"If it's a tragedy you want, then perhaps you should know that after the fire, I used to seek my death in battle with open arms. Rather naively, I thought that if I died, I could, at long last, beg Sarah's forgiveness." Gideon's lips twisted in a mordant smile. "A futile desire given that what I did to Sarah is as unforgivable in the heavenly realm as it is here on earth."

Tears pooled in Jessica's eyes, the anguish in his voice tearing at her heart. "Gideon, I know what happened at Highland House on November the 7th, 1863. And I also know how it happened. Which is why I can say with complete certainty that you aren't to blame."

Gideon slowly shook his head, his confusion plainly evident. "You weren't here. You can't possibly know what took place on that ill-fated day."

"You're greatly mistaken," she told him. "I know what occurred because I was here at Highland House...in 1863. I'm the woman whose forgiveness you seek." As she spoke, Jessica placed a hand on Gideon's forearm. "And I forgive you, Gideon. I forgave you a long time ago."

"It can't be," he said adamantly, shaking his head as he backed away from her. "Sarah died one hundred and fifty-one years ago."

"Yeah, about that. Um...this a toughie because—" Jessica shifted her weight from one sneaker-shod foot to the other, uncertain how to broach the topic of reincarnation—"as strange as it sounds, I was your wife Sarah Pemberton MacAllister in a prior incarnation."

"No!" Gideon bellowed, his voice thick with emotion. "Such a thing is not humanly possible."

Chapter 25

Hey, I used to say the same thing about time traveling, remember?"

Evidently, Gideon didn't because he proceeded to stare at Jessica as though she was a raving lunatic. The mad woman of Highland House.

Sensing that she was getting nowhere fast, Jessica said, "You want proof? Okay, let's see... um, we met at Sweet Springs when Sarah got her foot caught in a mole hole. Two nights later, you charmed me into climbing out of my window and waltzing with you in the moonlight. A few days after that, we eloped. A few months after that, the war started." Jessica stopped suddenly and wagged a chastising finger at Gideon. "And if you ever fight in another war, so help me God, I'll clobber you."

Gideon's eyes opened wide, his expression having morphed into one of stunned incomprehension. "How can you possibly be privy to this information?"

"Like I said, I lived through it," she reiterated. "All of it. The good times and the bad ones too." About to raise the taboo topic of Sarah's death, Jessica emotionally braced herself for Gideon's reaction as she said, "In the fall of 1863, you were wounded at the Battle of Bristoe Station. That's when you came home on a medical furlough. I begged you to remain at Highland House rather than return to active duty. But you refused to tender your military resignation because—"

"My God," Gideon murmured, profound astonishment written all over his face. "There have been many times that I've seen a haunting resemblance between you and Sarah. Indeed, it has often baffled me as to how you could both possess the same passionate nature, the same generous spirit."

Jessica gnawed on her lower lip, her heart beating a mile a minute. "So then you...you actually believe me?"

Extending a hand in her direction, Gideon cupped one side of her face. As he gently smoothed the pad of his thumb over her trembling lips, he slowly nodded his head. "There's no doubt in my mind that you are telling the truth. Although I'm confounded as to how such a thing is even remotely possible."

"I'm a little confounded by that myself. It's called reincarnation, and it has to do with the transmigration of the soul." Then, with a shaky smile, she offered a more pedestrian explanation. "As best I understand it, when we die, the soul packs its bags and moves out, only to take up residence in another body. All of which means that rather than driving in the express lane, our souls take the scenic route to heaven."

"If I understand what you're saying, the soul lives on in a different body." Gideon took several moments to digest that before he said, "Although the idea beggars description, some things in life must be accepted on blind faith. Clearly, this is one of those instances." Verdict given, Gideon gaped at her like an awestruck groupie, clearly bedazzled.

"Is something the matter?" Jessica asked, unnerved by his rapt scrutiny.

"To think that Sarah resides in your body is truly—"

"You can stop right there," she interjected, horrified to think that it was Sarah he wanted, not her. "I hate to be the bearer of bad news, but I'm not Sarah. I used to be, but...but that was a long time ago. All that remains of Sarah are little bits and pieces. In this lifetime, I'm Jessica. And if you can't accept that fact, then—" Suddenly aware that she was on the verge of delivering a "take it or leave it" ultimatum, Jessica clamped her mouth tightly shut.

Jeez, Louise. Am I really jealous of...me? How absurd was that?

"Jessica, whatever would make you think that I want you to be anyone other than who you are?" Gideon asked with a look of utter sincerity. "Since coming forward in time, I've felt like a resurrected man. And that is solely because of you. Not only are you the woman who pulled me from the grave, you are also the woman who gave me a reason to live."

His ardent declaration filled Jessica's heart with a rush of emotion so potent that she swayed slightly, having to put a hand on Gideon's chest to steady herself.

Raising that hand to his mouth, Gideon pressed his lips against her knuckles. "In truth, you saved me from myself."

As she thought about the near-dying man who'd mysteriously shown up on her doorstep, Jessica choked back a sob. If Gideon hadn't traveled through time, he would have died of pneumonia in the year 1864. But he did cross the threshold of time. And, in so doing, he'd given Jessica something that she'd long been searching for: love. That simple, four-letter word which had the power to make a person whole, and good, and beautiful.

"You saved me too," she whispered. "More than you'll ever know."

With a tender smile, Gideon pulled Jessica into his embrace. "I am fully cognizant that you are different from Sarah," he murmured in her ear, his warm breath sending a tingle down her spine. "You are a woman of this time and place. But, for one moment, may I address those 'bits and pieces' of Sarah which you still carry inside of you?" When she wordlessly nodded, Gideon set her at arms' length, enabling him to better hold her gaze. "I want you to know that had I been here at Highland House on that long ago day, I would have done all in my power to prevent the terrible accident that took Sarah's—"

"The fire wasn't an accident," Jessica blurted.

Gideon's brows instantly drew together. "If the fire wasn't an accident, then what, pray tell, was it?"

Now that she'd opened her big mouth, Jessica dismally realized she had to reveal everything she knew about Sarah's murder—something she hadn't intended to do just yet, having planned to ease Gideon into the unsettling revelation.

Her good intentions now thrown to the wayside, Jessica said, "Oren Tolliver forced me—Sarah, that is—into the barn. After which he…he set it on fire."

In the aftermath of that horrific disclosure, Jessica observed the progression of emotions that flashed across Gideon's face as his eyes first opened wide with shock. Then, a few seconds later, those beautiful blue orbs watered with anguished tears…just before they narrowed with an unadulterated rage.

"I'm going to track that bastard down and kill him," Gideon hissed between clenched teeth.

Jessica placed a placating hand on his chest. "I'm afraid that vengeance isn't possible."

"Don't you understand? He killed—"

"Oren Tolliver is dead," she stated baldly. "And has been dead for more than a century."

"No!"

That single word, bellowed to the heavens, was like the agonized cry of the damned. And it nearly broke Jessica's heart to hear it.

"Gideon, please don't be upset. That tragic episode is over and done with. It happened so…so long ago…and…" Unable to convince even herself, Jessica's voice trailed into silence. While the hideous incident may have happened decades ago, because of her past life regression, Sarah's death seemed all too recent to her.

Seeing the abject grief on her beloved's face, Jessica knew that she had to be strong. Later she could fall apart. But right now, at this critical juncture, Gideon needed her.

"Please, listen to what I'm about to say as it's vitally important that you hear this." When Gideon refused to meet her gaze, Jessica placed a hand on either side of his face, forcing him to look at her. "We can't change the past. Because we live in the here and now, we can only affect the future. Which is why you need to let go of the anger. Don't you see? We've been given a second chance. Please don't destroy it with recrimination or dark thoughts about what happened long years ago. This may be the only chance we ever have to get our relationship right."

* * *

Disoriented, Gideon dropped to his knees, the emotional upheaval more than he could bear. His head spinning, he instinctively reached for Jessica, wrapping his arms around her waist. At that moment, he was like a drowning man grasping for something, anything, to save himself from the swirling undertow.

As though she was standing a great distance away on the shoreline, Gideon faintly heard Jessica repeatedly utter his name. But he was too far gone to respond, trapped in a place where there was neither comfort nor redemption.

Battling to free himself from the dark, pitiless force that had seized his soul, Gideon tightened his hold on Jessica, smashing his face against her lower abdomen.

With each deep breath, he filled his senses with the smell of her—vanilla, autumn leaves, lemon balm. And underlying it all, a scent more full-bodied, more earthy than the others—a musky tang that incited his baser instincts. Incited by that feminine scent, Gideon burrowed his chin, his mouth, his nose against Jessica's lower body, wanting nothing more than to lose himself in the arousing distraction of that one highly erotic scent.

But even that wasn't enough.

Driven by an almost frantic need, he unzipped Jessica's jeans. Shoving the denim aside he nuzzled his face against her silken undergarment, filling his nostrils with her fecund aroma. With each deep breath, his manhood lengthened and swelled. This was the scent that drove a man to rut.

Leaning over his shoulder, Jessica yanked his shirttails free. Tenderly she stroked the muscles of his back before raking her nails across his flesh.

Gideon groaned aloud, the pain she inflicted far more arousing than the gentler caress.

"Undress me," Jessica rasped, her voice little more than a breathy whisper. "I know we're outside but…" Mewling softly, she left the thought unfinished.

Impatiently Gideon removed first one, then the other sneaker. Finished with that, he pulled off her jeans and panties. Next he removed her sweater and T-shirt, as well as the lacy undergarment that bound her breasts, the name of which eluded him.

Still on his knees, Gideon appraised Jessica's nude body from head to foot as she stood before him. Her breasts—gorgeously flushed with passion—were a sight to behold. But it was the auburn nest between her legs that garnered his undivided attention. Purposefully he placed a thumb on either side of her sex. Pushing the outer petals up and out, he exposed every lush inch of her. Barely able to pull air into his lungs, he gazed upon the glistening, velvety folds, certain he'd never beheld a more potently carnal sight.

Holding her open, he dredged his tongue through her moist folds, greedily lapping at her tangy juices. When he found her hidden nubbin, he suckled it. As Jessica began to buck and writhe, he grabbed hold of a rounded buttock and held her in place.

Determined to leave his mark on her, Gideon kept at it until he had her wet and ready. Only then did he pull away from her.

"Please, Gideon…don't stop. I'm so close."

"As am I," he muttered, tugging at his zipper. He shoved the denim fabric off his hips, unwilling to take the time to shuck the garment completely. With his right hand, he palmed his testicles. From the tight feel of them, he knew it would be a hard, fast ride. "Lay down in front of me."

Jessica did as bidden, taking the unasked measure of spreading her legs wide open, the sight of which was more than he could handle. Without preamble, Gideon angled his hips between her legs and thrust himself to the hilt. Relentless, he pushed as hard and deep as he could. Over and over.

How long he kept at it, he had no idea.

Suddenly, Jessica clutched his upper arms, her fingers digging into his biceps. "I love you, Gideon."

Hearing that, his breath caught in his throat…*she loves me.*

As if Jessica had uttered some magical incantation, Gideon's rabid lust ameliorated, becoming a different impulse all together. Gone was the anguish, the fury, the grief. Gone the frantic need to satisfy a primal, bodily urge. In that instant, he became aware of the color of Jessica's eyes, the texture of her skin, the feel of her warm breath fluttering across his face.

And with that awareness came deliverance, their lovemaking a reaffirmation of life's creative potential. Vital. Powerful. Uplifting.

Awestruck, he saw, heard, and felt Jessica reach her climax. No sooner did her orgasm end than his began, the seed sapped from his body in one long, cathartic burst of pure ecstasy.

In love's aftermath, Gideon watched, spellbound, as Jessica's hazel-colored eyes turned a verdant shade of green—just one of the "bits and pieces" of Sarah that lived on in this extraordinary woman.

Love. Reincarnation. Eternity. As he continued to gaze into Jessica's eyes, each word took on a heightened meaning.

"I love you, Jessica Reardon," Gideon avowed in a reverent voice. "Forever and a day."

His lady love smoothed a hand over his flushed cheek. "Not even death can separate us."

"'Then was a time of joy and love. And now the time returns again,'" he whispered, quoting from his favorite poet. Made whole by their union, Gideon pressed his forehead to Jessica's and closed his eyes, the pain finally gone.

* * *

Staring at the orange flames that hissed and sparked in the living room fireplace, Richard Bragg forcefully jabbed the iron poker against a glowing log.

For the last four weeks, he'd constantly obsessed over how he would punish Jessica for her defiance. Her disobedience. For the loss of prestige that he'd suffered at her hand. For the laying to waste of all his dreams and aspirations. But most of all, for her betrayal of their wedding vows, having caught her red-handed in a flagrant act of infidelity.

And while thoughts of retribution had somewhat diminished the burning pain in his heart, they did nothing to alleviate the all-consuming desire for revenge.

Sweet, life-affirming revenge.

To that end, he'd spent the last month plotting. Planning. Meticulously reviewing how he would punish his whore of a wife, not about to leave a single detail to chance.

Needing to vent his fury, Richard snatched his Smartphone out of his trouser pocket. After making certain that he blocked his number, he placed the call. Bounced to voicemail, he ground his teeth as he listened to Jessica's recorded message.

With growing impatience, he waited for the prompt before he hissed "Bitch!" in a lowered tone of voice.

Enraged that his wife refused to answer the phone, Richard yanked off his wedding band. On the verge of hurling it into the flames, he instead clutched it tightly in his hand, unable to follow through on the impulse.

Shoving the ring back onto his finger, he marched out of the living room and made his way to the master bedroom. In dire need of a cleansing purgative, he threw open the closet door and grabbed an armful of Jessica's clothing, including his favorite green silk evening gown, roughly yanking the garments off of the clothing rod. His arms laden, he strode back to the living room and shoved his booty into the roaring fire.

As he watched the flames rapaciously consume the bundle, Richard envisioned his wife wearing the green silk dress. He then imagined that he could hear her agonized screams for mercy as her flesh seared on the bone. He smiled, the vision filling him with a deep sense of calm purpose.

Soon, Jessica. Very soon.

Chapter 26

There it is," Jessica murmured as she reached for the canister in the back of the kitchen cupboard. "Enriched white flour," she read aloud from the label. "All right. On with the show."

Never having made biscuits from scratch, she was using a recipe she'd found in an old cookbook. While fairly adept in the kitchen, baking wasn't her forte. To date, she had yet to bake a cake that hadn't collapsed in the middle. Hopefully, she'd fare better with buttermilk biscuits.

As she measured and stirred, Jessica reflected on the earlier turning point with Gideon. They'd weathered a tough storm. But together they'd gotten through it. To her mind, there could be no greater testament to their love. And she did love Gideon. Not only was he was her lover, he was also her companion, her partner, and her lifetime mate. Just thinking about the two of them growing old together put a smile on her face. After the tragedy that had befallen them in the nineteenth century, they certainly deserved a little happily ever after.

Removing the large ball of dough from the mixing bowl, Jessica placed it onto the floured countertop and rolled it out. She didn't have a biscuit cutter so she used an empty tin can to cut a dozen biscuits, which she arranged on a baking sheet before popping them in the oven. If all went according to plan, in a few minutes' time, twelve flaky biscuits would be coming out of that same oven door. Along with the biscuits, she was serving a chicken and veggie stir-fry, watercress salad, and homemade, jasmine-coconut ice cream for dessert. Fusion cuisine, her specialty.

As she hummed along to Adele's "Set Fire to the Rain," Jessica carried china plates, cloth napkins, and flatware to the dining room and set the table. Because she wanted everything picture perfect for what might well prove the most important dinner of her life, she lit the two candles that she'd earlier set in crystal holders. Sometime during the meal, she planned to tell Gideon that she was pregnant with his child. Special occasion, indeed.

Suddenly hearing the tinny peal of the oven timer, Jessica rushed back to the kitchen. A few seconds later, potholder in hand, she opened the oven door.

"Oh, God," she groaned at seeing the twelve rock-like objects.

As if on cue, Gideon stepped into the kitchen. "Are those biscuits I smell?"

"Um, not exactly," she hedged, mortified by her baking disaster.

Undeterred by her less than enthusiastic reply, Gideon snagged a biscuit from the hot tray. "There is nothing I enjoy more than a biscuit right out of the oven," he informed her, just before he raised it to his mouth.

Grabbing hold of his wrist, Jessica said, "That might not be such a wise idea. You don't have dental insurance."

With an amused chuckle, he took a large, hearty bite.

As he chewed, a strange look crept into Gideon's eyes. When he made a gagging sound, Jessica hurriedly grabbed a glass and filled it with water. Handing it to him, she watched as he swished a mouthful before swallowing. Wordlessly, he placed the remainder of his half-eaten biscuit back on the tray.

"That bad, huh?"

"I have tasted worse," he diplomatically replied, too much of a gentleman to come right out and say it—her biscuits were god-awful.

"Believe it or not, I actually used a recipe," she told him.

"I will be only too happy to share Beulah's biscuit recipe with you." Stepping over to the cupboard, Gideon proceeded to remove the very ingredients that Jessica had put away minutes earlier.

"And who, may I ask, is Beulah?"

"Beulah was the cook at Highland House when I was a young boy," Gideon said over his shoulder as he removed a quart of buttermilk from the refrigerator. "Back in those days, the kitchen was separate from the house. And in the winter months, there was no place warmer than Beulah's kitchen."

Grabbing the baking tray, Jessica unceremoniously dumped the remaining eleven and a half biscuits into the trash can. "Let's just pretend that first tray of biscuits never happened."

As he measured out the flour, Gideon shot her a sideways glance. "To which biscuits are you referring, madam?"

"I knew I had a reason for loving you." Jessica said warmly, rewarding him with a loud, smacking kiss on the cheek.

With a courtly sweep of the arm, Gideon handed her a mixing spoon before motioning her to the counter. "Only the one reason?"

"There are a few other reasons, but in the interest of getting dinner on the table in a timely manner, I think it best if I wait until after biscuit-making class to reveal them," she teased. "And just so you know, I intend to do you and Beulah proud."

A tender smile animated Gideon's handsome features. "I

would certainly hope so, as I can't have a wife who doesn't know
how to make a proper batch of biscuits."

Surprised that he'd just broached the "W" word, Jessica said,
"I thought we'd agreed that we'd live together first before we,
um, take the relationship to the, you know, next level."

Gideon took hold of both her hands. "While others may be
content to live together, I hail from a century when a man and a
woman first committed themselves in marriage. Only then did
they live together." Raising her right hand to his lips, he pressed
a warm kiss in the center of her palm. "You will make me a very
happy man if you would do me the honor of becoming my wife . . .
yet again."

At a sudden loss for words, Jessica worriedly gnawed on her
lower lip. More than anything, she wanted to marry Gideon
again. But before that could happen, she had to first make an
unpleasant confession.

"For a woman so full of good cheer, you've become noticeably
quiet."

"There's something that I, um, have to tell you," she nervously
sputtered. "First of all, I need to apologize because I should've
told you sooner, but . . . well, the truth of the matter is that I'm a
divorced woman. Or at least I will be in a few days' time."

Gideon shook his head, clearly stupefied. "I beg your pardon?"

Hoping she had the inner fortitude to get through the next
few minutes, Jessica reluctantly elaborated. "I was married for
seven years to a man named Richard Bragg. Because he ill-treated
me, I left him and filed for a divorce. Which should be finalized
sometime next—"

"Do you actually mean to tell me that you're still married to
this man?" Gideon thundered, his eyes darkening to a stormy
shade of blue.

"Uh-huh," Jessica admitted with a shaky nod, forcing herself to meet his gaze. "Although for the last seven months, I've been legally separated from my *soon-to-be* ex-husband," she said with added emphasis, hoping to mitigate the damage. "And, you should be happy to know, according to my lawyer, the final divorce decree will be issued any day now."

"It matters not," Gideon retorted. "You've already made an adulterer of me. A fact for which I am not the least bit happy. Why in God's name didn't you tell me before now?"

"Lest you forget, you weren't so forthcoming about your own marital status," she pointed out in a snarky tone of voice, hoping to knock him off his sanctimonious high horse.

"Ah, but the difference is that I am a widower. Your widowed husband, to be precise." Gideon paused a moment, his lips twisting in a mocking sneer. "Or was your fantastical tale about reincarnation also a deception?"

"How dare you insinuate that I lied to you!"

Realizing, too late, that her ire had gotten the better of her, Jessica took a calming breath. The situation had all too quickly escalated to the point where, in the heat of anger, someone could very well say something he or she would later regret.

"I wanted to tell you about my first marriage," she continued, taking a more conciliatory tone. "But, in all honesty, I was terrified of how you'd react."

"That doesn't excuse your lamentable lapse."

Immediately retracting the olive branch, Jessica folded her arms over her chest. "You want the straight scoop? Here it is. I didn't tell you about my divorce because you're a Victorian prude," she lashed out at him. "In fact, I'm surprised you didn't wag your finger and accuse me of being a fallen woman."

"Damn you, Jessica."

"Right back at you, Gideon."

Spinning on her heel, Jessica turned her back on him. To stop her hands from shaking, she gripped the counter top. As she stood there, desperately trying to get a grip on her runaway emotions, several stray tears trailed down her flushed cheeks and plopped into the flour bowl.

God knows, she'd had every intention of telling Gideon about her marriage to Richard. She'd simply been waiting for the right moment to present itself. Obviously, she waited too long. And because of that, she was now in so deep that she didn't know if she could dig her way out.

Wiping her tears on her shirt sleeve, Jessica turned back around. "When you first came to live at Highland House, it seemed like an irrelevant omission. I thought, 'Why should I tell him I'm getting divorced? It's none of his business.' But then… we grew closer and…and I was afraid you'd think less of me," she hesitantly confessed.

"I admit that being a divorced woman does not raise you in my estimation."

"Well it should," she snapped, Gideon's stodgy proclamation making her livid. "If I hadn't walked out on my husband, I would never have ended up at Highland House. And without Highland House, it's doubtful that you and I would have ever met. This house is the conduit that brought us together across the boundary of time. In other words, my divorce happened for a reason."

"But you didn't know that when you originally broke your marriage vows, did you?" he goaded. "Now if you will excuse me, I seem to have lost my appetite."

"Oh, that's rich," she sniggered, refusing to let him sidestep around her. "Since the dawn of time, men have fled to their caves at the first sign of emotional duress. My guess is that it has something to do with having a penis."

Gideon's eyes opened wide, the man obviously shocked. "In my day, a woman would never speak so brazenly."

"Just get over your bad self, will ya? In this day and age, a woman can say anything she damn well pleases."

"Given your shrewish tongue, I suspect your husband was mightily relieved when you—" Without warning, Gideon groaned in pain as he reached up and clutched his head with both hands.

Oh my God. Draygan is back.

Her ire instantly forgotten, Jessica grasped hold of Gideon's forearm. "Are you having a spell?"

"Leave me be, woman." It was the last thing Gideon said before he stormed out of the kitchen.

Jessica stood rooted in place as she watched him leave, concern and bitter regret bombarding her in equal measure.

Suddenly feeling a queasy roil in her belly, she lurched toward the sink and promptly vomited a mouthful of stomach acid. As she splashed cool water onto her face, Jessica heard Gideon stomp up the staircase.

Moments later, he stomped back down the stairs…and right out the front door.

Hearing the resounding echo of that slammed door, Jessica experienced a *déjà vu* moment, recalling with perfect clarity Gideon's angry departure from Highland House. Almost one hundred and fifty-one years ago to the day.

Chapter 27

May God damn him for being a dunderheaded fool. And an overly proud one at that.

Outraged over Jessica's revelation regarding her previous marriage, Gideon had donned his Confederate tunic, armed himself with his revolver and saber, and departed from Highland House. Since he could not do battle with Jessica's first husband, Richard Bragg, he would instead do battle with the infernal beast Draygan.

His heart now heavy because of the acrimonious exchange with Jessica, Gideon tugged on the reins, setting Blaze on a northwesterly course toward the stand of white pine known as Archibald's Wood. The land was named after his grandfather who, taken with the magnificent wooded tract, had refused to put it to the ax. On one memorable occasion, he'd overheard his grandfather remark that the tiered pine branches resembled an oriental pagoda, an accurate if somewhat whimsical observation for so staid a Scotsman.

Entering the ancient grove, Gideon veered toward the abandoned saltpeter mine located near Devil Run's Creek. Overhead, a ponderous full moon illuminated the woodland.

His teeth chattering together, Gideon braced himself against the biting cold. The day, which had dawned so balmy, had turned decidedly wintry, making him think that the plummeting temperature was a punishment of sorts.

Have I learned nothing from the travails of my life?

Since Sarah's death, he'd suffered many a sleepless night, guilt-ridden that he'd callously abandoned her. Yet, once again, he'd reacted in like manner, turning his back on the woman he loved.

Full of shameful remorse, he recalled that last heated argument with Sarah, an argument that had ironically occurred nearly one hundred and fifty-one years ago to the day. As always, the memory was a bitter reminder of how he'd failed his wife. And because Sarah died soon thereafter, he'd never been able to beg her forgiveness.

In similar fashion, he'd earlier betrayed the love that he bore for Jessica, having succumbed to a heated jealousy when he learned that she'd been previously wed. Although, as Jessica had adroitly pointed out to him, leaving her cad of a husband had been the impetus for her purchase of Highland House. If that was true, should he not then be relieved, elated even, that she'd dissolved her marital union? Anything that transpired before his fantastical journey across the boundaries of time should not matter.

A conclusion he wished that he'd arrived at much sooner.

While Gideon wanted nothing more than to return to Highland House and make amends for his loutish behavior, he knew that, in order to truly live life to the fullest in this new century, he had to rid himself of the beast who took such delight in bedeviling him at every turn. If he wanted to carve a place for himself in these hills and mountains that he loved so well, Draygan must be destroyed. Gideon did not intend to live another day in the infernal creature's dark shadow.

Splashing across the swift-running creek, Gideon and his mount started up the first of several switchbacks that led to the abandoned saltpeter mine. As he made his way through a stand of hemlock and red spruce, he heard a high-pitched keen that sounded like the death lament of bereaved women mourning their slain kinsmen. Spooked by the unnatural sound, Blaze nickered softly.

Moments later, the foreboding air intensified when the moon, now hidden behind a veil of clouds, cast a strange blue light onto the landscape.

Gideon reached into his vest pocket and removed his watch. Thumbing it open, he noted that it was twelve o'clock. *The witching hour.*

Nearing the entrance to the mine, he removed a flameless torch, what Jessica called "a flashlight," from his saddlebag. Shining a golden beam of light, he spied several conspicuously broken tree limbs, evidence that someone, or something, had recently traversed this same trail. Reining Blaze to a halt, he dismounted so that he could better examine the broken limbs. Directly beneath them, he discovered a cluster of animal prints which had clearly been made by a beast that had large, clawed feet.

Just then, Blaze began to skittishly paw at the ground.

"Don't worry. You can stay put," he assured the horse as he looped the reins around a low-hanging tree limb.

Flashlight in hand, Gideon proceeded on foot. Pushing aside a dried cluster of prickly pear, he discovered the entrance to Hell's Hole. As he perused the opening to the mine, he noticed that there was a gnarled grapevine spanning the gaping entryway, to which a sturdy length of rope had been tied. Since the hemp "ladder" appeared to be the only way to reach the cave below, he tucked the flashlight into his vest, enabling him to grab hold of the rope with both hands as he made his descent.

When his booted feet finally touched solid ground—some fifty feet below where he'd started—Gideon found himself standing in a chamber of monumental proportions. Massive stalagmites formed columns that put him in mind of an ancient underground ruin. From this central nave, there were several corridors, each leading in a different direction. Hearing a faint gurgle, he aimed the flashlight toward the far side of the chamber where a stream of water cascaded over a large limestone slab.

Awestruck, he turned full circle, mesmerized by the cavern's majestic, roughhewn beauty.

Only belatedly did it occur to him that his chances of scaling up the rope to the cave entrance were slim to nil.

"Oh, Jessica," he murmured bleakly as he stared at the dangling length of rope. "What have I done?"

No sooner had he posed the question than the answer hit Gideon like a well-aimed Minié ball—he'd let his obsession with Draygan take precedence over all else. Just as he'd let his obsession with duty drive a wedge between him and Sarah.

Am I doomed to repeat the same mistake over and over again?

He'd been given a second chance, yet once more he'd failed to make love his first, his only, priority. Love was not something to be brought out on special occasions, like a piece of fine china. Love was the embodiment of all that he felt for Jessica, all that he'd felt for Sarah, and it was to be cherished, each and every day. He'd learned in the most painful way imaginable that this world was a lonely place without the woman he loved by his side.

Lost in his sad musings, Gideon was taken aback when the scene around him suddenly began to shimmer and undulate, before everything within visual range fragmented, the broken pieces weirdly shifting as they condensed into a blue pinprick of light. The pinprick exploded with a brightness so intense that Gideon had to shield his eyes with his coat sleeve.

When he finally lowered his arm, he stared in bewilderment at the scene before him, wondering if he'd taken leave of his senses as he gazed upon the smoldering remains of what had once been the barn at Highland House. The scene was so real that he could smell burnt wood, even as he tasted ash in his mouth.

To his horror, Gideon belatedly realized that he was peering at Sarah's funeral pyre.

Propelled into action, he rushed toward the fiery debris. "Sarah!" he hollered, the full-throated bellow catching on a ragged sob.

The cry was answered by the harsh caw of a raven, one of a quartet that ominously circled overhead.

Caught in the throes of a painful heartache, Gideon closed his eyes to block out the ghastly scene, certain that Draygan had conjured the gruesome illusion. Although to what end, he could not fathom.

"Damn the beast," he hissed, inundated with a grief so potent that his heart muscle painfully tightened. Had he stayed at Highland House, he could have saved Sarah from—

Suddenly hearing a high-pitched cackle, Gideon opened his eyes. Although his vision was blurred by tears, he saw a shimmering, diaphanous specter, immediately recognizing it as the ghostly image of Oren Tolliver.

A burning rage instantly welled within him. "What in God's name is going on?" he hoarsely muttered. "What manner of trickery is this?"

"You couldn't save her then. And you can't save her now," the apparition taunted, its pale lips twisted in a malevolent sneer. "Because she belongs to me, I will take her away from you each and every time."

"You bastard!"

Gideon lurched toward the ghostly image, but it immediately faded into a fuzzy blur that soon vanished into thin air. Within seconds of the apparition's departure, the entire scene fractured into myriad pieces, much like a shattered mirror. Those pieces, in turn, compressed into a tiny prism of blue light.

As before, the blue light exploded. Gideon shielded his eyes with his forearm.

When he lowered his arm a few moments later, he was again standing in the middle of the darkened subterranean cavern.

Shaken by the vision, Gideon staggered toward the nearest corridor, determined to find his quarry, finish what he'd set out to do, then return to Jessica. Come hell or high water. And given his present location—somewhere deep in the bowels of the earth—he might very well have to brave the former rather than the latter.

Ignoring the endless mounds of bat droppings, he continued along the passageway. As he neared the end of the corridor, he began to feel a dull throb in each of his temples. A dull throb that turned into an acute burst of pain as he entered a large chamber, this one housing a dark pool of still water.

Draygan is near.

Shining the flashlight across the chamber, Gideon discovered the skeletal remains of half a dozen men, all of whom still held their weapons—repeating rifles, muskets, and a bow and arrow in the case of one skeleton—in an eternal death grip.

Had they, like him, come to slay the beast?

Gideon had no time to ponder the question, suddenly hearing

an ominous rumble that emanated from a corridor on the far side of the chamber. Beneath his booted feet, the ground began to vibrate as dust motes and other loose debris fell from the lime-stone ceiling. Shifting the flashlight to his left hand, Gideon unholstered his Colt pistol. Despite the unbearable pain in his head, he held his weapon steady as he aimed it at the passageway opposite.

Just then, Draygan entered the chamber.

Its red eyes gleaming, the beast came to a shuddering halt as it took Gideon's measure. A mammoth, winged chimera, it stood nearly ten feet in height with a leathery, gray hide. An abomination if ever there was, it looked as though it had been conceived in the fiery pits of hell.

"I am Gideon MacAllister...and I have come to kill you," he announced, wincing from the burst of pain that ricocheted from one temple to the other.

His announcement made little impression on Draygan, and the beast stared at him with eyes that eerily glowed in the dim light cast by the flashlight. In that chilling moment, he realized that his nemesis was a mythical creature whose very existence disproved the laws of science and defied the dictates of enlightened reason.

Able to hear Draygan's sonorous voice inside his head, Gideon flinched as he listened to the oft-spoken words, "Evil will descend upon the land of the Greenbrier. The red man cometh. Those in high places will perish in the flames of hell. So sayeth the Beast."

"Damn you and your nonsensical utterances," Gideon hissed between clenched teeth. Bracing his legs, he leveled his weapon and took aim, intending to fire a silver bullet straight into the dragon's heart.

In the next instant, Gideon pulled the trigger, horrified to hear an impotent *click* echoing off the walls of the stone sanctuary, the bullet having jammed in the chamber.

Cursing under his breath, Gideon flung the useless revolver aside before he unsheathed his cavalry saber. If this was how it was to end, so be it. He'd looked death in the face innumerable times on countless battlefields. As on those brutal occasions, he was filled with an insatiable bloodlust. An unholy desire to kill or be killed.

Draygan, staring at him with a preternatural awareness, suddenly extended his wings as he lumbered forward. Acting purely on instinct, Gideon raised his saber and swung it toward the beast's neck, intending to decapitate his enemy.

Draygan is only a reflection of you. What you do unto Draygan, you do unto yourself.

As though he'd just plucked those words from the ether, Mother Maebelle's cryptic warning from several weeks prior came to Gideon in a flash.

Not giving himself time to think, Gideon suddenly pivoted on his heel, purposefully striking a large boulder just to the right of Draygan. The sword blade snapped in two, orange sparks flying through the air. No sooner did the broken blade hit the pitted floor of the chamber than Gideon was blindsided with an excruciating burst of pain. No different than if he'd been shot in the head point-blank.

But that pain in no way compared to the agony he suffered when Draygan opened his mouth and struck him with a fiery burst, the red-hot flame hitting Gideon in the center of his chest. A scalding blast, it lifted him off his feet and sent him hurling through the air.

As he slipped into what he feared would be an eternal sleep,

Gideon yearned to tell Jessica how much he loved her. *Forever and a day.*

That was Gideon's last thought before his world turned dark, the beast having won the bout.

* * *

"Come back to me, Gideon…come back to me," Jessica murmured anxiously as she stepped onto the back stoop.

On most days, she took an unabashed delight in the awesome view, but today she only saw the bare, leafless trees that dotted the desolate landscape. Like so many stark effigies.

Gideon had been gone all night. Unable to sleep, Jessica had tossed and turned as she'd listened for him to walk through the front door. Several hours before dawn, she'd finally fallen asleep, only to wake up with the sunrise and discover that five inches of snow had fallen. Old Man Winter had arrived with a bone-chilling abruptness.

What if Gideon left the house without a coat? He could be stranded somewhere, suffering from frostbite or hypothermia.

Beset with fearful thoughts, Jessica once again scanned the horizon, hoping to see a speck of movement on the snow-covered hills. With the exception of the four black ravens that circled overhead, it was as though that part of the world had come to a complete standstill. Frozen in time.

Having waited as long as she could, Jessica removed her Smart-phone from the back pocket of her cargo pants. Although it was early to be calling someone, especially on a Saturday morning, this was an emergency situation.

"I'm sorry that I woke you," she apologetically blurted when a noticeably sleepy voice answered the phone.

"What's the matter?" Darlene Malone demanded, suddenly sounding exceptionally alert.

"It's Gideon...He's been gone all night, and I'm worried to death about him."

"The two of you had a little tiff, huh?"

"Calling you is like phoning The Psychic Hotline," Jessica muttered. "Although there was nothing 'little' about it. In fact, we had a humdinger of an argument. After which, Gideon stormed out of the house, saddled Blaze, and took off for God knows where."

"I'm sorry to hear that, honey. But if it's any consolation, the makeup sex will probably be incredible." The other woman laughed, the hearty sound temporarily lifting Jessica's spirits. "How about I call J.W. and send him out to search for Gideon?"

"And how about I thank you from the bottom of my heart?" Jessica gushed. "While I'm not altogether certain, I've got a sneaking suspicion that Gideon may have ridden out to Hell's Hole."

There was a noticeable pause on the other end of the line.

"You don't think he went looking for Draygan's lair, do you?" Darlene said at last.

"Maybe...I'm not sure. A few weeks ago, he expressed an interest in finding Draygan, but—" Jessica stopped in mid-stream, too overwrought to continue. If there really was a dragon out there, Gideon could be in an enormous amount of danger.

"Don't worry, honey," Darlene said in a soothing tone of voice. "We're gonna find him."

"Please make it sooner rather than later." Again, Jessica scanned the horizon, hoping to see an approaching horse and rider.

"Gideon will come riding down that mountain soon enough,"

Darlene stated matter-of-factly, having correctly intuited the direction of Jessica's gaze. "So I suggest you go inside, put on a pot of coffee, then get busy knitting some baby booties."

"First of all, I don't know how to knit. And secondly, how the heck did you know I was standing outside?"

"How do I know anything?" came the enigmatic reply. "And by my count, you've got eight months to learn how to knit one, purl two."

"On that note, I'm hanging up," Jessica grumbled, not in the mood to make coffee, let alone teach herself how to knit. "And Darlene...thank you. You're a true friend."

Relieved that J.W. would search for Gideon, Jessica hit the disconnect button and slipped the phone into her back pocket. Then, forcing herself to put one snow boot in front of the other, she headed for the carriage house. Fretting over Gideon's absence wouldn't bring him home any sooner so she decided to tend to the morning chores—feeding the birds, shoveling the snow off the back steps, forking some hay into Blaze's shed—anything to occupy her time and alleviate her troubled thoughts.

Opening the set of double doors on the front of the carriage house, Jessica stepped inside. Propped in the far corner were the snow shovel and a large bag of rock salt. After loading both items into a wheelbarrow, she trudged back through the snow toward the back stoop. There she ripped open the bag of rock salt, picked up the shovel, and began to clear the snow from the top step.

Several minutes later, she was halfway through shoveling a path between the stoop and the carriage house when she heard a vehicle pull into the front driveway.

Hallelujah! That must be J.W. dropping off Gideon.

"I'm back here," she called out, anxiously smoothing a hand over her cable-knit sweater and readjusting her wool cap.

Hearing a footfall, she turned around with a welcoming smile on her face—a smile that instantly fell flat.

Oh, God. Jessica's stomach queasily lurched at finding herself face to face with her estranged husband, Richard Bragg.

"Richard…Wh-what are you d-doing here?" she stammered.

His thin lips twisted into a nasty sneer. "I would think that's obvious. I've come to claim what's mine."

Chapter 28

Sarah slowly approached him. With an almost funerary air hovering about her person, she raised an ornately carved picture case. Gideon immediately recognized the hinged frame—it was the same one that contained the daguerreotype they'd sat for on their wedding day. He'd had the case specially crafted and delivered all the way from Richmond.

Gazing directly at him, Sarah unlatched the case and held the two opened halves in front of her chest. But this case did not contain their wedding portrait. Instead, it contained a curious pictogram of an upright triangle encircled by an Ouroboros, a dragon biting its own tail.

"Your end is your beginning," Sarah whispered as she raised the case and offered it to him. "As is mine. But only if you return to me. This is the day, the only day, that you can ever relive. For this is the day of atonement."

Gideon took the proffered case. The seconds silently slipped past as he tried to decipher the meaning of the pictogram, certain that it contained a hidden message of great import.

"*Please tell me what it means,*" he pleaded, his gaze riveted by the upright triangle contained within the Ouroboros.

"*The answer lies within your own heart.*"

Startled, Gideon glanced up, taken aback to see that it was Jessica Reardon who now stood before him. He craned his neck from side to side…but Sarah was nowhere in sight.

And then he remembered—Sarah and Jessica were one and the same.

Gideon shook his head, still baffled by the pictogram's cryptic symbols. "*The only thing contained within my heart is my undying love for you.*"

"*Then act on that love, Gideon. Let love be your guide.*"

"*I will. Just as soon as I find the beast known as Draygan. I have taken a vow to slay the—*"

Jessica placed a hand over his mouth, silencing him. "*Draygan is the conduit, the portal between worlds. Only a chosen few are given the chance to live again. I beg you not to squander Draygan's gift.*"

"*Ha! A fine gift I've been given, when the beast bedevils me at every turn,*" Gideon scoffed, angered that she would come to the creature's defense. "*I will slay the dragon; after which, we shall live ever more in love's light.*"

"*Do that and we will once again live in death's shadow,*" Jessica replied.

Her pronouncement filled Gideon with a dark foreboding. He'd lived in death's shadow once before—when Sarah died—and he did not think he could withstand such torment a second time.

"*Then tell me what I must do to safeguard our love,*" he entreated, willing to do whatever was necessary to keep their love alive.

"*All you have to do is come back to me, Gideon…simply come back to me,*" Jessica murmured before she turned and walked away.

"Please don't go," he implored, lunging forward to grab hold of her arm.

But he was too late. She had already vanished into thin air.

* * *

Gideon awoke with a start, gasping for air.

To his surprise, he found himself reposed beneath a sturdy pine tree, covered in a thick mantle of newly fallen snow. He peered at the tree that hovered above him, the branches drooping with the weight of their wintry burden. A few seconds later, as he roused himself from what had been a deep, enchanted sleep, a light breeze rattled the sturdy pine and sent a limb's worth of snowflakes wafting to earth, dusting his face.

Baffled as to what he was doing there, Gideon lurched to his feet. He surveyed his surroundings with his hands on his hips, noting that the snow-clad hillside was as still and quiet as a grave.

Which was precisely where he thought he'd find himself on this snowy morn, certain that he'd met his demise. Certain that he had joined those other lost souls whose skeletal remains littered Draygan's lair. While he could not recall in any great detail his encounter with Draygan—as most soldiers cannot recall the minutiae of a battle just fought—he did have a clear recollection of the beast exhaling a fiery blast, inflicting a wound of excruciating pain. At the time, it'd felt like the dragon had ripped his still-beating heart from his chest.

Curiously enough, this morning he suffered no pain whatsoever.

If the near-deadly encounter in the cave really did occur, how had he come to be sleeping beneath a pine tree that was situated at least a mile away from Hell's Hole? Even more puzzling, his horse Blaze was tethered to a nearby branch.

As he turned full circle to get his bearings, Gideon noticed his cavalry saber sticking upright in the snow not far from where he stood. Frowning, he stomped over to retrieve it.

"How can this be?" he murmured as he grasped the hilt and pulled the saber out of the ground.

Raising the completely intact weapon, he closely examined it. The sword shone as though newly forged, yet he distinctly remembered the blade breaking in two when he'd swung it against the stone wall of the cave.

Had it been nothing more than a dream?

Bewildered, Gideon slid the saber into the scabbard belted around his waist. That was when he noticed that the front of his uniform tunic was scorched with a black circle.

So it did happen. He did enter the cave, and he did meet Draygan in mortal combat. Moreover, he'd survived to tell the tale. But to what end?

Anxious to return home to Highland House so that he could sort through the curious conundrum, Gideon untied his horse's reins from the pine tree. As he did so, he noticed a strange marking incised into the bark of the tree trunk—an upright triangle encircled by a dragon biting its own tail. *An Ouroboros*, the same symbol that he'd been shown in his dream. The same symbol that he'd also seen in the vision given to him by Mother Maebelle four weeks ago.

"Who went to the trouble of carving this where I'd be sure to see it?" he wondered aloud as he fingered the marking. Unless he was greatly mistaken, an upright triangle was the alchemical symbol for fire.

Those in high places will perish in the flames of hell.

As Gideon pondered the meaning of the carved symbol, he suddenly wondered if there was a connection between the pictogram and the unintelligible message that Draygan continually tried to communicate to him. Was it possible that "high places" was a veiled reference to Highland House? Or more specifically, a reference to Sarah's tragic death in the fire that had occurred at Highland House one hundred and fifty-one years ago to the day?

That it was the anniversary of her death took Gideon by surprise. In his dream, Sarah had told him that this was the day—indeed, the only day—that he could ever relive.

But how could anyone relive a day that had come and gone fifteen decades ago?

And what did the Ouroboros have to do with Sarah's death? He knew the ancient symbol of a dragon biting its tail represented eternity and—

—*the repeating nature of life*, he realized with a start.

In that instant, it suddenly dawned on him that both the pictogram and Draygan's cryptic message could be a dire warning that another fire would occur at Highland House. Except this time, it would be Jessica, not Sarah, who would meet a fiery death at the hands of the "red man."

"No," he croaked, assailed with a deep, visceral pain. Tears stinging his eyes, Gideon feared that he might be too late. He'd been gone all night—plenty of time for disaster to have struck.

Estimating that he was a good thirty-minute ride from the house, Gideon hefted himself into the saddle, chastising himself for having left Highland House in the first place. All he wanted, all he'd ever wanted, was to spend his life with the woman he loved. And had loved for so many lifetimes. *Forever and a day.*

But this time he would not take forever in vain. If God would only grant him a second chance, this time, he would put love above all else.

* * *

Still in a state of shock, Jessica stared at her estranged husband. As she did, she took note of the perfectly pressed chinos, Maine duck boots, white button-down shirt, and walnut-brown barn jacket. Not a red hair out of place.

Lips turned down at one corner, Richard, in turn, gave Jessica a perfunctory appraisal, his gaze traveling the length of her body before resettling on her face. "You've changed. And for the worse, I see."

Although Jessica would never admit it, the snide remark hurt. But then, Richard had always been skillfully adept at emotionally hitting below the belt.

"Wh-what are you d-doing here?" she stammered. All of her old hang-ups, all of her old fears, were instantly resurrected. "You're not welcome here."

"Are you deaf?" he sneered. "I told you already...I've come to claim what's mine."

The put-down that prefaced his pronouncement made Jessica painfully recall how, for seven long years, Richard had turned her life into a dysfunctional hell. During the course of their marriage, he'd repeatedly demeaned her, always managing to find fault.

But I don't have to take it anymore, she told herself. Richard could only hurt her if she ceded him the power to do so.

"You're here because of the secret slush fund that I discovered in your desk drawer, aren't you," she stated without fanfare, summoning the courage to look him directly in the eye. "Granted, I didn't take time to count, but I'm guestimating that you had a few million dollars stashed away."

"Who have you told about the money?" Richard demanded, a harsh cast to his features.

"I've told no one. And just so you know, I don't care how you acquired your ill-gotten gains," she informed him. "My intention was never to expose you."

"Merely to steal from me, eh?"

"I was about to say that my only intention was to escape from you," she calmly replied, refusing to buckle under.

Richard's thin lips twisted into a nasty sneer. "But only after you helped yourself to a hundred and fifty thousand dollars of my money."

"If you've come looking for restitution, you're knocking at the wrong door. I've already spent the money." Pausing a moment, Jessica took a stabilizing breath, admittedly perplexed as to why he'd waited so long to make a stink about her divorce settlement. "After my parents died in the automobile accident, I gave you my entire $300,000 inheritance. The way I see it, I was entitled to half that amount." Money that she knew Richard would never voluntarily return to her of his own free will.

"While I came here for restitution, monetary recompense isn't what I'm after," he replied, punctuating the remark with an indifferent shrug.

Jessica stared at him, uncomprehending. "So what the hell are you doing here?"

"*Tsk tsk.* Such coarse language." Peering over his shoulder, Richard cast a disparaging glance at the house. "I take it that you used my money to buy this ramshackle wreck."

"Highland House belongs to me," Jessica retorted, pointing to her chest for emphasis. "The deed is in my name. And you can't have it."

Richard chortled softly, as if her assertion greatly amused him. "Again, you've jumped to an erroneous assumption."

"Then what exactly did you mean when you said that you've come here to claim what's yours?"

"We are still married, are we not?"

"In a manner of speaking," she conceded grudgingly. "But if you think for one instant that I would ever consider going back to you, then you're barking—"

"I will not let you sever our sacred marital bond."

Jessica felt her jaw slacken, bowled over by his arrogance. *What a schmuck.*

Given that Richard Bragg was a man of average height and slender build, Jessica wondered that she'd ever been intimidated by him in the first place. As she took his measure, she noticed all the small details which she'd long since put out of her mind—the well-groomed strawberry-blond hair; the thin, lifeless lips; the pale hands and skeletal fingers. To her surprise, she saw that he still wore his wedding ring.

"Our divorce is a done deal," she told him point-blank, unnerved by the sight of that gold band on his left hand.

"Word to the wise: while we don't always get what we want, we usually get what we deserve," Richard quietly intoned.

Still holding the snow shovel, Jessica tightened her grip on the handle, starting to get a very bad feeling in the pit of her stomach, an uneasy premonition that something was terribly awry.

Leaning the snow shovel against the wheelbarrow, she reached into her back pocket and removed her Smartphone. "I have the sheriff's office on speed dial," she announced as she held the mobile aloft. "If you don't vacate my property this instant, I won't hesitate to make the call."

No sooner had she issued the threat than the back of Richard's hand came flying in her direction, making contact with the right side of her face.

Momentarily stunned, Jessica staggered backward. Taking advantage of her disoriented state, Richard snatched the Smartphone out of her hand and hurled it across the yard, where the device disappeared from sight as it landed in several inches of soft snow.

"I trust that, from here on out, you'll be more cooperative." Licking his lips, Richard clenched and unclenched his fists.

Frightened by the sinister look in his eyes, Jessica wordlessly nodded.

"Now that the preliminaries have been dealt with, I want you to tell me where I can find him."

"F-find who?" she nervously sputtered. "I live alone."

"I won't tolerate your lies," Richard hissed. "I saw the bastard with my own eyes four weeks ago."

"Oh my God! You've been stalking me," she accused, the fear factor instantly spiking.

"I'm your husband. You belong to me." Richard paused a moment, treating her to a mirthless smile. "'Until death do we part.'"

In that instant, Jessica suddenly knew, with horrifying clarity, the true purpose of Richard's unexpected visit—he had come to Highland House to kill her.

"You'll never get away with it," she croaked on a serrated breath, brave words that belied her terror. As she backed away from him, she bumped into the side of the wheelbarrow and her hand landed in the plastic bag of rock salt. Without thinking about it she scooped up a handful.

Intent on taking him by surprise, she tossed a hefty amount of rock salt directly at him.

"Argh!" Richard screamed, his mouth agape as his hands spasmodically flailed at his face.

Seizing her chance, Jessica ran toward the house and scrambled up the back steps. She made a wild grab for the rail, but not before stumbling near the top and painfully banging a knee against the wooden stoop.

Her kneecap throbbing, she pushed the back door wide open and rushed inside the kitchen. She slammed the door closed and hooked the chain latch, then frantically scanned the kitchen. A weapon! She needed to get her hands on some kind of weapon.

Suddenly, at the other end of the house, she heard a loud clamor. With a fearful gasp, she realized that the front door had been left unlocked.

Choking back a sob, Jessica rushed toward the nearest kitchen drawer, nearly pulling it off the runner as she yanked it open. There was no time to be choosy—she grabbed the first knife her hand happened upon, never having been so terrified in all her life. As she heard Richard charge down the hall, her panic swelled to new heights. There would be no escape. This was where she'd have to make her last stand.

Just then, Richard rushed into the kitchen, his eyes rimmed in red, his hair and face glittering with rock salt. She was stunned to see that he'd taken the time to don gloves.

"It would appear that you're cornered," he snickered, managing to sound sinister despite his ridiculous appearance.

"Not quite." She raised the knife so that he could see it, the blade gleaming in the early morning light. "If you take another step, I will not hesitate to kill you."

Ignoring the warning, he took a step in her direction. "What happens if I take two steps? Will you kill me twice?"

Rattled by his smug condescension, Jessica's hands shook as though palsied, and her breathing became short and uneven. When he took yet another step in her direction, she gripped the knife in both hands and charged forward.

She stopped instantly when Richard pulled out a gun.

"I suggest you put down the knife; otherwise I'll be forced to pull the trigger. And in case you're wondering...I would dearly love to see a bullet rip through your body."

Having lost the bout before it even began, Jessica tossed the knife into the kitchen sink. Granted, she didn't know much about weapons, but a loaded gun most definitely trumped a plastic-handled paring knife. Her only recourse now was to play along with Richard and hope to God that she could find some means to disarm him.

As he stepped toward her, Richard's face suddenly contorted with a maniacal anger, a wrath unlike any Jessica had ever seen before. Following the direction of his narrowed gaze, she saw Gideon's blue plaid shirt hanging off the back of a ladder-back chair.

"You whore!" Richard exclaimed as he snatched hold of the shirt. Then, like an enraged bull, he charged toward her, thrusting the garment in her face. "Tell me his name."

With nowhere to run, Jessica cowered against the wall. "It's not what you think," she told him, desperately trying to think of an innocuous reason for why there would be a man's shirt hanging off of the kitchen chair. "He's my, um...my tenant. He pays me rent. That's all it is."

Richard flung the shirt to the floor. "You're nothing but a

bitch in heat," he snarled just before he smacked her again. The blow slammed Jessica's head against the kitchen wall. "Now tell me his damned name!"

Jessica stubbornly shook her head.

This time when the back of Richard's hand flew in her direction, Jessica feebly tried to parry the blow with her forearm.

Brutally seizing her by the wrist, Richard jerked her arm away from her face and smacked her once more, his open palm smashing her lips against her teeth. Groaning in pain, Jessica spat out a mouthful of blood, splattering red droplets on the green-checked kitchen tablecloth. Without giving her time to catch her breath, Richard yanked her cap from her head, grabbed a fistful of her hair, and dragged her out of the kitchen and down the hallway.

Now Jessica feared that Richard's intention was to completely break her spirit before he killed her. He'd practically foamed at the mouth when he struck her, clearly taking sadistic delight in inflicting pain.

I need to rile him into losing control of the situation, she thought desperately, not about to be led like a lamb to the slaughter. If she could force a fumble, she might then be able to finagle the gun from him.

When they reached the library, Richard glanced around the room with disgust. "It appears that your housekeeping has gotten a bit slipshod."

After threatening to shoot me, you're now trying to make me feel bad about a dust bunny? Get real, Richard. Jessica bit back the retort, not wanting to bait him just yet.

Gesturing with the pistol, Richard motioned her over to the fireplace. "Build a fire," he brusquely commanded.

Jessica wordlessly complied, going down on bent knee to pile paper, wood, and kindling on the grate. Once she had a respectable blaze going, Richard motioned her to the sofa with exaggerated politeness. As she obediently seated herself, he hitched his hip against the edge of her desk.

"Have you gotten around to telling your mystery man that you're barren?" Richard inquired. He tucked his left arm against his waist and crossed his ankles in what she supposed he thought was a nonchalant pose.

Because her plan was to goad him into losing control, Jessica shrugged her shoulders and said, "Why would I do that?" With slow deliberation, she cast a disparaging glance at his crotch. "As it turns out, you were the inadequate one in our marriage, not me. If you must know, I'm carrying his child."

Immediately a blue vein throbbed in Richard's temple, a sure sign that he was thoroughly incensed.

Before she could lob another insult at him, the break that Jessica had been praying for occurred. She heard a loud *whoosh* followed by a noisy bang and immediately surmised that the unlatched French doors had just been blown open.

The instant that Richard turned his head, Jessica lurched from the sofa. Drawing back her right foot, she shifted into position, determined to kick his testicles to kingdom come.

Maybe it was male instinct, but for whatever reason Richard pulled his legs together as he bent at the waist, effectively shielding himself.

Her plan foiled, Jessica shrieked with frustration and darted past him, making a run for the French doors. She'd gotten no more than a few steps when he barreled into her from behind and tackled her to the floor.

Attempting to cushion the fall, Jessica instinctively pulled her arms to her chest—big mistake. Not only did Richard land on top of her, but she hit the carpet face down and the impact knocked the wind out of her. With her arms now pinned beneath her own body, she was completely immobilized.

Straddling her back, Richard raised himself to his knees before flipping her over. Petrified, Jessica lay beneath him unable to catch her breath. Against her cheek she felt the merciless prod of the gun barrel.

"Please…please don't k-kill me," she begged, tears streaming down her face.

"Maybe you should have thought of that before you shacked up with another man." Digging his fingers into her shoulder, Richard yanked her up with him as he rose to his feet. "Now sit down and shut up," he snarled as he roughly shoved Jessica toward the sofa.

Once she'd retaken her seat, Richard removed a plastic baggie full of pink pills from his jacket pocket and tossed it toward her.

"Start swallowing," he ordered.

Jessica glanced at the roaring fire, suddenly realizing the fate that awaited her. "Once I'm unconscious, you're going to set fire to Highland House, aren't you."

Gesturing to the ripped and faded floral wallpaper that covered the library walls, Richard said, "An old shack like this is a four-alarm fire waiting to happen. I'm guessing such fires happen all the time. Since you've already done me the favor of building a blaze, it should be relatively easy to set your ramshackle residence aflame. By the time someone notices the smoke, it'll take the buffoons in the volunteer fire department a good thirty minutes to get here. You're what, ten miles from town?"

"Eleven and a half," she murmured forlornly.

Because there was nothing she could do to stop Richard's diabolical plan, Jessica opened the Ziploc bag and reluctantly scooped up several pills. Slowly, she raised one of them toward her mouth. As she stared at the brightly colored capsule, she envisioned herself convulsing on the floor while Richard gleefully looked on. He had plotted her death so that it would look like a suicide. The perfect murder.

"Swallow it," he barked, angrily waving the gun at her. "I don't have all day."

Jessica vehemently shook her head. "I won't be a willing accomplice to my own murder. If you want me dead, you'll have to man up and shoot me," she said defiantly, refusing to cave in.

Just then a shadow fell across the room. Out of the corner of her eye, Jessica detected somebody standing near the open French doors.

"What in God's name is going on?" a familiar voice bellowed.

Chapter 29

No sooner did Gideon step through the doorway than Jessica hurled a handful of capsules onto the Oriental carpet.

Gideon quickly assessed the room's ransacked state—a broken lamp, a smashed vase, a wooden chair upended on its side. Obviously, a physical altercation had taken place between Jessica and the stranger who stood at her side.

Catching sight of the bright red welt that marred Jessica's cheekbone, Gideon rushed forward, ready to kill the man who'd dared to strike his beloved.

"Go back outside!" Jessica shrieked.

He drew his saber from its scabbard. "I will do no such thing."

"Put down the fancy sword or I'll put a bullet in her brain."

The dire threat caused Gideon to immediately come to a shuddering halt. In that instant, he noticed what he'd not seen before—the stranger aimed a gun at the back of Jessica's skull.

"You contemptible bastard," Gideon snarled as he set the saber on the floor. His chest heaving with a barely repressed rage, he took the measure of the pale-complexioned intruder. At seeing the thatch of ginger-colored hair, his gut painfully tightened.

The red man, Gideon realized, thunderstruck.

"Well, well, well...your *tenant* has seen fit to grace us with his presence," the red-headed bastard jeered. "Perhaps you'd be kind enough to introduce yourself. Though I tried to wring it out of her, my wife refused to divulge your name."

"My name is Gideon MacAllister. And I take it that yours is Richard Bragg," he grated between clenched teeth, trying his damnedest to keep a cool head. While he had no idea what had precipitated this dangerous encounter between Jessica and "the red man," he would do all in his power to safeguard his beloved.

Jessica, seated on the settee, wrung her hands together, her eyes glimmering with unshed tears. "Oh, Gideon...why did you return to Highland House?"

"I returned because I love you," he stated, heedless of the fact that Richard Bragg was privy to the declaration. "When you told me about your estranged husband, I lost my head to jealousy."

"You were actually jealous of *him*?" Jessica raised a hand to her mouth as she tried, unsuccessfully, to stifle a hysterical burst of laughter. "You're twice, no, three times the man that he is."

"Shut up," Bragg ordered. "One more word out of your whore's mouth and your lover boy will end up a dead man."

"Even dead, Gideon would still take top prize for being the better man," Jessica snickered as she scornfully swept her gaze up and down Bragg's person.

"I don't want to hear another word from you," Bragg hissed, so furious that his face was a deep shade of crimson.

Gideon shot Jessica a quick glance, wordlessly entreating her to hold her tongue. She, in turn, pointedly looked in Bragg's direction. From that brief, silent gesture, he deduced that she was deliberately attempting to provoke her estranged husband. No doubt in the hopes that he would then act injudiciously. During the war, Gideon had seen many men commit fatal errors when driven into a blind rage.

Suspecting that was Jessica's game, he said in a deprecating tone, "You were right to file for divorce from this man. It's obvious that he is naught but a jackal."

Baited by the insult, Bragg stormed toward him. "I'm going to enjoy killing you, MacAllister!"

Gideon made no reply. Instead, he carefully scrutinized the man standing opposite him. From the awkward way that he held his pistol, Gideon surmised that his foe had little experience in firing a weapon. He intended to exploit this inexperience if an opportune moment presented itself.

As Gideon kept his gaze focused on the gunman, he began to feel a niggling twinge of familiarity. There was something about Richard Bragg's demeanor and mannerisms that, strangely enough, put him in mind of Oren Tolliver. Granted, Jessica's estranged husband looked nothing like Oren Tolliver, but what he saw reflected in the depths of Bragg's hate-filled, brown eyes made Gideon suddenly wonder if Richard Bragg, Oren Tolliver, and the "red man" weren't one and the same.

"Can that possibly be true?" he murmured to himself. "After a century and a half, have I actually come face to face with my nemesis of old?"

An uneasy look crept into Bragg's eyes. "What are you yammering about?"

"Reincarnation," Gideon said simply.

When Bragg shot him a questioning befuddled glare, Jessica clutched her throat with her right hand. "Oh my God," she gasped as she gaped at Richard Bragg. "You don't actually think he's Oren Tolliver?"

"That's precisely what I think," Gideon confirmed with a terse nod before he turned to the red-headed bastard and, in a commanding voice, said, "You must allow Jessica to go free. It's me that you want, not her."

"Damn you," Bragg hissed as he clutched his weapon with both hands. "Who are you to give me orders? In case it's escaped your notice, I'm the one holding the gun."

"Go ahead," Gideon taunted, more than willing to sacrifice his life to save the woman he loved. "Pull the trigger."

Bragg's lips curved in a malevolent smile. "Ladies first," he said, and pivoted toward Jessica.

"No!"

In the next instant, Gideon hurled himself at the other man. As in battles past, he knew this would be *une lutte à mort*. A fight to the death.

His attack fueled by brawn not brain, Gideon grabbed Bragg's right wrist and yanked his arm upward, but not before his enemy had squeezed the trigger. The bullet went high, into the plaster ceiling overhead, showering both of them with powdery debris.

Gideon jerked Bragg's arm that much harder, not stopping until he heard a sickening, bone-scraping *pop*.

"Argh!" Bragg screamed as his shoulder dislocated, dropping the gun.

"For the atrocity you committed against the woman I love, then and now, you will die," Gideon avowed.

His revenge had waited a long time; Gideon savored the feel of his fist connecting with Bragg's face. From the telltale crunch and copious spurt of blood, he knew he'd broken Bragg's nose. Not content to stop there, he grabbed his foe by the neck and yanked him several inches off the ground. Grunting loudly, he heaved Bragg toward the nearby oak armoire.

Bragg let out a pain-wracked shriek just before he slumped to the ground in an unconscious heap.

Out of the corner of his eye, Gideon saw Jessica rush toward him.

"Don't you think this is a good place to call it quits?" With a worried expression on her face, she placed a restraining hand on his forearm. "He is, after all, down for the count."

Disdainfully glancing at Bragg's sprawled body, Gideon said, "Honor demands that I avenge Sarah's death."

"You can't do that," Jessica said in a pained voice. "It would be an act of cold-blooded murder." She frantically clutched at the front of his jacket when he moved to retrieve the gun. "If you kill him, the authorities will send you to prison." Tears pooling in her eyes, she begged, "Please, Gideon. Don't do it. I can't bear the thought of losing you."

This last tearful utterance felled him. While he could all too easily assuage his need for vengeance, he refused to forsake his one true love. They'd been given a second chance, their aching hearts having sought each other across the boundaries of time. He wouldn't let his damnable pride destroy their love. He'd made that mistake once before and had lived to regret it.

Gideon exhaled heavily. "You must think me a brute of a man," he said, overcome with shame.

"If you must know, I think that you're—"

"Gawd Almighty, Ol' Man Winter hit this place with a vengeance," a voice exclaimed from the open doorway.

* * *

As J.W. Malone strode into the library, Jessica cast a glance at her battered, soon-to-be ex-husband, who was still out like the proverbial light.

"Old Man Winter certainly does pack a powerful punch," she murmured, unable to drum up an ounce of sympathy for Richard.

Peering behind the sofa, J.W.'s brows instantly shot upward. "What happened to the fella sprawled on the floor? He looks like he went two-steppin' with a two-by-four."

"As you can see—" Sweeping an arm across the ransacked library, Gideon gestured to the smashed lamps and upended furniture. "We were embroiled in a bit of a ruckus."

"A ruckus, huh?" J.W. nudged Richard in the ribs with his boot tip. When he got no response, he glanced at Gideon and said, "I've seen roadkill that looked more lively."

"What would you have me do with an armed intruder?" Gideon countered.

"Point taken."

Relieved that the violent ordeal was finally over, Jessica slumped against Gideon's shoulder, her internal battery pack completely drained. "How did you know that Richard would be at Highland House?" she asked, awed to think that Gideon had proven his love in the most elemental way possible—by putting himself between her and the madman's loaded gun.

"I had no idea that he would be here," her knight errant replied as he placed a protective arm around her shoulders. "But soon after awakening this morning, I sensed that you were in grave danger. From who or what, I knew not."

" 'The red man cometh,' " Jessica whispered, suddenly making sense of what heretofore had seemed a nonsensical phrase. "If you hadn't charged to the rescue when you did—"

Gideon put a silencing finger over her lips. "Let us not speak of things that did not come to pass."

"You're right," she conceded, loathe to ponder the deadly

"what-if" scenario. The confrontation was over. That was all that mattered.

Inclining his head, Gideon brushed his lips against her forehead. "This day, this lifetime, Oren Tolliver was soundly defeated. He can never again harm you."

"And hopefully the karmic cycle has finally been broken." Suddenly curious about something, Jessica pulled her head away from Gideon's shoulder. "By the way…where did you sleep last night?"

His expression somewhat like a Cheshire cat's, Gideon said, "That story is best saved for later, I think."

"We were all worried as hell, buddy," J.W. chimed in as he retrieved Gideon's cavalry saber from the floor. "When I heard that you rode out to Hell's Hole, I figured—" He broke off in mid-sentence as the entire room suddenly began to shake.

In the next instant, Jessica's breath caught in her throat as the two-hundred-year-old windows began to rattle in their equally old panes.

Seconds later, all three of them turned toward the French doors. In stunned amazement, they watched as a cherry-red Dodge Ram pickup truck roared across the snow-covered front lawn, fishtailing to a stop just outside the library. J.W.'s sister hopped out, her cheeks flushed the same vivid hue as the truck's paint job.

"Jessica, honey, are you all right?" Darlene shouted as she dashed into the library. "I had this terrible premonition that you were in danger. When I got no answer on your cell, I decided to hustle on over here."

"My Smartphone and I got separated," Jessica told her, deeply touched by Darlene's concern. She'd never before had friends like J.W. and Darlene Malone, ready to drop what they were doing and rush to her aid.

Glancing behind the sofa, Darlene didn't so much as raise a plucked brow. "Who might that be?" she inquired, her blasé reaction the complete opposite from her brother's startled response.

Appearing equally blasé, Jessica said, "That's my soon-to-be ex-husband."

"Truth be told, I've been tempted to do that to a couple of my exes." Catching sight of Gideon's expression, Darlene shot him a dimpled grin. "Hey there, big fella. I'm glad to see that you made it back to Highland House in one piece. And I hope Jessica read you the riot act for not coming home last—" Darlene's smile abruptly vanished as she pointed a finger at Gideon's chest. "How did you come by *that*?"

Jessica and the two Malones stared at the large scorched circle that was prominently centered on the front of Gideon's uniform.

Due to the ruckus, Jessica hadn't noticed the strange anomaly earlier. "It looks like you were hit by a bolt of lightning," she remarked.

"In a manner of speaking, that's precisely what happened to me." Gideon placed a hand over the scorched fabric. "This is a remnant of my meeting with Draygan."

J.W. whistled, clearly impressed. "Are you shitting me? You actually saw the dragon face to face? Now that's a story I can't wait to hear."

Just then, the blare of a police siren sounded in the near distance.

"When no one answered the phone, I got worried and called the sheriff's department," Darlene said by way of explanation.

"Time to face the music," Jessica muttered, worried that once Richard regained consciousness, the situation would deteriorate into a he said/she said harangue. Artful liar that Richard was, Gideon could end up being charged with assault and battery. Or worse yet, attempted murder. And the fact that Gideon possessed no driver's license, no Social Security number—no identification of any kind—would only complicate matters. "When the sheriff arrives, he needs to know that Gideon had absolutely nothing to do with the, um, ruckus that took place," Jessica instructed everyone, willing to do or say whatever was necessary to protect the man she loved.

"Why would you tell so blatant a falsehood?" Gideon asked in an indignant tone of voice.

"I think I know," Darlene intervened, her eyes narrowing as she shot Jessica a level stare. "And just so we're all singing from the same choir book, when Sheriff Dowd gets here, he's gonna want the truth, the whole truth, and nothing but the truth."

His feathers clearly ruffled, Gideon said, "I have every intention of being forthright with the authorities."

"Which is exactly what has Jessica worried," Darlene said astutely.

In the next instant, a county patrol car pulled up beside the red pickup truck. Darlene assumed command and led them outside. Back straight, shoulders squared, the bleached blond marched up to the unsmiling, uniformed man who stood next to the squad car and planted a loud, smacking kiss on the sheriff's left cheek.

"Don't worry," Darlene said over her shoulder, grinning from ear to ear as the sheriff swiped his hand across the lipstick imprint left in the wake of her affectionate greeting. "We're kissin' cousins."

"Damn it, Darlene. I'm on duty," Sheriff Dowd loudly complained as he hitched his holster from his hips to his waist. "Now what's all this about? I'm up to my jawbone in emergencies, what with that overturned timber truck out on Route 219."

Still grinning, Darlene motioned for Jessica and Gideon to

step forward. "Sheriff Reuben Dowd, I'd like to you meet Jessica Reardon and Gideon MacAllister."

The lawman acknowledged the introduction by politely nodding at Jessica. As he shook Gideon's right hand, he said, "I know everyone in this county, but I don't recollect ever having seen you before."

"And there's a perfectly good reason for that," Darlene piped in, her brown eyes twinkling mischievously. "Do you remember that story Mother Maebelle used to tell about the oddly dressed fella who mysteriously came down off the mountain, claiming he'd been lost in time?"

Sheriff Dowd nodded brusquely and said, "Yeah, what of it?"

"Well, it just so happens that Gideon…"

Chapter 30

Arm in arm, Jessica and Gideon stepped off the back stoop, both of them in dire need of a quiet respite.

Once Sheriff Dowd had been apprised of the "unique" situation, Gideon managed to avoid arrest. Richard Bragg was not so fortunate, and Jessica was optimistic that the sheriff's office would be able to make today's attempted murder charge stick despite Richard's vehement denials. Hopefully, cosmic justice would prevail, and Richard would end up sharing a prison cell with a big, horny, tattooed inmate named Bubba.

As she and Gideon trekked across the field adjacent to the house, a westerly wind whistled past, dislodging a wet clump of snow from a spent thistle. Gideon put his arm around her, pulling Jessica close to his side to shield her from the chill breeze. The scene before them was one of profound beauty, the late-day sun casting a myriad of shifting gray shadows onto the snowy palette. Beneath their boots, the pristine snow crunched and compacted into two sets of deeply incised prints, while overhead, leafless trees raised their gnarled arms heavenward. In the southern sky a pair of wild geese honked a noisy greeting.

Jessica clearly recalled the first time she'd walked this field soon after buying Highland House, and how she'd instantly been enthralled with the stunning vista. Almost heaven. Granted, she couldn't lay claim to being a native West Virginian, but her spiritual roots ran deep. As deep as her love for the man who now walked at her side.

"How do you feel?" Gideon asked, the inquiry punctuated with a light squeeze to her shoulder.

"Exhausted. But strangely enough, I also feel lighthearted." Her addendum put a smile on Gideon's face. Jessica realized then that he no longer resembled a sad-faced crusader. Like a blithesome knight-errant, his smile extended all the way to the depths of his cerulean blue eyes. "I know this is going to sound a bit off the wall, but there's a remarkable change about you. It's as though you're now filled with..." Her voice drifted into silence; she was unable to think of the right word.

"A spark of celestial fire, perhaps?"

Jessica laughed softly. "I wasn't thinking in such flowery terms, but you do seem full of good cheer." Not unlike the man she'd first fallen in love with in her dreams.

"I suspect the change is due to my strange and enchanted wanderings last evening."

Intrigued, Jessica came to a complete standstill. "Enchanted? How so?"

"It was enchanted in so far as I found myself caught between two worlds." As he spoke, Gideon smoothed several strands of windblown hair from Jessica's face, tucking the wayward tresses behind her ear. "To my astonishment, I discovered that not only is there this world, the one that we see with our eyes, but there is yet another world, one that we perceive with our souls."

"Do you mean to say that out there—" Jessica gestured to the snowy landscape spread before them—"there's an enchanted world peopled with otherworldly beings?"

Gideon verified with a nod. "That is precisely what I mean to say." Placing a hand on the small of her back, he prodded her forward so that they could continue with their stroll.

"I know about Draygan, of course," she said. "But what other kind of beings are we talking about?"

"When I first wandered into this realm, I happened upon Mother Maebelle, who—"

"You've got to be kidding," she interjected, making no attempt to hide her astonishment. "According to Darlene, her grandmother died nearly twenty years ago. That would mean that Mother Maebelle paid you a visit from beyond the grave."

"In all honesty, I did not think to ask from whence she came. I only know that I shall forever be in the old woman's debt for her wise and generous counsel."

"Chalk up another one for the Malone women," Jessica quipped.

Cupping a hand around her elbow, Gideon ushered her forward as they continued their stroll across the snowy field.

"There was a time, not long ago, when I mistakenly thought that death was the only curative for the pain lodged in my heart," Gideon said quietly, his confession so unexpected, the words filled with such pathos, that Jessica instinctively reached for his hand.

"I had no idea that you were so tormented," she murmured. "Believe me, if I had known I would have⊠"

"Saved me from my dark reveries?"

"Yes," she quickly assured him. "That's exactly what I would have done."

"And so you did," Gideon informed her, a tender smile hovering about his lips. "Ever since I first arrived in this century, your love has proven to be the most potent elixir of all. From the very beginning, you have been my refuge from the storm. Not only did you nurse my ravaged body, you mended my battered heart."

"Yours isn't the only heart recently mended. I'm just grateful we've been given a second chance to get it right." As she spoke, Jessica watched a cardinal alight on a weathered fence post. Perhaps it was the pensive tone of their conversation, but for whatever reason, its crimson red plumage looked like a pool of blood splashed onto the snowy backdrop.

And that in turn made her think of Draygan.

"I'm still curious about your, um, scorched uniform," she said tentatively. Then, because she couldn't think of a diplomatic way to phrase the question, she asked point-blank, "Did you kill Draygan?"

"No, I did not kill Draygan. And though I did slay a dragon, it was the one that resided within my own heart." Gideon's shoulders heaved with a plaintive sigh. "In the past, I'd always let duty, and what I thought of as my sacred honor, determine my actions, placing both before the dictates of love. That was why I was so determined to kill the beast, seeing it as my duty to do so."

"So what made you see the light?"

Gideon steered Jessica around a snow-covered patch of prickly pear. "It was the realization that love is all that matters. Nothing else in this world is of greater consequence. Once I surrendered to that, I was able to conquer the beast within me. Had I not done so, I would never have been able to return to Highland House and save you from the true monster that lurked amongst us."

"After my past life regression, I wondered why it was that you came forward in time instead of traveling backward. Now I know." Jessica placed a protective hand over her abdomen. "You came forward so that you could save us."

Gideon stared at her slack-jawed. "Do you mean to say that… that you are with child?"

"I like to think that *we're* with child," she corrected. "And I don't know how men did it back in the good ol' days, but here in the twenty-first century, you guys are expected to pull your fair share of the diaper detail."

Gideon came to a sudden halt. As he turned toward her, tears fell unchecked down his cheeks.

"I didn't mean to make you cry," Jessica said, her own eyes beginning to water. "And please tell me that those are tears of joy."

"Joy. And love. And heartfelt gratitude that we are together once more," Gideon told her, his voice thick with emotion. Smiling, he pulled Jessica close to him, wrapping her in his arms. "Who would have thought a day that dawned so bleak would usher in such glad tidings?"

"Yeah, who would have thunk it?" Jessica playfully retorted as she pressed her cheek against his chest, awed by the knowledge that theirs was a bond so strong, so sure, it transcended the ages.

The next few moments passed in a rapturous silence while they stood together in the snow, wrapped in one another's arms.

Suddenly reminded of something that had transpired in their previous life together, Jessica tilted her head so that she could look Gideon in the eye. "With everything that's happened in the last twenty-four hours, I haven't had a chance to mention that, during my past-life regression, I was privy to an interesting tidbit: Sarah buried some silver beneath the azalea bushes. A thought that excited me to no end…until I realized there are no azalea bushes anywhere on the property."

"There used to be a clump of pink azaleas on the eastern end of the porch," Gideon informed her as he pointed toward the house. "And the silver in question was part of my grandmother's dowry."

Jessica gaped at him, absolutely floored by the disclosure. "Do you mean to say that there actually might be a two-hundred-year-old silver set buried in the front yard?"

"If you must know, the silverware and tea set are considerably older than that," Gideon clarified in an almost casual tone of voice. "As I recall, the silver had already been in the family for some years when my grandmother wed. Interestingly enough, her family was from Boston. All of the silver was crafted for them by a rather famous member of the Revere clan."

Placing her hands squarely on Gideon's chest, Jessica said, "Catch me. I'm about to faint. For your information, not too long ago, I watched an episode of *Antiques Roadshow* in which a set of eight Revere-marked tablespoons were valued at—get this—eighty thousand dollars. We're talking ten thousand dollars a spoon."

"I take it then that the sale of the silver will provide us with ample funds to refurbish Highland House."

"And generously pad our retirement account to boot," Jessica told him, having yet to get over the shock. "Wow. What a neat little trick. Bury some treasure in one lifetime and retrieve it in the next."

Smiling warmly, Gideon said, "You were always a clever woman."

As she peered at the horizon, Jessica could see that the hour grew late. Pewter clouds were trimmed with the castoff remains of a shell-pink sunset.

"There is a beauty, a grace, to these mountains that touches the soul," Gideon murmured, his gaze having also turned to the western skyline.

"I've often thought it's like being in an open-air cathedral."

"An apt description, to be certain." He took a deep breath, his chest slowly rising and falling against her cheek. "After witnessing so much carnage during the war, I lost my faith in everything. But coming home to Highland House has restored that which was lost. And it has made me realize that there is far more mystery to God's creation than I ever supposed."

"Darlene says there's magic in these old mountains. And I'm beginning to think she's onto something." Peering at Gideon from beneath lowered lashes, Jessica impishly smiled and said, "How about we head back to Highland House and conjure a bit of our own mountain magic?"

Her blue-eyed knight gallantly swept his arm toward the red brick house in the distance. "With pleasure, my lady love."

Please see the next page for an excerpt from

Chloe Douglas's Time Wanderer novel,
A Love for All Time

Chapter 2

*S*hit!" Mick bellowed at the top of his lungs, nearly blinded by the swirling beams of brilliant light that encompassed the two of them in a whirling vortex of energy.

One instant he'd been standing in the alley off Larimer Street; the next he was being sucked through some sort of illuminated vacuum. All around him, Mick saw blurry images of people whizzing past at a dizzying speed. Who they were, and what they were doing in this supersonic funnel, he had no idea.

Moments later, as the bright light faded, Mick struggled to catch his breath. Grateful that he was once again standing on solid ground, he slowly turned full circle. He felt like he'd just cannonballed through a particle accelerator at the speed of sound. Or even faster if such a thing was possible.

Lettitia, still holding the strange disk in her hand, warily took his measure. "I trust you made the journey without incident?"

"Freakin' unbelievable," he muttered in a stunned whisper. "Where in the world am I?"

"You, sir, are in London." She inclined her head in a queenly nod. "I bid you welcome."

Surprised that it was daylight where before it had been early evening, Mick peered heavenward. Thick streams of black smoke shadowed the sky, the dark billows emanating from innumerable chimneys and smokestacks. "Welcome to Hell is more like it," he said in a husky voice.

Suddenly hearing a loud clamor, Mick turned his head toward the nearby street. The straw-covered lane teemed with horse-drawn wagons, carriages, carts, and buggies. Scores of pedestrians dodged the wheeled onslaught, more than a few offering up a choice curse as they nimbly crossed the cobbled thoroughfare.

As he eyeballed his squalid surroundings, Mick quickly deduced two things: he wasn't in Kansas; and he sure as hell wasn't in Oz.

A bow-legged man wearing a pair of leather chaps strolled past. Across the top of his shoulders, he balanced a long stick from which dangled four dead rabbits. Mick grabbed him by the upper arm, stopping him in his tracks.

"Am I really in London?" he asked, disinclined to believe anything Lettitia told him.

"Piss off, you gin-sodden bugger!"

Since Mick could barely understand the thick Cockney accent, he figured he had his answer.

Still holding onto the other man's arm, he asked the next logical question. "What year is this?"

The man shrugged free of his grasp. "As if you don't know it to be the year of the three eights," he hissed before continuing on his way.

Stupefied, Mick turned toward Lettitia. "'The year of the three eights. What does *that* mean?"

"It means that you are in London, this being the year 1888," she calmly informed him as she stuffed the silver disk into her beaded purse.

"Well, send me back to Brooklyn circa 2013. Now."

Rather than comply, his companion straightened her shoulders. In the short span of time since he'd made Lettitia Merryweather's acquaintance, Mick had seen a multitude of emotions in her smoky gray orbs. *Trepidation, anger, obstinacy.* But this was the first time that her eyes glimmered with a conniving intent.

"I will return you to your own time and place *after* you locate my sister."

Mick let that soak in a moment…before he ripped into her.

"If you think I'm gonna let you pull me around by the short-and-curlies, think again!" Snatching the handbag off of her wrist, Mick ignored her indignant outcry as he broke the Eleventh Commandant—*Thou shall not rummage through a woman's purse.* When he found what he was looking for, he flung the beaded bag back in her direction.

"Okay, tell me how it works," he ordered as he opened the disk that she'd used to activate the time portal. One side housed some kind of old-fashioned watch rimmed with Roman numerals and astrological symbols. At least that's what Mick thought they were. The other side contained what looked like a compass needle submerged in an aqua-blue liquid. On both sides of the device there were small nubbins similar to those on a wristwatch.

Mick thumbed one of them.

"Don't touch that!" Lettitia screeched, trying to snatch the device out of his hand.

He held it aloft, out of her reach. "Why? What'll happen?"

"There's no telling what calamity will befall us if you reset the device. Those settings have to do with time and place." Clearly worried, she peered over her shoulder.

Mick craned his head to see what had garnered her attention. In a niche set within a brick wall, he saw an iron ornament exactly like the one in the alley on Larimer Street.

"Let me guess," he said. "One activates the other."

"In a manner of speaking."

"Can you be more specific?"

"Not until you ascertain my sister's whereabouts."

"Shit. That's extortion. You can't—"

"Yes, I can," she said over him, her expression resolute. "And so that we are clear on the matter, I will do anything, *anything,* to find my sister. The time portal can only be accessed during the seven days of the lunar cycle when the moon is at its fullest. Which means that you have seven days to find Emmaline."

Physically shaking—he was that pissed—Mick relinquished custody of the time device. Until he could figure out a way to escape, he had no choice but to surrender the field.

"Earlier, you kept mentioning some madam person."

"Madame Mazursky is a well-known spiritualist. In fact, it was she who gave me the time device and sent me to the future in order to secure your assistance."

Christ. What do they think I am, a damned bloodhound?

Mick was stumped as to why this mysterious Madame Mazursky would send Lettitia one hundred and twenty-five years into the future to find him. He was just a New York City cop, not freakin' Sherlock Holmes. Determined to find out what the hell was going on, he made a mental note to have a little chat with Madame Mazursky. Sooner rather than later.

What he needed now was a stiff drink.

"Come on." He cuffed a hand around Lettitia's elbow. When she balked, he tightened his grip, not in the mood to play nice. She'd tricked him into taking her to Larimer Street, and now that she'd transported him to Merry Olde England, she was holding him prisoner until he found her missing sister.

"I demand to know where you are taking me," Lettitia huffed in an imperious tone of voice.

His fury still at a fast boil, Mick stopped in mid-stride and pivoted toward her. "I've had about all I can take of your demands," he growled. Invading her personal space, he pressed his chest against her well-endowed bosom, a move that instantly caused a life-affirming swell in his boxer shorts. "It just so happens that I'm in need of a stiff drink and that bar across the street has my name written all over it." Given the large tankard of frothy ale painted on the sign over the door, there was no mistaking the establishment for being anything other than a drinking hole.

Lettitia turned her head, her gaze narrowing as she peered at The Ten Bells. "Sir, do you realize what time it is? Why, it is only—" she glanced at the small silver watch pinned to the front of her jacket—"eight o'clock in the morning."

Mick consulted his wristwatch. "Maybe in your neck of the woods, but according to *my* watch, it's seven o'clock in the evening. Which means that happy hour is still under way."

"Under no circumstance will I accompany you into that den of sinful inequity!"

"Fine by me. In fact, it's probably better that you not accompany me."

"Surely you do not mean to leave me standing in the street while you—"

"Is this bloke givin' you trouble, miss?"

At hearing the unwelcome intruder, Mick glanced behind him. Standing at the ready was a big, burly, blue-suited constable slapping his nightstick against the palm of his hand. Mick instantly released his hold on Lettitia, taking the unasked measure of stepping away from her.

"This gentleman is…is an acquaintance of mine," Lettitia sputtered, her chest heaving.

The constable jutted his chin at Mick's ripped coat sleeve. "'e's dressed a might queerly to be associating with a lady such as yourself."

"He's from America," Lettitia said, as if that explained everything.

Evidently it did, and the constable bid them both 'G'day' before continuing on his beat.

"Really, Detective Giovanni. You must learn to control your temper. As well as your repugnant vices," she added, pointedly glancing at The Ten Bells.

Ignoring her, Mick crossed the cobbled street, maneuvering around a large, two-wheeled buggy as he made a beeline for the bar.

Out of the corner of his eye, he saw Lettitia primly raise her skirts several inches as she crossed the busy thoroughfare.

"Need I remind you, Detective Giovanni, that a gentleman *always* assists a lady across a street? To not do so demonstrates a lack of—"

"Can it, Lettitia. In case you haven't figured it out yet, you're not one of my favorite people right now."

"Sir, you cannot mean to go in there!"

"Just watch me." With exaggerated politeness, he held the tavern door wide open. "Coming, dear?"

Huffing indignantly, Lettitia marched across the threshold of The Ten Bells in a swish of black taffeta and frilly white petticoats. Following in her wake, Mick took the lay of the land: there was an old-fashioned, mahogany bar; an aproned barkeep cleaning glasses with a hand towel; and a buxom woman serving beer to a table full of early morning revelers.

Yeah, this will do.

As he seated himself at a corner table, Mick hollered at the barkeep, "Give me a bottle of your best Irish whiskey."

"And just how do you expect to pay for your demon spirits?" Lettitia harped, looking down her nose at him. "Your money is worthless here."

"But yours isn't."

"I will not pay for your evil vices!"

Tuning out the temperance harangue, he motioned to the empty chair opposite his. "Have a seat."

Not budging so much as an inch, Lettitia stared at him, an obstinate gleam in her eyes.

Uh-uh, sweetheart. Nothing doing. Mick folded his arms over his chest, refusing to lunge to his feet to assist her.

"Must you be so uncouth?"

"Yeah, I must. It's encoded in my caveman DNA."

"Sir, your remark is nonsensical."

Forced to seat herself at the table, Lettitia sat with her back ramrod straight, her spine a good six inches from the back of the chair. When the barkeep placed a bottle and two empty glasses on the table, she glared at the man as though he were the devil's minion.

Mick reached for the whiskey bottle. Pulling the cork, he took an appreciative sniff before pouring a healthy measure of amber-colored booze into his glass. "Hey, Lettitia, lighten up, will ya?"

"Henceforth, I would prefer that you address me as Miss Merryweather," she intoned, stone-faced.

"Care for a snort?" He held the bottle aloft, intentionally egging her on.

On cue, Lettitia exclaimed, "Most certainly not!"

"Suit yourself." Mick drained the glass in two swallows.

"It is obvious that you are no stranger to strong drink."

"Must be the Irish in me," he deadpanned, refilling his glass. Before the Kingsborough Massacre, he used to have an occasional beer on the weekends. Now he polished off nearly a fifth of Jameson's a week. It was the only thing that put him to sleep. Even with the nightcap, he only averaged four to five hours of sleep on any given night.

"Okay, let's get down to business." Mick pulled a notebook and ink pen out of his jacket pocket. "Tell me about your sister."

Judging by the way her gray eyes opened wide, Lettitia was obviously surprised by the request.

"What? Did you think I was gonna drink myself under the table? The sooner I find her, the sooner I can go home."

"What exactly do you wish to know about Emmaline?" Lettitia countered in a circumspect tone of voice.

"For starters, when did you see her last?"

"Tuesday, the seventh of August. We met for tea."

"At what time?"

"As I told you already, it was at tea time. That being four o'clock in the afternoon," she clarified when he irritably pointed to his watch crystal.

Mick jotted down the date and time. "Did the two of you routinely have afternoon tea?" he asked, glancing up from his notepad.

"We met only on the days that I volunteered at St. Ursula's Hospital."

"Why did you only see your sister on the days that you volunteered at the hospital?"

Acting like a guilty perp, she dropped her gaze to the table. "I will not divulge the intimate details of my sister's life. To do so would be unseemly."

"Hey, if you want me to find your sister, you better start divulging."

Lettitia's head instantly snapped upward. Wordlessly, she glared him, a picture that was worth a thousand words, and not a civil one among 'em.

"And stop throwing daggers my way, will ya? Seeing as how I'm doing you a *huge* favor. Any other woman would be kissing up to me right about now."

Splaying a hand over throat, Lettitia recoiled. "How dare you suggest that I—"

"I wasn't," he interjected. Mick left it at that, not in the mood to give a lesson in twenty-first century slang. "Now how about answering my question?"

A long pause stretched into an awkward silence. Fast losing his patience, Mick repeatedly tapped the end of his pen against the notepad.

"If you must know, my sister is no longer received in society," Lettitia finally divulged. "That is why we meet surreptitiously on the days when I go to the hospital."

Suddenly feeling like he'd crash-landed into an episode of *Downton Abbey*—every red-blooded man's nightmare—Mick had to ask the asinine follow-up: "Why is she, um, no longer received in society?"

"My father had gone to great lengths to arrange a marriage between Emmaline and Lord Wortham. While my mother is of noble birth, my father's antecedents are not nearly so exalted. Although between my sister's great beauty and my father's great fortune, such an impediment hardly mattered. At least it wouldn't have mattered if my sister had shared our father's lofty ambitions. Emmaline, however, refused to marry a man that she did not love."

"So I take it that Emmaline broke off her engagement to this Lord Wortham fellow?"

The question elicited another lengthy silence during which time Lettitia began to nervously fiddle with a button on one of her gloves.

Mick silently counted to ten then repeated the question.

"It pains me to confess that my sister ran off with the Welsh stable master," Lettitia murmured bleakly, unable to look him in the eye. "In retaliation, my father cut Emmaline off without a cent. She was then forced to…to—" Pausing mid-sentence, Lettitia wiped a wayward tear with a gloved finger.

"Okay, I've got enough details for now," Mick said abruptly, unnerved by Lettitia's agonized expression. He didn't do distraught women. At least not well. Stuffing the notebook into his pocket, he rose to his feet. "You can give me a list of addresses later."

After grudgingly paying for his two drinks, Lettitia beat a hasty retreat from the pub.

Mick caught up to her a few moments later. "I need to speak to your good pal Madame Mazursky. This time portal thing is—" Suddenly noticing a skinny kid standing a few feet away hawking newspapers, he momentarily lost his train of thought.

Christ Almighty, I don't frigging believe it.

Fishing a quarter out of his pocket, he handed it to the newsboy. Although the grimy-faced urchin eyed the coin suspiciously, he nonetheless handed Mick a newspaper dated November 4, 1888. The banner headline, set in bold, old-fashioned typeface, read: Jack the Ripper Still At Large.

About the Author

Chloe Palov, writing romance as Chloe Douglas, was born in Washington, D.C., and graduated from George Mason University with a degree in art history. Although she began her writing career in the romance genre, Chloe switched gears several years ago, making the leap to thrillers, written under the name C.M. Palov. Chloe is excited now to be returning to her romance roots. Chloe lives and writes with a menagerie of furry family members from her home in Virginia.

ChloeDouglasBooks.com
http://facebook.com/ChloeDouglasBooks

You Might Also Like...

Looking for more great digital reads?
We've got you covered!

Now Available from Forever Yours

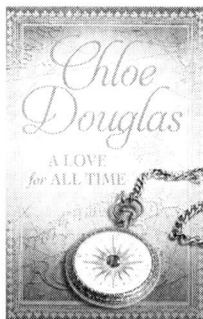

*From modern-day New York to Victorian London,
one thrilling mystery brings together two passionate
souls—for all time...*

Homicide detective Mick Giovanni has seen lot a strange things
in the NYPD—but nothing like Miss Lettitia Merryweather.

Waltzing into his precinct dressed like some actress on *Masterpiece Theater*, the stunning British beauty implores Mick to find her missing sister. The strange part is, she disappeared in London—in 1888. Of course, Mick doesn't believe Lettitia. Until he steps through a time portal onto a gaslit street and sees a newspaper headline that reads: *Jack the Ripper Still At Large...*

For Mick, it's the dream of a lifetime—a chance to hunt down the most notorious killer in history. But for Lettitia, it's all too personal, and Mick is her only hope. The tough, handsome cop has only seven days to solve the world's greatest mystery before he loses his chance to go home. But the closer Mick gets to the truth, the deeper his feelings for Lettitia grow. Even if he solves the case, can these two soul mates say good-bye to a love that was meant for all time?

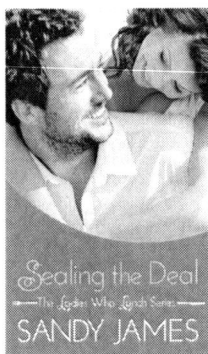

Sealing the Deal
SANDY JAMES

After losing her sister, Bethany Rogers needs a shoulder to lean on more than ever—though she never expects that shoulder to belong to her new boss...

Bethany has been in love with Robert Ashford since they were teachers at the same high school. After Robert leaves to start his own construction company, Beth puts her feelings aside to focus on her goals. When she finally lands a gig as a part-time designer, she is shocked to find her new boss is none other than Robert... and he's hotter than ever. But Bethany's happiness is short-lived when she receives word that her sister has been killed in combat.

With the success of building homes for one happy family after another, Robert is finally ready to settle down. When Beth is left to care for her nine-month-old niece, Robert can't help but step in. And before long, the trio are inseparable. Yet convincing the cautious, bereaved Beth to let him in proves difficult—but Robert will give everything he's got for the chance at his own happily ever after.

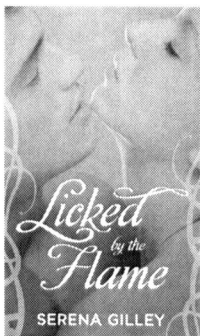

One hot kiss from a smoldering Dragon and all her thoughts go up in flames...

Lianne McGowan is a scientist on a mission. As brilliant as she is beautiful, she believes the key to the Earth's future is a new energy source. To find it, she'll delve deep into the fiery heart of an imposing mountain—and take on an even more imposing man: the sinfully seductive Nic Vladik.

Shape-shifting dragon Nic has sworn to guard the secret to

his brethren's insatiable power. He must stop Lianne's search, yet the moment he feels the soft silk of her skin, his soul is set on fire. Unable to resist, Nic and Lianne submit to desire and experience an exquisite passion unlike either has ever known. But their pleasure is short-lived. Lianne has made a discovery that endangers herself, Nic, and all dragonkind. With his world at stake, will Nic save his clan—or the woman he loves?

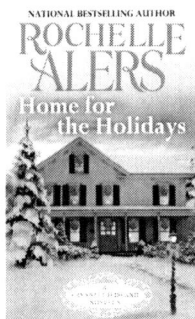

NATIONAL BESTSELLING AUTHOR
ROCHELLE ALERS
Home for the Holidays

Love is always in season.

There's no place like home for the holidays, especially for divorced pastry chef Iris Nelson. After escaping an abusive marriage, she's found peace on charming Cavanaugh Island. As the holiday approaches, Iris looks forward to spending it with her newfound best friend's family...and their very handsome visitor.

On leave from Afghanistan, Army Master Sergeant Collier Ward is excited to be reunited with his family for Christmas. But the best gift of all may be this warm, beautiful stranger who joins them for the festivities. With his visit coming to an end, Collier can't deny the heat smoldering between them. Yet Iris can't help but wonder if it's just the glow of the season—and one night of passion—or a true miracle of love that will change their lives forever...

CPSIA information can be obtained at www.ICGtesting.com
Printed in the USA
LVOW12s1407311214

421083LV00001B/3/P